T0131056

"As fizzy, sharp, and delicious as a bottle of vintage Veuve Clicquot, *The Winged Tiara* offers readers a caper full of glamour, romance, and intrigue. I'm not sure which of our suave, screwball thieves I fell for most, just that I tore through the pages, desperate for them to finally fall back into each other's arms. A total delight."
—Jennifer Thorne, co-author of *The Antiquity Affair*

"An exhilarating, immersive cat-and-mouse adventure, with exquisite period details, pitch-perfect pacing, a glittering prize, and a swoon-worthy, star-crossed romance. I absolutely inhaled this novel. Mesmerizing, from start to finish."
—Lee Kelly, co-author of *The Antiquity Affair*
and author of *A Criminal Magic*

"Ciesielski delivers truly memorable characters and high-stakes action rendered with remarkable realism. Readers will be riveted."
—*Publishers Weekly* for *To Free the Stars*

"*To Free the Stars* is a fast-paced, thrill ride of a spy novel, tempered by moments of profound tenderness and emotion. J'nell Ciesielski writes with energy and passion, bringing brilliant life to two dynamic characters battling extremes on every front. A star-bright story of perseverance, devotion, and above all, love."
—Mimi Matthews, *USA TODAY* bestselling author of *The Belle of Belgrave Square*

"*To Free the Stars* is *Captain America* meets *The Alice Network* in this final unforgettable installment in the Jack & Ivy series. A sweeping romance comes alongside an intense adrenaline-inducing mission around the world to create a story that will steal your heart from the first page. As Jack and Ivy fight for peace and each other, a most important truth emerges clearly—that war may wrap its evil tentacles around our necks, and peril may meet us at every breath, and memory may fail. Even so, love WILL remain."

—Joy Callaway, international bestselling
author of *All the Pretty Places*

"I love a heroine who can beat the men in hand-to-hand combat, and Ivy is the best! This is a fast-paced, unputdownable adventure story with a strong emotional core."

—Gill Paul, *USA TODAY* bestselling
author of *The Manhattan Girls*

"From thrilling fight scenes to tender romance, *To Free the Stars* races off the page, dropping readers into the middle of a desperate fight between good and evil set against the glamor and danger of the Roaring Twenties. You won't be able to put this one down!"

—Julia Kelly, international bestselling
author of *The Last Garden in England*
and *The Lost English Girl*

"Ciesielski starts off her new series with a kiss and a bang, and neither the romance nor action slows down from there."

—*Library Journal*, starred review,
for *The Brilliance of Stars*

"Ciesielski launches her Jack and Ivy duology with this captivating and immersive tale of espionage and romance amid the dangers of World War I."

—*Publishers Weekly* for *The Brilliance of Stars*

"An epic, Bond-style tale set during the First World War, *The Brilliance of Stars* grips the reader from the first page. With mesmeric settings, nonstop action, and witty dialogue, Ciesielski crafts a thrilling love story of powerful equals working tirelessly to save the world from darkness."

—Erika Robuck, national bestselling author of *Sisters of Night and Fog*

"Action! Romance! Spies! Secrets! *The Brilliance of Stars* has it all. This electrifying read from J'nell Ciesielski comes to life with historical details and sparkling descriptions that will leave the reader begging for book two!"

—Amy E. Reichert, author of *Once Upon a December*

"Excuse me while I go read *The Brilliance of Stars* by J'nell Ciesielski a second time. The intrigue of master assassins, a secret society, a cat-and-mouse game, all while the world is teeming with tension from the Russian Revolution and the First World War. Not to mention while Jack and Ivy are falling in love. Who knew a grenade pin could be so romantic? This thrilling historical novel has it all, and I look forward to more 'Jack and Ivy.'"

—Jenni L. Walsh, *USA TODAY* bestselling author of *Unsinkable*

"[*The Ice Swan*] is well written, with superb similes and metaphors. Highly recommended."

—*Historical Novel Society*

"Ciesielski delivers an intense love story set during World War I. Fans of historical romance should snap this up."

—*Publishers Weekly* for *The Ice Swan*

"A Scottish lord and an American socialite discover love during World War I in this gorgeous historical romance from Ciesielski . . . The undercurrent of mystery and Ciesielski's unflinching approach to the harsh realities of wartime only enhance the love story. Readers are sure to be impressed."

—*Publishers Weekly*, starred review,
for *Beauty Among Ruins*

"*Beauty Among Ruins* is an atmospheric, engrossing romance for fans of *Downton Abbey* and *Somewhere in France*. A real gem!"

—Aimie K. Runyan, internationally bestselling author

"Ciesielski has created a fresh and original tale in this inspiring World War I romance about a dour Scottish laird and an American socialite."

—Tea Cooper, author of *The Fossil Hunter*,
for *Beauty Among Ruins*

"With sweeping romance and evocative prose, Ciesielski transports readers to World War II–era Paris, where a British aristocrat loses her heart to a Scottish spy . . . Ciesielski's vivid characterizations and lush historical detail quickly draw readers into this expertly plotted tale. Readers looking for an immersive, high-stakes historical romance will be wowed."

—*Publishers Weekly*, starred review, for *The Socialite*

"Smart, savvy, and seductive, *The Socialite* shines bright as the City of Light and then some!"

—Kristy Cambron, bestselling author
of *The Italian Ballerina*

"In the tradition of Ariel Lawhon and Kate Quinn, *The Socialite* immerses readers in the glamour and destruction of Nazi-occupied Paris. This impeccably researched love story stands out in a sea of World War II–era fiction with its distinctive crystalline voice and unforgettable hero and heroine."

—Rachel McMillan, author of *The Mozart Code*

"Readers will devour each moment leading up to the satisfying ending."

—*Publishers Weekly*, starred review,
for *The Songbird and the Spy*

"*The Songbird and the Spy* is a must-read!"

—Kate Breslin, bestselling author

THE
WINGED
TIARA

THE WINGED TIARA

A NOVEL

J'NELL CIESIELSKI

THOMAS NELSON
Since 1798

The Winged Tiara
Copyright © 2024 J'nell Ciesielski

Published in Nashville, Tennessee, by Thomas Nelson. Thomas Nelson is a registered trademark of HarperCollins Christian Publishing, Inc.

Thomas Nelson titles may be purchased in bulk for educational, business, fundraising, or sales promotional use. For information, please email SpecialMarkets@ThomasNelson.com.

Publisher's Note: This novel is a work of fiction. Names, characters, places, and incidents are either products of the author's imagination or used fictitiously. All characters are fictional, and any similarity to people living or dead is purely coincidental.

Library of Congress Cataloging-in-Publication Data

Names: Ciesielski, J'nell, author.

Title: The winged tiara : a novel / J'nell Ciesielski.
Description: Nashville, Tennessee : Thomas Nelson, 2024. | Summary: "Diamonds and danger dazzle in Ciesielski's latest enchanting romp through post-war Europe as estranged spouses and jewel thieves hunt an elusive Valkyrie tiara"—Provided by publisher.
Identifiers: LCCN 2024007619 (print) | LCCN 2024007620 (ebook) | ISBN 9780840721204 (paperback) | ISBN 9780840721211 (epub) | ISBN 9780840721297
Subjects: LCGFT: Romance fiction. | Christian fiction. | Novels.
Classification: LCC PS3603.I33 W56 2024 (print) | LCC PS3603.I33 (ebook) | DDC 813/.6—dc23/eng/20230222

LC record available at https://lccn.loc.gov/2024007619
LC ebook record available at https://lccn.loc.gov/2024007620
Printed in the United States of America

24 25 26 27 28 LBC 5 4 3 2 1

To Lettie:
One chicken of doom just for you.

PROLOGUE

Paris, France
12 November 1918

HANDSOME MEN ALWAYS MADE FOR the most delicious dreams. Even more divine when they were real.

Head fuzzy and limbs still weighted from remnants of sleep, Esme Fox snuggled into the soft pillow as her mind lingered on the man. There had been crowds all around, music playing, bells ringing, and then without warning the press of bodies parted and there he stood. Buffed and pressed in his army uniform, hat tilted dashingly to the side, and a grin that stopped her heart in its tracks. She had no choice but to sway straight up to him and kiss him.

Curling her legs under the bedsheets—odd that her nightgown wasn't tangled as it usually was—her mind flipped to a quiet booth tucked in the back of a pub. Holding hands, her fingers lacing perfectly with his. Quiet laughter over their shared sense of spiky humor, her giggling as he pulled her from the depths of her hidden self. Talking as if their souls had been waiting to meet and share a lifetime's worth of hopes and dreams of becoming more than what their pasts dictated. A whispered confession of wanting to fall in love, to see what they could make of it. Her question of why not find out?

A slow throbbing began to drum through her head, distorting the images. A large room with rows of benches and lovely windows of stained glass. A man in a long black frock standing with them. He held a book of some kind and droned on while she lost herself in a pair of magnificent brown eyes that gazed at her as if she were the sun and stars.

She pressed her hand to her forehead as the throbbing paraded around her skull.

The man—the handsome one, not the black-frocked one—had smiled at her, kissed her until she melted against him. Happiness had danced through her. *Let's see what we can make of this.*

Then he was holding a key and fitting it into a door lock as she urged him to hurry while cradling two bottles in her arms.

Then . . . What? The smarting pain blocked out all coherent thought. She tugged her hand free of the blanket and rubbed her temple. Cool metal brushed against her brow. What was that?

Easing upright, Esme blinked groggily at the unfamiliar ring on her finger, then promptly rolled over and vomited a rousing night's worth of champagne into a silver bucket. It had been an excellent vintage, but the exquisite taste was soured upon reemergence. She groped for a linen napkin from the bedside table and patted her mouth before draping it discreetly over the bucket. She blinked several more times and passed a hand—not the one with the band—over her eyes to dislodge the gathered grit.

Bright yellow light poured through the window in blindingly irritating radiance. It wasn't like her to keep the blackout curtains open. But wait, there were no more Germans. Well, that was not to say that Germans didn't exist, because they certainly did, but there was something about them going home. What was it? The dull ache behind her eyes wrapped around the front of her head as her mind revolted against being bullied into coherent thought.

She glanced around the room, which seemed to tilt oddly to the left. She tipped her head to the side to accommodate. It was a decent room with sturdy furnishings and watercolors hanging on the walls. There on the table, wadded between dinner plates— why were there two?—was a flag of blue, red, and white. A single cotton stocking dangled over the back of one chair while its mate fluttered from the bedpost. Her shoes had been kicked off near the door while her clothes were scattered about the floor like delicate land mines. Well, that wasn't unusual—but the man's uniform hanging from the curtain rod certainly was.

Shifting in bed, she found him. He was stretched out on his stomach with his arms hooked under the pillow. Thick golden-brown curls sprang wildly over his head. His face was turned away, making it difficult to suss out his looks, but going by the tanned neck and white back stretched with taut muscles, he seemed a manly specimen indeed. Judging by the hint of bare, rounded flesh visible just before the sheet had the audacity to cover him, her bedfellow was naked. A quick peek at herself beneath the sheet confirmed she had joined him. Clearly the result of the excellent champagne.

How to break it to the poor fellow? *My dear boy, while I do not recall the nuptials, our time together will be remembered fondly.*

Or perhaps, *Your kisses were pure magic so it's best not to ruin them by making further plans.* She nodded to the sleeping form with satisfaction. Yes, that explanation would do nicely.

Carefully slipping out of bed so as not to disturb him, she reached for her chemise and stopped cold as the sunlight glinted off the gold ring. The one resting on the fourth finger of her left hand. Somewhere in the distance a tinny gramophone played "Pack Up Your Troubles in Your Old Kit Bag And Smile, Smile, Smile!" Her gaze skittered to the celebration flag on the table and the champagne bottles rolled beneath.

Armistice Day. Yesterday the war had finally come to an end and all of Paris had erupted in celebration. There was singing, dancing, music, drinking, and kissing. She held her trembling hand up to her face. The bold blighter of a wedding band was still there. Perhaps too much kissing.

No, no, no!

She dressed faster than a matinee dancer between numbers, not caring that her blouse was missing two buttons or her hair tumbled in a mess down her back. Rounding the bed on tiptoe, she peeked at the man—the word *husband* sent nerves skittering up her spine, and she had more than enough to deal with at present—still sleeping soundly. He had a fine nose and full lips that were slightly parted to release soft breaths of air. Blond lashes rested against his cheek into which a dimple curled.

Who are you?

A curl flopped across his forehead. For a second she had the exhilarating urge to flip the lock back in place, but a slight stirring of his legs that shifted the bedsheet a tad lower stopped her.

She needed to leave. Now.

She wriggled off the ring and placed it on the bedside table next to a photograph of what could only be them in inebriated bliss and a marriage license signed by Esme Fox and Jasper Truitt.

Jasper Truitt, her hus— *No! No, no, no!*

She grabbed the photograph and bolted for the door. Before closing it, she dared one final peek at Jasper Truitt and sighed in regret. A shame. He looked rather a dish.

1

A BALMY BREEZE LADEN WITH salt and surf trickled through the glass doors that had been thrown open. Party guests flowed in and out of the villa in continuous waves, the women as gaily dressed as tropical fish in their pinks, silvers, and greens while the men resorted to the tried-and-true blacks and whites of formal wear.

Jasper Truitt swirled the ice melting in his scotch as a bead of condensation rolled down the glass and plopped to the travertine floor, narrowly missing his shoe. If only he were a fish. At least then he could jump into the Mediterranean for a cool-off from the miserable heat and none of the stuffed shirts would spare him a second glance.

"Enjoying yourself, Mr. Truitt?" An elegant woman dressed in soft blue with silver hair framing her delicate face floated over to him. A small fox terrier trotted obediently next to her.

"Very much indeed, Madame Rothschild," he replied with a small bow. "Your home is quite stunning."

Madame Rothschild smiled comfortably at her surroundings as if she had been accustomed to wealth all her life. Because she had. A member of the French banking Rothschild family, she was a collector of fine arts, fashion, parties, and homes dotted around the world. Including the posh Villa Ephrussi in which they now gathered.

"Do you enjoy fine art, Mr. Truitt?" she inquired as the six-piece orchestra shifted into a Louis Armstrong number.

"It catches my attention."

"Then you must return sometime and browse my collections when fewer people are ogling them and trying to estimate how much I paid for each." She waved a dismissive hand. "As if one could place a price on art."

"I would be only too happy to return and examine these works to better understand their true value."

"*Bon.* In the meantime be sure to visit the stone garden. I just added a gargoyle that was saved from one of the churches in Amiens during the war. He is quite fierce, and I adore him. Enjoy the show later."

"Thank you, Madame Rothschild. I will." Jasper offered another bow as his hostess departed to be swallowed into the swell of her party guests. Each person grasping to touch even the hem of the famous Rothschild fortune. But for him there were rules to follow. Protocol. An honor code. Strangers were preferable, galleries and exhibits top-notch, and passing acquaintances acceptable, but one must never steal from a friend.

It was fashionable for coming-of-age gentlemen to partake in a tour of the Continent. Leaving behind the dreariness of England, a lad could experience gondola racing in Italy, bull-fighting in Spain, the nightlife of Paris, and every other frivolity money could buy, all while tallying it up to a fine education in the ways of the world. His grandfather, that sly old sinner, had taken him on such a tour.

On the refined soil of England, the seventh Duke of Loxhill was a prominent figure among the nobility and would not acknowledge the out-of-wedlock fruits of his notoriety, but across the Channel no one gave two gold crowns for the upper-crust rules of respectability. In fact, the more notorious one was, the more welcomed they were. So off to Europe they went—Jasper, the bastard son of a bastard; and his grandfather Duke. Duke introduced him to princes, queens, generals, master painters, novelists, dancers, and every colorful character imaginable. It was indeed a great education.

Jasper reluctantly turned away from a gilded-framed Fragonard hanging on the wall. Duke had introduced him to Madame Rothschild ten years ago, making her a personal friend. So despite the easy fifty thousand pounds he could collect from one of his discreet buyers for the painting, rules were rules. That and if he was caught lifting one more item, he'd be sent right back to jail.

For years Jasper had slipped beneath the authorities' noses, earning himself the rather stylish moniker of Phantom, and not once had they come close to catching him. Until a year ago when his trouser pocket caught on a doorknob and out spilled a ruby necklace and three gold rings. Right in front of a police officer. The police wanted to make an example of the infamous Phantom to discourage all would-be thieves, but Duke had stepped in, and with a few words, Jasper was a free man again.

While he couldn't deny his preference for freedom over a lifetime behind bars, it had chafed him raw to be forced to rely on another man's standing rather than his own. Ah, the complexities of being a thief with a sense of pride.

Of course, such pride didn't keep him from slipping off from time to time to pursue jobs—such as enjoying a stunning collection of jewelry at a party on the French Riviera. One piece in particular.

"Mesdames et messieurs! Ladies and gentlemen!" A man dressed in a starched butler's livery stood in the indoor patio, a squared-off space in the center of the villa with marble columns and arched spaces that greeted visitors upon arrival. Tipping up his chin, he raised his voice to be heard over the din. "If you will all make your way to the garden, please. The show is about to begin."

A flurry of excitement carried Jasper outside into the evening air, only a degree cooler than inside. The sun setting in the west cast its last orange rays across the crystal blue waters of the Mediterranean while washing the sky in pinks and purples, smattered with stars. The lights glowing from inside the pink villa flooded out to mingle over the deep green grass and palm leaves from which dangled hundreds of light strings. Down the center of the yard stretched a long rectangular basin of water dotted by lily pads. Torches and lanterns had been placed to highlight the many gravel paths leading deeper into the perfumed gardens of lavender and lemongrass.

"Jazz! Jazz!" A familiar voice called through the throng, followed by a sharp whistle. "Oy! Over here."

From the terrace Jasper made out a waving hand down by the water basin. Desmond Walsh. A degenerate second son of a viscount Jasper had met while serving together during the war.

With Desmond's penchant for scotch, cards, and good music, they had become immediate friends.

Jasper zigzagged through the crowd and grinned at his old comrade. "Mond, how are you? Didn't expect to see you here."

"You know me. Wherever there's a party." Wearing an eager grin, Mond offered him a lazy salute with his left hand. His right arm had been blown off at Verdun. "Heard a whiff of it from the gambling tables at Monte Carlo and had to come see the shindig for myself."

"How did Lady Luck treat you?"

"Well enough at first." Mond patted his breast pocket where a formidable bulge pressed beneath the fine black jacket. "She's a fickle mistress, though, and started batting her lashes at an Italian count before long, but I fully expect to entice her back tomorrow night. Care to join me?"

"Perhaps."

Mond tilted his fair eyebrows with interest. "Unless you have your eye on something here."

Jasper swirled his scotch. The melting shards of ice pinged the glass. "Perhaps."

"Got a buyer yet?"

"I have a client," Jasper said evasively.

Another reason for their friendship. Mond was well-connected in aristocratic circles, and rich people loved nothing more than becoming richer and earning the jealousy of their peers. There was only so much money to go around, but artwork and treasures were an entirely separate level, and Jasper knew how to provide. During the war Mond had noticed Jasper's unique gift of acquiring goods for the soldiers—goods not even the quartermaster could finagle off the black market. Food tins, socks, cigarettes, photographs of dance hall girls in their scanties—Jasper knew how to get it all, and soon enough, for a small percentage of the cut, Mond began introducing him to generals and colonels, men who, outside the trenches, were referred to by titles.

Perhaps the greatest strength of their friendship was that Mond never raised an eyebrow when Jasper got the itch to try his hand at a new prize, and on more than one occasion was there to aid in scratching it.

"All right, keep your secrets." Mond grabbed a glass of champagne from a passing waiter and sipped. "But know this, there's chatter around the craps tables. A wealthy Prussian is searching for a valuable artifact that belongs to his family and has been missing for sixty years. The reward is said to be substantial."

"I'll keep that in mind."

At the far end of the rectangular water basin, a small hill protruded with stone steps leading up to a rotunda. Torches ringed the structure and highlighted the petite figure climbing the steps to stand within the circle of columns upholding the roof.

"Good evening, my friends," Madame Rothschild said. A megaphone was stationed in front of her so the audience lined along the basin and closer to the house could hear. "I am very pleased you have joined me here tonight to celebrate beauty, art, and life. After four horrible years of death and destruction, we must learn to live again."

As her speech carried on, Jasper sipped his drink and surveyed the crowd. Women outnumbered the men six to one. Men too old or too fresh-cheeked to fight. Those left of middling years were sparse and often accompanied by missing limbs, eye patches, blasted-off ears, or canes. At least, those were the visible scars. Jasper's hand trembled, nearly upsetting his glass.

Some scars were buried too deep to be seen. Unless one knew where to look. A man across the way had shoved both hands in his pockets but couldn't stop his feet from twitching. Nerve shakes. Another fellow pressed his hand to his ear as the megaphone droned on. Loud noises. Back home, people said these were the lucky men, the ones who still had their looks and all their arms and legs. But what did they know?

He shook himself from that maudlin thinking. He'd survived; others hadn't, and that was simply that.

". . . have gathered the world's finest collection of jewels in a rainbow of colors to celebrate all things that glitter," Madame Rothschild continued. "Many of the items you will see are on loan from private collections. However, take heart. Several of the pieces are up for sale. The proceeds will go to a displaced children's hospital in Nice, so dig deep into your pockets, gentlemen, and buy the ladies something pretty."

At her signal the orchestra dove into a classical piece by Debussy, and at the far end of the basin stepped a figure, moving as if gliding atop the water. The crowd pressed forward with oohs and aahs. The woman was costumed as Marie Antoinette, the infamous French queen, wearing a revealing caged skirt and a towering wig. Draped around her throat were enough diamonds and sapphires to fund an entire country.

"This sapphire-and-diamond parure," Madame Rothschild said, "is thought to have been made for Empress Josephine and later acquired by the House of Bourbon."

The model sashayed to the end of the basin where Jasper stood. She did not walk upon water as the crowd was made to believe, but on a thin layer of glass fitted over the top. Still, the illusion was quite something.

Smiling a pink smile, the model offered her hand. "Care to help a girl down?"

Mond shoved his glass into Jasper's hand, then leapt forward with gallant determination. "At your service, my queen."

By the time her slippered feet touched the ground, a new lady was paraded out on a whirl of Tchaikovsky. This one was dressed in all white with a fur cape tied to her shoulders and sported a crown that looked like a diamond egg cracked open with pearls rolling down the center. She carried a scepter of gleaming ivory topped by a ruby the size of a walnut and a matching ruby brooch pinned to the center of her bodice. It was a miracle she didn't tip right over from the weight.

"And now we journey to Imperial Russia," Madame Rothschild said. "This crown was crafted for Catherine the Second, and the scepter was used by the last Romanov czar, Nicholas II."

As the model neared the end of her walk, Mond was there with eager hand extended to graciously help her down to walk among mortals on the ground. The string of jewels kept coming. Strands of creamy pearls, rich emeralds embedded in tiaras, icy sapphires winking from earlobes, and blood-red rubies dripping from fingers, all encrusted with diamonds and more diamonds.

"What a feast, eh, old boy?" Mond grinned back at Jasper as he assisted a Bavarian beauty whose shortened dirndl left little to the imagination, never mind the Dresden Green pinned to her corset.

Behind her floated Miss Britannia draped in the British flag and— Hullo, what was this beauty? It couldn't be. The Bagration Tiara was said to have been lost in Russia before the revolution, but here it was, complete with matching necklace, hair comb, and earrings dripping in pink spinels. The entire set sold to the right buyer could set him up nicely for years.

Jasper edged his way past Mond, ready to help this particular jewel, er, lady down from her walkway. A few delightful words in her ear and they'd slip off to one of the darkened garden paths where it would be only too easy to slide the pieces off one by one into his pocket. Of course, the lady would need to be distracted while this was going on, but who said the evening had to be all work and no play?

As he raised his hand to her with his most charming smile, the music suddenly changed. Richard Wagner's "Ritt der Walküren." A triumph of brass and galloping horse hooves and warrior shield maidens—and triumphant she was.

The model strode down the walk as if it were her field of victory. Her diaphanous gown slinked over her shoulders and came to a V just above her navel before draping into a skirt that sliced open to reveal long legs laced up in sandals. Enormous wings made of wire and downy white feathers extended from her back and trailed the ground at her feet. If the costume hadn't sufficiently impressed the audience into stunned silence, a crown lifted straight from the brow of a Valkyrie adorned her head. The crowd gasped in delight.

His intended prize.

"And now for our showstopper," Madame Rothschild continued, a bit breathless by this point. "The Valkyrie Tiara. First performed in 1876, Wagner's opera *Der Ring des Nibelungen* is the story born of Norse mythology where in the third act we are greeted with 'The Ride of the Valkyries'—women who choose who lives and dies on the battlefield. The opera immediately sparked a fashion for all things Norse, including the treasure you see here before you."

Circling the model's head, the diamond bandeau sprouted two glittering wings shooting straight up—ethereal, majestic, and terrifying—as the stones glimmered like fire. Slowing her pace so her hips swayed to each side in rhythm with her steps, she glanced neither left nor right but seemed to take in her rapt audience all at once. Her deep red lips curved in pleasure, her bobbed black hair glowing as dark as an onyx under the torch-light. Entranced, Jasper took a step closer and bumped the tips of his shoes against the low basin wall.

". . . comprised of 2,500 cushion-shaped, single-cut, circular-cut, rose-cut diamonds and set in a frame of gold and silver. The *en-tremblant* diamond wings are constructed using wire-coiled springs so they move slightly when worn. Observe."

The model turned her head gently from side to side, encouraging the diamond wings to flutter and earning another impressed *aah* from the crowd. Her smile broadened, one side of her lips tipping up just a bit farther than the other, prodding something in the back of Jasper's mind. Like he'd seen that quirk before.

She was nearing the end of the walk. The audience grabbed at the tiny feathers that loosened from her wings and drifted through the air. Grown men and women squealed with delight as they jumped and snatched for the fluffy bits, then waved them high in the air when at last their treasure was caught. Indeed, the Valkyrie was the treasure of the event, and all eyes would linger on the magnificent piece for the rest of the evening. Not that he was worried; he was rather good at lifting things right from under the spotlight. It all came down to a matter of finesse.

The crowd pressed in around him, but he held his ground. A few more steps and he could take her hand, offer her a refreshing drink, then suggest a cooling walk among the secluded garden paths to—

The prodding in the back of his mind slammed into him full force.

It couldn't be.

The woman's tilted smile flashed over him to the next person but screeched back to him. He saw the recognition in her eyes the same instant it hit him.

Yes. Yes, it could be.

It *was*.

His glass of watery scotch slipped from his hand and smashed on the gravel, sending shards of crystal tinkling over the smooth pebbles. The people around him yelped and jostled away.

Or at least, he thought they did. Every quivering bit of his attention was centered on the woman before him. She blinked and the shared look of disbelief disappeared. With another flash of her tilted smile, she whirled at the audience's resounding applause for a second look and sashayed back the way she'd come.

A hand waved in front of his face. Mond.

"Seems you made an impression on the lady. As you did my shoe." Whipping the silk handkerchief from his breast pocket, Mond wiped specks of scotch from his shoes. He straightened and tucked the handkerchief back into his pocket. "Who is she?"

Jasper rubbed at the heat dashing up the back of his neck.

"My wife."

He darted after her, following the trail of downy feathers as he moved away from the drag of guests clogging the main lawn as they clustered around the bejeweled models for closer in-spections. He rushed down a parallel path that veered off behind a scrim of thick-leaved bushes and trees that sheltered a small squared space to showcase a single piece of art.

And there she stood, leaning her back against a marble ped-estal with a Grecian hero perched atop. She looked exactly as she did in his dreams, yet nothing at all like what he remembered. Her skin was still the milky color of alabaster, her legs long, and her hair as black as midnight. The last time he'd seen her, those dark strands had brushed her waist after he'd pulled the restrictive pins from her hair on their wedding night. He'd delighted in run-ning his fingers through it to stroke the soft skin hidden beneath. Now she sported one of those fashionable bobs all the women were raging over. On most women the cut resembled a young boy who'd yet to grow into his chest hairs, but on her it was perfection. Shorter in the back and tapering longer in the front to brush her jaw like a razor's edge.

All right, Truitt, my lad. You can play this one of two ways. First option: the long-lost husband still nursing a broken heart after waking up to find his wife had run out on him. Or the second: cool and calm as if he barely remembers their whirlwind romance and has not spent the past four years searching for her face in every crowd.

At the sound of his intrusion into her sanctuary, she turned her head in his direction.

"It's you." Her voice was collected with the barest hint of surprise. As if the world had not just stopped spinning and tossed them on their heads.

Second option it was then.

Jasper slipped his hands in his pockets and affected a non-chalant shrug of one shoulder.

"Hello, Esme."

She turned fully around to face him in a graceful swirl of her sheer skirt.

"It's been a long time."

"Four years."

Her thin eyebrows lifted as if the passing of time caught her off guard. "Has it really been that long? My goodness . . . Well, you certainly look swell. What a surprise to see you here tonight. Of all the places in all the world."

He moved farther into the private space where the scent of blooming jasmine hung heavy among the dark green leaves. "The world is smaller than we typically think. After all, how could you explain this reunion?"

"Serendipitous good fortune." She smiled brightly as if to convince him to ignore the obvious topic thundering below their flippant words. At last her smile dimmed and she sank her teeth into her lower lip in capitulation.

"I suppose this is as good a place as any to have it out. Darling, I am sorry for what happened, but you must admit it was all rather rushed and we fumbled into a mistake. Commitment was never my strongest feature and surely you see by now that my leaving was for the best."

He nodded, not in understanding or agreement but rather at finally confronting the unanswered questions haunting him. That morning after their wedding he had sat in a stupor for a good half hour wondering where his bride had vanished to. Realizing she hadn't merely popped out for tea and crumpets, he'd run—all right, more like stumbled due to the lingering effects of champagne—down the street shouting her name and asking every person he saw if they'd seen her, but most were still too sodded from their Armistice carousing to notice a runaway wife.

At first the constant whys had harangued him morning, noon, and night, but time had sanded away their cutting roughness, leaving little scabs for him to pick at when the mood struck. A bottle of champagne often did the trick. Seeing Esme again ripped off the old scabs, and out poured a hundred fresh whys with their stinging edges.

"Did it occur to you to mention that before we signed the marriage license, or did the notion seize you after our wedding night?" The abrasive whys softened to a memory. A smile toyed with his lips. Several memories, in fact. "If I recall correctly, you had no qualms about . . . ah, our time together."

She plucked at the hair curling near her cheek, covering the pink stain beneath. "Our time together was spent drunk on champagne. Surely you see the folly in our overexcited actions, spurred on by youthful celebration. Really, darling, you should be thanking me for saving us a lifetime of regrets."

"How do you know there would have been regrets? You left too early to find out."

"I had no choice. Better to have made a clean cut than drag out the inevitable. No hearts broken or tears shed."

In that she was probably right. Their marriage had ended before they could discover if there was anything true about it. Anything worth fighting for. His heart may not have broken, but it had certainly been bruised by her cold disappearance. To say nothing of his wounded pride.

"You might have left a note."

The last rays of the sun peeked through the bushes behind her and dusted her shoulders, setting the gauzy material of her dress aglow like that of a Grecian goddess come to life.

"I am sorry about that, but I was terrified you would wake up and want to hash things out, and I simply couldn't allow it. Clean cut and all that."

"Yet you took our wedding photograph."

"A memento. For the lovely time we spent together, though I remember it mostly through a haze." She stepped closer to him. The hem of her gown swayed over the tips of his shoes. She was quiet for a moment as she examined him, barely needing to look up to meet his eyes due to her exaggerated height. "So your eyes are brown. I've often wondered."

Her gaze dropped to his mouth and for a second, he thought she might kiss him. Despite the desire it kindled in him, he dragged his attention away from her lush, inviting lips to the wings atop her head and took half a step back.

"The first time we met you had long hair and wore a nurse's uniform," he said, collecting himself to business he had actually come for. "Now look at you. Chic and crowned with diamonds. You've come a long way in four years. Or were you a princess in disguise and neglected to tell me?"

She, too, took a step back into cool reserve. "Hardly royalty. With the war over I put aside my starched apron and rolled bandages—you remember me telling you I was never very good at it to begin with?—and decided to try something new. I couldn't go back to what I had been doing before the war." A brief shadow clouded her face but lifted just as quickly as she pressed on with her story. "A few odd jobs here and there until I found something I'm rather good at, and it brought me here tonight. Modeling precious jewels most women can only dream of. Such as this." She lifted her hands to either side of her head, indicating the Valkyrie.

"It's a stunning piece. May I?"

She tilted her head forward so he could better see all the angles. The sun now dipped beneath the horizon, and the silver-and-gold metal no longer stood separate but melted together into a rosy hue that burned through the diamonds like pink fire. Beautiful, but not what he was looking for.

He tried another tack. "I imagine it's quite heavy."

"Then you would be wrong. It's certainly no heavier than that tin hat you wore in the trenches. You told me it weighed a ton."

"I was trying to impress you." It slipped out. He was finished with that line of thinking and had shut the door to carry on with his intended purpose, but the heat pressed around them, heavy with memory and laden with the mingling scent of her perfume—an intoxicating blend of orange blossoms. He kicked the mental door shut before the perfume wreaked havoc. "But a tin hat is nowhere near as impressive as a winged crown."

She glanced around quickly, then slowly lifted the tiara from her head. "We're not supposed to remove these, but if you don't tell, then I won't."

"Cross my heart." He made a quick X over his heart, then held out his hands to accept the tiara. As simple as that. His treasure handed to him on a silver platter. He could turn on his heel, vault over the wall, and be off scot-free before she could utter an alarm. Yet something in him resisted, and the door cracked open. It was too easy, and she was too near. After four years of wondering why, he couldn't simply walk away, not as easily as she had, not yet.

"See the wings here?" She leaned forward, nearly touching her head to his to point to a red-painted nail at the wings. "The coiled-wire springs allow them to move as if in flight without adding any unnecessary weight." She carefully rotated the piece on his flat palms and pointed to where the thin wires had been attached to the headband.

"The craftsmanship sure is something, as is the myth behind it." Jasper tilted the tiara slightly to catch the light twinkling from the electric bulbs strung through the trees. The yellow light glided along the headband's smooth metal backing, catching slightly on the screws holding the wings in place, but not on the scrolled *R* that was supposed to be stamped just under the left wing. Blood throbbed in his head. The tiara was a fake.

"Cartier made a number of these back when they were all the rage, but the famous jewel house crafted the Valkyrie to be the most exquisite of them all."

"Who was it crafted for?" He kept his voice neutral despite his entire plan having gone belly-up. Duke would not be pleased. Where was the real Valkyrie?

Esme shrugged. "There's a rumor about it belonging to a posh aristocrat's mistress, an Italian opera singer, long before it went to his bride, but who can untangle the affairs of the rich? Would you mind helping me take these off?" Tugging at the straps over her shoulders that tied the wings on, she turned and presented her back to him. "The tiara may not be heavy, but these certainly are. My back will be sore for a week."

Jasper reached for the strap only to remember he still held the tiara. Correction, the fake. He cursed silently. The only option now was to start hunting again from scratch. Esme quickly plucked the tiara from his fingers and slipped it back on her head.

"Is it straight?" she asked, feeling the diamond-encrusted band sitting crookedly across her brow.

He gently straightened it, careful not to let his fingertips linger too long anywhere near her face. There was no telling . . . Well, actually there was a telling of precisely what they would do so close to that smooth cheek. He snatched his hands back and indicated for her to turn around.

The straps were white leather made to blend into her barely-there gown. Three in total, one for each shoulder and a center one that held them together to form a sturdy H. He unbuckled the center one first, then the shoulders, and helped ease the massive feathers from her back.

Holy smokes! The pair of them had to weigh at least three stones.

"Ah, much better." She rubbed the back of her neck. The short black hairs bristled softly against her pale, exposed skin.

"It's a wonder you didn't topple backward." He draped the wings carefully over the statue, transforming the marble man into Icarus.

"If I had, I would have played the part of a Valkyrie slain in battle. Keep it as part of my act." Smiling with amusement, she stared up at the statue, idly twirling one of the feathers around her finger.

Her back was to him, and their tête-à-tête had dragged on long enough. Any longer and Madame Rothschild might wonder where her showpiece had gone and come in search. Poor woman. She had no idea she'd been duped.

Why was there a fake circulating to begin with? And then there was Esme. His wife. How was he to go about that, and more precisely, *what* did he want to do about seeing her again?

Boom!

Jasper ducked, throwing his arms over his head as red flares filled the night sky.

A cool hand touched him. A soft voice filled his ear. "Fireworks. Look!"

He glanced up to see bursts of red, white, and yellow. Not starbursts to cut charging soldiers in half, not artillery shells whistling down for explosion, but fireworks. Harmless, frivolous fireworks.

Slapping on a smile to cover his thundering heart, he straightened, but not before catching the sympathy in her eyes.

"Yes, fireworks," he said, pushing away her sympathy as he forced himself to watch the sparkling display over their heads.

There had been fireworks the night of the Armistice. Everyone in Paris went out to see them, including him and Esme, but it hadn't been long before they could only see each other.

He turned to her. "Do you remember—"

She was gone.

2

"WHAT DO YOU MEAN IT'S a fake?" Esme didn't know whose cry of surprise was louder. Her own or that of the aging opera diva standing next to her. Though, to be fair, the old lady's squawk trembled with a high-pitched vibrato Esme could never hope to achieve. If any patrons at the hotel casino below heard, they would most likely chalk it up to one of the exotic birds flapping about in the lobby's aviary.

The jeweler, a small mole of a man draped in entirely too much starched black for the Mediterranean climate, looked up from his examination of the tiara. One brown eye squinted from the glare of the lamp desk while the other peered at them through the glass of his loupe.

"I assure you, ladies, this is indeed a fake. LeRoi is a prestigious jewelry house in operation since the reign of King Louis the Fifteenth, who marked us as the royal jeweler when he first commissioned a piece for his mistress, Madame de Pompadour, in seventeen—"

"Do not presume to speak to *me* of mistresses." The diva flapped a wrinkled, impatient hand as she paced the room. "I know all too well about them."

Countess Rossalina Accardi was not a woman to waste time on inconsequential matters, such as the opinions of others or facts. She demanded her own narrative with an iron will that had broken her free of the chorus when she was only fifteen years old, cast her as a leading lady by eighteen, and made her known as a singing legend by twenty. She had wrestled fame to her bidding and was now past the prime of her long life, lounging over her stardom as if the world should fall at her feet and praise her for bestowing such a gift upon them. A musical Prometheus straight from the Olympic opera houses.

Once upon a time, perhaps she had been great. She certainly had the wealth to claim so, but whatever talent of range and charm she once possessed had been lost under eighty years of wrinkles, a sagging bosom, and enough layers of theater makeup to prop up an entire stage of ingenues.

"Madame Rothschild went to great lengths to ensure each of the pieces for her show were without question." Esme toyed with the sleek hair curving her jaw as she propped a hip against the desk. Only on the very rare occasion was she wrong about a jewel, and the sensation did not sit well with her pride. Though she would be the last person to admit it. "How could this one have slipped in?"

The jeweler's mouth puckered. "It is an easy enough mistake when one does not know what to look for in real stones."

Countess Accardi's black pencil-drawn eyebrows arced like an irate beetle. "I have scores of jewels at my palazzi. All three of them! Men used to throw emeralds and rubies at my feet. Rubies! Other singers were given flowers that wilted within a week, but not I. Rossalina Accardi, world-renowned soprano, was gifted gems and furs and carriages. Do you think I do not know what a real diamond looks like by now?"

The jeweler dabbed at the sweat beading on his pasty forehead. "I do not doubt your knowledge, Countess, but some flaws only make themselves known to a practiced eye."

A polite way of saying the old woman was blind as a bat. It was a wonder she could see anything past the thick black kohl lining her eyes.

Esme leaned across the desk for a closer look at the headpiece. Despite her wearing it for nearly two hours at the party, she'd had barely a moment to examine it for herself. Though Jasper had . . . She pushed away that bedeviled thought before it had time to prick her.

"What kind of flaws?" she asked.

"The glass kind." His magnified eye blinked at her. "There are a few real diamonds interspersed, but the majority are glass, I am afraid to report. Along with the gold metalwork being dipped."

"Dipped?" Countess Accardi clutched at the triple strand of jet beads looped around her neck as if this bit of information was the last nail in the coffin. "Dipped!" Snatching the tiara from the table, she threw it on the tile floor and stomped on it with her red T-strapped heel. Tiny bits of glass shattered and spewed across the floor like sugar granules.

"Oh! Do not do that, s'il vous plaît!" The mole extracted himself from behind the desk and scurried around to brush the broken bits into his doughy palm. His fingers barely missed being stomped on in his fervor.

Sighing, Esme crossed the hotel room and dropped into a scrolled-back chair covered in a material of blue-and-white print that reminisced the scenery out the large windows. Well, she imagined they did, as the countess had locked tight the windows and balcony door and drawn the curtains should any-one have binoculars that could angle up to the fifth floor.

The whir of the roulette wheels, shuffling of cards, and tossing of dice was muffled beneath the plush rug, marble bathroom with its gold fixtures, and silk-draped bed large enough to roll around on and never find the edge. Pure luxury. But while Esme enjoyed a soak in a claw-foot tub as much as the next girl, she'd rather be sinking herself into a Gin Rickey. Ice-cold with condensation collecting in tiny bubbles on the glass. A thick lime wedge balanced on the rim. If she swirled it hard enough, the clinking ice might drown out Countess Accardi's tirade.

It was but one of many tantrums Esme had witnessed since coming into the countess's employ, though of late they had in-creased in fury. More screeching, more smashing of valuables. The woman's theatrics could rival any of London's East End brawlers Esme had grown up watching in back alleys, but that was home, where she could settle into the comfort of knowing those same brawlers would be sipping pints together at the pub once they'd had their licks. With the countess there was no such comfort, and Esme had to keep her wits about her lest she end up with a flowerpot flying at her head.

"I have paid enough to do as I like." The old woman huffed as she pulled a case of cigarettes and a lighter from the bright red sash tied low around her hips. Attaching the cigarette to a long black holder, she lit the end and drew in a breath of smoke. "Just as I pay you enough to forget your moral scruples to LeRoi."

The jeweler, who had been gathering up the tiara's broken bits, straightened on his knees with a haughty sniff. "LeRoi is a dignified employer."

"But not one that pays enough, which is why you take on side jobs for me."

The mole's eyes drifted to Esme, who merely shrugged. She had come to work for the countess a year and a half ago, lifting some of the most glamorous pieces in her portfolio, but the jeweler had been enrolled only nine months ago. After all this time working together, she really should learn his name, but then, the countess had never bothered to learn it either. In this line of work, the less personal information offered, the less it could pin one down. A thief never wished to be pinned down.

"The real one is still out there," Esme said, crossing her long legs and enjoying the feel of real silk stockings against her skin after suffering through the war years with scratchy cotton. "I'll find it."

"Oh will you indeed?" The countess rounded on her, beetle eyebrows raising. Smoke curled from her dark lips, which were stained a deep berry color that did little more than exaggerate the feathery lines around her mouth. "I already sent you to find the prize for my collection and you return with *i rifiuti.*"

"Hardly rubbish when LeRoi claims it has some diamonds to its worth."

"Specks of dust." The countess raised her foot again to stamp on the stones but found they had been swept safely away by the jeweler. She settled for grinding cigarette ash into the rug in front of Esme's shiny shoes.

Resisting the urge to swivel her feet away lest the countess think to stomp on them too, Esme smoothed the skirt of her ivory-and-ebony dress over her knees. "You hired me because I'm the best. I have yet to fail in procuring prestigious additions for your collection, and I don't intend to sully my reputation now."

"This is more than your silly reputation." The countess's eyes narrowed to kohl slits. "This is my life. It is a matter of personal honor to have it returned."

While a sparkler could certainly enhance a lady's life and joy, Esme could not understand the dogged determination and near obsession the countess had with obtaining the Valkyrie. It was all the old woman had talked about for months as they waited until it finally revealed itself as the headline piece for Madame Rothschild's event. Esme never bothered wondering the whys of who bought and sold on the black market. Most were rich eccentrics with too much money, and as long as they paid her, it mattered not what they did with a first-edition Dickens or ruby-encrusted bracelet.

Countess Accardi was different. She'd first bought an emerald brooch in the shape of a panther before asking if Esme could locate a specific ring. Esme hadn't worked for clients directly as she preferred to lift what caught her eye and then sell to the highest bidder, but the countess had offered a sum too tidy to turn down. Since that first ring, she'd been paid to locate and procure more items for the diva, and the earnings had set her up quite nicely, enabling her to hop from one exquisite hotel to the next—as far away from Wilton's Music Hall in the East End as she could get.

Esme didn't back away from the old woman's stare. "I'll find it."

"My grand return to the stage is two months away. It is imperative that I have the Valkyrie in hand for my performance."

Ah yes. The performance to top all performances, when the grand dame planned to pluck herself from retirement and reclusiveness and foist herself into the stage's spotlight for one glorious, delusional evening to perform her most beloved rendition from Wagner's *Die Walküre*. Hence the need for the Valkyrie tiara.

Perhaps the sparkler was intended to distract from her soprano now sounding more like the song of an aged owl with its wing caught on a branch.

Smoke curled from the countess's lips. "After such a stinging failure, how do you plan to retrieve my tiara?"

"Leave those details to me. It's what I'm good at."

"So you said about this catastrophe." Countess Accardi cut her smoke-rimmed glare to the broken metal bits and stones the mole was carefully separating into piles on the desk. She wouldn't be surprised to find a few of those pieces in his pocket by the end of the evening.

Eager to leave before the woman's stare could sear her to the chair, Esme stood. "A temporary setback. One I shall rectify at once." Right after that drink at the hotel bar.

"See that you do. The Valkyrie belongs in my hands. It is the culmination of everything, the *pezzo forte* to what I am owed. The wrong done by the one who stole it from me will finally be righted." A malicious light glowed in the old woman's eyes.

Well, that was alarming. "What do you mean 'righted'?"

"In my younger, benevolent days I had a distinct pleasure in ruining the reputation of anyone who dared to cross me, having their names smeared to worthlessness. It often drove them to the despair of leaping off a balcony or throwing themselves in front of a carriage. If they made themselves my enemy, there was nothing a drop of poisoned honey in their tea or suffocation with a pillow in their dressing room could not resolve in my favor.

"Sadly, I no longer possess the patience for such endeavors, but for the Valkyrie I will make an exception. Poisoning is too gentle; suffocation not nearly satisfying enough." Her eyes blazed.

"This particular double-crosser deserves something spectacularly violent for an ending, as befitting the legend of a Valkyrie."

Esme's stomach lurched. "I've never found violence to be the answer for anything."

"I have." The smile of a snake slithered across her face. "As I said, my patience for recompense has grown thin over the years, and I have been forced to assign the deeds to another—with the exception of the Valkyrie, as only my personal touch will suffice."

She grasped the long rope of pearls dangling from Esme's neck and tugged, sawing the baubles back and forth across the back of her neck. "Pirazzo's particular skill is strangulation, did you know?"

Throat dry and skin burning raw, Esme shook her head.

"Quite an art. I've watched him work a number of times, and the finesse and strength required in the fingers is astounding." Dropping the pearls, the countess motioned to a shadow near the door. "Pirazzo, see our pennyweighter out."

Esme didn't bat a mascara-caked eyelash as the threat hit her square in the heart and slid into her cold belly. She had clawed her way tooth and nail to escape destitution, hunger, and fear. Her street smarts had provided a way of survival and earned her a prime living, but not only that, they had provided a life. A life of hopes and dreams where she wasn't begging for scraps. With one snap of the countess's bony fingers, it could all end.

If Esme didn't find that tiara . . . How she wished to slip away and never deal with the old woman again, but she wasn't foolish enough to pull such a stunt with the countess. Not when the shadow by the door stepped into the light and took the form of a hulking man with a gun and a long silken cord strapped beneath the immaculate cut of his suit jacket.

Esme smoothed the front of her dress to cover the shaking of her hands. "No need to escort me, darling." She breezed out the hotel room door that Pirazzo held open for her. "I know the way."

"You better find it, Miss Fox." He stood at the door, immovable as a mountain, his dark eyes following her down the hallway. Having worked as Countess Accardi's bodyguard for years, he was not a man to be crossed. "But if you don't, I'll enjoy showing you how tight a silk rope can cinch."

Ice skittered through her veins despite the warm night air. She covered the alarming sensation by waving over her shoulder. "Work on your sweet talk, Razz. That's no way to get a girl."

After rounding the corner, she slipped into the elevator and took a deep breath to calm her racing heart.

"Floor, mademoiselle?" the operator politely asked as he shut the cage doors and hovered a white-gloved hand over the operating handle.

"Three— No, lobby, s'il vous plaît." As much as her silk sheets and a hot bath called to her, so much more did a strong drink to shake the tremor from her bones. Never had she been threatened with Pirazzo's particular talents in all the time she had worked with the countess, but this tiara seemed to have everyone in a bother. The sooner she found it, the better. Straightaway after that drink.

At ground level she stepped off the elevator and into the lobby, which put the title Grand Hotel into perspective. Designed to invoke the Belle Époque, the room boasted marble pillars, pale-green and white walls with gold trim, cascading chandeliers, and painted frescoes. Fresh flowers blossoming in glazed pots perfumed the air with sweetness as the salty evening breeze spilled through the dozens of open doors leading to the terrace and, beyond, the midnight blue of the Mediterranean.

Esme's heels clacked across the marble floor, drawing stares from hotel guests lounging on the swanky couches and chairs. She kept her gaze forward, her head tilted, knowing the striking image she displayed in her svelte black-and-ivory gown and sleek bob. It wasn't vanity, merely truth. Above-average height made a girl stand out no matter her surroundings, so she'd decided long ago to embrace it and never looked back. Or down, as it were.

She glided into the cool recess of the bar, slid onto a barstool, and ordered a Gin Rickey with double lime wedges. It was that kind of night. The muscles strained along her shoulders and back from carrying the weight of those wings despite the sense of awe they had imbued her with. It wasn't everyday she took on the role of a mythological warrioress, but she could certainly see the appeal of such power.

"Here you are, mademoiselle." The bartender placed a tall glass filled with ice and pleasure in front of her.

She slid a generous tip across the bar. "Merci." As she took a long sip, the refreshing blend of gin, lime, and soda water glided down her throat in an explosion of sparkly bubbles that melted her cares away.

A gentle breeze kissed the exposed skin of her back where her dress dipped dangerously low. Turning on the stool, she surveyed the intimate clustering of small tables and chairs, column-lined walls interspersed with towering palm trees, and the stained glass domed ceiling. The entire back wall had been opened to a terrace that extended the space to outdoor seating where most of the crowd was gathered to listen to a band.

"Good band."

Esme jumped, catching her drink just in time, and swiveled to face the man who had appeared on the barstool next to her. She covered her surprise with a cool smile.

"Jasper. Fancy seeing you here."

"A notch above many of the holes I've stayed in."

"Oh?" My, that black jacket and tie were the perfect touch for his charming smile. She took another sip for composure, but this time the fizzing bubbles were more frenzied than refreshing. "Are you staying here?"

"I came for you." He met her gaze straight on. Confident and decisive with none of that wishy-washy uncertainty too many men employed. It was one of the traits she had found most intoxicating about him during their whirlwind courtship. He was a man who knew what he wanted, and he had wanted her. The thought had made her dizzy with desire. Even now, her heart gave a little twirl. But she had been drunk on champagne and the victory of war then. There was no excuse now to trap herself into commitment. Not when relationships were as reliable as candy floss in the rain.

Seeing him again at the party had been unexpected, to say the least, and terrifying at the very most. The man she had raced to stand before a priest with and raced even faster to the nearest hotel, only to sneak out in the morning without a word. Without a reason offered to him—her husband.

She had stood in that garden tonight arrayed in a warrioress's finest and waited for him to slash her with accusations and anger. All of which she deserved for her cowardly abandonment, but she had again stepped into her customary retreat of leaving before the other person left her.

She had wronged him by saying yes in the first place, but it was a mistake she was set to rectify. In the meantime she would enjoy returning his gaze, as handsome men were difficult to come by these days. "However did you find me?"

"I followed the trail of feathers."

"I wasn't wearing any feathers when I came here. Remember, you assisted me in removing them?"

He plucked a delicate feather from his front jacket pocket and twirled it between his fingers. Tan, long, and masculine. The feather was but a white blur between them.

"Oh, I remember." That bronzed stare again.

Esme sipped her drink to cool the molten yearning swaying in her belly. "So you followed me?"

"Let's just say I'm rather good at locating things."

"To what purpose?"

"I figure we have a few things unsettled between us, and I hate loose ends." He released the feather and it floated to the polished floor between them.

"Such as our marriage," Esme said.

"To state the obvious."

"A divorce would tie that up nicely." Best to cut him off quickly in case he had the dastardly idea of attempting marital bliss. Or worse, trying to force her to it.

"It would."

The knotted ball of anxiety in the pit of her stomach eased. Good. He didn't entertain illusions of shoving a wedding ring back on her finger. This might turn into the most amicable breakup of the age.

He signaled to the bartender and ordered a scotch, neat. The bartender poured the amber liquid into a squat glass and shot it down the wood bar where Jasper caught it deftly in one hand. Passing the glass beneath his nose, he inhaled deeply and sipped.

He had a strong profile, the kind that turned a woman's head. Cut jaw with the faint darkness of end-of-day stubble. Straight eyebrows with just the right amount of thickness. Aquiline nose hovering above perfectly molded lips, the bottom slightly fuller than the top. And those golden-brown curls that urged her to tousle them into unruly bits. The way she had last seen them flopped over his forehead while he slept.

"Like what you see?" He swirled his glass.

"As a matter of fact, I do." Propping her elbow on the counter, she cupped her chin and settled in for a proper appreciation. If she was going to set him free, she might as well drink her fill now. "You look different out of uniform and sepia tones. I've always thought that if a man can't don a uniform, then he should be in evening wear. Rather dashing, the looks, and no better way to get a woman's heart thumping."

"You told me music does that too. I remember dancing in the Place de la Concorde when a brass band paraded down the Champs-Élysées an hour or so after armistice was announced."

She smiled. A happy day it was after four long years of mud, blood, and death. Laughter and music had filled the air. Jasper had taken her in his arms and not let go. She had not protested. "They played 'Daisy Bell.'"

The band on the terrace glided into a jazzy tune with swinging notes and a hot trumpet that melted through the salty night air.

"Would you care to dance?" A dimple flashing in his right cheek, Jasper stood and held out his hand.

Her fingers flittered out to grasp his, but then pulled back. She had one too many strings with this man, and it was best not to tie any more. "My pins ache after balancing those wings tonight. Another time perhaps."

With a gentlemanly incline of his head, he settled back onto his barstool and lifted the glass to his lips. Two sips, as if he was rationing them.

"It was quite the frenzy tonight after you ducked out. Madame Rothschild was beside herself when the tiara couldn't be found."

The knot in her belly clenched again. She ignored it with a lift of her eyebrows. "It's missing? Oh, poor Madame Rothschild! To have the showpiece of her charity event disappear is horrible indeed." She rubbed her temples. "It was giving me such a headache that I needed to take it off. I returned it inside the villa where the models had dressed. There were jewelers waiting with secure cases to return the items to their proper owners or new buyers. After I took off the tiara and placed it on a velvet tray, the man put it in his case and locked it tight. I can't imagine what became of it after that." She shook her head in sympathy. Or what she imagined was sympathy since taking from the rich had never burdened her. "I do hope they find it. Such a magnificent piece."

"So the crowd believed." Meeting her eyes over the rim of his glass, he drained it dry.

That was quite enough of that topic for the evening. In fact, his inquisitive brown eyes were far too direct for her peace of mind, particularly during the evening.

Uncrossing her legs, she slid off the barstool and summoned a petite yawn. "Well, this has been enjoyable, but I'm afraid the night's activities are catching up to me. Are you in town long? Perhaps we can do brunch and iron out the wrinkles for a divorce. It's really for the best. Well, good night, darling."

She forced her pace to remain sedate as she left the bar and crossed the lobby to the elevator when all she wanted to do was tear toward the nearest exit. Jasper put her in a tailspin and if she wasn't prudent, she would nosedive straight into destruction. A fate she had sensibly avoided since birth. No strings. No commitments. No heartbreak.

The elevator doors opened and out stepped Pirazzo. He dipped his oiled head in acknowledgment. "Thought I would find you at the bar."

"You only just missed me." She moved to step around him, but he placed a heavy hand on her arm. The alarming ice from earlier that she had managed to melt in her drink came rushing back to freeze her insides.

"Do not act so glib, Miss Fox. The countess grows impatient."

Esme nodded calmly as if in perfect agreement and reached to smooth the dark hairs behind her ear, effectively dislodging his meat hook from her arm. "I'm doing my best. Tonight was a minor setback, nothing more. Tomorrow I start a new search, and before long I'll return, prize in hand."

"It is in the best interest of your neck if you do. Something so *bellissima* should not be broken, but your necklace . . ." His eyes dropped to her rope of pearls. "Should we see how many times it can loop around your neck? White pearls against the blue and purple of your face as they cinch tighter?"

Her throat constricted. "Purple has never been my color," she said hoarsely.

"We leave tomorrow for Milan. Contact us there when you have it. And not before. Here. You forgot your bag upstairs." He handed her the black velvet clutch and stepped back into the elevator. The gun flashed beneath his jacket. "Going up?"

Shaking her head, she backed away. "I'll take the stairs. Stretch my legs." How odd her legs were becoming the most convenient excuse for avoiding awkward situations. "*Grazie* for the purse." *And the ever-increasing threats on my neck.*

She would not dwell on the bad. Not only did it spoil her mood, but it slowed her down, and if there was anything of value to a truly talented thief it was quickness. Once this tiara—the real one—was secured, she could hand it off in exchange for payment and skedaddle, leaving the countess and her beast in the dust for good.

The hotel stairs were a marvel. White marble with thin pink veins running through its creaminess and a gold runner sweeping up the center. Lady hotel guests were known to use it simply so they could sway dramatically while the enthralled lobby looked on. Esme had done it once or twice herself for her own amusement, but this time she rushed past the women posing in their finery to the third floor where the bustling sounds faded away into a long hallway with lush palms and bright white doors with brass numbers. Hers was all the way at the end.

"Are you going to follow me all night?" She turned at the sound of hushed footsteps several paces behind her.

Hands in pockets, Jasper grinned at her, the dimple digging deep into his cheek. "Isn't that what all ladies desire? A man trailing her."

"Not this lady." Flirting was all well and good in a darkened garden and bar, but near her room was quite another matter. "I understand we are still legally married; however, I intend to enter my room alone. Apologies if this upsets your marital intentions, but as we have not been living as man and wife, you can hardly expect otherwise."

"It may interest you to know—instead of assuming—that I'm not here for that."

She ignored the slight flag of disappointment. "Oh?"

He closed the space between them. "Why were you talking to that man?"

Her disappointment sallied into amused irritation. "I never pictured you for the jealous type." Turning on her heel, she continued down the hall. "It doesn't do you justice."

"A confident man need not dabble in jealousy," he said, following. "Unless it's something worth his attention."

"Ouch."

"Nothing you should take personal. After all, you're not really my wife, are you?"

Clever. She'd forgotten that about him. A smile tugged at her lips as she pulled her room key from her purse. "Then what are you here for? In the bar you claimed to be looking for me, but now you claim I'm not worth your attention. Do make up your mind, darling. You make a girl dizzy." Stopping at her door, she inserted the key.

"The man. What did he want with you?"

"I really don't think that is any of your business. Estranged husband or not—"

His hand shot past her, twisted the key, and opened the door. He'd shuffled her inside before she could blink. Stepping in behind her, he closed the door and locked it.

She took a step back into the sudden darkness that flooded them. "Now just a minute. I made it perfectly clear that this is *my* room alone. You cannot barge in here—"

He whirled on her so quickly she was forced to take another step back.

"Gio Pirazzo is a hired thug. A torpedo. His business is strong-arming people to do as his employer says, and if they don't deliver as promised, Pirazzo blips them off. Dead." He didn't move from the door, but he seemed to soak up all the air in the room. "Tell me truthfully, what are your dealings with him, or rather, his employer?"

She crossed the room and switched on a table lamp. Golden light spilled across the softly colored sitting space. Tossing her purse on the low-slung couch, she poured herself a glass of water from the decanter on the side table before easing into a wicker chair as her mind spun for a reason plausible enough for him to believe while getting him out the door as quickly as possible.

"As I told you, I've been modeling. His employer is an eccentric artist who wishes me to try on her latest creations." A lie was best when it stuck close to the truth. "I have no idea or interest in the security she hires."

"Nor the type of jeweler, I suspect."

"This artist does have expensive tastes."

"Ones that run to the black market it seems." He was watching her entirely too closely.

She draped her arm over the back of the chair. Languid, cool, precisely as her actress mother had shown her, and completely opposite to the knot of panic tying up her chest. "Whatever do you mean?"

He gave a dry laugh and strolled over to the couch, dropping the room key next to her purse. "You'll forgive me, but this has been a rather odd night. First, seeing you again. Imagine, putting a ring on a woman's finger and then four years later discovering her strolling down a pond with wings and a tiara—a tiara that winds up missing. Then, the same night, you see a notorious hit man and a jeweler who is known to take bribes for ascertaining pieces and their value on the black market." Perching on the arm of the couch, he loosened the black tie from his throat. "The Valkyrie tiara is worth a small fortune. On the black market it could fetch triple its originally commissioned price."

She shuddered on cue. "The black market, what a horrid thought."

"It would be if the tiara from tonight wasn't a fake." Tie loosened, he slipped the first button of his shirt free. "But you didn't know that, did you? Not until you brought it to this so-called artist and her bribed jeweler."

"How did you know it was a fake?"

"Because I'm hunting the real one. Same as you."

Esme's mouth dropped open to a very unrefined O. Not much in life surprised her after watching every possible scenario play out on London's East End stages, and even more backstage as a child, but this took the cake. While Mimsy—the name her mother preferred as she refused to be called anything as horrid as mum—taught her there was always another act to play, Esme was quick enough to realize when it was time for the curtain to close on a performance.

Closing her mouth, she dropped the doe-eyed innocence. "Very well. I'm a jewel thief if you must know. The best, in fact."

"I beg to differ. Have you ever heard of the Phantom?"

"I take it that's you. An impressive résumé you have. Paintings from the Musée d'Orsay, artifacts from Cairo, diamonds from the throat of a duchess. I heard you seduced her in her husband's opera box during the second act of *Don Giovanni*."

"Intermission actually, and it was a bauble she hardly missed, considering the duke was at the time sailing on his yacht with his mistress."

The absurdity of it all. Esme laughed. "Well, this is a pretty pickle if there ever was one. Two thieves. One tiara. Which of us will claim the prize?"

"Depends on who is better at tracking down leads."

"And those would be?"

He matched her laugh. "What kind of thief would I be if I offered that information to my competition? No matter how beautiful she is."

Charming, handsome, and flirtatious. She saw right through it. "You don't know where the real one is."

He shrugged as if that made little difference to the outcome. "I will soon enough."

If anything was more mesmerizing than a man's confidence, she had yet to find it. Standing, she arched her back against the aching muscles. Who knew feathered wings were so heavy?

"Make yourself a drink. I'm going to kick my shoes off. When I return we can discuss location possibilities for the tiara. I'd like to imagine it's locked in a Swiss bank. I've always wanted to try breaking into one. A girl needs a challenge from time to time."

He gave her that secret smile again, the one that offered a glimpse of his amusement while coyly hiding his thoughts. "May I use your telephone while I wait?"

"Of course. It's just there." She pointed to the piece sitting on a low table next to the window before gathering her purse and walking into the separate bedchamber and closing the door behind her. Sinking onto the fluffy bed piled high with pillows, she let out a lengthy but quiet sigh. How many more ways could this evening go bottom-up?

Jasper's voice rumbled through the door as she kicked off her shoes and unhooked her stockings from their silky garter straps, then draped them carefully over the foot of the bed. Having spent the war years in a starched nurse's uniform and rationed cotton stockings, she would never take for granted the luxury of pure French silk. Though, to be fair, she wasn't a true nurse, not in the way those sour old matrons in white wimples were, but she did volunteer at the hospital changing sheets, rolling bandages, and reading to the soldiers as the task demanded. She didn't care much for the sight of blood, but king and country called, and she'd answered like the rest of the womenfolk left behind. It was either that or take to the stage like Mimsy suggested, for the boys. Oh, there was no losing one's knickers or hip swiveling in those places, although one girl did split her pantaloons after a dizzying number of cartwheels down the center aisle. Tickets sold out for weeks afterward in hopes she would do it again.

Behind all the glitz and glamour of the lighting, costumes, and music, Esme had grown up seeing the cracks and the weariness such a life put on the soul. Premature wrinkles cracking makeup. Graying, dirty hair stuffed under wigs. Smiles that dropped as soon as they stepped backstage. They only time those actors and actresses felt alive was on the stage. Everything else was a disappointment as they survived from one performance to the next. Esme never wanted to live like that. She wanted to set her own terms of comfort, and so she had. One stolen diamond at a time.

Now she was after the biggest prize of her life, only to run smack-dab into the man she had been avoiding for four years. She flopped back on the bed and stared at the gilded sea creatures chasing one another around on the ceiling. What was she to do about Jasper? Not get distracted from the tiara by his charming smile, that's what.

Excellent plan, Esme. Men were for flirting, not keeping. Now, what about the tiara? She frowned at a particularly lascivious starfish who watched the ceiling chase from his painted corner with voyeuristic pleasure. *Well, for starters—*

The front door opened.

She bolted upright on the bed. Had Jasper left?

No, a second male voice entered the room followed by the door shutting. What sort of high-handed game was he playing by inviting visitors into her private hotel room? She marched to the door and prepared to fling it open in dramatic fashion when the stranger's excited voice stopped her cold.

"Valkyrie. New lead. Train tomorrow."

She dropped her hand from the doorknob and pressed her ear against the door to listen.

3

JASPER CLOSED THE DOOR BEHIND Mond. "Keep your voice down."

"Afraid of your *wife* overhearing?" Mond's eyebrows twitched at the closed bedroom door.

Jasper crossed the room and switched on the wireless. Music drifted out that sounded close to what the band played downstairs. "Of anyone hearing."

"What, your surprise reunion not copacetic?" Mond strolled around the room, taking in the opulent surroundings with an assessing eye. "Being in her hotel room is a promising start."

Jasper had come close to not finding her at all. Luckily, one of the cabbies at Madame Rothschild's overheard where Esme instructed her driver to take her. Jasper had arrived not five minutes behind his fleeing bride.

"It would be a promising start if she wasn't the one who stole the tiara from the party."

Mond's brow wrinkled in surprise. "That does put an interesting spin on things." His brow dropped. "With this kind of hush-hush information we should have met downstairs, not have it out with the competition a wall away."

"I would have joined you in the bar, but there's a hit man running loose and if he overhears us discussing the tiara, we're likely to end up as fish bait. Besides, the lady has a habit of slipping the hook and I doubt she would allow me in here a second time. I have a few wrinkles to iron out with her before putting this marriage out of its misery, but first I need to know what else you've found out."

Jasper dropped into the chair Esme had previously sat in and rubbed a hand over the back of his neck. In this line of work one was forced to adapt quickly while navigating the unexpected twists and turns with practiced ease. Of course, one never expected their estranged spouse to get one up on them.

Settling onto the couch across from him, Mond struck a cigarette and inhaled, streaming the smoke through his nose. "After you hurriedly informed me that the tiara was a fake and rudely rushed out of a perfectly good party, I made a few discreet inquiries." In other words he spoke to his reputable contacts who dealt in trades of ill repute. "The recent release of this incredible tiara is shrouded in mystery and has quite the collector enthusiasts shivering with delight at the prospect of obtaining it."

Thirty years ago the Valkyrie, the real one, had disappeared from public view with Duke hinting at having sold it after his wife died. Too sad a memory to keep, he'd claimed. Then two months ago a whisper had reached Duke that the tiara had resurfaced. The news sent him into a desperate tizzy, ordering Jasper, newly released from jail, after it. Who better than his bastard grandson and pinnacle of all thieves to retrieve the family crown?

When Jasper had questioned Duke why he suddenly wished to have the tiara again after selling it, Duke rambled on about not being in his right mind due to grief all those years ago and that time had allowed him to find sentimental value in the piece. The tiara was a Roxburgh heirloom and belonged in Roxburgh hands. Perhaps that was why Duke trusted Jasper to fetch it—to prove himself a true Roxburgh and not some shameful family secret, someone worth welcoming into the fold.

"A new whisper arose from Venice," Mond continued. "A collector of the rare and beautiful has a shop near Ponte delle Tette. Signor Campano. He doesn't like parting with his collection unless the offer is well over asking price, so be generous."

"Generous is for those intending to pay," Jasper countered.

"Be that as it may, dealing with Campano is likened to peeling a turtle from its shell."

"I've dealt with my fair share of turtles." Jasper's gaze slid to the bedroom door. *Minxes too.*

"So you'll be off then?"

"First thing in the morning I'll catch the train out. I'll stay at my usual haunt if you need to get in touch with me."

"And, ah . . ." Mond grinned, smoke curling from his mouth. "Until morning?"

"Make divorce arrangements, it seems." At Mond's look of confusion, Jasper settled back to explain—though what he was trying to explain was still foggy to him.

"We married in the craze of a celebration. Passions were high and we didn't think beyond the next sunrise and were fueled by a great quantity of champagne. Having gone into war and come out the other side alive, I figured the next best thing to survival was finding love. Well, I was young and foolish and captivated by a pair of blue eyes."

"A mistake from the beginning."

He'd not thought so at the time. Imagining settling down to wife and home, all of which he could claim for his own. As a bastard, nothing had been his own. Not even his last name, as Duke had forbidden all of his illegitimates—of which there were many—from using it. Douglas, Jasper's father and Duke's only son, had chosen their surname from a favored box of cigarettes.

"Why did you never tell me?" Mond asked.

"And say what? After a whirlwind of passion my bride left me mere hours after I placed a ring on her finger? Better to swallow the shot to my pride alone."

"Sometimes I think that's all women know how to do. Break hearts."

"Never said my heart was broken." Cracked, perhaps, but still mostly intact. Jasper pushed the thought aside as he had numerous times over the past four years, and stood.

"Thank you for the information about the tiara. I'll let you know when I arrive, but in the meantime I'm sure you'd like to jaunt down to the bar where I noted no less than six blondes."

Mond settled more comfortably into the couch and propped his ankle atop his opposite knee as he lit a fresh cigarette.

"All in due time, but not until I meet the mysterious Mrs. Truitt. The only woman who managed to snag and then leave in the dust the most sought-after playboy north and south of the English Channel."

Jasper knew from experience that once his friend got that look there was no chance of getting rid of him until he was appeased. Even if it meant putting off talking to his wife in private. Crossing the room, he knocked softly on the bedroom door.

"Esme? Might you come out here for a moment? There's someone I'd like to introduce you to."

No answer.

He knocked again. "Esme?"

When no answer came, he cracked open the door and stuck his head inside. "Apologies for disturbing you, but—"

The room was empty. He swung the door open. The bathroom was dark and the chest of drawers gaped open. As did the window.

He rushed over and thrust his head out to find two silk sheets tied together to form a rope, one end hooked to the bed's headboard while the other dangled a few feet over the grass.

Laughter took hold. Deep and unbelieving, it smothered the curse struggling to fly loose.

That woman. Gone again.

4

"What do you mean the train is not running?" Esme dropped her suitcase with a no-nonsense *thunk* and leaned closer to the partition separating her from the ticket manager. With her towering height, slash of deep red lips, and lack-of-sleep-crazed stare, she aimed to be the most intimidating force he had yet to encounter.

The little man was not impressed. That or he'd witnessed too many hysterical tourists after they'd lost their money at the gambling tables at nearby Monte Carlo to give much attention to her. Leaning his elbows on the counter in front of him, he gazed over the morning newspaper at her. "That is what I said, mademoiselle. The train is not running."

"How long will it be before it is running again?"

He shrugged and turned a page.

"That's it? The mass transportation of the Mediterranean coast is determined by a shrug of the unknown?" She leaned closer, her nose nearly touching the glass between them. "I need to reach Venice by tomorrow. It's imperative."

"I'm certain the railroad workers think it imperative they go on strike for unionization, but they're no doubt sorry for inconveniencing you and your little trip."

"My little tr— Is this what passes for helping one's customer?"

"No, that was the handwritten sign saying, 'No Train Tickets Sold.'" He turned another page and doffed an imaginary hat without looking up. "Good day to you, mademoiselle."

Esme huffed. She'd traveled enough to learn that most countries ran on their own schedule and not the quick, precise march that England set. Most days she enjoyed the rather laid-back feel of the Continent, but today she would pay a pretty farthing for a bit of good old-fashioned British efficiency.

Readjusting her white net gloves, she plucked her suitcase off the floor and stepped out of the dingy ticket office and into the brilliant morning light. No train. Now how to get to Venice?

Her silver patent shoe tapped as she raced through half a dozen options and discarded them. The Mediterranean waters sparkled a deep blue far off in the distance. Tiny yachts with their blinding white sails skimmed over the waves caused by larger ships pulling into and out of port. Ships. *Perfect!*

After hailing a taxi, she arrived at the harbormaster's office in half an hour and in another half hour had a ticket in hand to sail aboard the *Carpe Diem*. A rather fitting ship name. She wasn't built for speed but satisfied herself by sailing rich passengers around the warm waters from one coastal city to the next.

With no luggage large enough to check, Esme carried her small suitcase to her room, which was on the small side of luxury. But it was tidy and clean with a porthole that gazed to the western, er, port side. She was lucky to snag the accommodation at all as most of the cruise had been bought up by a group traveling to Greece.

"Beggars cannot be choosers," she muttered to herself as she stepped out into the tight corridor and locked her door behind her. "And you are in no position to be choosy."

Winding her way up the stairs to the public spaces of the ship, she glided past the dining room set with fine silver and snowy linens, a fully stocked library, and a lounge area dotted with cushioned wicker furniture. The other passengers had gathered along the rail to wave at anyone and everyone standing on the docks, but Esme slipped past them to the bow and settled on a lounge chair thoughtfully propped there.

The engine started, rumbling the deck boards as the ship pulled away from port. The passengers raced to the stern, eager for one last parting adieu. What was the point in looking back? The future was all that glittered and beckoned far from the dregs of the past.

"Drink, mademoiselle?" A waiter appeared with loaded tray in hand.

She selected something red and slushie with a pineapple wedged against the rim. "Merci."

A briny breeze tickled her skin as she took a sip of the fruity drink, wholeheartedly supporting the idea of drinks before noon while on a cruise. She tipped her head back against the chair and closed her eyes as the morning's warmth glided across her face and arms. One might assume she was on holiday, and it would be too easy to slip into that fantasy, if not for one tiny thing. It was all a lie. She was on the hunt, and train tickets aside, she would not be deterred from seizing her prize. Especially not with her neck on the line.

A wrinkle marred her tranquility. It was a prize she might have been too slow in obtaining if not for Jasper. The tiniest sliver of guilt attempted to wriggle into her good graces. She had sneaked off on him. Again. After eavesdropping on his private conversation. Which was conducted in her room, so that was his own negligence. Before which he'd accused her of unladylike common thievery. As if she would stoop to ordinary nabbing of baubles and bits. She had taste after all.

Still, there had been that moment in the bar when heat had arced between them. A rekindling of something she'd felt only once, so fleeting it had scared her right out of the honeymoon suite. And what was her first act upon seeing him again? Stealing the tiara right out from under him. Well, he should expect nothing less as the so-called Phantom, and if he did, he was in the wrong trade.

"Mmm, sure is a nice view."

Esme's eyes snapped open to find Jasper himself lounging in the chair next to hers with a tall glass of what appeared to be orange juice. He wore a straw fedora and a white linen suit with a pale-blue shirt, the essence of Mediterranean travel.

"Good morning." He raised his glass in salute, then took a sip.

She tilted her glass in recognition. "I see you found me."

"I see you were eavesdropping last night."

Smiling, she sipped her drink. "Guilty. Though can you blame me when you so conveniently laid bare the facts in my room?"

"I suppose it would be hypocritical of me to scold you or hold a grudge when I would have taken precisely the same action."

"I appreciate your ability to recognize the futility in seeking a different outcome." She tilted her head to block the sun with the thin rim of her cloche and stretched out her legs, crossing them at the ankles. "Since we are to be in close quarters for the next few days on this ship, shall we call a truce?"

He nodded in good humor. "I see no reason not to have an enjoyable cruise for as long as it lasts. Once we make port in Venice we can return to every man—or woman, as it were—for themselves. Deal?"

"Deal."

They clinked glasses and drank.

Silence stretched between them, the empty space filled with the lull of waves lapping against the ship's hull and seagulls crying as they floated through the soft blue sky. If she were a woman of cozy imagination, she might believe the brilliant weather and warm sun was good fortune smiling down and fling her cares as far as the horizon. However, she'd been raised by actresses and prop masters around gas-illuminated stages, and she'd learned that the beauty in front of the curtain was cut as soon as the red velvet swung closed.

Beneath the tranquil sunshine and cawing birds and icy drinks of a perfectly staged day buzzed a current. It was the same feeling of standing in the stage wings with all eyes glued to the diva's closed dressing room door. Waiting. Any second she might emerge and bring the house to their feet or down around their ears. Except instead of a heavily girdled woman with too much rouge, two simple words had Esme holding her breath.

Their marriage.

Now, there was a center stage act she wanted to shove in a broom closet and bolt the door against until she was good and ready to unleash it. And held something stronger than the slushy drink in her hand.

Veering as far away from that topic as possible, she settled on a much tamer subject. "How did you know the tiara was a fake?"

The linen material of his jacket flowed smoothly over his shoulders as he shrugged. "A good thief can weigh the value of his wares almost immediately."

Ha! "When I took it off my head you examined it rather closely. There was no way of you knowing some of the gems were made of glass without a jeweler's loupe or good lighting. Neither of which you possessed there in the garden, which means you knew to look for something else, a mark of some kind perhaps. What did you seek but not find?"

He swirled his drink. Bubbles fizzed from the bottom. Orange juice and champagne? Delicious. "Do you really think I would so easily give away my advantage?"

"If you claim that's the only advantage you have, then you are a poor thief indeed."

White teeth flashed against his tanned skin. "I never claimed it was my only lead, just one I'm not imparting to you."

"Very well. Then tell me something else. Why are you after the Valkyrie?"

His expression was as smooth as glass, a trick of the trade. As was lying through one's teeth. "Our profession needs only a monetary reason. The Valkyrie is worth a fortune. However, I don't have Italian hired guns breathing down my neck if I fail." He sipped his fizzing orange juice as seriousness touched his tone. "Who are you working for?"

Seriousness she was not having. She wagged a finger at him. "No, no. Some secrets must be kept, as you just pointed out."

"My secret advantage doesn't threaten me in a hotel lobby." The humor had faded from his expression and in its place flashed a direct alertness. "Pirazzo is dangerous. I've seen his handiwork before. Whoever he is working for must be a real pip. You may be in over your head."

She waved away his concern with a manicured hand. "Darling, I've been in over my head my entire life, but as you can see, I've learned to float."

He swung his long legs off the lounge chair and pinned his entire attention on her. "Esme."

What was that little shiver running over her skin when he said her name?

"You need to be careful."

"I am always careful, but it's sweet to have you worry about me. Besides, none of this will be a concern once I find the true Valkyrie."

That did the trick. The corners of his mouth quirked in amused confidence and shuffled out the seriousness. "You're assuming you'll get to it before me."

"Of course I will, but it'll be entertaining to have you along in second place. It does a lady good to have a handsome man chasing after her." Uh-oh. Did she not just tell herself to keep the broom closet locked? Here she was, dangerously fiddling with the key.

She stood before he could take that accidental flirtation and run with it—and from the look on his face he was more than happy to—and offered him an apologetic smile. "If you'll excuse me, I think I'll have a lie-down in my room. The past evening's activities left me with little beauty sleep."

He stood and elegantly inclined his head. Always so well-mannered. She remembered that about him. How it enhanced his attractiveness. Oh no. Not again. Truly, her thoughts had a wayward mind of their own.

"Will I see you for lunch?" he asked as she skirted his lounge chair. "Crab salad is on the menu."

For some reason the mention of food tipped her stomach sideways. No, wait. That was the boat rocking from an agitation of waves propelled by a passing cargo ship. She grabbed for the handrail.

Jasper leapt to her side and took her elbow. "Are you all right?"

She nodded, but the motion made her dizzy. "Right as rain. The sun must be getting to me."

"Allow me to escort you to your room."

"No, I shall be quite all right once my sea legs return."

They were standing awfully close. His hand was warm under her elbow and his eyes were a rich nutmeg under the shade of his hat. He smiled, dimpling one cheek. Her stomach fluttered as a smile slipped to her lips in return. The flutter turned to a heave.

His smile wavered. "Are you unwell?"

"Please do excuse me," she said, then bent over the rail and neatly tossed her cookies.

5

THE SILVER LINING WAS THAT Esme wasn't dead. The more concerning part was that she had sent back each tray of food Jasper had delivered to her stateroom over the past two days. The ship's porter said not to worry; he had not lost a single passenger to seasickness yet. Drunken toppling over the rail, yes, but not seasickness.

The knowledge did little to assuage Jasper's fretting.

He swirled his after-dinner drink, watching the ice clink together and water down a perfectly good scotch, leaving condensation dribbling onto the snowy-white linen tablecloth. Then again, what was he fretting for? Her recovery meant she would slip off again to snag the tiara before him. A foolish attempt on her part for she had no idea who she was up against.

He was the best obtainer on and off the market with a network of buyers and contacts that stretched deep underground while simultaneously climbing into the palaces of royalty. Everyone knew the Phantom. He had worked hard to establish his reputation as never failing. And so far he had succeeded by living by three golden rules: keep it entertaining, forgo making enemies if possible, and never allow the game to be personal. Rules one and two were going swimmingly, but number three was doing its best to sidetrack him with memories of lingering champagne kisses.

Dancers spun on the floor as the last remnants of supper were cleared away by gloved servers and the ship's band edged into more lively tunes that would be of little help to digestion. He adored a good turn around the wood, especially with a beautiful woman in his arms, but this evening the music did nothing to encourage his feet. He was content to sit at his table and watch while drowning his thoughts in scotch. Or what was left of it from the ice.

Lifting the glass to his lips, he stopped short. There, perched on top of one of the ice cubes, was the image of a mini Esme. Full red lips curved in seduction as she stared up at him through sooty lashes.

"*Forget the way I crushed your heart,*" she seemed to taunt. "*Forget that I abandoned you without care, and let's have a drink for old times' sake.*"

He shook the glass, overturning thoughts of her to the watery bottom. Two could play that game.

"Monsieur, telegram for you." A server appeared at his side with a folded paper balanced on a silver tray.

Jasper took the telegram. "Merci." Knowing what it said and from whom was a forgone conclusion. Only one person knew how to contact him at any given moment. Smoothing out the paper, he read the sparse lines from Mond.

Duke a pest. Stop. Hurry and locate.
Stop. Am not your secretary. Stop.

His friend may have been the only one who knew how to get ahold of Jasper at any time, but Duke knew how to put the squeeze on Mond to get to Jasper. His grandfather wasn't known for his patience, and it seemed he'd placed retrieving the Valkyrie at the top of his priority list and for reasons he declined to disclose. The old twister.

"Shall I bring you another, monsieur?" The waiter indicated the diluted drink on the table before whisking it away at Jasper's nod.

Striking a match from the matchbook provided on the ashtray, Jasper touched the flame to the telegram's corner. Bright orange flared on the yellow paper, eating it away to blackened edges. He tossed it in the ashtray as the ashes crumbled against the crystal with cool satisfaction.

"There's a rumor about it belonging to a posh aristocrat's mistress, an Italian opera singer, long before it went to his bride." That was what Esme had said of the tiara. Could it be possible? Could Duke and this singer—

"Looks like you could do with another one of these." A glass slid into his hand with soft fingertips tapering over his. The knuckle-fisted waiter didn't have hands like that.

His pulse thumped an extra beat as he looked up to find Esme smiling down at him. Dressed in sharp black with silver trim, she was the most striking woman in the room. "The waitstaff has grown uncommonly pretty in the last few minutes."

Her deep red lips curved into a smile. Paleness clung to her cheeks and a slight dimness to her eyes, but at least she was no longer green. Standing, Jasper gestured to the chair on the opposite side of his table. "Will you join me?" Once she settled across from him, he returned to his seat. "You are looking much improved."

"I have determined to rally my spirits and escape those four prison walls they call a room."

"Are you hungry?"

She shook her head, sending the sleek black hair gliding along her jaw. "I managed a few water biscuits, but I shall not tempt Fate with anything more substantial tonight." A waiter walked by with a tray wafting of roast beef and cream sauce. Esme's gaze followed with hunger. "As tempting as it might be."

"Something to look forward to tomorrow."

"Thank you for sending trays. They were untouched, but the gesture was appreciated."

"My pleasure. I couldn't allow my travel companion to suffer without sustenance, though I admit it may have done more harm than good." He brushed away a fleck of ash that floated too close to his drink.

"Travel companions, are we?"

"Would you prefer archrivals, or perhaps husband and wife?"

She arched a thin dark eyebrow. "A bit of the same thing, are they not?"

"They don't have to be."

"From what I've witnessed they are often synonymous. The bickering, the lies, the backstabbing, and of course the inevitability of one going off to success while abandoning the other to dry up in their wake. Nothing more than a husk of broken promises."

She was right. He'd seen it enough times in his life to deny that happiness rarely lasted in relationships—if it began there at all. Love was nothing more than a rifle with a bullet in the chamber ready to put a beating heart out of its mournful existence. His own parents never married and died hating each other. Mother swept away by the Spanish flu, and dear Douglas shot dead by a jealous husband.

Then there was Duke, who preferred to live by the passion of his loins rather than the steadfastness of genuine affection. Hardly examples to follow. His experience of dissension in the marital ranks should have turned Jasper away for good, but for some unnerving reason it simply made him want to buck the trend all the more. Brokenness was not the life he wanted.

Dipping his unused salad fork into the glass, he scooped out the offending ice and dropped the cubes in the ashtray. It didn't matter how hot it was, scotch should never be abused in such a manner.

"Would we have turned out that way?"

"After a bit of reckless passion, the magic would wane as it does with time."

"So a breakup is inevitable."

She tapped her lacquered nails over ripples in the tablecloth, smoothing them flat. "Have you seen it work otherwise?"

"No, but that doesn't mean we couldn't have started a new fad. Make them all wonder what we're about."

"You could not possibly want me as a wife."

"Clearly I did at one time since I offered you my name, but I want a wife who wants me. I'll not beg after a woman listing all the reasons she should adore me."

Esme leaned forward, a devilish curl to her lips. "Pity. I love to see a man begging."

He matched her devil. "Get a dog."

She threw her head back and laughed, a free, jubilant sound that had him joining her. Couples at nearby tables looked over and smiled at the darling pair of them enjoying a private joke.

It was a coziness he couldn't afford to be tempted into. She was a rival.

Standing to break the spell, he buttoned his dinner jacket and stepped around to her side of the table. "No begging, but rather a favor. Would you care to dance?"

She flicked a glance over her shoulder to the couples spinning around the floor to a boozy trumpet. "If you don't mind," she said, sliding her fingers into his offered palm, "I'd prefer to take the air."

"Your wish is my command."

Outside, the hot air had cooled over the Mediterranean waves. Moonlight glinted silver across the cresting deep blue waters as the ship prowled along, with the coast of Italy hunkered dark on the western horizon. They strolled slowly around the deck, nodding to other couples in passing. After a full circle, they stopped at a quiet spot. Splashing water below mellowed the brass notes crooning from the dining room.

"The last time I visited Italy it was *Carnevale*," Esme said, leaning against the rail. "Venice dazzled with colors I hadn't seen since before the war. Everywhere there was gold, and purple, and green flashing like brilliant kaleidoscopes. Costumes and water floats, fire-breathers, jugglers, and dancing troupes." She rubbed her hands against her bare arms as a cool breeze skipped across the waves. "It was wonderful to slip behind a mask and pretend to be someone else for a night."

"A trick you still seem fond of." He slipped off his jacket and placed it around her shoulders.

"Mysterious is always more fun, and *Carnevale* is nothing if not theatric. A shame we won't be in town for the celebrations, but then, you could always linger to console your loss when I take the tiara before you." She flipped his jacket collar up to her ears, but not before hiding a teasing nose twitch.

"Nursing a loss for six months is not my style, but then neither is losing, so I'm afraid it is you who will be in need of consolation." He leaned his forearms against the rail. The metal's coolness reached through the expensive weave of his shirtsleeves. "Not to fear. Midsummer in Norway is fast approaching to celebrate the summer solstice. I hear there's a maypole to dance around. Not quite the drunken revelry of Venice, but in your soon-to-be-dejected state I doubt you'll notice."

"What spurs on your confidence?"

"Experience."

"Not a secret plan you wish to tell me?" She peeked at him over the edge of his jacket collar.

Reaching over, he pulled the edge of it down. "Why? Because you have none of your own?"

"If I did, I would hardly tell you."

"Which means you have none."

"I'm an opportunist. Planning is for those who wish to live safe."

"Planning can be highly strategic. Especially if one knows how to play their opponent."

"Are you implying you know how to play me?" She turned to face him. Bold and challenging.

He matched her stance. Their verbal sparring intoxicated him far more than any scotch. "I wouldn't dream of such a presumption."

"Good. I would be disappointed in myself if I were to become predictable." She twisted one of the jacket's buttons. The garment was too large on her slender frame yet she made it look intentional. As if she required the extra space in which to stow her mysteries. "When we dock tomorrow, I shall miss our comradery and truce."

"As will I."

Slipping his coat from her shoulders, she handed it back to him. "May the best thief win."

She walked away, the black beads dripping from her gown's shoulders swaying over her exposed back, much as her long hair had done when they first met. He remembered pulling handfuls of pins from it, tossing them carelessly to the hotel floor in eagerness to feel the soft heft of inky waves in his palms. She was the girl who had stolen his heart. The one he could flip the world on its head with.

"I wouldn't have left," he called, draping his jacket over the rail.

She stopped and turned back. "They all say that."

"I never say anything I don't mean."

Like a wave rolling to shore, she closed the distance between them. Her gaze roved over his face as if finding something unexpected and not quite sure what to make of it.

"After all this time, cynicism hasn't chipped away at your romantic heart. It's one of the things about you I fell hard for. It was so lovely to lose myself in after all the war and death." Reaching out, she grazed her fingertips along his jaw.

A shiver ran over his skin. Wanting, needing. It would be all too easy to fall into that temptation, but he'd been burned before. No way was he going into that inferno again without her cast into the flames right beside him. "And now?"

She dropped her hand to her side. "Now, I've woken up. Romantic hearts belong to returning soldiers, champagne bubbles, and soft midnight hours."

"People like us do our best work at midnight."

"True, but harsh daylight is just on the horizon. Best to remember that, darling." With that, she turned and left him in a haze of perfume that lingered far too enticing in his nostrils.

Shifting his gaze to the dark shore, he sucked in a lungful of salted air to clear his senses and made peace with his next move.

Esme stretched in bed. To her delight it had ceased rocking. Her head wasn't pounding, her stomach remained still, and for the first time in countless hours the thought of food was a welcomed one. Brilliant sunshine poured in the round porthole and soaked her exposed toes in warmth. Actually, the entire bottom part of her body lay uncovered due to her wild sleeping habits, which had tossed the majority of the covers to the floor.

She flung aside the remaining corner of blanket and sat upright, waiting for the wave of queasiness. All was well. Her constitution was most often ironclad, but occasionally the right wave motion or train lurch would have her kneeling before the porcelain. She got out of bed and quickly completed her morning ablutions, patting her face with rose water and rubbing in moisturizer before slipping into a linen blue-and-white number with a dropped waist and two long satin ribbons that curved around her neckline and dropped into a loose knot over her flat chest. Well, mostly flat, and thank the gods of fashion for that. Bandaging her breasts was not a style she wished to suffer.

After buckling her navy T-straps into place, she rummaged around the room for her purse, lifting up stockings here, shoving away knickers there. She picked up her beaded gown from the night before and aimed to drop it on the bed when a scent stopped her. Spicy. Woodsy.

She held the dress up her to nose and inhaled. Cedarwood.

Jasper.

His smile in the moonlight. The warmth of his body lingering in his jacket pressed against her skin. The way his words flirted with her pulse, coaxing her with temptation. Of their own accord, her eyes slid to the velvet case where she carried her jewelry and the one token she couldn't seem to part with. Their wedding photograph.

As if burned, she dropped the dress in her suitcase and tipped the lid shut. Enough of that. A girl could get distracted, and she was far too busy to entertain that complication. She picked up her straw wide-brimmed hat and left her room, taking the stairs up to the main deck. A spot of toast and jam sided with green tea was just the ticket on this glorious morning of adventure.

The ship boards were smooth beneath her shoes as she entered the dining room. Passengers sat dotted around tables with plates of sandwiches and tall frosted cocktails. She wasn't one to raise an eyebrow at another's drink of choice, but at so early an hour one might at least consider a Bloody Mary.

Wait. The ship wasn't moving. Why wasn't the ship moving?

She rushed outside and gripped the rail. The docks of Venice bobbed gracefully mere yards away. They had already made port, and judging by the slant of the sun it must have been some time ago. She cursed herself for oversleeping and grabbed a passing steward.

"Pardon *moi*, is Mr. Truitt on board?"

The steward shook his head. "*Non*. I am sorry you have missed him, mademoiselle. He took a small boat in early this morning just before we dropped anchor."

"Oh he did, did he?"

Esme grinned, then raced back to her room and threw her clothes into the suitcase.

The game was on.

6

Venice, Italy

THE SHOP WAS LOCATED DOWN a tiny waterway across the small arched bridge of Ponte delle Tette. Jasper wove his way around workmen hauling ladders and buckets of plaster to patch up the ancient crumbling buildings that seemed too exhausted by the centuries to continue standing straight. Children toddled along oblivious to the water drop-off inches away while mothers carried knitted bags full of groceries. A simple luxury not seen during the war.

"Buongiorno!" Two scantily clad women lounged against the bridge with cigarettes dangling from their painted lips. "Lost your way, signor?"

Jasper politely doffed his straw fedora and quickly switched languages in his head. Duke had paid for the best tutors, but Jasper had picked up a great deal more from his travels. Usually phrases the tutors considered too impolite to instruct.

"I'm looking for Signor Campano's shop, Il Negozio Meraviglie. Might one of you ladies point me in the right direction?"

"'Ladies' he says." The women doubled over in a fit of laughter, slapping each other on the shoulders until their threadbare blouses threatened to slip off entirely. Finally, they collected themselves long enough for one to answer. "Down that way. Third door."

"Grazie." Reaching into the pocket of his cream checkered linen suit, he took out two generous coins and placed them in their hands.

"Sure we can't interest you in something more?" they called after him as he stepped off the bridge.

"I'm afraid not, but here." He turned back and flipped them two more coins. "For your help and delightful offer of company."

"Anytime! We'll be here all day."

Waving at their renewed fit of laughter, he continued down the way he'd been directed and stopped in front of the third door. It was short and squat with peeling blue paint and a faded sign declaring it to be *Il Negozio Meraviglie.* He seized the handle and opened the door, stepping into another world cloaked in Renaissance musk and faded memories.

The shop was a maze of shelves stuffed with oddities that glimmered and sparkled. *Carnevale* masks. Theater costumes. Scrolls, paintings, suits of armor, animal skins, stuffed animals, bottles of every size and shape, banners, and chests overflowing with all manner of valuables. An Aladdin's cave of wonders with absolutely no tolerance of organization to its treasures.

A muffled voice scratched from within the labyrinth. "Who is it? What do you want?"

Removing his hat, Jasper peered through the gloom that could not be dispelled by the single rectangular window high on the wall above the door. "Signor Campano? My name is Jasper Truitt. I'm here to inquire after an item you may have."

"Be gone. I do not have time for oglers." The irritated voice moved, though it was difficult to track, pinging off the bric-a-brac like a cracked billiard ball.

"I assure you, signor, I am quite serious about my inquiry."

"Allow me to guess. You are here after the fabled golden fleece."

"As it turns out, I am not in need of a fleece." Jasper frowned as he stepped around a shelf in hopes of capturing the elusive voice but found only more stuffed cases.

"Perhaps the champagne glass modeled after Marie Antoinette's right bosom?" the voice continued, this time to the right.

"Um, no, although such a piece would be the highlight of any party."

"Caesar's death mask? The quill of Shakespeare? Joyeuse, Charlemagne's personal sword? No, I cannot give you that. It was purchased last month by a private buyer from India. How did you find this place? I chose this location precisely so I would not be bothered."

Why open a shop in the first place if the man wished to be left alone? Jasper batted away a dusty cobweb he'd stepped straight into. "I met two ladies outside. They were kind enough to give me directions."

"That's not all they'll give you if you are not careful. The clap being their favorite parting gift." Boxes shuffled. "Donne delle Tette, named for the prostitutes who would stand topless on the bridge to entice customers. They still do in honor of their predecessors. A shame you did not come to see them at night."

"Yes, a real shame. Next trip perhaps." Jasper swatted the last shreds of the cobweb from his shoulder. Hopefully its resident hadn't decided to slip down his collar in the upheaval.

"Tell me what you seek so I may turn you away and return to my overworked schedule."

"The Valkyrie tiara."

The movements stilled, followed quickly by short-tempered footsteps. A second later a dwarflike man with chalky skin and tufts of salt-and-pepper hair sprouting over his knobby head popped out from behind an elephant foot serving as an umbrella stand.

"Which Valkyrie? There were several made when the fashion was for all things Wagner." He snorted. "As if the Germans have offered the world anything of remark when the Italian masters hold superiority in all manner of art."

Regaining his composure from the possible spider invasion, Jasper stood tall with his hat tucked neatly under his arm. It was best to appear confident in all situations. Not only did it allow one to feel in control, but it also presented an air of authority. One of his many lessons from Duke on how to get ahead.

"There is none like this tiara. It was the last one. Handcrafted by Pierre Cartier himself."

"The last one you say." The dwarf stroked a tuft of hair over his ear. "What year?"

"It was commissioned in 1889 by a duke using his own family's jewels to adorn it but was sold after the death of his wife."

"Women." The gnome made a derisive noise. "As if they aren't given enough baubles to fascinate them. Nothing ever satisfies them." The shelf to his left caught the man's attention. He turned to it with a frown and began rearranging the items.

"You are known for obtaining the most valuable of antiquities, signor." Though the bent trumpet and broken shield he currently held gave little credence to that statement. Then again, one man's trash was another man's treasure, and Jasper wasn't about to question what some considered treasure. Not when acquiring it for the right buyer paid well. "This item returned to the market a mere two months ago."

Campano continued rearranging, each movement stirring up a sneezable amount of dust. "It's not here. Not anymore. It came to me, along with several other items, last month upon the passing of an old acquaintance. A jeweler he was and a favorite among the bluebloods for his discretion. That scrap of sparkling metal was hardly worth my consideration. Its monetary value was unmistakable, but what is money to me? Did it once grace the head of Catherine the Great? Did Zheng Yi Sao loot it from a sinking East India Company vessel that her own pirate ship downed? Are the diamonds tilled from the blackened coal of King Solomon's mines? If no, then it is of little interest to me."

Jasper tried breathing through his mouth. The air settled with bitter age on his tongue. "Despite its lack of cultural and historical relevance, it is a rare collector's piece—"

Campano whirled, hair standing askew and nose quivering. "Do not enter my shop to tell me what pieces are of interest to a collector. I have been in this business longer than you have been out of short trousers. Now, be gone with you for you have wasted time enough of mine. I have work to do."

"Forgive me, Signor Campano. I meant no disrespect to you or the admirable work you do. I was only hoping to purchase the tiara for my own collection."

"Treasures galore I have on my shelves, too many sitting for years collecting not admiration but dust, yet this worthless headpiece has garnered more attention in its short time here than deemed fair. Just yesterday a man—I suppose you might call him that, though he shared more resemblance with an egg—came snooping around for it."

An egg? That description fit only one person Jasper knew. Lamb. That no-necked prankster had the rather bad habit of sniffing around right under Jasper's feet when there was a prize to be found. They'd been in friendly competition for years, but Jasper trusted the man as far as he could throw him. If Lamb was after the tiara, there was more to this game of cat and mouse. That wild eccentric would ensure it.

The dwarf shook a nubby finger. "I'll tell you the same thing I told him. 'You're too late. I sold it and glad I am to be rid of it. It was taking up valuable shelf space.'"

Disappointment knocked at the tiara being just out of reach once again, but Jasper didn't linger. An elusive acquisition was part of the thrill that kept his skills sharp. Lamb he would deal with later. "And the buyer?"

"I'm a respectable businessman who doesn't give away private information, but as the man himself was less than respectable I do not mind so much telling you." Signor Campano looked around as if greedy ears might be listening from the stacks of collectibles and dropped his voice. "A showman." He paused for dramatic effect.

"*Orribile.*" Jasper gasped on cue, which unfortunately filled his lungs with drifting dust.

Signor Campano nodded gravely. "Claims he was making a traveling collection of opera bits. A wedding veil from *The Marriage of Figaro*, Roman armor from *Norma*, and Parisian scenery from *La bohème*. All trinkets. *Rottame.* Stagehand castoffs to entertain the masses."

How Duke would snort and rave to hear the illustrious Roxburgh jewels assessed as little more than trinkets. "Did this buyer mention where he was traveling next?"

"North. Prussia or some such miserable place. He babbled on about showcasing Wagner's and Mozart's masterpieces in their home countries. Masterpieces." He snorted like a riled horse. "The Italians are the only masters of anything."

Jasper moved to the door, the jingling bell cutting off another tirade from the old man. "I thank you for your time, Signor Campano, and wish you a pleasant rest of the day."

"Pleasant," the dwarf grumbled as he disappeared behind a portrait of Napoleon. "As if that's possible with customers in and out disturbing me."

Jasper shut the door behind him and breathed in deep to clear his head of mustiness and crankiness. It would be easy to feel defeated after walking away empty-handed, but that was part of the job. Following clue after clue, each one drawing him closer as his mind flashed to piece them together and instinct drove him on until the trail was hot enough to burn through his veins.

There was no feeling in all the earth quite like that of tracking a prize until at last it gleamed before him, begging his hand to lift it from its spot and place it among the exalted. Well, no feeling perhaps save that of holding a woman in his arms. Especially one with hair the color of midnight and eyes that could melt his soul.

He shook himself out of that wayward thought and tapped his hat more securely atop his head. Esme was not a daydream. She wasn't even his wife save in name alone. She was a rival. A competitor to beat for the prize. A prize he would be winning, and once the champagne was popped in honor of his victory, they could get about the business of a divorce.

He'd dreamed of having a wife to love, a family to care for. Growing up, he'd never had one, and he wanted nothing more than to fill that longing, to have someone care that he walked through the door each night, to whisper good night to someone and have them wake next to him. Not flee in the early hours of the morning without so much as a goodbye note or payment on the nightstand. As if it were a one-night stand!

He huffed, startling two elderly ladies feeding pigeons as he crossed Campo San Polo. Somewhere along the way he'd taken a wrong turn west instead of proceeding south. Venice was a city of languid desire and broken hearts, masterfully seducing all who entered its inviting embrace. He needed his mind to stay on track and not wander off the rails every time Esme crooked her finger at his imagination.

After making his way to the Grand Canal that flowed through the heart of the water city, he jumped on a flat-bottomed rowboat serving as a taxi and asked the striped-shirted gondolier to take him to the Aman Hotel.

Palazzi lined the canal like grand dames awaiting their next affair. Dressed in colors of cream, rust, salmon, and butter, they gathered the passing centuries about them in regal cracks and gracefully sagging lines, unobliging to the water creeping ever upward around them. Here in their alcoves lovers embraced, through their windows celebrations cheered, and upon their terraces art was created. It was a city to love and one that gladly loved in return as long as it was treated right. As with any lady, heaven help the one who did wrong by her.

The gondolier guided his boat to the dock stretching out front of Aman Hotel, a four-story structure made of white limestone and lined with windows on each floor. The entrance was arched with glass through which glowed the grand foyer's chandelier and to the left boasted one of the few private gardens in the city. The perfect place for an afternoon aperitif.

After generously tipping the gondolier, Jasper hopped onto the dock and strode from the dazzling sunlight into the sumptuous coolness of the hotel. A checkerboard floor of white and terra-cotta stretched beneath his feet as he crossed the grand lobby where wrought iron sconces and priceless tapestries hung from the cream walls. Little tables and chairs gilded with rococo finery dotted the space as fashionably dressed couples sat sipping tea and espresso from elegant chinaware.

"*Buon pomeriggio*, Signor Truitt," one of the hotel clerks said as he passed the front desk.

Jasper held up his hand in greeting. "*Buon pomeriggio*, Tommaso. Beautiful day." Another lesson from Duke was always to know the staff of any establishment by name. They were more likely to prove useful when they were made to feel important. It was a calculated approach Jasper despised as he preferred to treat all, servant or master, with the same politeness. Manners were the only thing truly separating man from beast, and he'd seen enough dogs parading as gentlemen to spot the difference.

Tommaso scurried around the desk, adjusting his tie. "Do you require anything, signor? The dining room is serving scallops in wine sauce today. Would you like me to set up a guided tour of the Frari? No? The garden is lovely at this time."

"Thank you, no. I'm most in need of a *telefono*."

"Ah *sì*. Follow me, signor." Tommaso led him out of the grand foyer and along a short corridor lined with marble columns to a room surrounded on two sides by windows and drenched with sun. A sitting room in cool greens and whites with a trim of gold. Frescoes lavished the ceiling in scenes of pastoral tranquility while large paintings adorned the walls.

Dodging cozy groups of satin-covered couches and chairs, Tommaso led him to a table divided by four velvet screens, each a private wedge fitted with its own telephone.

"Grazie," Jasper said, pulling out the curved-back chair to one of the sections.

"Is there anything else I can do for you, signor?"

"Not at the moment, but there's a fair chance I'll be checking out this evening or first thing in the morning."

The skin between Tommaso's black eyebrows creased. "You've only just arrived, signor. Surely you wish to take in the sights of our fair city."

Sighing, Jasper pulled his hat from his head and dropped it to the table. "As much as I wish to, this is a short business trip. Next time I'm in town I'll take you up on one of those guided tours."

Tommaso inclined his head and left, and Jasper focused on the business at hand. Phoning Mond. After several minutes of connecting operators, Mond's irritated voice crackled through the line.

"Jasper, this better be you because if it's not you are extremely rude for disturbing my peace and quiet, and I shall curse your inconsiderate carcass with unforgiveness and festering." He paused, swished something in his mouth, and swallowed. "If this *is* Jasper, you are still extremely rude and inconsiderate, but I shall forgive you if you have good news."

"No good news, I'm afraid."

"Then I'm hanging up."

"Wait. I've got a new lead." Jasper leaned forward, keeping his voice low. "The item is no longer here. It was sold two weeks ago to a collection of opera memorabilia traveling around Europe. The next stop is Germany."

"Well, *guten tag* and *auf wiedersehen* to you, *mein Freund.*" Mond's yawn rattled down the line.

"I'll stop in Munich first and put inquiries about. Can't imagine a collectable exhibit travels fast." Jasper fanned his hat over his face. The cool marble surrounding him did little against the Italian heat pouring in the glass windows. "In the meantime, don't let Duke get a bead on you. He's antsy about this piece and more than willing to take it out on anyone caught in his crosshairs if he doesn't have it in his hands by August."

"What's so important about August?"

"His birthday party. Every year he throws an elaborate bash to make all the bluebloods jealous. He's most likely planning the item as a showpiece."

"I wish he would tell you why he's so obsessed over this one crown."

"It's worth a fortune."

"Yes, but the Roxburgh family owns thousands of priceless jewels. Some worth more than a winged headpiece."

"Sentimental value? He adores Wagner?" Jasper paused, then a chuckle escaped, quickly followed by Mond's laughter. There wasn't a sentimental bone to be found in Duke's body.

Mond's laughter subsided and the faint sound of ice clinking in a glass followed. "Speaking of sentimental. Found your wife yet?"

As if conjured, a whiff of orange-blossom perfume danced on the air. Jasper turned, half expecting to find Esme standing there, but all he saw were ladies in wide-brimmed hats with men carrying shopping bags trailing after them. He flapped his hat to dissipate the scent, real or imagined.

"As a matter of fact, we sailed together, but I've since given her the slip. No doubt she's fuming while still struggling to get ashore. I'll be on my way to Munich by the time she realizes the prize is gone from Venice."

"A shame you don't team up. She seems the kind of woman to make things more interesting."

"I work alone. You know that. No distractions, and Esme Fox is an undulating distraction if ever there was one." Undulating, swaying, dancing, teasing, Cheshire smiling, and any other manner of complication she wielded that could drive a man clean out of his senses.

"Distractions can be fun."

Sure they were, but they could also leave one feeling . . . well, left. Jasper flattened the brim of his hat against the table. That was all in the past. He'd managed to stay one step ahead of the rest of the world all these years, and he wasn't about to let her outstrip him again. This time he would be the one leaving.

"Keep your ear to the ground about this traveling exhibit. No telling where they might set up. I'll be staying at the usual place in Munich."

"When you get there, do me a favor. Cable or telephone or send a carrier pigeon, I don't care which, to Duke. That man is tying up my line and I'm quite tired of his nagging." He paused for a yawn. "I hope the old man is paying you enough. It better be worth risking a lifetime in jail because I doubt the judge will give you a second chance."

Duke was paying enough for Jasper to live in luxury for the next few years, but the payout Jasper truly desired was a respectable name tied to a welcoming family. Duke had never promised such a thing, but Jasper hoped that by the time he had the Valkyrie in hand, Duke could hardly say no.

Ringing off, Jasper signaled a nearby waiter for a glass of water, took a long swallow in preparation, and connected to the operator. "Blackheathe-492, please."

The line crackled for a long minute until at last a starchy voice pierced through the receiver. "Linton Hall." Corby. Duke's over-starched butler.

"This is Jasper Truitt. May I speak with His Grace, please?"

"What is this pertaining to?"

"Your position if you don't put him on."

Sniffing, Corby disappeared. He made no bones about detesting Jasper. Detesting everyone, really, but he was smart enough to play along to keep his employer happy, and nothing delighted Duke more than the prospect of seizing his prize.

Minutes passed before Duke's voice barreled through the line. "Jasper, my boy! Do you have it?" His words thrummed with excitement.

"Nearly. There have been unforeseen complications." That was putting it lightly.

"What sort of complications?"

Jasper shifted on the chair as the litany of problems unrolled in his mind. Best not to muddy the waters with talk of competitors and his soon-to-be ex-wife. "Apparently the fake kind. Care to elaborate on why there's an exact replica floating about?"

A muffled curse. "I, well . . . What can I say? Objects of beauty are coveted by the masses. Some measly jeweler most likely saw my piece and decided to make a pretty farthing for himself by duplicating it." By the end of his speech, Duke's annoyed tone had returned to its calm, cultured drawl. Jasper could picture the old man buffing his gold signet ring against his silk tie. "How much longer do you anticipate?"

"I have a lead. Should be soon."

"Jasper." Duke sighed in that benevolent way meant to make others feel as if he were doing them a great service. "I do not believe you understand the importance of this occasion in August and why the tiara must be returned to me with all due haste."

"August, yes. That marvelous month when the stars aligned and you graced this world with your birth. Is that the occasion you speak of with such import?" He shouldn't take so much pleasure, but Jasper didn't often hold the upper hand when it came to Duke, and he wasn't about to turn down the opportunity when it fell in his lap. "Don't worry. Your guests will be able to gasp with delight over the precious bauble at your festive shindig."

"No doubt they will, but my astounding them with all that glitters is only part of the celebration. There is a particular announcement I should like to make, one I should like very much for you to be in attendance for."

Duke was rather fond of making announcements. His birthday, his winning horse at the track, his latest automobile purchase, but never had he requested Jasper's presence. His palm dampened against the telephone's earpiece. He quickly switched it to his other hand. "What does this announcement pertain to?"

"It has been in the making for some time and will lead the Roxburgh name into the future."

Did Jasper dare to hope this was the moment he had dreamed of? When Duke would finally call him from the bastard shadow and into the light of legitimate kin? Did it all hinge on him locating the Valkyrie and returning it to Roxburgh hands, his family's hands? Perhaps Jasper was merely spinning scenarios he desperately wished to come true, but even if Duke was building up hope only to dash it, Jasper couldn't turn away from the possibility.

"Well," Jasper drawled despite the tripping of his heart, "I'll be sure to wear my top and tails when I deliver."

His hand shook as he replaced the receiver in its cradle. *Don't get ahead of yourself, old boy. That's how you get burned.*

With new purpose lightening his footsteps and the next leg of the mission mapping out in his head, he strode to the lobby and found Tommaso behind the front desk. "When is the earliest train bound for Munich?"

"Eight o'clock this night, signor," Tommaso promptly answered.

"Impressive. Do you know all the train schedules off the top of your head?"

"No, signor, but it was recent that I looked up schedules for Germany." A smile crept across his face.

"That many folks heading north, eh?"

"Perhaps a few seeking a romantic getaway." Tommaso's smile widened until it pushed his cheeks nearly up to his eyes.

"Don't know if I'd classify Germany as romantic in comparison to Venice, but to each their own."

Leaning forward, Tommaso lifted his thick black eyebrows in a show of conspiracy. "It is more about the company you keep, *sì*, Signor Truitt?" His eyebrows wiggled like caterpillars.

"Um, yes. I suppose so." Jasper leaned back, feeling as if he weren't quite caught up on a jest. "Have a water taxi ready for me at seven." He started for the marble staircase.

"As you wish, signor. Would you like me to have refreshments sent to your room?" Tommaso was practically sprawled across the front desk to call out to him.

"No, thank you."

"Have a *molto* pleasant afternoon, Signor Truitt," Tommaso sang out.

Jasper hurried up the stairs to his third-floor accommodations. What was that all about? Tommaso was friendly but always properly courteous. Romantic getaway? Company you keep? A *very* pleasant afternoon? Why would—

Jasper stopped cold. There could be only one reason.

He bounded up the remaining steps two at a time and marched straight to his room, fit the brass key in the lock, and swung open the door.

"Hello, darling!" Esme stood at the open door leading off to the balcony. Dressed in a nautical number of crisp blue-and-white, she was the picture of Mediterranean summer. And she was encroaching on his day.

"Hello, yourself." He stepped inside and kicked the door shut, then leaned back against it, slipping the key in his pocket. "You look much refreshed. I take it you enjoyed a good night's sleep?"

"Indeed, I did. A bit too good, which caused me to awake rather late. You're a lout for sneaking off without me before the sun rose."

"The sun had already broken the horizon when I left our slumbering ship. The early bird and all that jazz." He noted the shopping packages and boxes scattered across his bed. "I see you made good use of your time in the city."

"The other night you forced me to clamber from my window with little more than I could carry in a single suitcase. Of course I had to stop and purchase wardrobe reinforcements." She peeled a wide-brimmed straw hat from her head and carefully patted her sleek black hair into place.

Shopping bags. Wide-brimmed hats. Elegant ladies traipsing through the sitting room while he telephoned Mond. Jasper's eyes narrowed. "How much did you overhear?"

"Only that we're off to Munich next. I thought of following you to Signor Campano's shop, but then I reasoned you would root out the pertinent information there, and I could simply wait for you to return. After overhearing our next destination, I had the front desk telephone the Venice train station on my behalf to purchase a ticket before making my way here to your room. Sorry, only a single ticket, but before I'm off I thought we could have a drink on the balcony."

A serendipitous knock sounded on the door. "Ah, that'll be the refreshments now. Tommaso was terribly kind and helpful. I hope you tip him well."

Jasper opened the door and took the drink tray from the dining staff. A carafe of red wine, two empty glasses, and a plate of biscuits in the shaped of the letter S. Slipping the boy a tip, he closed the door and turned back to Esme. "You know I have no intention of allowing you to get ahead of me."

He carried the tray across the opulent hotel room, soothing in its draped silk and tones of champagne and cream, and out to the balcony overlooking the private garden below. After placing it on the small café table, he pulled out one of the chairs for Esme before taking the other for himself.

She peeled off white net gloves and placed them in her lap. "Good intentions are not made for people in our line of work."

"I never said they were good." Pouring them each a glass of wine, he held his aloft. If they were stuck in together, he might as well apply one of his rules: keep it entertaining. And Esme's company was nothing if not entertaining. "Salute."

Grinning, she touched her glass to his. "*Cin cin*," she replied, offering the favored toast that mimicked the glasses clinking.

The wine was a 1912 Barbaresco. Aromas of rose and violet drifted under the nose while notes of truffle, cherry, and licorice tingled over the palate. He was by no means a connoisseur of fine wines, despite Duke forcing him to every vineyard in France and Italy. *"Every gentleman should know his drink,"* the old man would say, but Jasper had always been better at knowing who to sell which coveted bottle to at the highest price. Still, something of that inebriated summer had settled into his memory to differentiate the bitter licorice from the tart cherries.

"Tell me," Esme said, swirling the red liquid around the glass as afternoon sunlight bounced off the windows across the waterway behind her. The gondoliers' voices drifted up to the balcony from where they prowled along the water. "What are your intentions for the Valkyrie?"

"I have a client eager to take possession of it."

"How diplomatically evasive of you."

"I've always been good at finding things. The best." She scoffed and he ignored it. "My clientele are the cream of society with the most expensive tastes. I find what they want, and they send me off with a large paycheck. Everyone is happy. There are no intentions beyond getting paid. Well, that and the thrill of the hunt."

"There's nothing quite like seeking an elusive find." She leaned forward as a new light danced across her face. "The thrill in your blood as you get closer, the trip in your heart rate at catching a first glimpse of the item. Your breath tight in your lungs as you reach for it and the sudden rush of adrenaline once you have it. You almost hope to peek over your shoulder and find someone watching you, wondering if they'll give chase."

With each word he felt the pull in his blood. The desire to seek and find. A desire reflecting in her own eyes. "A bit like wooing a woman."

She met his gaze head-on, locking them into charged silence. The dynamism between them was palpable, electrifying the air around them with memories of champagne, whispered words, and the adventure of being alive. She had made him feel alive again after climbing out of four years of death and mud. She had made his heart start beating again when he'd thought it broken from war. She had given him reason to hope for brighter things, and he had pursued her like a shining star streaking across the sky, reckless in his attempt to catch her. He'd held that brilliant star for but a moment, and then like all fiery things, it had burned him. Yet here she was again, filling the sky with wonder, and he couldn't help feeling the pull toward her light.

But burns left deep marks and he would not give himself over to such flames again.

Without breaking away from the hypnotic blue of her eyes, he slipped off his jacket and tossed it onto the empty chair next to him. He rolled up his sleeves while discreetly smoothing down the golden hairs on his arms that seemed to pulse in the ongoing charge. If he didn't mind his good sense, they might burn the place down around them.

He took a biscuit and bit into its sweetness, chewing long enough to reorder his thoughts. "How did you come to work for Countess Accardi?" he asked, seizing back control of the conversation.

She blinked. It was a languid motion that swept down her thick black eyelashes before swooping them back up, but it was enough for him to note that it was her way of clearing the electricity from her own pulse. So she was not so untouchable as she wanted to appear.

"Over the past few months, I've found odds and ends for her. Jewelry, paintings, and such. Wilhelm's dinner plates from when he was kaiser of all Prussia."

"Did he not take them to the Netherlands when he abdicated at the end of the war?" He polished off the last of the biscuit. Why couldn't English food have flavor like this?

She shook her head. "If you saw them, you would understand. They're positively hideous, but the countess demanded them, and if there's anything I've learned, it's that she always gets what she wants."

"And her hired gun Pirazzo sees to it."

"Pirazzo has never bothered me because I always land the deal. Unlike you, I don't care if my clients are cream of the crop, nor am I selective. I find a valuable I think will fetch a pretty price and I take it, then sell it to the highest bidder. The countess became the highest bidder for many of the items I brought. That's why she hired me for the tiara. It's one of the rare times I've gone after a specific item, but the game is still the same."

It would be easy to become dazzled by the marvel of her sophisticated savvy. If it weren't for her sheer disregard of mortal harm. Taking risks was one thing—a spike to the blood like a stolen kiss with a stranger under the midnight clock—but traipsing about as if all were a lark was akin to crossing a tightrope over a shark tank. One wrong move and that toothy jaw would clamp around her.

"The game is not the same when men like Pirazzo are involved." Pushing aside his glass, he leaned forward. He didn't want to care, didn't want to get entangled with this unreliable woman again, but coldhearted indifference had never been his style, and though he made his golden rules for himself, he should have very much preferred keeping Esme from making enemies as well.

"The man has assassinated a slew of royals, burned down a monastery, kidnapped dozens of heirs from the casino business to the vice admiral of the navy's nephew, and is wanted on three continents."

"I've been taking care of myself for a long time. This lift is no different." She crossed one long leg over the other, dangling her foot inches from his. "Don't tell me you've never had muscle breathing down your neck."

"I have and I never cared much for it. This powder burner isn't like any I've come across. He won't think twice about snapping your pretty neck if his master doesn't get her way."

Her red lips curved up. "Think my neck is pretty, do you?"

"I do, and like any pretty thing, I'd hate to see it destroyed." Slipping into familiar waters of flirtatious banter, Jasper relaxed back into his chair.

"Well, it won't be harmed in the least because I'm going to snag the Valkyrie before you and collect my payment. Which is an obscene amount that I'm debating how to spend. A tour of Europe sounds delightful, but I doubt many of the cities have recovered after the Hun destroyed them. Perhaps a long voyage around the world. Or my own villa on the south coast of France. I could retire in style and never have to scrape together a living ever again."

"We could split the profits and sail around the world together, visiting every exotic port and indulging in whatever it has to offer."

"I told you before, I don't like entanglements."

"Think of it more as a proper farewell filled with tantalizing memories that might erase the one of waking up to cold, empty sheets." It was a whim, a fantasy built on sand that would quickly wash out with the next tide, but oh the fun to be had while it lasted.

She stared at him through veiled lashes, considering. "And then we part ways?"

"And then we part ways."

"Your offer is intriguing despite knowing neither of us would ever split anything. It's all or nothing for people like us."

"True enough, but that's a predictable sentiment. People like us are anything but predictable."

She laughed, clear and loud. "I knew it wasn't only your looks I fell for. Those are reason enough, but there's a clever sense of wickedness that I find wildly attractive about you."

There it was again. That spark threatening to burn everything between them and to hell with the vicinity catching flame. "It's good for a wife to find her husband attractive."

"If only for a short time. Wife, that is. I have no doubt you'll remain devastatingly handsome long after the ink has dried from our divorce papers."

Jasper lofted his glass. "To dried ink."

"To dried ink." Esme joined his toast.

Downing the contents of his glass, Jasper enjoyed the red liquid coating his throat and sloshing delightfully in his belly. Life wasn't always easy, and he'd learned quickly to grab hold of the good moments before they slipped by. What could be better than a moment filled with Italian sunshine, mouthwatering cuisine, and the presence of a beautiful woman? By tonight the moment would have vanished like the sun below the horizon, and he was no fool to let it go without seizing the last rays of enjoyment.

Putting aside his napkin, Jasper stood. He wore the lightest summer suit he owned, but it was no match for the city's heat. Nor the sweat trickling down his back.

"Now, before the train sets off for Munich with me and not you, how about we go down to the dining room? It's too early and too hot for a full meal, but they serve the most refreshing shrimp risotto with diced cucumber you have ever tasted."

"Sounds heavenly. I'll slip on the new peep toes I bought."

"And I'll just change my shirt. Excuse me for a moment." He went inside the room, then turned back before crossing into the washroom. "Oh, and if you're thinking of making a run for it, know that I've paid well to have all the exits watched. It was only a matter of time before you breezed through the hotel doors, and the staff has been given strict instructions not to allow you to leave without me."

ESME SCRUNCHED HER CHEEKS IN exaggerated adoration. "Darling, you think of everything." He smiled back at her, that heart-skipping one that flushed her all over. She grabbed their wineglasses and handed his drink to him. "To ingenuity."

"To ingenuity," he said, tipping his glass in salute to her before taking a sip.

She took a sip from her own glass, then set it down before moving to the shopping bags on the bed, but whatever she had been about to search for slipped clean from her mind as Jasper began to hum from the other room. "When My Baby Smiles at Me." Music from long ago pinched her heart. Those chords had wrapped around two young lovers, weary from war and longing for the promise of happiness in each other's eager arms.

What if she were to seek his arms again and let him fill that hole that had been buried deep inside her for so long that she no longer knew where to find the bottom? He was everything a woman could want. Handsome, clever, witty, thoughtful, resourceful, and all hers if she wanted to stake marital priority. But want and need were two very different beasts, and only one could be mastered at a time.

Right now the need to return with that tiara outweighed any need a man might be able to fulfill.

Shaking herself, she picked through the shopping bags. "Now, when we arrive in Munich I expect you to behave as the perfect gentleman and not get in my way."

"This foolish thinking is precisely the kind you need to forget about. Believing you have any chance at all against me is a laughable notion."

"Use all the flowery words you like, but you cannot convince me otherwise."

Flicking a glance up, she caught him unbuttoning his shirt in front of the mirror. "I will use any manner necessary to convince you. Irritate you, charm you, or blackmail you. Any way is fine, but I do hope it's charm. I love a challenge." His eyes met hers in the reflection as he slipped the shirt off his shoulders.

She held steady his gaze. "And how I love to defy them."

He blinked heavily. Again and again. Then tilted slightly and grabbed the sink.

"Oh dear." She hurried into the washroom and gently led him out to the bed. "That took hold faster than I anticipated. Here, have a lie-down."

"Y-you drugged me." He glared up at her while slurring.

"Only a tiny sleeping pill. Seeing as I'm to be your wife for a little while longer, I must look out for your well-being, and I insist you sit this one out, darling."

"I-I'll c . . . ome af . . . ter you."

"Perhaps, but not until I'm long gone."

He flopped back, sound asleep.

"Thank goodness you held it together until I got you to the bed." She wriggled her hand out from under him. "I don't know what I'd have done if you decided to go down in the loo."

Rounding the bed, she upended one of the shopping bags. Out came a hotel maid's uniform, sturdy black stockings, hideously practical black shoes, and a graying wig tied into a severe knot. Growing up behind a stage had taught her many valuable lessons that were perfected by the life of a thief. One being the art of disguise—in particular, the unnoticed servant who could slip past the tightest security measures. Another lesson was how to shimmy through a costume change in under thirty seconds. One second she was young and glamorous. Twenty-eight seconds later, she was the frumpy help.

She gathered up her bags and stopped next to Jasper's sleeping form. Giving in to one minor indulgence, she reached down and brushed the flopping curl from his forehead.

"Still a dish."

Sighing, she blew him a kiss and slipped out the door.

7

Neuschwanstein Castle, Bavaria

AFTER TWO DAYS OF SPORADIC train schedules that seemed to be suffering a hangover from the war era, Esme finally made it to Munich, only to be informed by her black-market gossip line that the traveling opera relic exhibit had been invited to Neuschwanstein Castle, home of the once fairy-tale king.

King Ludwig II had departed his mortal coils some thirty years prior, but his eccentricity had left an indelible mark in this southwest corner of Bavaria where he had dreamed of his romantic castle perched high on a rugged hill above the picturesque village of Hohenschwangau that would allow him to live out his fantasy of grand knights and maidens depicted in Wagner's operas.

At least that was the story Leggy Joe told her when she was a girl. Leggy Joe was the gaffer at Wilton's Music Hall and he knew how to light a stage better than anyone in the business. With one tweak of his lantern, the girls would turn into unearthly beauties, the scenery would spring to life, and villains would lurk in shadow. He'd been a teacher of history once but found the schoolroom too stifling and traded his chalk for grease paint, though every once in a while he would recite one of his old lectures for Esme's amusement. It was as close as she got to a formal education.

Esme moved around the throne room with its arched doorways, red marble columns, exquisitely tiled floor, and colossal chandelier. The place resembled a cathedral more than the seat of reigning royalty. She tilted her head this way and that, nearly blinded by the amount of gold and colorful depictions of Christ's apostles. This room alone was enough to prepare a person for atonement, but the guests that evening had no time for confession, taken in as they were by the spectacle in the center of the floor. A tableau of Rome and a half-finished painting of Mary Magdalene propped on a church altar. A placard on a gold easel read *Puccini's Tosca*.

The people around her stared and murmured appreciation as if the painting had been done by Michelangelo himself and was not merely a play prop. Esme stifled a yawn behind her black lace fan. Rather mundane compared to a tiara.

The Cultural Edification of the Arts of Bavaria was bankrolling this shindig and they had spared no expense. The courtyard had been converted into a biergarten with thousands of lights strung from the castle walls to glitter against the hundreds of tankards. A full orchestra played in the Singers' Hall. Waiters and maids with loaded serving trays ducked between political officials, war heroes, and titled nobility who wandered from chamber to chamber like gloriously decked-out swans from the nearby Alpsee.

For her own transformation, Esme had chosen a black satin drop waist gown with a handkerchief skirt of soft pink panels peeking out from beneath the top row of black. A strip of black velvet wrapped around her forehead in the fashionable bandeau style with a pink feather attached to float just above her right eyebrow and curve around to her ear.

Plucking a chilled glass of champagne from a passing server, Esme strolled through an anteroom into the dining hall, which was drowning in red silk and gold trimmings. The art here showed a courtyard in sunny Spain with colorful scarfs draped every which way. Nestled among the scarfs was a gleaming set of barber tools. The plaque read *Rossini's Barber of Seville*. Next came the king's bedroom in heavily carved woods and blue silks with the legend of Tristan and Isolde gazing down upon the royal occupants. A sword from Wagner's *Tristan and Isolde* lay majestically in the bow of a ship with waves painted on thin cuts of wood sawing back and forth to resemble moving water.

Up next, the grotto. Her pulse quickened as she stepped down three rough-cut steps and into a darkened cave. A dripstone cave to be exact. Stalactites dripped from the ceiling into a seemingly crystal green river. A waterfall rushed down the far wall while colorful lights splashed around the rock surfaces like craggy rainbows. In the center of the river drifted a boat unlike any other kind of boat. This boat was made of dreams and carved into the shape of an opened shell with a cupid perched on the bow, readying to strike all who dared step aboard with his arrows of passion.

A flash of sparkle caught her eye. Scooting around the other finely dressed gawkers, she moved closer to where the rock ledge ended and peered across the water to the boat. There it sat. The Valkyrie. Like a warrior queen upon her pillow and surrounded by festoons of rose garland. Her fingers itched to reach for it. Patience. Always patience in this game.

"I don't know who had the fool idea of roses. That jewel of fabled heroics should be lifted upon the mounds of the fallen brave. Shields and swords. Not a floral display."

For the second time in a matter of minutes her pulse tattooed a fast beat as Jasper's arm grazed her elbow. "Ah, here you are. I was wondering when you'd turn up."

"I'm afraid I had to crawl out the bathroom window after you jammed the lock on my room door, traverse the ledge— three stories up, mind you—and jump onto the balcony. A bit late, but I'm here nonetheless."

Hands tucked casually into his trouser pockets, he was the picture of bored refinement. He wore the tuxedo jacket and black tie that had recently become all the rage, the crisp white shirt setting off his mild tan to perfection, an unheard-of condition on pasty British skin. His golden-brown curls had been combed and slicked to the side, though one obstinate coil draped dangerously over his brow. The same curl she had brushed from his forehead while he slept.

She detested interruptions while working, but part of her thrilled at their game. Thieves and opportunity seekers abounded, especially after the war when noble titles and wealth were left unclaimed after young heirs had given their lives for king and country, but no one else had been on equal footing. They all snatched at the lower rungs filled with grandmother's pearls and corner store robberies, almost all being caught and thrown behind bars. Esme would laugh and tut over their incompetency.

Then this man showed up, the infamous Phantom. Respected by all thieves—an honor not easily gained—and trusted by the black market. A man who could finally keep up with her. And not only keep up but keep her on her toes. A situation she had never expected, just as she never thought to see him again. Heaven help her; he was exhilarating.

"Have you decided how you'll do it?" he inquired politely.

Pay off one of the waitstaff to tip his drink tray into the orchestra as a distraction. Use the conveniently long cord attached to her fan as a lasso and swing the fan around the cupid. Draw the boat near. Snatch the tiara. Hide it beneath her skirt's handkerchief pieces. Walk straight out the front gate.

"A lady never reveals her secrets."

"Must be something grand considering its held captive under the adoring eyes of every person here." He shifted closer as a new throng descended into the tight space, clamoring for a view of the show-stopping tiara. "Then again, you're one for decidedly simple yet bold moves."

"How well you think you know me."

"We may have spent a limited amount of time together, but I've spent a lifetime observing people. What they want, what makes them tick, and what those traits foretell concerning how they'll go about achieving their desires."

"If you're so knowledgeable, pray tell, what is my greatest desire?"

"Your greatest desire I'm still piecing together, but I know you're a woman who refuses to be pushed into the margins. Such makes for a bold woman. A warrioress." He leaned close. "A Valkyrie."

For once her wit failed to rise in response. It was held hostage by the warmth of his chest brushing against her arm. The scent of cedarwood toppling over champagne. The brush of his breath on her ear. She tried to turn away but was pinned in place by the wall of people. The euphoria was quickly turning against her.

No entanglements. No dependency on anyone but herself. No getting thrown off course by a handsome face. No turning into her mother.

"Excuse me a moment," she murmured and pushed her way through the crowd.

Ignoring the orchestral strains, the exclaimed comments over artwork, ladies in their glittering jewels, and old men bantering about one another's medals, she hurried through the chambers but could not find what she sought. A moment of fresh air.

A man brushed by and grabbed her arm.

Esme jerked her head to see his face. "Unhand me—"

Pirazzo.

"You're following me?"

His fingers squeezed into the tender flesh on the back of her arm. With his other hand, he reached up and tugged on the velvet choker wrapping around her neck. "What I could do with this." With a final yank, he let go and slipped into the crowd like a snake slithering through the grass.

Esme jerked the choker from her neck with trembling fingers. Jasper's warning flashed through her head. *He won't think twice about snapping your pretty neck if his master doesn't get her way.*

The room closed in around her. Laughter rang in her ears. She turned in a circle, seeking escape. Air was difficult to draw.

"Allow me." Jasper appeared once again at her side and took her elbow, guiding her through the maze of carved furnishings and upper elite to a heavyset door at the back of the throne room.

Swinging it open, he ushered her outside to a long, covered balcony with towering arched windows.

Esme grasped the railing and dragged in a grateful breath, willing her heart to calm. She would succeed tonight and Pirazzo would crawl back into his hole. Never again would she have to look over her shoulder in fear of him.

"Better?" Jasper asked.

Esme moved to stand by one of the stone pillars framing the arched window and tossed the choker over the rail. "Between the champagne and the boat on the water I do believe I was reliving our days on the ship to Italy." After taking another deep breath, she flashed a smile to cover her moment of weakness.

"Right as rain now." She spread her hands over the stone ledge. "And how could I not be with this view?"

The view beyond was, in a word, *spectacular*.

Towering mountains enrobed in mists of purple as the sun sank slowly behind their peaks while green hills bedded down at their feet, readying for a coming night's slumber. A lake glistened like a bowl of water cupped between the rolling hills as the sun's last rays mingled with the thin veil of rain across the blue surface. A tiny village nestled along the shore, lights flickering on in the windows as its occupants eked out one more hour of their day before retiring. Did they know they lived in a fairy tale?

Jasper joined her. "I've traveled a great many places in this world, and I believe none so transportive as Bavaria. Though the Scottish Highlands might have something to say about that." Leaning forward, he rested his forearms on the ledge. "That's Alpsee in front of us. The one over to its right is Schwansee. Swan Lake. I wonder if that's where Tchaikovsky found his inspiration for the ballet."

"It's rumored he took it from the folktale of 'The Stolen Veil' by Johann Musäus and then modeled the dreamer Prince Siegfried after King Ludwig himself. All hearsay, of course."

He lifted a surprised eyebrow. "Where did you hear such sayings?"

She shrugged, toying with the fan's silken cord. "Theater talk. My mother was a performer on the East End stages, and I grew up behind the velvet curtains. I learned everything from King Lear's death rattle to making false lashes stick with nothing more than Vaseline to impersonating the posh set."

How valuable those lessons had been for her chosen career. She could float like a duchess, speak with a crystal-cut accent, and knew which fork to eat from, but it never seemed to diminish her sense of fraud. She could act like an aristocrat all she wanted, but she would always be that East End theater scamp playing pretend. An actress for her role in life. Someday she hoped to put away the makeup and lights and simply be Esme. Whatever that looked like.

"I never knew you grew up with the theater."

"Before you start getting grand ideas of me perched in an opera box, you should know they weren't those kinds of stages. *Swan Lake* was performed with little more than strategically placed feathers."

He threw his head back and laughed. Curls broke free of the oily Brilliantine trap and sprang about. He raked them out of his face with careless ease. "And who would you perform as? Odette or Odile?"

"Odile. She has more fun. Poor Odette just swam around mourning her situation instead of doing something about it." Mourning, moaning, and complaining was for the weak, and

Esme had never been allowed to be weak. Weakness got you killed on the streets, and she had no intention of ever going back to shivering in doorways and stealing food while her mother begged at any stage door looking to hire.

"I didn't grow up with grandness either," Jasper said.

"Says the man who was able to afford an army officer's commission." She brushed away the mist collecting on the fine hairs of her arm. "You don't get that number of pretty coins by delivering milk."

He took off his jacket and draped it around her shoulders. A habit of his she found very much to her taste. "My father was a womanizer and shot dead by a jealous husband. My mother was a lady's maid who was charmed by my father. She died in the first wave of the Spanish influenza. I am the bastard product of their brief union."

Not alone in that.

"It wasn't until I turned thirteen that my grandfather made himself known and sought to bring me up in the world."

"Why did he wait so long?"

"He could never formally recognize an heir born on the wrong side of the blanket, and had only daughters by his wife, Clarice. They in turn had the audacity to produce only daughters. He's getting older, and I suppose an illegitimate grandson is better than no grandson at all. He took me under his wing, gave me a formal education, and tutored me in the ways of the world. When the war came, I was eager to do my bit and he was eager to support me. Not in a grandfatherly way but in a way that benefitted him. Always an angle for himself, the old blighter."

"So he's using you for his own gain."

A flicker of a frown edged around his mouth as he glanced down at his hands then out to the falling night vista. Under the finely woven shirt, his straight shoulders bunched and stiffened. She knew the stance well, having adopted it herself whenever the ugly truth dangled before her nose.

"You could call it a mutually beneficial relationship," he said. "I had schooling and now live a rather comfortable life. Delivering milk or hauling crates at the dockyard was all the future I could look forward to without him."

"But you're indebted to him. Don't you long to break free?"

"I did during the war. I'm a man who knows how to obtain things, and during a crisis that's a profitable commodity. Over time I built up enough contacts, and now buyers seek me out." The stiffness left his shoulders, but they remained straight and proud. "The old man may have pulled me from the mire, but I stood on my own two feet."

The sun sank behind the mountains, withdrawing its final glow of warmth. The mist creeped around, filling in the pale oranges and greens with silver grays and watered blues.

Esme tugged closer the collar of Jasper's jacket as mist tickled her neck. "Will you stay a thief forever?"

"Haven't you heard the saying 'once a thief always a thief'?" he smoothly replied. "You?"

"As long as it's amusing."

Brushing the gathering wetness from his hands, he straightened and leaned against the stone pillar. "Tell me, what was the first thing you ever stole?"

"Apple."

"The last?"

"A woman's sapphire bracelet in the powder room. She had three others and won't miss it." She hadn't intended to take it, but honestly it was the smallest of the bunch and the woman had eyed Esme's vulgar use of lipstick with old biddy disdain.

Jasper grinned and crossed his arms over his chest. She did her best not to notice how the movement caused the material to strain appealingly across his muscles, but then, she'd never been one for denying herself the simple pleasures in life.

"The most selfless?" he asked.

"A gramophone from the officer's ward to give to the enlisted. The rich shouldn't have all the nice things. Especially not in hospital after what those boys went through." She'd never learned to make proper hospital corners on the bedsheets, and her rolled bandages left something to be desired, but she'd done her best without complaint. What was there to complain about when soldiers lay there covered in bandages and missing arms and legs? "Only time I nicked anything during the war."

"I see patriotism flows in your veins."

"Working in that hospital was the only honest job I've ever had, and I wasn't about to spoil it with light fingers. You men deserved better than that."

"A lot of those men deserved better than what they got. A bullet to the stomach. Drowned in a mud crater. Gassed and blinded with their lungs shredded. I felt ashamed for returning home with little more than a scratch. They all kept saying we were the lucky ones. Well, I never felt lucky. Not until I saw you coming through the crowd. I knew then what I'd been fighting for." He hadn't moved a muscle, but the space between them shrank. Their own tableau of restrained attraction.

Heat swept her cheeks. She gave a playful laugh to defuse the sensation. "I was one of the first cleanly dressed girls you'd seen in a long time. It wasn't difficult to impress you."

"No, it wasn't just because you were a woman, or devoid of mud, not even because you were standing there like an angel. It was simply you."

The heat surged again. "Perhaps it would have been better if I had turned around and disappeared back into that crowd."

"Perhaps." His voice turned husky, drawing her further in. "But could you have?"

She remembered that day in a series of vignettes. The announcement of the armistice. The throng of cheering crowds in the Tuileries. The deafening clapping and shouting. Flags waving. Her hat being knocked off and not caring enough to retrieve it beneath the crush of feet. And then it seemed like the crowd knew, as if sensing a lightning strike. They parted and there he stood. Blindingly handsome in his rumpled uniform that he managed to make look debonair, and a smile that rocked her off her feet. A smile aimed right at her that soundly dissolved her willpower of detachment. He gave her no choice and drew her as decidedly as he did now.

"I—"

Explosions burst over the top of the castle. Sparks of green, red, and gold twinkled like gems as they collided with the mist.

Jasper glanced up with a wry twist of the mouth. "Always fireworks."

Esme stepped back. Cool air chilled her cheeks and scrubbed away the warmth that had come too close to making her lose her head. The one thing she'd vowed to herself never to do—lose her head over a man—and there she was about to fall into a deluded moment's embrace.

Fool!

"Here." She pulled off his jacket and thrust it back at him, then hurried inside before she had the chance to . . . to . . . She wasn't certain, but it was bound to be utterly idiotic and regrettable.

The castle hummed like a kicked-over beehive. Voices clashed against the gilded ceilings as bodies pressed together. Esme was quickly folded into the flow and carried along like a twig on a rushing river toward the main entrance. Out the front door she was rushed down a set of stairs—built oddly to the side against a flanking wing instead of in the center of the main castle—where she spilled onto the upper courtyard.

Fireworks dazzled overhead, their booms muted among the wet droplets and cheering crowd. Pushed from behind, she kept her feet moving lest she be knocked down and trampled until she bumped into a stone rail that separated the upper courtyard from the lower courtyard some seven meters below where a crowd was clapping and shouting.

A gleaming white carriage pulled by four matching bays with gold plumes attached to their harnesses was parked on the cobblestones in the lower courtyard. A driver dressed in powder-blue breeches and frock coat, white stockings, powdered and curled wig, and tricorn hat perched atop a cushioned bench patiently holding the reins.

Next to Esme stood a man quietly observing the riotous scene. Pudgy about the jowls and on the shorter side with spindly legs that gave the impression of propping up an egg, his lips pursed in amusement.

"What's happening?" she asked.

"You did not hear the announcement?" His English was heavily accented. French.

Esme's French was spotty at best, and the few phrases she had picked up over the years weren't meant for polite company. "I was on the balcony and saw the fireworks. Then before I knew what had happened, I was swept along with the crowd."

"You see this gentleman there, *oui*?" He pointed to a towering man with a rotund belly and red face who was sauntering down the steps that curved to the courtyard where the carriage awaited.

"The comte de Laval. The sixth wealthiest man in France. And there is his newest wife." He pointed to a petite woman with bleached-blonde hair who swayed along next to her husband, her mouth opened wide with laughter.

"His previous two wives had aged too much for his liking. Barbette Nicole de Mortemart is not only a younger model but a champagne heiress. Her family has owned one of the most successful champagne companies for generations. Together, they make quite the influential couple."

The name clicked in Esme's head. "Mortemart, as in Mortemart Champagne."

"Ah, I see you have heard of it."

"Heard of it? We practically bathed in it after the war. The Fontaine des Mers was filled with the bubbling brew, and we girls kicked off our shoes to—" At his far too interested look, Esme stopped her explanation. "Ahem. It's devilishly delicious."

"That it is"—he glanced down at her bare left hand— "mademoiselle."

She snapped open her fan and batted it to clear the air of his impertinence, then turned her attention back to the glamorous couple basking in their limelight. The castle was choked to the gills with important starched collars. Not even Prince Rupprecht, the last heir apparent to the Bavarian throne before his family was removed from power, had received more than a smattering of applause at his earlier arrival.

Then the answer to all the hullabaloo came into view.

Sparkling like a crescent of stars, the Valkyrie glided through the crowd on a red velvet pillow held by a servant dressed in the same ridiculous powder-blue getup and wig—straight toward the waiting carriage and French champagne fops.

Dropping her fan, Esme curled her fingers over the stone rail. *No, no, no.*

"Seems the comtesse cast her eye upon the most glittering item she could find and wanted it," the little man next to her chirped. Fingering an unusual spray of golden feathers pinned to his lapel, he appeared to be having entirely too good a time observing the spectacle. "Never able to resist her pouting charms, the good comte acquiesced to her desire, and now the magnificent tiara that once graced the grandest of opera halls shall perch atop a spoiled head."

Esme watched as the couple stopped next to the awaiting carriage. The comte lifted the tiara from its pillow and held it high for all to see as his little wife clapped and jumped up and down behind him like a kitten springing for a feather on a string. Gathering all the pomp he could muster, the comte turned and held the tiara above her head.

The crowd breathed in. After tossing a wink back at his audience, the comte solemnly lowered the Valkyrie and settled it atop that silly little head. The crowd exhaled with a cry of excitement. The crowning of royalty.

Esme's nails dug into the stone as the twit climbed into the carriage and waved her diamond-ringed hand, no doubt imagining all before her as adoring subjects.

"Bloody hell."

"Pardon?" The man bounced next to her, eyes crinkling in delight.

"Nothing, I was—" Esme flicked a dangling feather from her cheek and composed herself. "I hate to see a work of art intended for the arts sold away to private collectors and buried deep in their family vaults." A lie. She would be out of business if not for those twittering snobs always grasping for more to stuff in their golden hordes.

"*Oui.*" He sighed with dramatic flair as his feet finally flattened. "That magnificent piece is now off to the de Mortemart estate near Reims where she'll flaunt it before her party guests for a few days, grow bored, then move on to the next bauble."

Settled in the carriage, the couple waved as the driver flicked the reins, and off the horses trotted. The comtesse spun around on her knees to wave over the back, knocking the tiara askew with her wiggling fingertips. She giggled and tapped the tiara back into place before the carriage passed through the gatehouse and out into the fireworks-filled night.

There was nothing more exhilarating to the blood than a challenge, but this was becoming positively bloody ridiculous.

Well, we'll just see who's great enough to truly wear the crown.

Smoothing the damp hair curling at the back of her neck, she turned to the Frenchman. "In Reims did you say—"

But her bouncing egg companion was gone.

She looked all around, but he was nowhere to be found. The crowd deflated after the departing fanfare and meandered back inside where the orchestra kicked into a lively polka and the champagne poured freely. There was nothing rich people loved more than free entertainment. Esme wasn't titled, but she certainly enjoyed champagne as much as the next heiress.

Tonight, however, the grapes would without doubt sour on her tongue. The Valkyrie had been within her grasp. It had dazzled before her eyes. And it was gone. Again. Whisked away. Again. All because she'd allowed herself to be distracted by cologne and a husky voice.

Damn that man. Damn all men.

She'd trained herself to be better than all those witless women who fell for the first pretty face or whispered promises. Too many made that mistake and paid the price of heartbreak or dishonor and a belly swollen with child or forced from one man to the next. Like Mimsy. Mimsy claimed it was her choice, but she'd always been weak when it came to men. Needing their affection, their attention, almost as much as she craved the spotlight. Esme had thought herself above such trappings.

Until tonight.

Jasper Truitt may have smuggled his way into her heart during a moment of celebratory weakness four years ago, but she wasn't about to let that thorn fester. To Reims she would go and not give him another thought until she could finally sign her name to that divorce paper.

As she turned away from the castle, a rough hand grabbed her and shoved her back against the stone rail.

"The countess will not be pleased." Pirazzo's stale breath reeked across her face. His dark eyes were nothing more than black beads as his fists pushed hard into her chest.

"I will get it." Fear strangled the air in her lungs.

He ground his knuckles into her sternum until she bent backward. "You know what happens if you do not."

Esme flung her hands out to grab the rail to keep from tipping over.

"This is a temporary setback. Nothing I haven't dealt with before." Her feet scrambled to grip the ground.

He leaned forward until his nose smashed against hers. "The next time, *I* will deal with *you*."

Then he was gone.

8

WHAT HAD BEGUN AS A typical German mist quickly turned to a full-on English bucketing down. The timing couldn't have been more perfect to match Jasper's foul mood as he ducked under shop awnings to ward off the worst of the wetness.

The sooner he signed those divorce papers and rid himself of the irksome soon-to-be ex-Mrs. J. Truitt, the better. The woman had him all tied up in knots. One minute teasing and gazing at him with fond memories, and the next snatching the security out from beneath his feet. Security he had built brick by brick to lay a foundation that gave his life meaning and purpose.

Then she came along and called out the cracks he'd been able to excuse. *"He's using you for his own gain."* Of course he was! Duke used everyone, and he certainly wasn't above contracting his own grandson if the purpose suited him. Not that Esme knew he was Duke's grandson. She would have used it as further ammunition. Only Mond knew that dirty family secret. For the obscene amount of money Duke offered him to take the job, Jasper was the one making out with the greater payment.

"Don't you long to break free?" Ha! Says the woman chained to a dusty countess's leash. She was no freer than he was, both with masters to answer to.

Darting across the street, his foot landed in a hole. Water poured into his Italian-leather oxfords. Par for the course that evening. Back at the castle, he'd bummed a ride from the inebriated British Minister of Arts who had kindly dropped him off in Füssen. The nearest train station was located some three kilometers away, but the auto had suffered a flat tire a few blocks from the depot, and Jasper was forced to walk the rest of the way. Ordinarily a walk would clear his mind, but at that particular moment his mind roiled as dangerously as the thunderstorm.

Spotting the red blinking lights of the train in the distance, he jogged the rest of the way to the station and found a single attendant on the platform guiding straggler passengers with a torch.

"Entschuldigung," Jasper said, swiping the rain from his face. "Is this train going to France?"

The attendant helped a lady up the stairs to the last train car. "Stuttgart, Luxembourg, then you will change trains for Reims."

Setting down his travel bag, Jasper dug into his pocket for coins. "How much to Luxembourg?"

"Apologies, sir. The ticket window is closed for the night, but you can purchase one on board." The train whistle blew. "Hurry along. The conductor on board will assist you."

"Danke!" Jasper grabbed his bag and scrambled up the steps into the train as the monstrous black wheels started to turn against the steel rail and the locomotive lurched into motion.

Finding his balance, he walked down the corridor stretching between the cars in search of an empty compartment. All seemed to be occupied.

"*Entschuldigung,*" he said to the uniformed conductor walking toward him without the slightest bit of unease on the jerky car. "I would like to purchase a ticket to Luxembourg, *bitte.*"

The conductor pulled out a small notepad and a change dispenser clipped to his belt. "Is Luxembourg your final destination?"

"*Nein.* I was told I would need to switch trains to carry on to Reims."

The conductor marked his notepad with a blunt-tipped pencil. "That will be sixteen hundred marks."

Jasper gave a low whistle as he handed over the appropriate amount. Inflation after the war was staggering. The conductor punched his ticket and told him to squeeze into an available seat as most of the train was completely booked with important persons making their way back home after the castle gala. A snort conveyed the man's opinion about the rich and their parties.

Dragging himself and his luggage along the corridor in search of an open seat, Jasper ignored the squelch in his shoes, his shriveling toes, his aching shoulders, and the hammer pounding right behind his eyes. A good night's sleep was what he needed. Then he could start formulating a plan for the Valkyrie. One that did not involve distractions by Esme Fox.

A compartment stood open three doors down. At last a break in his streak of bad luck. He could almost feel his eyelids tugging blissfully closed at the anticipated rest coming.

Just as he reached the compartment, the doors began to slide closed.

"*Entschuldigung.*" He grabbed one of the doors and tugged it open. "I'm looking for an empty seat— Well, well, well. Just my luck."

Clad in a splotchy wet silk traveling coat, Esme stared back at him. Her hair had been sleek and smooth at the castle, but the rain had turned it to a frizzy poof.

"More like a bad penny." She kept her hands firmly on the door handles. "This compartment is taken. Seek other accommodations."

He glimpsed behind her. "You have seats for six people."

"So I do." She didn't budge.

"I'm exhausted."

"As am I." She started to close the door. "I bid you good evening."

The night, all its disappointments, and its one massive failure had been teetering above his head propped up by one tiny twig of sheer willpower to keep going. In that instant a silver T-strapped shoe kicked at his twig and the whole weight crashed around his ears. He knew precisely whose shiny shoe was to blame.

Wedging his foot in the closing door, he eyed his opponent. "I've never missed a lift, yet ever since you breezed back into my life like an ill wind I've had one bad turn after the next. What is it about you that sends everything toppling off a cliff?"

"Me?" She reared back, sending her poof bouncing. She tried flattening it with one hand while holding tight to the door handle with her other. "You're the reason I lost *my* mark tonight. If you'd stayed out of the way, or better yet, far away, I could be halfway to Italy by now with a diamond tiara in my purse."

"You'd be better off snatching pocketbooks. Leave the difficult grabs to those of us who know how to pull them off."

"As you have so adeptly showcased this past week with your empty hands and empty pockets, *Phantom*."

One door down creaked open and out poked an old lady's head with tight iron-gray curls. "Shh!" She scowled. "Some people are trying to sleep." Muttering in German, she shut the door with a thud.

Jasper leaned forward and lowered his voice to silken danger. He'd found it more effective than any amount of shouting.

"For all your bragging and swanning about, I fail to see you raking in the profits."

"I would have tonight had you not interfered." Usually when he leaned forward, people had the good sense to lean away from his quiet wrath. Esme was not inclined to be one of them. "It was there. It was mine for the taking, and then you had to corner me out on the balcony, making me miss my opportunity. Now my intended lift is perched atop the empty head of some champagne heiress who is being whisked back to her estate aboard a private train while I'm forced to take this one where the smell of a hundred picnic lunches has soaked into the upholstery."

"Next time I'll leave you fainted dead away on the floor, shall I? How ungentlemanly of me to think you might need fresh air when all the color drained out of your face, but here's the rub. I have never been called anything but a gentleman. Just as I never cornered you. The door was there for you to waltz back inside at any time."

"Very well. I take back that accusation." She conceded with miffed grace.

"And the one about me interfering."

"No. The truth is never an accusation."

"A good thief never blames the circumstances. He succeeds or not by his own abilities." He leaned his shoulder against the doorjamb. She tugged on the door, but his weight pinned it in place. "You could have gone back inside, but you didn't. Why not? What kept you out there talking to me?"

He fought to keep an unaffected air, as if it mattered not what her answer was, and in truth it did not matter, for it would not change his plans. Yet there was that part buried deep inside that needed to know. A vulnerability that had been left waiting in a hotel room for a bride to return. A vulnerability that needed to know why he still carried around her wedding band like some sentimental fool.

She gave up trying to shove the door into his shoulder and held tight to the other one as the train swayed. "You're rather concerned for my reasoning. What of your own? Why were you not inside taking the prize right out from under their lofty noses?"

"I had my own plan and would have carried it through if not for you." The plan had been simple enough. Posing as the castle curator, he would have all the guests ushered from the grotto and the entrance barred due to a burst pipe. A quick lasso of the boat with the thin rope coiled in his pocket and the Valkyrie would have been his. No explosions, no sneaking into windows. A simple grab that had been blown out of the water because of his sentimental foolishness.

"Did you not just chastise me about blaming circumstances?"

"Forgive me if I find it loutish to leave a lady unattended when she is unwell."

"I can manage perfectly well on my own. This isn't the Victorian age where I need to be kept in proximity of a fainting couch at all times." The train lurched around a bend, and she grabbed at her stomach.

"Good manners never change, no matter the years that go by or whatever modern creed is being touted."

The next door over rattled open again. Out popped the same scowling gray head of curls. "If you cannot be quiet, I shall ring for the conductor. Remove your lovers hissing to private quarters and leave the rest of us to peace."

"Remove your own busy nose to private quarters," Esme hissed back.

The old woman's wrinkled jaw dropped, then snapped closed. Mouth pinching into a colorless line, she humphed her displeasure and retreated, mumbling about what the conductor would make of such impertinence.

Jasper straightened but kept his foot blocking the door from slamming in his face. "Short of stooping to desperate levels where only the unimaginative dwell by tying you up and tossing you in the baggage car with a stamp 'Berlin or Bust,' I'm going to give you the benefit of the doubt and assume you would slither out of a locked suitcase with barely a wrinkle to your frock."

"You assume correctly."

"Then we shall play by the rules of gentlemen. Each to their own and stay out of the other's way."

Her black eyebrows narrowed to haughty arrows. "Fine by me. Winner takes all." Her fingers whitened around the door handle as the car swayed. The color also seemed to be waning from her perfectly powdered face.

Jasper lifted his brow in polite concern. "Not feeling unwell, are you?"

"I'm perfectly well."

"The rocking of the train. The sudden turns on the tracks. The way the rails bounce us around like marbles in a can. All the jerky motions can unsettle even the strongest of constitutions."

Her lower lip trembled as she made a tremendous effort to swallow. "My constitution is none of your business."

"Forgive me. I only wish to offer my assistance should you have need of it."

"As I told you before, I have no need of it." She touched a shaky hand to the base of her throat, then tried to act as if she hadn't by smoothing the neckline of her dress.

"Very well, then I shall bid you a fair evening." He was loathe to give up the possibility of claiming one of those empty cushioned seats in favor of a wooden bench in the dining car, but staying would force him to chuck her out the window at the nearest river crossing. Once more, the gentleman in him—blight the sot—won the argument. Tipping an imaginary hat, he continued down the corridor.

"Oh," she called after him. "I'll need to know where to send the divorce papers before I return to Italy with victory in hand."

"Do not fret on that account," he said over his shoulder. "My summons will find you long before yours can trace me. It's a particular skill of mine. Finding things or persons before others can."

"I only hope you find a soft spot to lay your head tonight."

"As I hope you last the night. We have a bumpy track ahead of us." He turned back just in time to see her slap her hand to her mouth and rush into her compartment.

"Good night, darling!"

9

Reims, France

ANOTHER COUNTRY. ANOTHER PARTY. JASPER knew them by heart—the crush of wealthy snobs elbowing one another as they clung to the social ladder. Jewels and white bow ties. Hundreds of frosted drinking glasses. Mediocre food. Boring opinions, forced laughter, and mindless entertainment for the rich at play.

For once he was delighted to be proved wrong.

As he stepped out of the taxi into the warm night air, a ball of fire billowed before his face. Heat scorched his cheeks as red flamed in his eyes. A man bare-chested wearing satin harem pants crouched in front of him holding a long fiery stick to his mouth. With one puff on the stick another blaze shot in front of Jasper. The fire thrower jumped back as the man across from him spit his own blaze. Then another and another, forming a burning pathway to guide guests through the vineyard to the cave entrance where thick double oak doors inlaid with metal scrollwork swung outward with a red silk canopy draped over them. A man dressed in a vintage harlequin comic suit of black-and-silver diamonds with white cream smeared all over his face stood at one side of the entrance handing out masks. A woman in a matching harlequin dress stood opposite with more masks.

Dutifully taking an offered mask, Jasper then slipped it over the top portion of his face and followed the other guests down a long series of stairs deep into the earth as music strains beckoned them onward. Torches lit the way, warming the white chalky walls to cream. Chalk was a unique ground component in which to grow grapes, but it was what made Reims champagne famous. He'd learned a great deal about the substance during his tour with Duke and was still fascinated by it.

The Romans had dug a series of caves like this one in which to mine salt and chalk. Champagne makers later discovered that the caves were ideal for their own purposes because the chalk acted as a sponge to soak up humidity, keep the temperature steady, and protect against vibrations. Jasper ran his hand along the rough-hewn walls. Grooves from picks and chisels lingered as reminders of those whose marks upon the earth lasted far longer than their mortal bodies.

Much like the bones and metal guns that sank in the mud of the Somme, forever calcified in a history of lives spent and wasted.

At the bottom of the stairs, the earth split open into an enormous cavern that had been transformed into a fantasy of magic. Red silk strips hung suspended from the cathedral-style ceiling like a circus tent that looped and draped down the walls. Raised braziers in large golden bowls rose from the flagstone floor and threw their light high into the air where it was caught in the prisms of thousands of crystals dangling from chandeliers before showering rainbows of color upon the wildly dressed performers mingling among the crowd.

Contortionists in leotards, men in top hats standing upright on large balls as their feet moved quickly to keep the ball rolling, a woman in a bright pink tutu swinging from a trapeze, a tightrope act balanced on chairs on a thin rope strung from one wall to the other. Right in the center of the chamber was a ringmaster dressed in sparkling gold with a whip made of feathers that he lashed through the air, driving the entertainment ever onward.

Jasper ducked under the feather whip as it reached out to tickle his ear and made his way to the back of the chamber where a fountain bubbled away. Not just any fountain. A fountain frothing with golden splendor.

"So this is where they keep the good stuff." Plucking a crystal glass from one of the tables on each side of the fountain, he held it under a golden spout. Bubbles splashed onto his white shirt cuffs peeking out from his black jacket sleeve in expensive excess.

"Glamorous, is it not?" A petite woman with light brown hair and oxblood lips draped herself against the fountain's ledge next to him. The chandelier's rainbows danced off her sequin dress. "Why keep it in bottles stored away when you can flaunt it like this?" She waggled her empty fingers, the tips painted the same oxblood color, at his glass.

He offered it to her, and she didn't hesitate in trailing her fingers over his as she accepted the glass. She sipped and a smile curved her lips over the rim.

"Mmm, dreamy." Dark eyes rimmed with kohl liner blinked up at him from behind her mask. "Will you not join me?"

His intended drink now in her possession, he filled a second glass, but before he could take a sip the woman clinked hers to his.

"To life, hopeful lovers, and a night of revelry," she crooned, leaning her bare shoulder into him.

"To life," he conceded. Lovers were far too dangerous, and revelry was the last thing on his mind for the night.

"I have not seen you at out soirees before." Her shoulder pressed more intimately into him. Any second her head would fall onto his chest.

Pretending to adjust his jacket lapel, he angled away from her persistent leaning. "I was in Bavaria when the comte and comtesse de Laval traveled through and had the great pleasure of making their acquaintance. They were very kind to invite me on a tour of the vineyard. By chance I've only just arrived to this spectacle."

The woman flicked a bored glance around. Not one blackened eyelash batted at a trio of dogs jumping through a fire-laced hoop six feet off the ground. "It is enchanting. Then again, everything Barbette does is enchanting."

Her bored expression narrowed to their hostess, who floated among her guests on the arm of her husband. He was dressed from head to toe in gold with a long purple cape trimmed in ermine, a scepter, and a crown studded with gemstones. The comtesse glided in a swath of white tulle with delicate white feathered wings sprouting from her back. Her arms, fingers, and neck were encircled with diamonds, but only one piece drew Jasper's eye.

The Valkyrie perched atop that bleached puff of hair.

Patience was key in the heist line of work. One wrong step, one overeager reach, and it could all be lost. One didn't become king by striking at first encounter. No, Jasper retained his crown because he knew to bide his time for the opportune moment, yet at each failed turn on this particular wild-goose chase, he felt the crown slip. Just enough to scratch his confidence, and that was enough to break his third golden rule of thievery. Never let a job get personal. Allow it to become personal and the fun disappears, which would break rule number one. Keep it entertaining. Not a difficulty on almost all other jobs, but there was something about the Valkyrie . . .

The woman at Jasper's side breathed champagne vapors into his ear. "See how she enchants Henri?"

Tearing his eyes from the tiara, he watched as the comtesse tugged her husband's arm and pulled him to watch a long-legged man balanced on a unicycle while juggling. She clapped and laughed at the antics as the comte smiled indulgently at her.

The woman next to Jasper rolled her eyes and tossed back her drink. "Henri was once enchanted with me. Until he saw Barbette. She is the second richest heiress in the country while I am only the sixth. All I managed to snag was a dying war veteran. He'd better be dying. He's old enough to be Methuselah's school chum, but that's why I picked him. As a wealthy widow I will be beholden to no man and can pick and choose my companions based on what suits me best." She refilled her glass, then sidled up to Jasper, running her hand under his lapel. "I adore this new decade of freedom, don't you? No more of the stuffy old rules. Men and women doing as they please with whomever pleases them."

"The war certainly changed things," he said absently as a crowd formed around the comtesse. The Valkyrie bobbed in regal splendor above the heads.

How could he remove it in such a crush? One: a simple distraction. The cons: in a place this large not all attention would be diverted. He could easily be caught. Two: kill the lights. The con: impossible to douse every brazier in a timely manner. Three: seduction. The con: a jealous husband. He'd dealt with jealous husbands before and never once suffered a slapped face from the lady. More often than not they were quite happy to be whisked away to a dark corner, never once imagining that the fingers at the back of their neck were unclasping valuable necklaces.

He tipped the champagne down his throat. Number three it was.

Placing his empty glass on the nearest table, he held his hand out to the woman. "Would you honor me with a dance?"

Like a cat lapping up the cream, she nodded and placed her hand in his. Her other hand held tight to the champagne glass. Jasper whisked her into the midst of the other dancers as they spun around the costumed orchestra, propped upon large wine barrels all stamped with the Mortemart Champagne emblem of an arrow piercing an oak tree.

"Forgive my rudeness in not asking your name before," Jasper said over the crooning of a clarinet.

"Marie de Bourbon from the royal House of Bourbon."

"Aren't I the lucky man to have a princess in my arms tonight."

She shrugged and brought the glass to her lips for a sip as they spun under the tightrope walker. "A princess once, perhaps, had the rabble not guillotined most of my family during the Reign of Terror."

"I'm sorry to hear that."

"Why? I did not know them." Overhead, the tightrope walker popped open an umbrella and began to do backflips.

"*Magnifique!*" Marie raised her glass to toast the acrobatics and spilled golden liquid on Jasper's arm. She giggled and swiped away the drops, brushing her fingers up his bicep. "Pardon. How clumsy I become, but then excitement happens, and I cannot control myself. Do you ever feel that way, monsieur? Monsieur. I do not even know your name."

"Jasper."

"Jasper . . . ?"

"I prefer the mystery of simply Jasper."

"A more delectable mystery I cannot imagine. Jasper." Her French rolled the syllables of his name like a fine wine over the tongue, but unfortunately for Madame de Bourbon the champagne slurred them into a mesh of soured grapes. "Do you ever feel the control slipping from your grasp, Jasper? Do you ever feel the barrier giving way and you tumble into the exhilaration of it all?"

He'd lost track of a coherent line of innuendo—if there was one to begin with—but she made more than clear her intentions as she pressed firmly against him. Her warm alcohol-soaked breath fanned over him in a suffocating cloud as her toes stepped all over his as they tried to find the musical beat.

"As long as I am with a beautiful woman, I care not which way I tumble."

Turning his head away for a quick intake of fresh air, he spotted the Valkyrie bobbing near the edge of the dancers. The comte had moved away to talk to a group of new arrivals. Time to make his move.

"Do not tell me she has you under her spell too?" Marie tapped her glass against his cheek as the crowd shifted to reveal a sliver of Barbette. "The cherub cheeks and fair coloring. Those angelic looks can be deceiving."

The crowd shifted again and the comtesse was gone, her only beacon the tips of the Valkyrie wings floating above heads. A dancing couple passed in front of him, blocking his target. The man was short, giving the perfect view of his tall partner with slender long limbs, sleek bobbed black hair, and berry-red lips that tilted up higher on the left side. Only one pair of lips he knew did that. And right then they were smirking at him from beneath a mask as his wife waltzed by.

Esme was a sublime dancer. He remembered that much from their whirlwind courtship. She had a way of moving as if on water, with her steps effortless and in perfect harmony to the beat. She made her partner feel as if he were the only man who knew how to guide her across the floor, and she in return made him feel as if he could fly to the moon. At least she once had. Her current partner barely came up to her chin. He couldn't fly even if he got a running start.

Jasper had known she would be at the party and steeled himself accordingly. No more flirting. No more following after. No more trusting. He had a job to do and past sentiments were a quicksand he could not afford. No matter how much the scent of orange blossoms tempted him. He'd end up with nothing more than sand in his teeth for the trouble because he was on the verge of breaking one of his rules by allowing their interactions to veer dangerously toward personal.

He cut his attention back to where it belonged. Two sparkling diamond wing tips. "I've always been drawn to the dark-haired beauties. My curse it seems."

"I can prove to you it's anything but a curse, Jasper." Marie pushed herself to the tips of her toes and grazed her lips across his ear. "Meet me in the—ooh!"

Whirling her through the throng, he smacked straight into his intended target. The little blonde squealed in surprise as she teetered on her heels.

Dropping Marie's hand, Jasper reached out to steady the comtesse. "How terribly clumsy of me. I beg your forgiveness—

Why, Comtesse! I doubly beg your pardon for stumbling into our illustrious hostess." He sketched a humble bow.

Her eyes widened as he straightened, and she took him in from head to toe. It was a reaction he'd grown accustomed to from women since he was a young man. Not that his vanity anticipated it, nor his ego required it, but neither was he going to undermine his own looks by pretending they were anything less than they were. They were a gift just as some men were blessed with brawn and others with a keen mind, and Jasper had no intention of letting his gift go to waste. He flashed a debonair smile.

It worked like a charm. The comtesse's eyelashes batted in unabashed delight. "Oh my." She poked at the tiara tipping sideways on her head, then wriggled her bejeweled fingers at him. "Accidents do happen, Monsieur . . . ?"

His attention begged for the Valkyrie, but he kept it trained on the target. "Jasper." Taking her hand, he brushed a kiss over her knuckles.

She giggled and tapped her fingertips against his palm before drawing her hand back. "Well, Mr. Jasper, before I offer forgiveness, I require three things of you."

So the innocent cherub knew how to play the game as well. Jasper smiled. "I am at your command, madame."

"First, I require a drink. And second, I must know why we have not met before."

Marie pushed herself between them and shoved her half-empty glass of champagne into the comtesse's hand. "Here's one. As to the other"—she latched on to Jasper's arm like a grappling hook—"you have met before. In Bavaria. Isn't that right, Jasper?"

Ah, women and their power struggles for possession. "Indeed. At Neuschwanstein Castle a few days ago when they displayed items of cultural relevance to the arts. We were briefly introduced in the grotto." A brazen lie. The only time he had seen the silly twit was when her husband hauled her off in the carriage. "Where the tiara was being displayed, though I must say that its current presentation is far more fetching."

The well-turned lie earned a pretty flush of pink on the comtesse's face and a digging of the nails from Marie.

"Of course!" the comtesse said. "Now I remember you—at least I suppose I do. There was a great deal of alcohol that evening and so many people, but I should enjoy making amends for our initial brief encounter."

"I look forward to it, madame." He slid her another smile, almost wishing she would make this more of a challenge. "A moment ago you required three things of me. As the first two have been satisfied, I should like to know the last that I may earn your forgiveness."

"A dance."

"No." Marie fumed, stamping her little foot. "You always do this, Barbette. Take and take. For once you will not take what is mine. Go back to your rich husband. Do you not remember him, the one you snared with tricks?"

The comtesse smirked. Marie had been right. Those angelic looks were deceiving. "The only trick I have was Henri falling more in love with me than you."

"Jasper is promised to me this evening."

"I doubt your husband would appreciate such claims on his wife from another gentleman." Smile gleaming, the comtesse glanced over Marie's shoulder to a man whose next step seemed fit only for the grave as he wheezed into a handkerchief. "Shall we call him over and ask him?"

Marie bared her pretty white teeth. "I despise you."

"I know."

Good heavens. He'd had women paw over him before, but these two in a ring would sell out a stadium.

As Marie stormed off in the direction of her doddering husband, the comtesse waved goodbye, then turned to Jasper with giggling excitement. "I'm ready to bestow my forgiveness on the dance floor."

"At your service, madame."

It was like dancing with a bird who was testing her wings. The comtesse hopped and wiggled, kicked and swung with complete disregard for Jasper's attempts to lead. Halfway through the song he gave up and simply held his arm up to let her twirl beneath. More than once the Valkyrie's wing tips caught on his jacket sleeve, and he was forced to fight the temptation of ripping it off her silly head and making a break for it right then and there.

The song eased into a slow tune and the comtesse turned eagerly into his arms. Uncertain where those dainty flapping hands might try to roam on him, Jasper bent to whisper in her ear. "Might we find someplace quieter to talk?"

A gleam twinkled in her eye just before she snapped it in a wink. "I know the perfect place."

Offering her his arm, Jasper looked across the dance floor to find Esme watching him. Despite the mask concealing the upper half of her face, there was no disguising the flat set of her mouth. She was displeased, which couldn't have pleased him more. He offered her a scout's salute, which she took with all the grace of spinning on her heel and melting into the crowd. He had to bite the inside of his cheek to keep from laughing. Events were firmly back to entertaining.

The comtesse led him out of the main chamber and into a dimly lit antechamber. Without the heat of bodies and blazing braziers, the temperature cooled under a single lantern that hung from a peg in the wall to illuminate the dark green bottles stacked floor to ceiling.

"Our 1914 vintage," she said, trailing her hands over the bottles. "The last batch we made before Germany invaded."

"Astounding that these remained in such pristine condition when the Hun marched right overhead." And well worth a fortune. If any client came to him with an expensive thirst, he knew precisely where to quench it.

"They stole a great deal of our stock, but this we kept hidden deep in the tunnels. There are nearly eight kilometers of tunnels buried under here."

"The Romans were an efficient lot."

Her brow furrowed in puzzlement. "Romans?"

"The original builders of the chalk caves."

Her brow smoothed as she waved a dismissive hand. "My father mentioned something like that years ago. He was always one for the history of business and how he could turn it into a profit. Something he and the comte share."

Leaning against an empty rack, Jasper slipped his hands into his pockets. A man unhurried with his impending victory. Of course, if anyone were to peek in his pockets, they would spy hands twitching with anticipation. He could practically smell the diamonds from there. "And you, Comtesse? What are you always one for?"

"Barbette, s'il vous plaît."

She was beautiful, rich, and the fun kind of distraction needed for a night or two out. Precisely the sort of woman he would go after if it gave him any kind of thrill at all. But it didn't. Women like her made themselves too easy to chase, and there was nothing a man loved more than a challenge he couldn't conquer. Trouble was, the only woman he enjoyed flirting with was the one woman he'd vowed to stay away from.

But a job was a job, so he matched the flirtatious tone, bore that it was. "Barbette."

"Hmm, what am I always one for?" Moving slowly around the room, she tapped a long, tapered nail against the bottles as she mused over his question. "Fun. Extravagance. And beautiful things." Completing her circle, she stopped in front of him and looked up expectantly.

She sought a compliment, a smooth line rolled out with honey meant to entice her until there was little more between them than thrumming desire.

But there was only one thing he desired this night.

His gaze drifted over her upturned face and parted lips to the crowning jewel atop her head. "It seems you have been crowned with the most beautiful of all. How fitting for such a queen."

She blinked in momentary confusion as to why he wasn't sweeping her into his arms for a stolen, passionate kiss among the dusty bottles. "A queen? How funny. I imagined they were angel wings, hence my costume." She fluffed her frilly white skirt.

"They can be whatever your heart wishes. You are the one who wears them."

"I am, aren't I?" She poked at the tiara. The wings fluttered in agitation. "Though honestly, it's beginning to give me quite a headache. And the wings insist on bouncing around and catching on things whenever I walk. I've already told Henri to find me something less of a hassle to wear for my next gift."

"Tired of a tiara already?"

"Not a tiara, only this one. I never wear a piece of jewelry more than once. It incites favoritism. Drat this thing! It keeps snagging my curls." She fussed and tugged. The Valkyrie wobbled precariously. Hard as diamonds it may be, but one good crash on a stone floor and those tiny jewels would pop out and scatter. He'd have a devil of a time collecting them all.

"Allow me."

As he reached up to disengage a bleached curl wrapped around the tiara's band, the sound of angry heels stomped into the chamber. Esme stormed toward him. *Pock. Pock. Pock.*

"How dare you do this to me again? You cad!" Rearing back her hand, she slapped him across the face. The band on his mask snapped. It fluttered to the ground.

Esme snatched off her own mask and threw it on top of his, then ground them beneath the toe of her shoe.

"'Never again,' you said. Lies!" She turned to Barbette with tears sparkling on her lashes. "You can't believe a word he says. He'll break your heart just like he's broken mine."

"No one said anything about involving hearts." Barbette looked uncertainly between Jasper and Esme. "A seduction, yes."

A perfectly timed tear slid down Esme's cheek. "That's how he starts. With a seduction of charming smiles and sweet words. The next thing you know, he's hooked your heart for his own amusement. Now I know I was nothing more than a trifle to string along with the others he's captured. Don't let him do the same to you."

The woman had no shame. Jasper shook his head in warning.

"Men like him should be ashamed." She sniffed and dropped her voice to a stage whisper. "Passing around the Neapolitan disease so freely."

Now she'd gone too far. He took a step toward her. "Why you brazen—"

"*Goujat!*" Horrified disgust wrinkled Barbette's face. She spat at his feet, then gathered Esme to her side and escorted her away. "Let us see about blotting that mascara from your cheeks. There is no point in crying over a man, *ma choupette*."

"You are too kind. *Oui*." Esme sniffed. "The ladies retiring room sounds heavenly."

Heavenly enough for privacy in which to clobber the comtesse over the head with her shoe and make off with the tiara.

Jasper followed discreetly behind them to the main chamber ready to whack them both over the head should necessity call for it—which was becoming more the case with each passing second—when the braziers suddenly whooshed out. The red flickering of doused coals splayed against the walls in hypnotic waves.

The ringmaster stood upon his pedestal and spun his feathered whip around his head, gathering the attention of the room. "Mesdames et messieurs! Welcome to a spectacular evening of magic!" Glittering confetti erupted from his whip.

"Mystery!" Fire-eaters blew fiery plumes into the air, the reds and oranges gleaming off the chandeliers.

"And fantasy!"

Spotlights collided midair where a trapeze pair swung on two silver hoops high over the crowd's heads. The woman, clad in tight pink and silver, stood within one of the hoops smiling and waving at the crowd. In quick motion she looped herself over the hoop to hang only by her legs. Her partner in dashing green and gold hung by one arm then two from his hoop, then balanced with both legs shooting like arrows toward the cave ceiling.

The crowd oohed and aahed, encouraging the hoops to swing faster and faster until all of a sudden the woman let go, flipped through the air, and grabbed her partner's wrists for a stunning display of acrobatics and idiocy. Who lacked the common sense to fling themselves through the air with no safety net? The audience, not giving a single thought beyond being entertained, exploded with applause.

Edging through the distracted guests, he spied where the Valkyrie had stopped in the middle of the chamber to tilt upward at the exhibition. Esme staked her claim next to it, swiveling her head like an owl to assess the best possible escape route. She tugged on the comtesse's arm to get her moving again but was promptly ignored when the flying pair began to flip back and forth on their hoops.

Jasper stalked closer, his fingers flexing and eager for the grab. With all attention captivated by the acrobats, it would take a mere flick of the wrist to loosen the tiara from its perch with no one the wiser until it was too late. He slipped to the right to catch Esme's attention. A second was all he needed to have her spot him before he slipped back into the crowd. Then, while she scanned the area for him, he would come in for the tiara from the opposite side.

Classic misdirection. That was where the dime novels got thieving all wrong. They made the art of a lift all about disguises, moonless country roads, derring-do, and sacks full of rubies, when it almost always came down to the simplest of techniques. A sly hand and a pocketful of gumption was all one truly needed.

Moving into her eyeline, he waited for Esme's head to turn his way. *Three. Two—*

A new hoop swung into view.

The woman acrobat gave a startled cry as her partner twisted his hoop sideways to avoid crashing into the newcomer who apparently was not part of the act.

A round egg of a man swung gently back and forth in his disruptive hoop. Jasper frowned. There was something oddly familiar about those thin legs kicking for momentum.

The man was costumed all in black with a black ruffle around his neck, giving his head the appearance of a floating marble in the darkness. A strip of black satin with slitted peepholes was tied around his eyes.

"Forgive my interruption, but I simply could not stay away from such a splendid party. Not when you have brought out the greatest of temptations." He rolled around to dangle by his legs, surprisingly agile for a man of his shape.

"You see, gentle audience, I am like a magpie who must gather shiny objects. I simply cannot help myself." He swung right over Esme.

And the Valkyrie.

Stretching out spindly arms, he plucked the tiara from the comtesse's head.

She screamed. "My crown! He has my crown!" She jumped up and down as if to snatch it back, but the egg laughed as he swung out of reach.

"Our meeting has been short but sweet and now I must bid you all adieu." Streamers exploded from his ruffle, snaking and twisting through the air. The crowd screamed and ducked for cover as if they were spraying bullets.

When the last of the shiny detritus cleared, only Jasper and Esme remained unmoving and staring into the void where the little egg had disappeared along with the Valkyrie.

Once again.

Esme turned to look at him. She crossed her arms and tapped her toe with impatience. "Well, I didn't expect that."

"Neither did I." He ruffled his hand through his hair as a sudden weariness stretched along his bones. He needed a stiff drink. "Guess the party is over."

"Good. I didn't know how much longer I could continue with that crying bit." She swiped at the mascara flakes under her eyes, all pretense of wilting and sniffling gone.

"Did you really need to proclaim I had syphilis?"

"Would you have preferred the clap?"

"I would prefer neither, considering I'm free of venereal diseases."

"I had to think of something to get her away from you. Her moony face was becoming too much."

Stepping closer, he crooked an eyebrow. "Jealous of my attentions to another woman?"

"You are an egotist."

"I'm simply aware that I'm rather difficult to resist."

She matched his imperious eyebrow quirk with one of her own. "As if I would squander myself on the puerile misgivings of jealousy."

"That slap said otherwise."

"Acting, my dear fellow." She lazily raised her hand to his cheek. "Care to see what another one says?"

He caught her wrist, circling his fingers around the delicate bones and brushing his thumb over her pulse. "Only if you're prepared for the consequences."

Her face didn't so much as twitch, but the tick in her pulse told him everything he wished to know. Her cool nonchalance was as unsteady as his own. For all his resolutions in the name of better judgment, why did he have to be drawn to this maddening woman?

"Monsieur. Mademoiselle." With impeccable timing to break up the unwise temptation unfurling, a man dressed in the ridiculous de Laval livery of powder blue and curled wig wedged between the excited crowd and stopped in front of Jasper and Esme. Sweat mixed with powder from the wig streaked down his face. "Pardon, but this was left for you." He held out a folded paper sealed with black wax.

Dropping Esme's hand like a hot poker, Jasper took the note and cracked the wax. The letter unfolded into a square of parchment with elegant script penned across the surface.

"That sly little bastard." Jasper dug into his pocket and fished out two francs. "Here. Go buy yourself a pair of full-length trousers."

As the man retreated with coins in hand, Esme snatched the letter from Jasper. After reading it, her eyes snapped to his. "That cheeky monkey."

"That's one name for him. I can think of a few others."

"You know him?"

"I have the misfortune to say I do. Lamb, his name is, but he goes by Magpie for his love of all things shiny."

"Enemy of yours?"

"I make it a point to avoid having enemies. Competitors are preferable."

She tapped a fingernail against the hand-drawn magpie carrying a tiara in its beak. "He's playing a game with us."

"A game we have no recourse but to join." His gaze fell to the words again.

For the great admiration I have for your esteemed
selves, please allow me the pleasure of your company tomorrow
evening at my home where I may express my veneration in
person. A car will be sent for you at the Orlean L'Hotel in
Montgonne. Please do not consider coming one without the
other, for I would loathe to miss the opportunity of having
you both at my disposal.

I must also express my regret at taking the Valkyrie tiara
from your grasping reach this evening, but as previously
stated I do so adore shiny things. Perhaps if you both are
very good, you may hope to see it again.

Until next we meet,
Admiringly yours

Esme huffed and crossed her arms. "Should have pushed Humpty-Dumpty over the wall in Bavaria when I had the chance."

"You've met?"

"Briefly. When the de Lavals made their grand exit from the castle. He was probably there to case the tiara before he made his big move." Her expression turned livid. "Your friend was casing us at the same time!"

"Hardly my friend. More of a jovial opponent I prefer to keep clear of lest he pick my pockets dry."

"When I get my hands on him, I'll wring that fat neck . . . Well, he doesn't have a neck, but I'll find something to wring."

"Save your ire. We may yet have the opportunity to crack him apart."

"'We'? One stunt and suddenly we're a team?"

"Like it or not, we're in this one together." He plucked the letter from her hand.

"When it comes down to the wire, the Valkyrie won't split two ways."

"That would be too easy, wouldn't it? If there's anything we've learned in recent days, it's that you and I never do things the easy way." He wadded up the letter and tossed it into one of the glowing braziers, then offered her his arm. "Shall we?"

She considered him a moment, her long, dark lashes sweeping lazily up and down, but behind the polished pose spun a wicked-sharp mind, calculating. And reaching the same resolution as his own.

At last her mouth curved to the side and she slipped her hand into the crook of his elbow. "Shall we indeed."

10

At precisely six forty-five a knock rapped on Esme's hotel door. "Enter."

Jasper walked in looking entirely too handsome in his dinner attire and quietly closed the door behind him. "Ready?"

They were staying in the small village of Montgonne halfway between Reims and Paris. It was a sleepy place with little to recommend it except the exciting glow of Paris on the evening's horizon. After four years of darkness under wartime curfew, the grand old City of Love was blazing to life once more. Too bad she was not their destination.

"Finishing touches." She tied a navy satin ribbon around her head bandeau style and discreetly tucked the knotted ends under her bob, careful to keep the attached tassel of pearls dangling in front of her right ear. "Must you always look so drab every time we step out?"

He brushed at the sleeve of his impeccably tailored suit that made him look cut straight from the picture screen. "What can I say? I work with what I'm given. Not all of us can achieve the dizzying heights of fashion such as you manage."

"This old thing?" Standing from the vanity mirror that looked like it had been through a revolution or two, she twirled. The hem of her navy satin skirt flared around her knees. Something about a dress rippling out simply made a girl feel pretty. And this little number was a showstopper she'd picked up the last time she breezed through Paris. Cut on the bias, it had a deep V-neck with an even deeper V down the back. The entire thing was held up by gauzy straps looped over her shoulders.

"Yes, that old thing, and well you know it." He crossed the room and settled into a faded green-and-white striped chair and propped one ankle atop his opposite knee. How easy he made every situation appear. Even forced ones in stuffy hotel rooms. "Now that we've settled your vanity, let's proceed to business, shall we?"

"Such as how much rope we bring to string up this magpie?"

"A man with a neck ruffle that shoots confetti while he swings upside down thirty feet in the air craves adoration and stimulation. Playing hardball with Lamb won't work. Charm and finesse are his tools."

Returning to the dressing table, she rooted around her toiletry case for lipstick. "I don't have time to sit around fawning over this parvenu."

"Why? The countess tugging on your leash already?"

"You should know better than anyone that no one throws a loop around me."

"Yet you've managed to loop yourself into quite the pickle. If I had to guess, I'd say every day you don't return with the tiara is a cinch tighter in the choke collar she's put around you. For a woman who espouses independence, you certainly have signed yours away to that woman. Which signifies one of two things. Either you're hard up, but given your couture wardrobe and Louis Vuitton travel set that is unlikely. Or you simply got more than you bargained for and must deliver or else."

The memory of Pirazzo's knuckles pushing into her chest stifled the air in her lungs. Her fate was sealed to the Valkyrie. She would rise or fall based on this lift, and oh, how far she would fall if she failed. Every inch she had clawed herself from the mud would be for nothing. She would be nothing. A mere blot—a smear wiped across yesterday's newspaper: "Woman Found with Silk Cord Wrapped Around her Strangled Neck."

Jasper need not know any of that. She was a grown woman and had managed to survive without weeping on someone's shoulder her entire life. If Mimsy had taught her anything, it was that the entire world was a stage and an actor's job was to smile through it all. Especially when they were kicked low.

Finding her lipstick, she popped off the top and rolled out the dark red stick to glide across her lips. "My business dealings are my own, except in the case of this magpie. If you don't mind, I'd prefer to keep to the task at hand. The sooner it's over, the sooner we can return to Robin Hooding on our own."

"Except we don't steal from the rich to give to the poor. Lofty ideals do not often go hand in hand with keeping oneself from the poor house. Our skills simply go to fund our own pockets."

"Then it's a good thing we're both good at what we do." She blotted her lips on a tissue. "And why we should have no trouble outsmarting this egg."

"He does look rather like an egg, doesn't he? More so than when I last saw him." Jasper stretched out his long legs and laced his fingers over his flat stomach. "You say you've never heard of him before?"

She shook her head and recapped the lipstick. "I know every worthwhile thief in the business, and more than a few who aren't. Which means he isn't worthwhile."

"Perhaps not in the grand heist of things. Mostly he's been content with swindling old ladies from their heirloom pearls or nicking a museum piece or two."

"Why now seek the cream of society's attention? Along with ours?"

"Clearly his ambitions have grown in the past few years. He orchestrated performing the most brazen act right out in the open. And right under the noses of the world's best thieves. What better way to make a name for himself?"

"To what purpose? To claim he's better than us?" She snorted, sliding the lipstick tube into her beaded purse. "Beginner's luck was all it was."

"Luck or careful plotting, he won that round. He has the Valkyrie. And now we need to figure out a way to steal it back."

"He'll be expecting us to try."

Jasper shrugged, unruffled by the challenge laid before them. "Of course he will. So we'll use that, along with what else I know about him. He's arrogant, has a flair for the dramatic, and a need to prove himself."

"I would prefer stupidity."

"Arrogance is its own form of stupidity. It will do."

Esme dipped her puff into the pot of powder, then dusted her nose and forehead. "If I didn't know better, I would say it sounds an awful lot like we're becoming a team." She caught his eye in the cracked mirror and smiled.

"A team for one mission only." He didn't return the smile but turned his head to the open window. The sound of shop windows closing and doors locking for the night as neighbors bid one another *bonne soiree* drifted up. "During the war we paired up with the French for the big pushes. We didn't trust them and they didn't trust us, but we both hated the Germans more. Common enemies bring about the most unlikely unions. All that matters is the mission."

Misery dulled with time etched his words. A familiar tone to all who had lived through that hell. She swiveled on the stool. "You don't talk much about what happened over there—well, over here actually. None of the boys do."

Sighing heavily as if an invisible weight pressed him from the inside out, he leaned forward to the edge of the chair and dropped his gaze to the floor. "Not much to say. What happened is done. Those who were there know, and those who weren't cannot understand."

She would never boast to understand what those men experienced in the trenches. Yet those on the home front had not escaped unscathed. Theirs was an entirely different kind of hell. One of waiting and hoping, of making do and carrying on. Of wondering how they could ever pick up the broken pieces of their men, wondering how they could ever be whole again.

She'd been fighting long before an assassin decided to put a bullet through an archduke as he motored around town with his wife. Fighting to survive. Fighting to know who she was. Fighting other children who had been bestowed a father's last name. Fighting to make something of herself and for herself. But always the past came haunting with its taunts of never quite making the mark.

"There are far too many ghosts we carry in this life," she said quietly.

Jasper's head came up. His gaze was steady and deep. "How do you silence yours?"

"They refuse to be silent, but I do my best to drown them out."

"Do you succeed?"

"Sometimes. And sometimes they scream louder."

A moment knit with understanding and sharpened by years of survival passed between them. Fleeting in its existence, but palpable to the core of Esme's being. As if her very marrow lunged in recognition of another scarred soul and the weight of its loneliness shared, if only for that one blinding point in time. But that was all it was—blinding. And she had vowed long ago never to allow sentimental feelings to rule her. She would not become a cautionary tale like her mother, and if there was anyone she needed to use caution around, it was Jasper. He was the only one who came close to enticing her to throw it all to the wind.

So she did what she knew best to cover the temptation. She took back control and summoned her charms. Grabbing an opera strand of pearls, she stood and turned her back to him, dangling the pearls over her shoulder. "Help a girl out, darling."

From the reflection in the mirror, she watched as he unfolded himself from the chair and stood, then smoothed the wrinkles from his suit. After buttoning the single black button on his jacket, he tugged his cuffs into place just over his wrists and crossed the room to her.

"They look more than long enough to slip over your head." His brown eyes caught hers in the mirror.

She ignored the flirtations of his cedarwood cologne as it wrapped around her own orange-blossom scent like a warm summer night breeze. "True, but there is a single large pearl, and I can never center it down my back on my own."

Taking the pearls from her, he rubbed them expertly between his fingers. She waited for him to rub them across his teeth to test for authenticity, but he refrained. "South Seas?"

"Japan. They belonged to an empress who had the misfortune of losing them while on a diplomatic mission in Prague last year." There had also been a gaudy topaz, but yellow wasn't Esme's color.

"How irresponsible of her."

"Indeed."

Lowering the creamy strand of pearls over her head, he gently laid them across her shoulders to sweep down her back in a gentle V. His fingers brushed her skin as he adjusted the center pearl. Warmth tingled along her spine, threatening to undo the steel resolve she had fortified around herself.

"I once found a double strand of black Tahitian pearls," he said.

"Found?" she teased, returning to stable ground.

He smiled but didn't take the bait. "If you turned them in the light, they shimmered dove gray and peacock with a touch of cherry. They would have looked extraordinary on you."

And just like that, her teasing armor weakened at the joints. Turning, she found herself inches away from the very temptation that could destroy her. Those brown eyes that peeled her apart layer by layer until she had nowhere left to hide. Those lips that had once kissed her so tenderly and eagerly, even breaking Anglican tradition by kissing her right in the church before the priest. She'd felt alive as she never had before.

Children were taught not to touch fire, but danger of the forbidden often proved even more alluring. How close could she get to the flame without being burned?

Emboldened by curiosity, she traced a nail along his smooth jaw to the slight indention beneath his lower lip, the fullness of it resting beneath her finger. "I seem to remember you being a very thorough kisser."

"Is that so?"

"Mm-hmm."

"Do you know something else you should remember about me?" He leaned close, his voice rough silk gliding over every untouched part of her.

Eyelashes growing languid, she angled her face up. "I wouldn't object to you reminding me."

He brushed the back of his fingers over her cheek, sending tendrils of anticipation curling through her. If this was the flame, she could stand being burned. Her eyes drifted closed, waiting.

"I don't like being late." He tweaked her cheek and pulled away. Her eyes snapped open to the cold rush of reality, and she could have sworn she saw him smiling as he brushed past her to open the door.

Curse the man.

CLOSE TO AN HOUR LATER they sat together in the back of a Rolls-Royce gliding down a country lane. The spit-shined chauffeur had said not a word as he rolled the car in front of the hotel and held open the back door for them. He turned his head neither right nor left as they drove down seemingly endless one-lane roads that cut through fields growing wild with red poppies. Battlefields reclaimed by the wild and nourished with spilled blood.

Esme peered out the window at the cropped moon hanging low against a backdrop of black velvet spangled with stars. "How much longer, do you think?"

Jasper shifted next to her on the leather seat. "Not much I suspect. Our host wants to impress us with a dramatic journey, not push us to the edge of bored irritation."

"He has officially five more minutes before I cross that threshold."

"Are you feeling unwell? I can ask the driver to pull over for a moment." Unable to see in the darkened interior, she heard rather than saw Jasper's concern for her motion sickness and its ingenuity at arising during the most inopportune moments.

Thank heavens it was dark, otherwise he would surely notice the warmth flushing unbecomingly up her neck. "I'm perfectly well, but I appreciate your concern."

"I only ask because this is a Rolls-Royce. The cleaning bill would be more than what I'm carrying in my pockets."

And just like that the warmth vanished. "Don't fret over the seats. I'd be sure to aim for your shoes," she replied sweetly.

The auto turned and passed through a thick hedgerow to reveal a square-shaped country château. Symmetrical rows of windows lined the two-story facade of sand-washed stone that glowed yellow from the torches staked along the drive. A simple roof of clean lines and neatly trimmed bushes on the lawn offered an air of tidy elegance.

"Part of me anticipated a circus tent," Jasper mused as the car rolled to a stop at the front door.

"As his bosom friend, have you never visited before?"

"Arm's length competitor, remember? And no, we never so much as took tea together."

The chauffeur came around and opened the door. Jasper climbed out first before turning to offer his hand to Esme. The front door swung open, and a butler dressed in traditional black and starched white welcomed them into the receiving hall that was simply decorated with watercolor landscapes, fresh flowers, and a chandelier that brightened the wood-paneled walls.

"If you will follow me," the butler intoned, then led them to a room off the main entrance that was cheerful in yellow and cream. "Your host will join you shortly. Should you require anything in the meantime, do not hesitate to ring." He indicated a silver bell placed on a low table between two wingback chairs.

"Touch nothing but the bell." With that cryptic instruction he bowed and quietly slipped away.

"Touch naught but the bell," Jasper said with mock seriousness. "What does he take us for? Two-bit cons?"

"Our reputations precede us."

Esme wandered about the room taking inventory. A grouping of Queen Anne chairs on an Aubusson rug. Fifty thousand pounds on the black market. Artwork by two unknowns and three Adélaïde Labille-Guiards. One hundred thousand pounds. Two hundred if she could sell it to one of those suffragettes always bidding over female memorabilia. Silver tea set. Limoges ceramics. Engraved Spanish swords. All worth a pretty farthing.

"No hidden vault for his collection, I see," she said.

Jasper peered at a chair crafted in a traditional Indian style and inlaid with pearl and silver. Two thousand pounds. "He enjoys displaying his spoils. Thinks he's untouchable once he lays claim to them."

"Is that so? Perhaps we'll get lucky and he'll wear the Valkyrie to dinner. I can snatch it off his head after soup is served."

Footsteps pattered out in the hall. "*Mes plus sincères excuses,*" their host claimed as he rolled into the room. He wore a purple velvet smoking jacket with toggle fasteners, olive-green silk trousers, and black boots with white spats. Why spats when there wasn't a need to protect one's shoes from mud in the house, there was no logical explanation for except to claim it was perfectly within his odd character. "I hope you forgive me for not greeting you at the door."

"Your butler was most gracious in welcoming us," Jasper said smoothly.

"Ah, Jasper! *Mon ami!*" Lamb rushed forward, grabbed Jasper by the face, and pulled him down, planting a kiss on each cheek. "How delighted I am to see you again."

Jasper extracted himself. "It's been some time, Lamb."

"Indeed it has. Delighted to see you out and about as a free man again."

If she hadn't had her eye on him, she would have missed Jasper's infinitesimal flinch. Esme pounced. "Free from what?"

"The army," Jasper quickly replied as he laid his hand on Lamb's thick shoulder. "Where we met and have followed each other's capers ever since."

Lamb's eyes narrowed for a fraction of a second before fluttering wide once more. Whatever his true thoughts, they were gone in a blink of sparse lashes.

"The past is riddled with many twists and turns, though I'm delighted to see your company has improved." Pointing out his toe, Lamb bowed deeply to Esme. The dome of his head shone white under the electric lamps. "I am Felipe Auguste Constantine Lambert Boisseau. My friends call me Lamb, and I hope you will do the same." Straightening, he waited with expectation on his round face.

"Surely you know my name," Esme finally said as he continued to wait.

Lamb tittered, an abrupt noise, as if someone had seized him under the arms. "Most certainly, but proper introductions are what keeps a civilized society from succumbing into the Wild West. We three are civilized, are we not?"

She'd adamantly declared that she would not dance to this fool's tune, yet here she was going back on her own word.

"Very well." Esme pivoted one foot behind the other and bent her knees in a perfectly executed curtsy that would gain a standing ovation from the Royal Opera House in Covent Garden. Just as Mimsy taught her. "Esme Fox."

Lamb clapped with delight. "*Merveilleux*, Miss Fox."

Esme straightened. One distasteful task complete. "You and Mr. Truitt are old army comrades. Did you serve together for the entirety of the war?"

"Heavens no. We met during the truce of fourteen. I sat contentedly atop a fresh pile of snow sipping what passed as coffee, only to see this Brit striding bold as brass up and down no-man's-land sipping champagne with the poilus, trading cigarettes for chocolate with the Boche, and rounding out the exchanges with a fine tenor of 'Auld Sang Lyne' with the Sawneys and their caterwauling bagpipes. Never have I witnessed a man enjoy himself so on a battlefield."

"Wasn't a battlefield at the time," Jasper said.

The Christmas truce of 1914 occurred mere months after the war had started. Enemies from both sides of the trenches put aside their fighting and came together for a moment of respite. German and Allied soldiers played football, dealt cards, shared photographs of sweethearts, all forgetting for a single moment the misery in which they had been entrenched. Some of the men who had come to hospital had spoken of it as the finest Christmas they had ever spent. At least until high command got wind of the mingling and threatened court-martialing and worse if such spontaneous comradery ever dared to happen again.

Esme couldn't help smiling. "You were there for the Christmas truce? We all read about it in the papers afterward."

Jasper shrugged as if such miracles of ceasefire happened all the time. "Many were there."

"Just as many were not taking guard of their valuables while they fraternized." Lamb pulled a silver pocket watch from his breast pocket and shined it against his lapel, all the while watching Jasper. Jasper stared at the watch, then looked away. With one final satisfying buff, Lamb tucked the watch away.

Before Esme could form a thought on that interaction, a gong sounded quickly, followed by the silent appearance of the butler. "Dinner is served."

The dining room was grand enough for an emperor. Brilliant green damask clung to the walls, suits of armor were posted in the corners, a bank of floor-to-ceiling windows overlooking a garden filled one wall, painted scenes depicting various stages of a stag hunt covered another, and a four-tiered chandelier was suspended by multiple wires that crackled with the hissing of electric bulbs. In the center of the room stretched a walnut table long enough to seat twenty people with high-back chairs cushioned by gold satin pillows. Three formal place settings had been arranged at one end with Lamb at the head, Esme to his honored right, and Jasper directly across from her to Lamb's left.

Lamb had gone to considerable expense for the *petite fête* with a menu of exceptional French cuisine that had been hard to find since before the war. Hors d'oeuvres of salmon mousse with capers. Trout smothered in a white sauce, swiftly followed by a palate cleanser of lime sorbet. *Le plat principal* was a heavenly beef braised to perfection in a cherry wine sauce with seasoned vegetables on the side. A light salad, cheeses, and olives, and finally dessert with a decadent chocolate pots de crème topped with fresh cream and white chocolate shavings.

Esme dipped her silver spoon into her pot for the last scoop of chocolate and savored the creamy thickness on her tongue for a moment before reluctantly relinquishing her spoon. The temptation to lick the pot clean was overwhelming and she signaled for the server stationed behind her to take it away before she made a stuffed girdle of herself.

"A long line of bakers my family comes from," Lamb was saying as the dishes were cleared and a silver service of coffee was arranged on the table. The butler then carried in two trays topped by silver domes and presented them to Lamb, who whipped off the cover of the first to reveal a cherry-red fez with a black tassel, which he placed ceremoniously on his head.

"One cannot truly enjoy coffee without a head covering. It helps to keep the heat from evaporating." Then he reached to uncover the second dome. There, nestled among a leafy bed of lettuce, sat a chicken. Complete with puffs of silky fine feathers and a black beak that stuck out from pom-poms covering its intact head.

Without warning, the uncooked centerpiece raised its head and clucked.

Esme and Jasper jumped back. It was alive.

Jasper was the first to regain his composure. "I believe your chef has gone a bit far in preparing your food rare."

"Lettie is no meal to be served." Huffing, Lamb picked up the clucking feather duster and deposited it in his lap. "She is a Silkie. A rare breed known for their silken plumage and originating from China in the fourteenth century. She is also my dearest confidant. Is that not right, Lettie?" He plucked a bright green leaf of lettuce and stuffed it under Lettie's beak. She gobbled the treat. "My confidant, my adviser, my right wing, and my golden goose."

Collecting herself, Esme ventured forth into the absurdity. "Forgive my city-born ignorance—"

"And where was that?" Lamb interrupted.

"Pardon me?"

Lamb stroked the chicken as it settled onto his lap munching its lettuce with contentment. "The city you were born. You forgot to mention."

"Oh, Westminster. London."

"Your father?"

"My father?" Her brain scrambled to latch on to one of Mimsy's cockeyed fabrications. What did her birth details have to do with lettuce-eating chickens? "Sir Thane Macbeth. A member of Parliament."

"Thane Macbeth. Thane Macbeth. Why does that name ring familiar?" Lamb tapped the top of Lettie's pom-pom. "It shall come to me in due time. Now, you were saying, *mon cher*, before I so rudely interrupted."

"You mentioned Lettie as your golden goose. While the closest I've come to a farm animal has been served on a plate, is she not a chicken?"

"A chicken? Certainly, she's a chicken! What gave you the impression she's not?" Without bothering for a reply, he shooed the butler away and began to pour the coffee. Lettie continued to munch her lettuce in his lap.

"What was I saying before? Ah yes. Hard workers, the Boisseaus. We kept our noses to the ground, and when the war came, we were in the right position to sell our flour and wheat to the right buyers."

"The black market you mean," Jasper said, accepting the cup Lamb had poured for him.

Lamb nodded and poured a second cup of the steaming brew. "Though instead of staying on to assist in the transaction, my father forced me to don a uniform. To keep a sliver of honor in the bloodline, I suppose."

Jasper cleared his throat. A bit too loudly.

"So I marched for the honor of France, and the Boisseaus made a tidy sum," Lamb continued as he slid the cup across the polished walnut table's surface to Esme. "We became the most successful bakery in all of northern France."

Angling the cup in front of her, Esme added a dash of sugar and a splash of cream, then stirred until the black liquid softened to brown. "Even during the war years, that's quite a feat when most people were starving."

That fat, golden chicken sitting plump right among them would have been a feast. Lettie's beady black eye glared at her from under its fuzz as if it could read Esme's hunger-consumed memory.

Sighing, Lamb stroked Lettie's back and stared off into the distance. "*Oui*, our success was unparalleled, but scooping flour onto the black market was not enough."

"Nicking fellow soldiers' personal items not fulfilling?" Coolness sharpened Jasper's words to a knifepoint.

"If they were so mindless to leave them unattended, then why should I not make better use of them?" Lamb slipped out the silver watch and rolled it over his palm. "Finders keepers."

Ah, so that was the point of contention. Jasper had made his stance clear that those in service to their country were not to be taken advantage of by a pair of light fingers. A matter Esme entirely agreed with. A caveat of honor, if such a thing existed among thieves.

Tucking the watch away, Lamb poured his own cup of coffee. "As both of you will understand, I needed more. A new challenge that didn't involve flour or pocket baubles. I craved the art of heisting."

Jasper sputtered on his coffee.

"'The art of heisting,'" Esme mused. "How sophisticated that sounds when all along I've been calling it stealing."

Lamb scratched under Lettie's beak. Her long golden neck stretched out for better access. "Sophistication at all times. It is how we stay ahead of the beasts."

"You seem rather a paradox, monsieur. For all your words of sophistication and the understated tone of your home are not parallel to the man we saw swinging from a trapeze as if all the world were his stage."

"The world *is* my stage! How else would I shine so brightly if the items around me were not kept subdued? Barring your glowing presence, of course." Lamb inclined his head toward her. His fez slipped over his bald head and covered his brow. He quickly tucked it back on top.

"I began small. An heirloom teapot here. A lady's ring there. All to hone my skills, and I found the practice exhilarating because at any moment I might have been caught. But I was not, and the thrill of success drove me on to larger prizes. Paintings, crowns from assassinated royals, statues, a yacht. Yet always in the back of my mind was the craving for something more. To be the best. And to be the best I must compete with the best. *Et voilà!* The reason I insisted upon our acquaintance."

Jasper finished his coffee and pushed the cup away. "You're right in that the lady and I are the best at what we do, though there is a debate about who is formally the best."

"There is no debate. It's me." Esme hiked a superior eyebrow across the table before leveling her attention on Lamb. With each passing minute she felt more like the mouse batted between the cat's paws. This feline had his absurdities with his jacket toggles and fez, but an unmistakable predatory spark gleamed in his eyes hinting at the claws beneath his velvet attire.

Best of luck to him. She had claws of her own and they were well sharpened on miniscule tuft-hunters like him. "How did you know about us?"

"As I said earlier, I've had great success on the black market and many of my buyers were only too happy to offer the names of the grandest thieves in the business, under the assumption that I required your services, of course. The Phantom and a fox. Though I suppose *vixen* would be more apt as you are a lady."

"Isn't she just?" Jasper dabbed his mouth with the linen napkin and flashed a mocking smile at her across the table. "A vixen, that is."

It was the same tone he'd used in the hotel, but instead of wanting to beckon him closer she was inching her fingers toward the sugar bowl for a lob attack that was entirely warranted.

"Referring to myself professionally as a vixen has certain connotations I'd rather avoid."

"Why? I rather like that about you," Jasper said.

His hand rested on the table with nearly two feet of waxed walnut separating it from her own, his index finger slowly tapping the wood. The soft beat pulsed into her palm, strumming her to a rhythm with an awareness he seemed particularly adept at mastering. The scoundrel.

"Do I sense a *tendre* swirling under my own roof?" Lamb wagged a finger between Jasper and Esme, breaking the crescendo.

Jasper tapped his finger one final time, then stilled, his eyes on Esme. "Yes, but don't worry. It's nothing serious."

"Nothing serious at all. In fact, it was over before it even began. *C'est la vie.*" She waved a dismissive hand, clearing the air of electric possibilities and stifling disappointment.

Leaning back in his chair, a dreamy look passed over Lamb's face as he slurped his coffee. "*Quel dommage.* Love is rare, except in France where it perfumes the air."

Esme tapped her lacquered nail against the table, a challenging harmony to the previously struck melody. "Here I thought it was still smoking from trying to put out the fires after war."

"Would require a rather large fire for it to still be smoking after four years." Jasper's gaze pinned her to the current zinging between them. "Can't imagine the heat it put off when it first caught blaze."

Her nail tapped faster. "Perhaps it's wise to remember that those who play with fire often get burned."

A golden fuzzball came into view, cutting Esme off from Jasper. Her nail skittered to a stop, and she blinked at the chicken that had been thrust between them. Two deadly black eyes glared at her as a growl—could one call it a growl when coming from a chicken?—vibrated up the ruffled throat.

"I feel as if I have trod into a conversation that began long before I came upon it, and I must inform you now that there is nothing I loathe more than being left out of a game. Lettie feels the same." Lamb retracted into his seat with a pout. Hunching in the chair, he flicked his spoon into a spin. Tiny drops of coffee sprayed across the tabletop. Lettie sprang onto the table and pecked at the drops. "So I propose this: either I am allowed to join your game of secrets, or you may join mine."

Their host was nothing more than a petulant child, and spoiled children who did not get their own way often turned to destructive habits. A good hide tanning was what was needed here, but before that lesson was taught, Esme needed to smooth his rumpled feathers. It was the only way to get what she wanted from him.

She gently touched the sleeve of his velvet jacket and softened her voice to a purr. "I'm afraid this secret is just for two, Lamb dear. Professional courtesy, as it were. You understand."

Lettie eyed Esme's hand still touching his sleeve. Her beak pointed and aimed. Esme snatched her hand back just in time before being impaled.

Huffing, Lamb sat up and halted the twirling spoon by pressing his thumb into the shallow bowl. "Certainly, certainly." He popped his thumb in his mouth and licked off the last dregs of coffee before dragging Lettie back into his lap. The overgrown feather duster swiveled her neck to gloat at Esme.

"That means it's my turn for a game."

"What sort of game?" Jasper asked. It was a perfectly polite inquiry with just the right tinge of boredom. It could fool anyone who didn't have a high stake in the outcome of this bizarre evening.

"The best. Winner takes all. In this game we may truly discover who is the best thief among the two of you."

Esme's brow lifted in surprise. "Two of us? Will you not be joining?"

"I've already bested you both. It is now time to see who wears the second-place crown." Lettie squawked in agreement.

Second place indeed! By the end of this little farce Esme would get her hands around his little no-neck lump and rattle the unmitigated gall from his fat head.

"What's the mark?"

Lamb's pale forehead wrinkled in befuddlement. Like an eggshell being rolled and cracked against the side of a sink. "Mark?"

"The target, the prize, the object to be stolen."

Lamb smiled as he removed his fez and placed it next to his empty coffee cup. His mouthful of large, squared teeth glowed under the chandelier.

"The Valkyrie, of course. It is why you came, is it not?"

11

Bedlam ensued, complete with the Mad Hatter, the Queen of Hearts, and Jasper himself playing the begrudging role of the hedgehog bounced about by flamingo mallets during a curious game of croquet.

"If I didn't know better, I'd think our host was toying with us."

Esme gazed up at a longcase clock with a tiny golden coach galloping around the face as it struck the late hour. A prize that had once stood in the private chamber of King William III of England built by the legendary Thomas Tompion.

"Whenever did you get that impression?"

"Sometime after his ludicrous claim of besting the best and before he sealed us into this asylum."

After announcing the Valkyrie as the grand prize, Lamb had disappeared and events happened rather quickly. Jasper and Esme were ushered by a white-gloved servant into a room off the main hall and left alone. For nearly half an hour.

The room was small with dark-paneled walls and heavy red damask drapes drawn closely over the windows. Mounted sconces flickered with yellow candlelight, scattering dancing shadows about the darkened room. Tribal masks and animal heads stared down from their perches on the walls as if seeking their hunters among the potted plants towering in each of the four corners.

"Where do you think he's put it?" Esme poked into one of the potted plants.

"My guess is he's tucked it away for safekeeping unlike all his other trinkets. Less of a temptation for our sticky fingers. Barking he may be, but stupid he is not. This game has been thought out for some time. He and that chicken have it all planned."

"I hate that chicken or goose or whatever he wants to call it. Did you see the way it was staring at me? Calculating how best to claw my eyes out."

"Don't allow her to ruffle your feathers."

Raising a hand to her mouth, she tittered with fake laughter. "A real rib-clutcher you are. A second banana from the top leaf."

"I try." Hands in pockets, Jasper wandered slowly around the room as Esme riffled through plants and peered behind animal heads. "What are you doing?"

"Looking for a trapdoor. Any kind of escape should the need arise. Always best to have two routes should the first become blocked. Or locked. Which I wouldn't put past our bizarre host." She pulled apart a pair of drapes for the third time to expose a wood-paneled wall. "Who covers a wall with curtains? This is becoming rather tedious."

"If you're so bored, why not leave? Claim a headache or indigestion. I'm happy enough with the Valkyrie on my own."

"Because he's locked us in here. Did you not hear the key click after the butler shuffled us in here? There's only one possible reason a man with a killer chicken locks people in a room with no escape." Her gaze leveled on him. "He plans to murder us."

"Lamb is many things, but a murderer he is not. He's more likely to fake his own murder and then howl with laughter at the panic he induced."

She scowled at his blasé response to their possible deaths and tugged the drapes closed. "Did you hear that?"

Jasper listened but detected nothing. "Hear what?"

"Talking? Music? I can't tell through these thick walls." She crossed the room and pressed her ear to the door.

"Why not simply pick the lock with the toolkit strapped to your garter and be on your way?"

"What makes you assume I have a kit with me?"

"Because a good thief never leaves home without one." He patted his jacket pocket where his own kit was safely tucked, then grazed his attention across the small bulge resting against her thigh beneath her skirt. "Are you never worried about it falling out?"

"First of all, nothing slips from my garter belt unless I intend for it to. Second, my kit is secured in an empty lipstick tube tucked safely in my bag." Dangling her beaded purse by its silver strap, she swung it back and forth like pendulum. "Coppers never resist the excuse to frisk a woman, but for some chivalric notion deem her purse sacrosanct."

"Then might I ask what is pinned in your garter?"

"Wicked man." She inched the fabric of her skirt over her knee and flashed the top of her silky stocking where a thin length of rope was coiled into her garter straps. "Should the need arise to shimmy out of a second-story window, lasso a tiara, or tie up the competition." She dropped her skirt and smoothed out the fabric.

"Preparation. And here I thought you lived on the ecstasy of winging it."

Shrugging, she moved to peer at a zebra's head. "In most situations, yes. However, this game has been dragging on and I should like to draw it to a close as soon as possible. Wouldn't you?"

Would he? The answer was more complicated than he cared to admit. He'd gotten into this line of work because he was good at it, and he'd stayed because of the thrill. The adventure, the adrenaline-spiking danger of possibly being caught, the shimmer of a prize just out of reach, the consuming satisfaction of holding it for the first time. Indeed, it was the same rush as that of pursuing an intoxicating woman.

When it came to the Valkyrie, he'd sobered up somewhere crossing the Rhine River out of Germany. And when it came to Esme, he was a man drowning in drink with a desperation for sobriety, yet once dried out he longed to bend the elbow for one more heady drop. She was worse than any amount of hair of the dog. Her perfume more scintillating than a finely aged whisky. Her smile more illuminating than a full moon. Her intelligence more cunning than that of a jungle cat, and her actions more lethal than a German howitzer.

She could blast straight through him with a single shot, leaving nothing but a singed, gaping hole. He already carried scars from her first barrage, and though he'd shored up his defenses he would be a fool to think he could survive her full arsenal attack. So his armor remained in place, dented and heavy, to withstand the assault on his heart.

As for the Valkyrie, the prize was his no matter what his wayward wife lobbed at him.

"Ending this as swiftly as possible is best for all involved for a myriad of reasons." Restless from his thoughts and the awaiting task, he plucked a dead leaf from one of the plants and twirled it between his fingers.

"I'm beginning to think you don't enjoy my company."

"If you recall, you were the first to break ties with *my* company while I was still abed."

A maddening, all-too-pleased smile settled on her deep red lips. "I enjoyed the departing scenery if that salves the wound." And *she* called *him* wicked.

He strolled up to her and tapped the leaf against the string of pearls dangling over her ear. They swung back and forth with a soft *swish*. "Think of what else you might have enjoyed had you not departed."

He was in control when he was the one launching the attacks, but a simple parting of her lips for a quick inhale had his shored-up defenses shuttering. The space between them sizzled as a thousand thoughts, questions, and wonderings sparked from her eyes straight into his where they plunged down his throat to burn in his chest.

The muscles in her throat twitched as her mouth formed itself around a word. What word? A flirtation? A confession? A cracking retort? He did not have a preference which, but knowing her, it was sure to send the burning in his chest to an all-out firestorm.

Gwooong!

The metallic groan of a gong reverberated through the air as a hidden door clicked open, knocking the sparks right out of him. The leaf fluttered from his fingers and drifted to the floor.

Relieved to have escaped another too-close-for-comfort interlude, Jasper turned toward the noise—but not before he noticed the smoke taking a moment longer to clear from Esme's eyes. That proved more satisfying than whatever she had been about to say, but important matters being what they were, he forced aside his smugness and turned his attention to where their host had breezed into the room with the chicken at his heels. He had changed from his fez and purple velvet into a blue silk cape with gold stars and a gold turban perched atop his head with a single peacock plume attached.

"I trust I have not kept you waiting," Lamb said.

"On the contrary, your hospitality is a luxury to be savored," Jasper smoothly replied.

Lamb was a prime example of money and status luring a person's common sense to eccentricities simply because the concept of no was foreign to them. Rich whims were never put into check, instead left to swell to gargantuan proportions, twisting with temptations and never satiated.

Positively revolting. Jasper had learned to swallow his disgust and smile as they handed over their precious coins in payment for an absurd bracelet or painting. No good could come from confronting an eccentric moneybag. They were liable to take his head off with a stolen Napoleonic sword, or worse, refuse payment. Neither option was agreeable to Jasper, so he kept his mouth shut and his smile wide.

Lamb's eyes swiveled to Esme. "And you, *mon chou?*"

"Ready to place that tiara upon my head." Esme tossed him a wink. The more jittery she was, the more flirtatious she became.

"Superbe!" Lamb swished his cape in dramatic circles. "Then we may begin. Lettie and I have drafted a checklist for each of you. The game is simple. The first to complete their checklist wins." From a pocket in his cape, he pulled out two envelopes

stamped with green wax and handed one to Jasper and the other to Esme. "No, no, Miss Fox. You must wait until the timer begins before opening your envelope."

Esme flattened the envelope where she had bent it to crack the wax seal. "My apologies. The intrigue has me breathless with impatience."

"As it should. Please do not disclose the contents to anyone, especially not to each other—this is a competition after all. When you have collected your items, return them to this room so each may be ticked off the master list."

"That doesn't seem too difficult," Esme said.

"Indeed, it is not." Lamb smirked. "However, the most important rule is not to be caught. This is a game of thievery, after all, and a marvelous opportunity to showcase your skills."

The chicken eyed them with contempt. "*Bock. Bock.*"

"Lettie says to prepare yourselves. She is swift at spotting shenanigans."

"I beg your pardon?" Esme said.

"Lettie will be watching at all times. I would advise you not to draw her attention." Lamb cooed to Lettie in encouraging tones. Esme took the moment of distraction to turn wide, disbelieving eyes to Jasper.

Jasper leaned close to her and whispered, "Ready to duck out, are you?"

"Darling," she whispered back, "that little egg has no idea who he is up against. It's time to scramble him."

Lamb waddled to the room's main door, the chicken marching behind him. "Questions? No? Good." Swirling the cape over his shoulder, he threw open the door to reveal a party in full swing. "The timer begins now. You have one hour. *Je vous souhaite bonne chance.*" Waving his fat fingers, he sallied out into the throng and disappeared.

A cacophony of blaring music, tinkling glasses, and raucous laughter clamored into the room. Esme smugly tossed her hair. "Told you I heard something."

"That's not something. That's a full-blown diversion." Jasper crossed and stood in the doorway. A sea of people dressed in white-tie and glittering jewels filled every available space. "How did they arrive so quickly?"

"Most likely he keeps them stuffed in the dungeon and only trots them out to intimidate unsuspecting guests. Shall we join them?"

"We shall indeed. Best of luck to you, Fox." He sketched a bow.

She curtsied in reply. "And to you, Phantom." With a wink she slipped into the crowd and disappeared.

Jasper wasted no more time, ripping open his envelope and pulling out the thick cream paper. He scanned the items listed in a scratchy hand. Expensive champagne, artwork, jewelry. A rather mundane selection, but then again, there was nothing mundane about his old compatriot. The pieces were likely wired to explode with confetti.

Right. Jasper smoothed his lapels into place. Rule number one on the job: always keep it entertaining. Summoning his best party smile, he moved into the hall in search of the first item on the list. A bottle of vintage Veuve Clicquot. Following the steady stream of sauce was easy enough; the closer to the dining hall he got, the fuller the glasses became.

What had been an intimate space a mere hour before as the three of them dined among candlelight had been transformed into a rollicking feast of alcohol. Every possible bottle of whisky, gin, bourbon, vodka, wine, and champagne lined the entire length of the dining table. Amber, golden, and clear liquids shimmered under the chandelier as they flowed from bottle to awaiting glasses to parched throats, all poured at the guests' discretion with no waitstaff in sight to assist.

Circling the length of the table, he spotted near the far end the iconic green bottle with its elegant gold label. Most collectors stored the precious bottles safely in a cellar, bringing them out only for the most special occasions. Yet here it was, snug between Beefeater Gin and a bottom-shelf merlot. Not that anyone here would notice the difference in quality, judging by their glassy eyes and ruddy cheeks.

Jasper frowned. The lift was too easy, nearly an insult. Threading his way through the drinkers, he reached for the bottle. Before he could touch it, the bottle slid away from his fingertips and into the arms of a gentleman in top hat with his collar button undone, leaving the starched collar ends to slap open like wings.

"My good sir," Jasper said. "Allow me to pour you a glass of that drink."

"Noo. Jush wants to hooold it."

There were three types of drunks. The kind whose spirits soared in happiness with each sip. The kind whose spirits sank into tears of sadness. And the belligerent sort. From Jasper's ample experience in pubs and with rich people not getting their way, this man could easily resort to quarrelsome if provoked.

Clasping his hands behind his back so he didn't appear as a threat, Jasper nodded conversationally at the champagne that could pay off the debt of a small country.

"A very handsome bottle, don't you agree?"

"S'good dance partner." The man bounced unsteadily on his feet. They were in trouble if he attempted the shimmy.

"I spy a lovely lady in pink just over there who would make an excellent dance partner." Jasper pointed far across the room. "Shall I hold your bottle for you while you twirl her about the floor?"

"No ladies. Jush this." The drunk cradled it to his chest, tucking his chin over the gold-foiled neck like it was a baby. "S'all I need."

Very well. So much for pleasantries and finesse. The only skill required here was a bit of sleight of hand. Reaching behind the man's back, Jasper tapped him on the opposite shoulder. The man's head swiveled away. Jasper slid the bottle from his arm and quickly replaced it with the cheap merlot.

The man's head wobbled back to Jasper, confusion lining his brow. "D'you see who's tapping me?"

Jasper slipped the Veuve Clicquot behind his back. "I'm afraid I didn't. If you'll excuse me."

"Certainly." The drunk attempted a bow. His top hat tumbled off his head. Straightening, he kicked it away and happily rocked back and forth with his merlot.

Jasper hurried back to the paneled room and placed the champagne on a table. He spotted a medieval sword propped against a chair. Esme had gotten here first. Best not to think about her. He needed to remain focused on the task at hand, and the task facing him next was . . . He consulted the list. A crossbow bolt. Now it was getting interesting.

He ducked his head into several rooms until he came to one where swords, shields, maces, Lochaber axes, tomahawks, and katanas shared the walls with floor-to-ceiling bookshelves. The air was quiet and soft, filled with the scent of ink and paper. Red plush couches and chairs were scattered about in the dim lighting, beckoning to the dozen or so couples who found themselves canoodling upon the cushions with roaming lips and hands.

The memory of sitting in a dimly lit pub booth with Esme swayed before his eyes. Not an inch of space between them, her fingers curling through his hair, his knee pressed against hers. Neither interested in coming up for air.

He blinked the image away. No time for distractions.

Circling the room, he passed a number of first editions, armor that belonged in a museum, and a tribal spear twice his height. There, along the left wall behind a desk stacked with stationery and a blotting mat, was a wooden plaque with a mounted bolt the length of his forearm. An inscription on the plaque read, "The bolt to fell King Richard the Lionheart 1199."

After a quick glance to ensure the room's occupants were, well, occupied, Jasper grasped the bottom of the plaque and lifted. It was screwed to the wall. He reached into his inner jacket pocket and pulled out his toolkit. It had started as a hodgepodge collection of hooks and rakes jammed in an oilskin cloth he'd snagged off a fisherman. Now he boasted the finest toolkit specifically made for him in a kit of Italian leather and paid for.

He selected the slim flattop screwdriver and twisted the four screws until they retreated from their holes and the plaque pulled clean away from the wall. Prize in hand, he returned to the paneled room and dropped off his latest item. Esme had yet to leave a new addition.

"Not so crafty as we thought, are we?" After arranging his items with smug satisfaction so she would see them first upon entering, he set off to finish his list.

Half an hour later he had collected a ruby bracelet from an older lady who'd been whispering to a plant on the stairwell, a miniature sculpture of Athena from the garden, gold tongs with ancient Roman inscriptions on the handles, and a fourteenth-century Ming vase from the study. Check. Check. Check and check. Down to the last item on the list with ten minutes to spare. Frank Dicksee's painting *Romeo and Juliet*.

Lamb, that little scoundrel, knew just where to twist the knife for his wicked little game. Of all the paintings in the house, he had to choose the one of star-crossed lovers.

This game was nudging Jasper closer and closer to breaking one of his own rules. Don't make it personal. Then again, everything was more personal with Esme involved.

Nine minutes. The clock was ticking.

He moved to the rear of the house where the entire length was divided into a solarium and music room. Having already searched the solarium earlier for a Mesopotamian scroll, he followed the sound of a jangling piano and accordion to the music room. It was a beautiful space, constructed for the enjoyment of refined instruments with its pale-blue walls and gold-rococo trim. There was nothing refined about the swell of men and women jammed cheek to cheek as they bopped around the parquet floor in rhythm to the bouncing tune.

Keeping close to the wall, he skirted the perimeter, quickly passing artwork painted by masterful hands until at last he came to the far wall, and there it hung, waiting for him. Shakespeare's doomed couple kissing in final farewell.

Longing stirred in his chest. For what precisely, he wasn't quite certain, but he couldn't help admiring the star-crossed lovers' intensity for each other.

"I've always loved that painting." Appearing from the crowd, Esme stepped up next to him. "Incredibly romantic, yet ignorant of the coming tragedy. If that's not passion, I don't know what is."

"Perhaps they would have been better off never having met. No pain, no tragedy."

"And an empty life. Better to burn bright and hot for a moment than to live cold all your days."

He looked at her and the longing stirred once more in his chest. How brightly they had burned for a moment. If he had known from the beginning that they would come crashing down, would he have done it anyway?

She met his direct stare with a flirting tilt of her eyebrow. "Are you assessing the value?"

Jasper blinked. "I'm certainly assessing something." Tearing his attention from her, he pressed his face against the wall to look behind the painting. Hung on wire and nails. An easy lift. And with the dancers in a complete state of zozzled revelry, no one would notice him pinching it off the wall and carting it away.

On the other side of the painting, Esme lifted the frame.

Jasper tugged it down. "What are you doing?"

"This is the last item on my list," she said. "I intend to win. Now if you don't mind moving out of the way so I can—"

"This is my last item."

She looked over Romeo's shoulder and Juliet's sweeping arm, desperate to keep him close, straight to Jasper, and grinned. "That cheeky devil."

Jasper grinned right back. "Devil indeed."

"You realize this painting won't split two ways." She gripped the frame.

"Oh, I have no intention of splitting it." She could grip all she liked, but she'd need a step stool to lift the wire off the nails. A predicament his extra few inches provided an advantage for.

"You there! What are you doing?" A young woman in a silver beaded dress and smeared red lipstick stared at them. Her dance partner didn't seem to notice she'd stopped, and continued with his steps.

"Checking for hidden safes," Jasper said. Best to always appear to know precisely what one was doing and with great authority. People tended not to question confidence.

The woman blinked her unfocused eyes. Mascara flaked her rouged cheeks. "The kind with"—*hiccup*—"money?"

Esme laughed. "I bet there are diamonds hidden behind more than one of these paintings. Merely a question of looking for the right one. So far we've only found the wrong ones, but between you and me, I think this would look better in one of the bedrooms upstairs. Much more romantic for necking with your man." She winked over at Jasper.

"Good luck to you, sister!" The woman tipped her glass to her mouth, found it empty, and with no convenient place to put it down, stuffed it into her dance partner's pocket and carried on dancing.

For all his life, Jasper would never cease to be amazed at the gullibility induced by drink. "With everyone as boiled as an owl, I'm feeling slightly insulted that this is the supreme test of our skills. Like asking Achilles to win a footrace against a blindfolded primary school student."

"At least we're not competing against that chicken." Esme tugged again on the frame. "Now, returning to business—"

The piano jingled. The accordion droned to a halt, and the couples stumbled to stops. The piano player climbed atop his bench and clapped for attention.

"Honored guests, you have been enjoying his refreshments and hospitality, and now it is my greatest pleasure to present to you our generous host, Monsieur Boisseau!"

High above them on the west wall the curtains drew back on a minstrel's gallery, and there stood Lamb in his turban and cape like a conductor presiding over the play he'd set into motion. Lettie was tucked under his arm.

"I hope you have all had a pleasant evening so far."

The crowd cheered and clinked glasses, spilling golden drink all over the floor. No one noticed.

"We continue our festivities with a little game of *jeu de cache-cache*, and the first to catch me wins the grand prize." He plucked away the feathered turban to reveal the Valkyrie sparkling atop his domed head. Mouth cracking into a wide smile, he looked straight down at Jasper and Esme. "To make things even more interesting, this game is played in the dark."

The lights went out. A woman screamed. Voices collided in a rush of excitement. Glasses shattered to the floor and were trampled beneath heels as the crowd swarmed to the door—or tried to with a great deal of bumping into one another with each man and woman claiming the prize was theirs.

"That double-crossing, low-life, bottom-dwelling, twisted soul of a motherless trickster." Jasper kicked the wall. Or what he thought was the wall. It was too dark to distinguish furnishing from a leg. "Now he's got the whole bloody château playing hide-and-seek for the tiara."

"Are you quite finished?" Esme's voice came from somewhere to his right.

"I can always think of more insults."

"Very well. You stand here with your insults. I have work to do."

"Esme. Esme!"

"Good heavens, what is it?" Her voice was several feet away. She was on the move.

Rooting around in his toolkit, he found and extracted a lighter and flicked it open. A spark flared to life, blooming in a soft orange glow around him.

Esme, who had been feeling her way along the wall, stopped and looked back at him. "A lighter. How clever."

"Came in handy in the trenches as long as you kept it below the sight line. You'd be accused of trying to get yourself a Blighty." He strode toward her, grabbed her hand, and pulled her across the room. Others in the crowd were still groping about in search of the door. "Come on."

"Partnering, are we?"

"It's pathetic watching you grope the wall. Besides, if you think I'm going to allow one of these chowderheads to seize the tiara right out from under me, then I'm no longer worthy of calling myself a decent thief. If I have to knock a competitor out of the way, I'd prefer it to be you."

"How you sweet-talk a girl." Her fingers tapped playfully against his. "But just so you know, Jasper, as soon as my eyes adjust to this pea soup of darkness, it's every thief for themself."

"I expect nothing less."

The entire house crawled with antlike seekers roaming hallways to explore every nook and cranny. Women shrieked as they collided with one another. Jasper quickly put out his lighter before a passing sleeve caught fire.

"This is insane," he said.

"Because he's insane," Esme replied.

Something wet soaked through Jasper's sleeve. Whisky by the smell of it. He would get nowhere like this—shuffling about in corridors waiting to be mowed down by well-heeled partygoers.

Lamb was taunting him and Esme. He would loathe having the final showdown in a pantry with hordes of other guests milling about. Most likely, he would go somewhere private so all the attention might be focused on him and how he outsmarted a great pair of thieves.

Away from others milling about . . .

Jasper dropped Esme's hand. "Sorry, love. Duty calls."

As if pushing himself through a can of wriggling sardines, Jasper stumbled his way upstairs where windows offered the advantage of blue moonlight. On the first floor he found half a dozen guest chambers with the furniture covered by protective white sheets. From the scent of them, guests had not been in attendance for some time, minus the few couples who had found a quiet corner to paw at each other.

Moving on, Jasper discovered Lamb's best-kept collections. There was a private library chock-full of books on every subject from taxidermy to world religions. Another room housed priceless porcelain, while another displayed carved busts of Genghis Khan, Julius Caesar, Empress Suiko, Edward Teach, and Esther Lachman, a ruthless Russian-born courtesan nicknamed the Glamorous Monster for the way she tossed men aside after using them up.

And of course, no true collector's roster could be complete without jewels. Lamb's jewel room was impressive to say the least. Diadems of diamonds the size of quail eggs. Garnet necklaces dripping like blood. Emeralds surrounded by pearls. All cushioned on pillows of velvet and made to twinkle when the massive crystal chandeliers overhead were lit. Any one of the precious stones would be enough to set Jasper up for a life of luxury.

But they were no Valkyrie.

It would be dishonest to say he wasn't tempted. That their siren songs didn't call to him, telling him they were ripe for plucking. The rubies with their sultry promises, the diamonds with their elegant boldness, the amethysts with their secret allure. However, he had learned long ago the price of distraction and carelessness—a fellow soldier shot or an arrest—and pushed away the glittering pleas, moving out into the corridor.

At the far end a small, plain door stood ajar. He crept down and peered in. A wooden flight of stairs spiraled upward. Likely servants' quarters. It was bad form to go snooping through the servants' privacy as they had no control over being swept into the games their master played, but just as he was about to turn away, a step creaked.

Someone was up there.

Taking the stairs, he struck his lighter. Orange light danced against the stone walls and shimmered off cobwebs.

Above him, the creaking stopped. A face flashed over the rail. "Stop following me," Esme hissed.

"Stop going where I'm going." He hurried up, brushed straight past her, and burst into the room at the top seconds before her.

It was a small garret with dusty floors, bare walls, and a small round window that allowed a sliver of moonlight to shine in upon a single chair placed in the center of the room.

In the chair sat the shape of a man, and upon his head rested a circle with two wings.

The Valkyrie.

Jasper's senses tingled in warning. Something wasn't right. It couldn't be this easy—to simply walk in and pluck it off Lamb's head.

Yet even as his gut told him no, his feet moved of their own accord, his arms reaching. Esme's fingers stretched out next to his. They grabbed the tiara at the same time.

Feathers floated up and tickled his nose. He snorted them away.

"Chicken feathers! Glued together into wings."

Esme squinted at the circle to which the feathers were attached. "And a bandeau with glass stones. Costume jewelry."

The "man" upon whose head it perched slumped over and broke apart into two stuffed pillows.

A laugh erupted from behind them. "Ha! Caught you!"

A lantern blazed to life, illuminating Lamb's delighted expression. The Valkyrie, the real one, sparkled atop his head. Lettie pecked at the turban dropped between his feet.

"The game is over, and I won! You were not to be caught, but it seems you could not help yourselves in being seen in order to win." He clapped like a child on Christmas morning and did a jig, holding the tiara in place with one hand.

"It's mine! It's mine! I win!"

Esme scowled. "That was a dirty trick to cheat."

"Do not tell me you believe in that old adage of honor among thieves?" Lamb waggled a finger at her.

"Not anymore." She huffed and crossed her arms.

Lamb had proved himself a man willing to sink to the lowest of lows to obtain what he desired. Antagonizing him would do no good. The little egg would have to be cracked another way.

As Lamb flipped the edges of his cape, the moonlight outlined an unmistakable bulge on his hip. It was time to say goodbye.

"Ashamed though I am, I must admit defeat." Jasper inclined his head as any gentleman loser would do.

Lamb cackled with glee and swooped Lettie into his arms, placing a wet kiss on top of her pom-pom head. "Oh, *mon ami*. How delightful it is to revel with you once again in what we do best. Not to mention bringing this lovely addition to my attention. There aren't enough beautiful women in the world for my taste, but you surpass them all, Miss Fox. Beauty, brains, and a beguiling skill of thieving." He pulled out a whistle that hung on a chain about his neck and blew a shrill note.

Lights flickered up the stairs. Whoops of surprise echoed up from the main floor.

"Let us return downstairs for refreshments. Tea, coffee, and brandy. And a tray of petit fours and madeleines. We deserve it after such an exhilarating chase."

"Who was chasing who after all," Esme muttered.

Jasper unclenched her hand from its strangled fist and tucked it into the crook of his arm. "Patience," he murmured.

In a louder voice, he addressed Lamb. "Don't trouble yourself on our account. Miss Fox and I must take our leave if we have any hope of catching the morning train to Paris." A lie, but one Lamb needed to believe if Jasper had any hope of salvaging this mess. Not to mention he couldn't stand spending one minute more than necessary in this asylum.

The grin fell from Lamb's face. "No! No! No! Giving up is not how the game is played!"

Jasper squeezed Esme's fingers. She'd better not blow the lie.

"My dearest Lamb," Esme crooned, smoothing her expression into pleasantries as she squeezed Jasper's fingers. A little too hard. "The game is over. You have won and will keep the tiara."

Lamb's thin lips pressed into a white line as steam practically rolled from his nostrils. Grabbing his turban from Lettie's beak, he jammed it atop his head, covering the tiara. "You agreed to play the game. Not quit before it was over. That was only the first round."

Jasper shook his head. "I'm quitting before I cause myself more embarrassment. Logic that has saved my neck more than once while pulling a job."

Lamb jumped up and down, stomping his feet. The peacock feather quivered with agitation. "No! No! No!" Lettie squawked and flapped, but Lamb pinned her to his side. "This is not how the game ends. We will continue with the next part I have planned. It is not over—"

Footsteps pounded up the stairs. The butler rushed in and over to his employer, bending down to whisper in his ear.

"I do not care if there is glass all over the floors!" Spittle flew from Lamb's lips. "The game is not finished. Inform the staff that if they do not outfit themselves for the next part of the game, it will be their heads on the chopping block as sure as Marie Antoinette's!"

Holy horse feathers. Surely he doesn't have Louis XVI's guillotine in the back garden.

"Come now, Lamb. There is no need for such threats," Esme cooed in her put-on honeyed voice. The one she utilized to disarm wasp nests. If the amount of buzzing coming from Lamb was any indication, he was ready to sting.

"Mr. Truitt and I have sallied forth our most valiant efforts to no avail and now concede defeat. We beg your humble graciousness in accepting victory for the Valkyrie. Perhaps another time we may once again vie for the crowning glory of superb thief, but allow us now to retreat and lick our wounds in repose."

The off-tilt spark in Lamb's eyes dimmed. He wiped the spittle from his chin with the cords tying his cape and neatly tucked them below where a chin should have been.

"Quite right. Your graciousness scolds my impatience into submission, my dear lady." He turned to speak to the butler.

"Over-egging the pudding, aren't you?" Jasper leaned close and whispered.

"I've witnessed many groveling scenes enacted on the stage, and it never fails to win over the audience," she whispered back with a sweet smile aimed at Lamb.

Groveling or pleading may work its magic on a theater audience, but Jasper was certain it was simply her charm that did the trick here. Of all men, he knew its power of persuasion.

Lamb shooed away the butler. "Stand down your men for the evening and have my guests' cars brought around."

After a quick toast to their health and assurances of no hard feelings, Lamb personally ushered them to their waiting car and held open the back door. He kissed Esme's hand and bowed his head in chivalric acknowledgment to Jasper.

"I do hope to meet again one day," he said, shutting the door and leaning down to speak through the open window. "We can discuss old times and what valuable prizes there are left to take in the world."

Esme leaned forward to speak around Jasper. "How lovely that would be. Not as competitors but as friends."

"When we do meet, I will keep the Valkyrie well out of hand so there will be no temptation of reclaiming her. *Au revoir, mes amis!*" Lamb offered them a salute with Bonaparte flair, then snapped his fingers. A flurry of feathers exploded from the front seat of the car as Lettie rocketed out of the window and crashed to the ground at Lamb's feet. Scooping her up, he marched back inside the château.

Jasper rolled up the window and settled back against the leather seat as the car glided down the drive. Leftover raindrops speckled the glass and tree leaves beyond as a sliver of moon cut out from behind the shifting clouds.

"He cheated."

"Certainly he did. That's why I told him so." Esme huffed. "Do you care to tell me why you were pinching my fingers to keep quiet? If you hadn't had such a vise grip, I could have snatched it off his round head and been halfway to Paris by now."

"In your eagerness for justice at having been made a fool, I take it you failed to notice the gun concealed beneath his cape."

She grew still. "The absolute nerve. Shooting us at a party. I've never heard of such bad manners." She slapped at the wrinkles on her skirt, her profile knife sharp in the confining darkness. "And now?"

"Now we steal it back," Jasper whispered.

"There's that *we* again." Sighing, she sank into the seat next to him. "When do we start?"

Jasper smiled as he caught a downy chicken feather floating between them.

"Soon. I've got a plan."

12

FRESHLY WASHED, SHAMPOOED, AND SPRITZED with her orange-blossom perfume, Esme felt more like herself as she stood on the small wrought iron balcony watching the quaint town rub sleep from its eyes and yawn into the bright orange-and-pink beams of dawn. She dug her fingers into her hair, massaging her aching head, but no matter how hard she rubbed, the brutal truth of failure pounded in her skull. How much longer before the countess sent Pirazzo to finish off Esme for good? How much longer before she felt the sting of his fingers around her throat because the Valkyrie had slipped through her fingers? Again.

All because of that little egg.

After their stinging disgrace at Lamb's house, she and Jasper returned to the hotel in silence, collected their bags, and climbed back in the car to be deposited at the nearest train station. Lamb's driver waited and watched as they purchased tickets and climbed aboard the early morning train, before finally motoring off to report to his master that they had departed.

Jasper waited until the wheels began churning before chucking off their luggage and hopping down to the platform once more, swinging Esme down with him. Lamb needed to think they'd slunk away with their tails between their legs if the plan was to work. What plan that was, they had yet to discuss.

From the train station Jasper hailed a taxi and gave directions to a small village some ten kilometers from Lamb's house. In France, ten kilometers might as well have been another planet. Jasper seemed to know precisely where he was going when he led her up a slim flight of stairs to a flat over a café. It was an airy space with pale oak floors covered in rugs of light blue. White walls with pictures of delicate flowers and landscapes. Antique furniture in pristine condition and a bedchamber with enough mirrors to satisfy the vanity of a peacock.

From the balcony she heard the front door to the flat open and close.

"Breakfast is here," Jasper called.

Turning from the serene morning view, Esme walked through the double doors into the living space where he'd settled a tray piled with food on a low table in front of the settee. A single daffodil sprouted from a crystal vase on the tray.

"We have croissants, tartine, fresh butter, cherry marmalade, palmiers, sliced oranges, and cheese. Brie and Comtè, I believe."

Esme took one of the provided plates from the tray and chose a sampling of each as her stomach growled in anticipation. Of all the countries she'd stolen across, nothing topped a fresh French breakfast. After settling on the blue silk settee, she slathered her baguette with brie and cherries and bit into it. Decadence! She closed her eyes and savored the tangy sweetness of the bread, the warmth of the sun's rays peeking through the windows, and the slow softening of her muscles as they relaxed against the plump cushions. A delicious drowsiness swirled her thoughts together as her bones grew heavy, longing for rest.

"The English could learn a thing or two from the French about breakfast, though a rasher of bacon wouldn't go amiss," Jasper commented as he fixed his own plate. "Here is *le chocolat chaud* for you. Did she include tea? I thought I saw—ah! Here it is. Nice and hot. Do you know I used to dream about hot tea, well, hot anything, really, while I was in the trenches. The only hot thing soldiers encountered then were flying bits of shrapnel. I may go for a walk after I finish. Would you care to join? It might help clear the mind before we begin discussing the plan."

Esme's eyes pried open at Jasper's prattling. "Please don't tell me you're a morning person."

He sat in one of the matching accent chairs across the low table from her. His masculine frame dwarfed the spindly stick of furniture with its outturned clawed feet and velvet-covered armrests. An ordinary man would look ridiculously uncomfortable, but Jasper made whatever his surroundings fit. "I am a whatever-time-of-day-I'm-awake-so-take-advantage-of-the-moment kind of person."

"All-around good-natured. Even worse."

"Are you always this moody first thing in the morning?"

"As I haven't been to bed yet, I consider this a continuation of a rather long evening."

"Then I suggest you take a sound nap in the bedroom. It's quite comfortable and the sheets are silk. When I return from my stroll, you should be refreshed and we can begin formulating an attack." Placing a pristine linen napkin across one knee, he poured tea into a porcelain cup and added a dash of milk.

"You've yet to tell me what sort of place this is"—she fingered the gossamer frills on the robe she had borrowed from the bedroom's chifforobe—"or who it belongs to."

"It belongs to an old army comrade. For his mistresses. Currently, he is between ladies, leaving the apartment conveniently available for our purposes."

Fully awake at the risqué turn in conversation, she plucked a chocolate-drizzled croissant from the tray and pulled it apart bite by bite. "Mistresses. My, my." She met his sharp gaze over the pot of tea steaming between them.

"The answer to your question is no. I do not have a mistress."

She shrugged a shoulder as if the answer meant nothing to her. "It's none of my business."

"Isn't it?" His voice was deceptively calm, a honey-covered thorn. One she couldn't help pricking her finger to.

"How do you know what the sheets are made of?"

"I've overnighted here a number of times when I was in the area and the ladies were out. When you've stolen Empress Josephine's ruby brooch, it's best to lay low for a while and avoid the hotels."

"Ruby, ha. Try her emerald and diamond."

Jasper raised a questioning brow at her. *You?*

Esme smiled smugly. *Me.*

He returned the smile. Not one of mockery or even of being impressed, but one of deep satisfaction. As if they were the only two who understood what it meant to pull off such a feat and revel in the success. An understanding as intimate as a caress.

One that simply could not be allowed to continue.

She brushed crumbs from her fingers and sipped her *le chocolat chaud*, then got to the matter of business.

"I have decided that there is no other recourse but to combine our skills in taking back the Valkyrie. Without a doubt, that man is more than a few bricks shy, and your previous experience with him should help sort the order of said bricks into our favor."

"A logical assumption, but after meeting Lamb you should know that logic long ago gave up claim to him." Jasper set his cup on the table and leaned back in his chair, settling his gaze on her. Alert and entirely too focused on her. Precisely the way she preferred it.

"Be that as it may, we will find a way to our advantage."

"He's expecting us to try for the Valkyrie. He *wants* us to go for it."

"Then we mustn't disappoint." She grinned like a cat planning to dip a toe in cream and reached for a tartine. After living off rationed meals through the war, her belly never denied the prospect of food.

A silence stretched between them, broken by soft bites of eating and the trill of birds outside the window. She didn't dare go so far as to say it was comfortable, but it wasn't unpleasant. She had never found another person with whom to sit contentedly. Growing up behind a stage, life was never quiet with actors and musicians and stagehands bustling about readying for the next show. Always the next show, and any space between performances was filled with grumbling about torn costumes, missed cues, or an ossified horn player. Esme had learned to stave off possible lulls early on, never allowing her true thoughts to bubble to the top lest she give away some part of herself for the judgment of another.

"We all have a role to play," Mimsy had instructed as she overlined her lips with red color. *"Learn your lines and never let them see behind the mask, because life is waiting just beyond the footlights, ready to snatch at those pauses of weakness."*

Over the years Esme's mask had grown heavy, and in the small, quiet moments she longed to put it aside. Like now. She gazed over at Jasper, the pomade having long since acquitted his hair and left it to flop about. The top button of his shirt was undone. His long fingers were laced over his stomach as he gazed serenely out the balcony door. He, too, carried a mask. His was brimming with charisma, charm, and wit. But there were times, like now, when he let it slip and she glimpsed what lay underneath. And it called to her.

"Were you injured during the war?" she asked.

Momentary surprise flickered across his expression as his gaze rested on her, but then he slowly shook his head.

"Not like the other lads. Cuts and bruises mostly." His mask hitched down a notch. "Had the hairs singed off my neck when an incendiary exploded in the sandbag above my head. Not to mention a bucketload of sand in my ear."

She picked at the tartine crust, scattering toasted crumbs on the linen napkin draped over her lap. "Were you frightened?"

"Every day. Frightened of getting hit. Of dying." Each word was low and controlled as if he were pulling them from the far reaches of his mind. His mask slipped further. "Then, once you move past that, it's almost the living that frightens you. Living to hear your comrades scream in pain or be mowed down like wheat stalks in a charge. Living with starvation gnawing your insides. Living through pure hell on earth . . . Sometimes you pray for the peace of death."

"How did you keep going?"

"The men. I put on a good face for them, told them again and again that I would keep them safe and get them through until the last bullet fired. After a while you say something so many times that you begin to believe it." His mask fell away and there she found a mirror unto herself—the cracks, insecurities, distortions, and the desperate need to make them all appear whole.

The revelation should have summoned sadness, embarrassment perhaps, to see her own struggles laid bare so plainly on his face, but she felt only wonder. Wonder that another could endure the grueling performance of existing day to day seemingly without a care, all the while withering inside for a spark of hope.

"Life is easier speaking from behind a mask. Like a performer thrust onstage. He is no longer himself but what the audience expects." Appetite waning, she placed the half-eaten tartine back on the tray. "At least, so I've seen in my experience."

"Experience on the stage?"

"Me? Heavens no. I didn't have the voice for it, not after the time I played a page boy in Empress Sissi of Austria's court. I croaked the lines. Mimsy never allowed me in front of the curtain again. Especially not when my flub took the spotlight from her own empress impersonation, but that's Mimsy for you. The whole East London stage or none at all."

She brushed a crumb from the silky material covering her knee. Once upon a time rough cotton and patched wool covered her knee, castoffs from the stage costumes. It had been a long time since she'd donned threadbare cotton, yet the feel of it clung to her skin even beneath the layers of chiffon and satin, as if knitted to her always.

"Sometimes I feel like I'm still on that stage croaking lines and waiting for the hook to snatch me off and toss me back in the gutter."

"The gutter isn't an easy pit to crawl out of. It takes fortitude and moxie. It takes crawling over broken glass and slander, setback after setback. It takes looking the world straight in the eye when it claims you are not worthy of a place in it simply because you were born on the wrong side of the blanket." He gave a rueful laugh. "Apologies for not being much of a prospect for a lady. The bastard of an illegitimate son has little to recommend."

"I'm no lady. My father is one of a dozen theater patrons I've never had the misfortune to meet. A gentleman of some kind. If abandoning your child to grease paint is the mark of a gentleman, I'll take a bastard over the toffs any day."

A wide, boyish smile spread across his face as he raised his cup. "To bastards."

"Cheers." She raised her half-eaten tartine in acknowledged salute.

He returned his cup to its saucer and selected a baguette slice, then slathered it with cream before settling back in his chair. All ease and calm wrapped around the room in companionable comfort. "A gentleman, eh? 'Thane Macbeth.'"

"Caught that, did you?"

"You showfolk and your Shakespearean references."

She scoffed. "Hardly Shakespeare. More like overacting and bawdy pub tunes."

He threw his head back and laughed. "I'd love nothing more than to hear a bawdy pub number at eight in the morning."

"Oh no. Those songs aren't meant to be heard while the sun shines."

His brown eyes danced over the creamed bread. "My dear, we're in France. That sensibility doesn't apply."

The ease between them sparked to flirtation. A ground she was more than comfortable sauntering across with him.

"I'll make a deal with you. When we relieve Lamb of the Valkyrie, I'll sing one." She decided to ignore the use of "we" for now. It was simply a means to an end that would make the journey deliciously fun, but ultimately she would walk away with the prize.

"The bawdiest?" he asked.

"I shall scrape one from the bottom of the barrel just for you."

That wide grin of his again. "Deal."

Returning his satisfied smile, Esme settled back against the pillows as all needs for a nap wafted away. "Now, as to this plan of yours . . ."

13

The plan was simple. No tricks or gimmicks. No disguises or wrangling forged invitations. Just a simple breaking and entering.

"We're going to get caught." Esme's voice filtered out of the darkness next to him.

Jasper pulled down a branch from the hedgerow they were currently hiding in to better view Lamb's château. The moon-speckled night and heavy black air, thick with the scent of coming rain, did little to prove the grand structure more than a dark square slumbering one hundred yards away. Such a night was perfect for thieving, but poor for visibility.

"Have a little more faith in your skills."

"It's not my skills I question, merely the absurdity of this plan. Sneaking into Lamb's home in the middle of the night, rooting around for the tiara, and slipping out before he has a chance to rouse from bed to raise the alarm. What could possibly go wrong?"

"I'll have you know this *absurd* plan has worked for thousands of thieves the world over."

"Yes, ones with less finesse."

He let the branch snap back into place. "Tonight is not about finesse. We tried that. It's time to return to our roots. In this case simple is better. Two nights ago a chicken was used to swindle the Valkyrie from our grasp. Lamb excels in over-the-top. He'll never suspect a simple break-in. I doubt he'll suspect retaliation at all."

"The man knows we're desperate to have the tiara. How can he not assume we'd come back for it?"

"Arrogance. Since I've known him, Lamb has always had to be the cleverest, wittiest, most daring, and most cunning of them all. It doesn't enter his mind that someone can outfox him, especially on his home turf."

"Very well." She sighed dramatically. "I shall summon all my crasser skills from youth."

It was dark, but she stood close enough for him to take an additional observation of her statuesque figure draped in a black form-fitting top and trousers she'd borrowed from him and cinched tight about her waist with a silk scarf. Thieving was no excuse to be without a statement piece, she had declared before leaving the apartment. She was the loveliest cat burglar he'd ever seen.

"Were you a thief when we met?" he asked.

She stilled and he could feel rather than see the full weight of her gaze on him. "Not during the war. People were losing too much. It didn't seem right to take more from them."

"Why Esme Fox Truitt. I believe you *do* have a conscience." He hadn't meant to include Truitt, but it slipped out and he had no urge to reclaim it.

He held his breath waiting for a rebuff. She exhaled softly for both of them. "Memory lane another time. Let's get to work, shall we?"

She dashed across the lawn and flattened herself against the wall next to the servants' entrance. Jasper was beside her in a flash.

"All the servants will have retired by now." Kneeling in front of the keyhole, he pulled out his lock-picking kit. "We should have a good three hours before they rise, but hopefully we'll be long gone by then."

Three hours was an enormous stretch of time. The longer a thief took, the more likely he was to get caught. Jasper preferred working solo, but even he had to admit that—given the size of the château, Lamb's penchant for bric-a-brac in every room, and a complete lack of knowledge of where the tiara might be stashed—two thieving heads were better than one. Not that he had any intention of letting her snag it first and leave him high and dry. If it came to it, he'd force her to take the fall.

He cordoned off his heart and mind from the past two days they had spent together in the apartment planning and strategizing. Talking of nonsense and sharing meals. He enjoyed seeing the slips behind her defenses to the carefree girl who had caught his attention on Armistice Day, standing in the crowd as if she'd been waiting for him all along. It did him no good to linger there among the what-ifs and might-have-beens. Esme was not a part of him and he was not a part of her. The sooner they went their separate ways, the better.

After sliding a hook into the keyhole, he gently pushed up on the pins one by one.

"Were *you* a thief when we met?" She was much too near.

His hand slipped and the lockpin slid back into place. *Concentrate!* He wiggled the hook around and tried again.

"I've always had a talent for acquiring things, but it wasn't until the war that I honed the talent. I put the black market to work for my men. Socks, cigarettes, biscuit tins, whatever they needed. That network was easy enough to maintain after the war, but instead of soldiers in the trench, I went to work for wealthy clients looking for exclusive finds."

"Where you're doing quite well for yourself, *Phantom*."

That name had once been held in high regard, but one tiny slip had landed him right under the authorities' thumb as they used his knowledge and connections to bring down his fellow thieves. If the coppers found out he was working a job without their consent, he would never see freedom this side of iron bars again. All the more reason to complete this grab and return the tiara to Duke with the authorities none the wiser. Duke's influence was what had saved him from rotting behind bars. If Jasper succeeded in capturing the Valkyrie, Duke might finally offer what he had long denied him. A place in the family.

Pushing aside the sentimental notion, he focused on the task at hand. The last pin was proving rather stubborn. Another moment and it gave way and the lock clicked open. They crept inside the door and quietly closed it, finding themselves in a darkened passageway illuminated only by the glowing coals of a banked fire in the kitchen. Creeping along, they emerged into the main part of the house where all remained quiet.

"You take the main floor," he whispered. "I'll search upstairs."

"*I'll* search upstairs if you don't mind. You may take the main floor."

How easily he forgot he was working with someone as devious as him. They both knew Lamb would not have hidden the tiara on the main floor. He would keep it close in a place that could not be disturbed by a visitor coming round for tea in the drawing room.

"Lady's prerogative," he said gallantly.

She glided up the sweeping staircase on catlike feet while Jasper made quick work of the main floor. More of an obligatory search really, considering his honed intuition beckoned him upstairs. Satisfied that nothing was gained by continuing to look on that level, he hurried up the stairs to the first floor.

Rain dashed against the large window at the far end of the hall, the *plop*s woven with the scratching sound of metal on metal. A lock being picked.

Jasper followed the sound to the end of hall where Esme knelt on the red carpet runner in front of the last door.

She didn't break her concentrated rhythm on the lock. "Are you going to stand there or are you going to assist me?"

"It appears you have things well in hand." He leaned against the wall, noting the quality of the watered silk damask stretching the length of it. "I'm surprised to see you didn't pick up that pair of pearl earrings along the way."

"As much as I adore a sparkling distraction, I knew you'd be up here on my heels. Business first." The lock clicked. Esme quickly rebundled her tools and tucked the kit into her—or rather his— trouser pocket. "Unless he sleeps hanging upside down from a beam in the cellar, I'd wager this is our host's bedchamber."

"It pains me to say I believe you're right." He assisted her to stand, ignoring the spark of heat brushing between their hands—a far larger distraction than a pair of earrings—and slowly turned the knob to crack open the door. Heavy breathing punctuated with loud snorts drifted out.

Without a word Esme stole into the room like a shadow. Jasper followed silently behind. It was a large, opulent chamber fit for a king with thick rugs, heavy drapes that pooled on the floor, scroll-legged furniture, and gilt-framed portraits of none other than the master of the house in various costumes depicting himself as landed gentry, a sea captain, mountain climber, high judge, and Dionysus.

A massive fireplace stood along one wall with a fire burned down to a few remaining logs that cast off a soft orange glow. On the other wall was a door leading off to a private sitting room. But it was the massive four-poster bed sitting on the dais in the center of the room that drew the eye. Carved of white wood, screened off with thick red curtains, and topped with gold fennels, it could sleep an entire platoon.

Esme raised her eyebrows at him in humorous disbelief. Jasper shrugged. Rich people and their eccentricities. Taking opposite sides of the room, they prowled about opening drawers and inspecting shelves. Jasper's eyes kept wandering back to the bed, intuition notching in his chest. He searched the adjoining sitting room, rifling through correspondence on the teak desk, and lifting a collection of Napoleonic hats. All the while Lamb's voice rattled in his head, *"I will keep the Valkyrie well out of hand for there to be no temptation of reclaiming her."* He stepped out of the sitting room and stared at the bed where unbroken snores erupted. That devilish little imp.

Esme came to stand beside him. "No," she said on a breath.

"Yes." Motioning for her to go around to the other side of the bed, Jasper tiptoed up the three steps to the top of the platform. Collecting his nerves, he let out a steady breath and patiently peeled apart the curtains surrounding the bed. Lamb slumbered beneath a pile of silky sheets and cashmere blankets with pillows propped all around him like a fortress. A tasseled nightcap perched on top of his head along with the most beautiful sight to behold. The Valkyrie in all her glory. Atop the sleeping egg's head.

Jasper had a mind to smother him where he lay. All these weeks of searching, of being locked in hotel rooms, sleepless nights, an irritable Duke, and a conniving soon-to-be ex-wife, and here sat the grand prize being used as a sleeping ornament.

Across the way Esme parted the curtains and quickly took in the scene. Delight flashed over her face, followed by confusion, then outright irritation. Her gaze traveled the length of the bed and stopped on the basket at the foot where the chicken dozed on a mattress of peacock feathers. Her eyes snapped back to the tiara, then to Jasper. Who would go for it first?

He had to let her think they were in this together, but he was the one closest to the door. She wasn't stepping one foot out of that chamber with the Valkyrie in her possession.

The glint in her eye showed that she knew precisely what he was planning, and she was not about to let him have his way. Smirking, she leaned over and grasped the tips of the wings, gently pulling upward.

It didn't budge.

Lamb snorted and rolled his head. Undaunted, she tried again. Nothing. Her smirk flattened to determination. Jasper could help. But then he could also let her do all the work, which was satisfying to say the least. She dropped her hands to the band wrapping around Lamb's forehead and tugged. It came free.

And knocked the nightcap's tassel onto Lamb's nose.

"Cease that, Lettie," Lamb muttered, brushing the tassel from his face. "*Bête petit poulette.*"

Esme froze, the tiara in her hands hovering over Lamb's head.

"*Bock*," came a groggy noise from the basket. A tiny head with two flattened pom-poms poked over the edge. *"Bock."*

"Not now, Lettie." Lamb batted at the tassel. His eyes cracked open. "What— You!"

"Yes, darling. It's me." Esme blew him a kiss, took one look at Jasper and the door behind him, then sprinted toward the private sitting room.

"Intruders! Thieves! Scoundrels!" Lamb yanked a bellpull hanging near the head of the bed. "Servants! Man your positions! We are under attack."

Bells went off throughout the house. Shouts and racing feet rumbled up the stairs. Jasper took one look at the escape door that was about to be blocked by servants, then flew after Esme.

"Jasper! Return here at once!" Lamb jumped up and down on the bed.

"Let's do this again never, old friend." Jasper tossed his old nemesis a grin, then slammed the sitting room door shut on Lamb's screams of outrage. He dragged the teak desk over and blocked the door with it, hoping to buy a few precious minutes to make an escape.

Cool wet wind blew across the back of his neck. Double glass doors stood wide open to the balcony.

There was no Esme in sight.

He crossed the room and stepped out onto the narrow balcony where two pale hands clung to the wet rail. Leaning over, he spotted the rest of her dangling two stories above the ground. The Valkyrie was neatly tucked into her silk belt.

He pulled a length of slender rope from the back of his trouser waistband. "Might you be in need of this?"

"You thief." Rain dotted her face as she glared up at him. "When did you take it off me?"

"A good thief never reveals his secrets, but allow me to say I appreciate matching the knickers to the all-black outfit." He leaned out farther and frowned. "Did you really think to jump from here?"

"What other choice did I have?" She spat out the drenched hair sliding into her mouth. "Why must you stand there looking like the answer to my dilemma?"

"Habit." The blocked door rattled behind him as angry fists pounded against it. "Time to go."

He tied off a secure knot and unfurled the length of rope to the grass below, then swung himself off the balcony and grasped the rope before curling an arm around Esme.

"Grab the rope. I've got you."

She took hold of the rope and wrapped it around herself. Jasper let go of her waist and plucked the tiara from her belt.

"I'll take that," he said, shimmying down the rope. One quick look and he spotted the scrolled *R* stamped just above the left wing. At last, the true Valkyrie.

"I'll take it right back in a moment," she said, following him.

Above, wood splintered and shouts barreled onto the balcony as the footman yelled at them to stop. As if that ever persuaded Jasper. His feet hit the ground and he took off running, the Valkyrie tight in his hand and waterlogged grass squelching beneath his boots. Esme landed, her footsteps catching up to him despite the mud.

Until she cried out.

Jasper turned as she slid and landed in a puddle. He needed to keep going, *should* keep going, but the look of confounded surprise on her face and his chivalrous nature forced him to turn back before his better sense could stop him.

"Now is not the time for a lie-down, love." He grasped her muddy elbow.

"Your terrible jests exhaust me, so I had no choice." She scrambled to her feet, took a step, and threatened to go down again. He caught her as she pitched forward, but his own feet failed to find traction with the momentum and down they both tumbled.

"I told you it was unwise to fall for me," she said, black hair plastered to her forehead and muddy cheeks.

He whipped out a sodden handkerchief and scrubbed at her cheeks. "Now who has the terrible jests?" He grinned.

She took the handkerchief, smearing the mud even more, and grinned back at him.

There they were. Two grinning fools in the mud.

Bam! Bam!

Mud and wet grass spit up around them as footmen took potshots from the balcony.

Lamb jumped up and down screaming behind them. "Shoot them! Do not let them escape with my crown!"

Bam!

"We've officially worn out our welcome." Jasper jumped to his feet. "Time to go." Hauling Esme up, he grabbed her hand and took off running. Their feet slid over the wet grass, sloshing water as they sprinted through puddles toward the barn that stood just beyond the hedgerow.

It was a magnificent structure, painted white with black trim, and already Jasper could smell the warmth of hay and horseflesh. And a way out. Pulling Esme into the barn, he then slammed the door shut behind them and dropped the bar to lock it.

"Go open that wide set of doors on the far wall," he commanded, striding over to where the gleaming Rolls-Royce was parked. It had been some time since he'd driven, but it couldn't prove that difficult.

Bam! Bam!

Buckshot peppered the wall. Air hissed from the auto's back wheel where an errant ball lodged in the rubber. Scratch that idea. He'd never liked driving anyway. Turning in a circle, Jasper jumped at the only other mode of transportation available. He grabbed a nearby bridle and slipped it over the Thoroughbred's head, then led the beast out of the stall.

"What are you doing?" Esme stood before the open doors with the rain a soft gray curtain behind her.

"*We* are getting out of here."

"On a horse?"

"The taxi that dropped us off a quarter mile away has long since left, and we can't walk the ten miles back to the village."

Bam! A bullet ripped a hole through the side of the barn.

"Time to go." He swung himself up onto the back of the horse, then took the reins and guided the animal over to Esme. He held out his hand. "Hop up."

She stared in terror at the horse. "I've never ridden before."

"Since when has that stopped you?"

Bam!

Voices approached outside the barn.

She looked at him, the horse, the holes blasting through the walls, and finally the Valkyrie tucked in his belt. She plucked it from him and held it tight between her hands. Hesitation warred across her face. She had it. She could make a run for it, though she'd likely not get very far. Or she'd have to trust him.

The closed barn door rattled on its hinges. Lamb shouted on the other side.

"I'll stuff you both and mount your pretty heads on my wall!"

With a wicked smirk Esme popped the tiara atop her head and secured it with her silk belt. She took Jasper's outstretched hand and swung up behind him. After some grunting and wiggling, she situated herself and announced she was ready.

"Hold on," Jasper said.

He tapped his heels into the horse's flanks. The beast lurched into motion. Esme's arms swooped around Jasper and latched on for dear life as they streaked out the wide barn doors and into the rain.

Behind them shotguns exploded.

The clouds thinned to allow slivers of moonlight to speckle the ground, proving Fate was smiling on them. Jasper knew from experience the dangers lying in wait across a dark field. A buried mine. Tripwire. A Bosch sniper. Or a simple hole waiting to twist an ankle.

To avoid injury to the horse, and thereby themselves, he kept to the château's drive before galloping out to the main road.

"Where did you learn to ride like this?" Esme asked as the château faded from view. Her warm breath mingled with the cold rain rolling down the back of his neck, eliciting a shiver.

No longer hearing their pursuers, Jasper slowed the horse to a trot. "My grandfather had horses. He claimed it was the only pure means of transport for a gentleman."

He rarely offered information on his upbringing and certainly not his connection to Duke, but the admission slipped out freely. In that moment he realized how tired he was of holding back his past, of covering up the details that made him who he was. Tired of Duke dictating which parts of him were acceptable to acknowledge while the rest of it was kept hushed in shame.

"And he wanted you for a gentleman?"

"Never quite took to me."

"Being a gentleman is overrated."

"If you think that, you would have loved to watch the army races. Back during the war in the little spare time we had, the cavalry lads would set up bareback races. I had just enough champagne in me once from a village we liberated to make a go at it. I managed to stay on for a good fifty yards before the ground came up to meet me."

She laughed. "You're right. I would have loved to have seen that. Not you falling off a horse, but the thrill of it. That rush of excitement. Of being alive. It must be how a true Valkyrie feels." Loosening her arms from around him, she held them out wide and gave a high-pitched shout that echoed into the night sky.

The sound settled deep in his chest, reverberating through the empty cavities and filling them with a beating pulse. "What was that?"

Her arms wrapped around him once more. "A Valkyrie's battle cry of triumph."

He smiled. It was indeed.

14

THEY STOPPED IN A FIELD on the outskirts of the village where a silver mist softened the awakening light of morning on the far horizon. The field sloped down to a valley where sandstone homes and shops stitched with worn cobblestone paths slumbered. Soon the animals would stir, rousing the sleeping inhabitants from their beds and into another day of chores and commerce, but for now all was quiet. A moment suspended in time, soft around the edges and peaceful to the mind.

At least it would be if Esme weren't skipping and laughing through the grass, head thrown back in pure delight as the mist coated her face and hair and skin in pearly drops. Jasper found it rather difficult to remain peaceful when his heart thundered in sheer delight as he watched her. Inhibitions gone, laughing at being alive. He very much wanted to be alive. With her.

"What a night! Never have I been on such a thrilling heist."

"Never? You've been missing out." He smacked the horse's rump. The animal snorted and trotted away, nose in the air, searching for the scent of home and his stall of hay.

"So I have." She untied the silk scarf that had kept the tiara secured atop her head during the ride and fitted it around her trim waist once again. "Come dance with me."

"I'm enjoying the view from here."

"I dance much better with a partner, remember?" She sashayed toward him, conjuring memories of champagne, dancing around the Concorde, and a Victrola playing "Clarinet Marmalade" out a hotel window. The Valkyrie's diamond-speckled wings fluttered with each step.

"Oh, I remember all right."

She wiggled her fingers at him. "Dance with me, Jasper."

He could have held back with his waning thread of self-preservation but hearing her say his name snapped it in two and tossed it to the wind. He'd forgotten what those two syllables said in her warm honey tone did to him. The unchallenged power it gave her and the desperation it stirred to hear her say it again.

Not *boy*, not *bastard*, or *captain*, or *thief*, or *Truitt*. Those were all placeholders, titles of *what* he was and his position in the world. *Jasper* was *who* he was, all the parts of him that were overlooked in favor of what he was. *Thief* certainly didn't ruffle her, illegitimacy hadn't either, but his partnering with law enforcement was a sticky subject and one he was loath to bring up while she crooked her finger so prettily at him.

He met her in the field, the grass slick beneath their feet, and the chill of dawn a brush against their skin. He took her hand and spun her around like they were cutting a rug at the Italian rooftop garden at the Criterion in London. Hands shaking, legs kicking, and intoxicating exhilaration coursing between them. Together, laughing out loud and seizing the moment to be alive.

He spun her around again. She came back to him and pressed close, one hand slipping to his shoulder as the other brushed a soaked curl from over his left eyebrow. A gentle smile pulled at her full lips. Taking her right hand in his left, he slipped his free arm around her waist.

"I looked for you, you know," he said softly. "After you left."

Her smile faltered. "I didn't want to be found."

"And now?"

"I'm deciding." Her fingernails trailed over his collar, standing up the hairs on the back of his neck. Mist speckled her sooty lashes like tiny diamonds. They sparkled as they flickered up and down, her sky-blue gaze darkening between meeting his own and looking down to his lips.

Height had never been a discrepancy between them, so it took little effort or time for her to brush her lips to his. Over almost before he felt it, but it was enough to stir the words he had carved into his bones and tried to forget.

"Why did you run? Four years ago I woke up to the end of the war, a hangover, and no wife."

"Twelve hours of marriage doesn't make for a wife."

"It did to me."

"We collided in a star-crossed rendezvous. We never stood a chance. Like fools, we rushed in where angels fear to tread and wise men never go."

"Neither of us is an angel, and as for being wise . . ." He pulled her closer, thrilling in the way her body melted into his, betraying her words, and the way her orange-blossom perfume mingled with the scent of rain on her skin. "You're the kind of woman who defies all expectations, but I'm a different kind of man who makes his own rules. Would it be so terrible for us to fall in love?"

"Ask me in the morning."

Her arms circled his neck. It was all the invitation he needed. The moment held suspended until he kissed her and then all the world exploded in color and light, life humming between them.

Jasper was lost to it.

ESME CLIPPED ON HER PEARL earrings and stared down at her husband's sleeping form on the rumpled sheets. A late-afternoon breeze, still cool and gray from the earlier rain, blew through the open window, stirring the fine curtains and ruffling the golden-brown hair over Jasper's ear.

A memory of him lying like this stirred through her, but champagne bubbles proved too thick to entirely recall that night from four years ago. This time there had been no champagne to stymie the rush of blood in her veins, the thrill of their escape thundering in her heart, or the desire blazing through her. This time she recalled the way his mouth fit over hers, the strength in his arms as he held her, the soft whispers in her ear, the way she clung to him in need. Not need for the sake of intimacy but for the sake of needing *him*.

That was when she knew it was time to leave.

Jasper Truitt had a hold on her heart, and it wasn't one she was ready for him to lay claim to. Nothing good came from laying claim. It left brokenness and despair in its wake when that momentary tenderness abandoned her for good. And it would. Time and again she'd witnessed it. Her father, whoever he was. Mimsy, for all the mother she was. To Esme's own dreams falling victim to cold reality. She could not rely on a single thing but herself, so it was best to leave behind all attachments before they deserted her. Jasper might have been different, but why take the risk?

"It's better this way," she whispered. More to him or to herself, she could no longer say. She slid the Valkyrie into her suitcase and locked it shut. Soon enough she could put all this behind her and unravel her heart from Jasper's and walk free from the countess's death threats. Freedom, finally.

"Don't do this, Esme." Jasper looked up at her from where his head rested on the pillow. Not an hour ago her head had rested there too. Resignation pooled in those gorgeous brown eyes of his, but it was the disappointment that cut her to the quick.

She attempted to cover the pain by swiping lipstick across her lips, swollen from his kisses, and dropped the tube into her purse.

"I have to, darling. You should know that about me by now."

"I know that's what you want me to think. That these trysts mean nothing to you."

"But they did mean something. A fizzing afternoon of fun, but all good things must come to an end. Now, if you'll excuse me. I don't wish to miss my train."

He shifted on the bed. The bedsheet lowered to his waist, revealing his hands tied together with her silk belt while he still slept. "Say what you want, but deep down you know you keep running because of fear. What you should fear is that hired gun and his Italian mistress. Don't give them the Valkyrie."

If only he knew the consequences of such actions. Consequences she couldn't allow him to be anywhere near. She owed him that. "And give it to you instead?"

"Cut ties with them, Esme. They're dangerous."

"I'm a grown woman. I can handle myself, though I do admit you did an admirable job of it earlier." She swept an appreciative look over the length of him and steeled herself against the rush of emotions it whirled in her. Reaching into her purse, she pulled out his freshly cleaned and pressed handkerchief. The one he had used to tenderly clean the mud from her face. She moved to place it on the nightstand.

"Keep it," he said softly. "I like to think of you owning something of mine. Even if it's no longer my last name."

A swift cut to the heart as only he could deliver. She returned the handkerchief to her purse.

"I'll be out of these bonds in a matter of minutes," he added.

"Yes, but it's enough to give me a head start. Then I suppose you'll come after me again. Makes a girl blush having a man chase after her so determinedly."

"I will come, but not for you." He sighed and in it she could hear *not this time.* "I'm coming for the Valkyrie."

She was crossing a line with no way of changing course. They had sidestepped each other across Europe, playing cat and mouse for the tiara as well as their attraction to each other. She enjoyed the game, the teasing, the suggestive smiles, but it wasn't until she'd awoken next to him an hour ago, his warmth curling all around her like a comforting blanket, his arm possessively slung across her hip, and that curl of hair—applesauce and crackers! That curl! It was no longer a clever game of wit and skill. It had become a game her heart was tangled into. Curse its impractical longings.

Her impractical beating heart wished only to crawl back into bed with him while her sensible mind pushed her toward the door.

From the regret in his eyes, she knew she would not be welcome anywhere near him ever again. Her leaving the morning after their wedding had cut him. She saw that now. This leaving broke something inside him, and he was using the pieces to build a wall that would keep her out.

It was what she had wanted all along. No attachments, no responsibilities, nothing to hold her back or keep her down. Then why did a piece of her feel broken as well?

"Because what seemed like candlelight last night is only the light of a freight train coming straight on in the morning." Mimsy's astute advice echoed in her mind. *"Best to wake up before it lays you out flat on the track."*

Harsh as it was, Mimsy was right. Esme had no desire to be laid out on a track with the chugging wheels of tender emotion flattening her. She had enough worries with Countess Accardi and Pirazzo if she didn't hand over the tiara in time for the countess's performance.

With that in mind, she picked up her suitcase and started for the door.

Before opening it, she turned back. "It's been a swell time. Goodbye, Jasper." She blew him a kiss and left.

15

Paris, France

La Train Bleu in Paris's Gare de Lyon was a gem of a restaurant. Welcoming train passengers since the 1900 Paris Exposition with elegant fares, steaming coffee, and helpful waitstaff, it truly was a reprieve from the smoke and grit and bustle of the teeming platforms.

Esme sat on one of the blue leather banquettes in the dining hall, the table in front of her draped in white linen with shining plates of small sandwiches and macarons, and a divine tea with steam drifting from the pot's spout. Paintings from the world's most famous Belle Époque hung on the ornate gilt walls. Chandeliers dripped from the ceilings, catching light from the dozens of arched windows lining the paneled walls. Everywhere touches of luxury were set to the soft tune of clinking crystalware.

She enjoyed none of it. She might as well have been nibbling on a stale digestive biscuit washed down by wartime beef tea while sitting in the theater alley between performances for all she noticed of her current surroundings. Yesterday afternoon she had left Jasper behind. After arriving in Paris early this morning, she had wandered around the train station, but three hours was too long to wander without purpose as she waited for her next train. She'd found herself in the restaurant hoping a spot to eat would right the gnawing inside her. It didn't.

She stirred her tea. She was doing the right thing. Forgetting about Jasper. Completing the job for the dowager. Not getting bumped off by Pirazzo. She glanced down at her suitcase sitting on the bench next to her. Handing over the tiara and getting paid was the right thing. Not morally perhaps, but then, she didn't have the luxury of choosing morals. Not when those upright principles prevented her from being able to afford food or a roof over her head. Survival had its own code of ethics, and she had become rather good at deciphering it to her advantage. The teaspoon slowed its listless circling in the porcelain cup. Survival had offered her daring purpose. Only, it was starting to lose its zing.

"*Buongiorno.*" A meaty man slid into the chair across the table from her. Pirazzo. Somehow oilier and uglier than when he'd tried to break her over a rail at Neuschwanstein Castle.

Every nerve in Esme's body crackled with fear, but she quickly quieted them. It would not do to appear frightened. Men like him fed on it.

"Following me again?"

With deliberate slowness he plucked the black leather gloves from his scarred paws and laid them on the table. A stark contrast against the snowy tablecloth.

"The countess is anxious because of your delays."

"She should know that retrieving this item was not a smash-and-grab job. It required a delicacy of timing." She stirred a teaspoon of sugar into her tea. His untimely appearance did not bode well. Her nerves jangled into high alert.

"She is not paying you for your time. She is paying you to complete the job."

"As she pays you to hound me, it seems." As she raised her teacup for a sip, images of the countess poisoning her unsuspecting rivals flashed through her mind. The old woman was nowhere in sight, but it wasn't past her doing to have Pirazzo slip arsenic into the brew. She set the cup on the saucer with a *clink*. "You left me a bit bruised upon our last meeting."

"It is nothing to what I will do if you do not have the tiara. Where is it?" His eyes were as dark and bottomless as pits. Nothing escaped from them. Not sympathy, not patience, and certainly not mercy.

Esme swallowed the lump in her throat. "Safe."

"In your possession?"

She nodded, sliding her gaze to her suitcase then back to him. "If you haven't noticed, we're in a train station. I am on my way to deliver it to her in Milan today."

"Lucky for you, you now have a bodyguard to escort you the rest of the way. To ensure you do not become lost. Or allow phantom distractions."

Phantom. Jasper.

"Distraction?" She forced a laugh past the constricting muscles in her throat and crossed her legs. All easy appearances belying the tremor racing through her. "More of a passing flirtation. One he could not keep up with, for here I sit with the tiara. He's returning to wherever he came from to lick his wounds and hopefully find a woman more attuned to his slow pace."

Pirazzo was a dog set to do his mistress's bidding, but hopefully distracting him with the tiara would keep him from sniffing after Jasper. It was the least she could do after leaving him.

"Women and your petty flirtations." Pirazzo snorted with derision. "You turned out to be smarter than the others at least."

"Others?" A tremor crept into her voice.

One blunt finger scratched at a pockmark of scars on his bullish neck. "I have worked for the countess for many years. I have seen the younger and prettier *ragazze* come and go, flirting with the old woman's leading men and drawing them away from her. I have watched her eyes narrow with jealousy and her heart turn rageful with losing her place in the spotlight. She blames them all for taking it from her, but not you. You have been clever enough to offer a trinket of her famed youth. This tiara is her fountain of youth and with it she will take the stage once more, claiming the applause she lives for."

A diva's need for the spotlight never failed as long as she had her vanity to stroke her on. Not that many audiences turned up to watch an eighty-year-old sing sonnets from her youth. Supposedly eighty. Esme wouldn't be surprised if the old woman had shaved off a decade or two for the sake of vanity. Not that the public would notice. They might accept her performance invitation to drink her champagne and eat her canapes, but Esme seriously doubted that anyone would be enraptured by her aged voice. It was more likely to be a spectacle, a sending-off of the old dame before they cut the spotlight from her for good. Not that the countess would slink quietly offstage. She would screech her protest of being forgotten until her bones finally gave up after carting her around for so long.

"How does the Valkyrie factor into this celebration?" Esme asked. "Please don't tell me she intends to recreate a vengeful Viking solo to spite this former flame who left her and gave the tiara to his bride?"

"The countess does not let go of grudges easily, if at all. That is why she has me. To take care of the scornful lovers and *bella* little divas who cross the stage and mock her. My favorite is when they are together." He jerked his head, motioning her to lean forward. She did so by a terrified fraction.

"The impresario for *Don Giovani*'s revival fifteen years ago was once her lover until his attention swayed to one of the chorus girls. I found them taking a gondola along the Great Canal and made quick work of that affair."

The blood drained from Esme's face. On one of her first trips to Venice she'd heard rumors of a haunted gondola that had washed up on the shore of one of the many nearby islands. Two lovers had been knifed to death and left for the fishes to feed upon.

Pirazzo's dark eyes glittered. He tugged his leather gloves back onto his solid hands. "I see you know of this. It is why the countess hired me when she tired of using her own hands to poison lovers or drop weighted props onto her understudies. Her ruthlessness is an inspiration."

"I shall leave the inspiration between the two of you. I'm merely hired to fetch the prizes." Gripping her handbag with whitened fingers, she glanced behind him at the ornate clock on the wall. "My train arrives shortly, and I need to powder my nose. Can't embark with a shine."

She rose, purse in one hand and suitcase in the other, and summoned a brilliant smile despite terror crawling through her like ants. "It was good of you to see me off, but I can make the trip without fuss. I'm sure you have other more pressing matters to attend."

"You are my only matter." Rising with her, he took her elbow and steered her out of the restaurant and down the sweeping double staircase leading to the platform area.

Passengers carrying luggage and briefcases bustled by, eager to catch their trains before departure. Trolleys loaded with coffee and pastries were pushed among the crowd by enterprising bakers eager to sell their goods to hungry passengers. Uniformed gendarme patrolled the tracks with an eye out for trouble.

I've got trouble right here. If someone will just pay attention . . .

Pirazzo must have felt her tensing for action. His thick fingers dug into the tender flesh above her elbow. "Do not think on this."

Esme moved her eyes all around in search of an exit. She lit on the nearest possibility, a door with ladies streaming in and out of its perfumed sanctum.

"I am only thinking on how much you are wrinkling my sleeve. The ladies lounge will have an attendant to help smooth it. I'll pop in and—"

He jerked her away from the lounge and into one of the several small rooms that were popular in generations before where women waited to keep the soot and smoke from spoiling their fancy frocks and frothy chapeaus. A bench ran along one wall while a lightbulb fizzed overhead. The space smelled of cigarettes and peanut shells.

"Whatever needs smoothing or powdering, you can do it in here," he said, releasing her arm.

"Sir, really." She resisted the urge to rub away the burning pain from where he'd gripped her arm and instead rolled her fear into indignation. "This waiting room is hardly appropriate for a lady to prepare herself for the journey."

He reached a hand in his pocket. "Only one journey you need concern yourself about now. The final one." He yanked out a thin cord and lashed it around her neck, then pulled the ends tight.

"The countess doesn't want loose ends like you. It's my job to tie you up, and then I'll be taking the tiara to her." Esme bucked and scratched at the cord cutting off her air, but Pirazzo merely pulled tighter. "She told me to tell you *grazie*."

The cord cut into her neck. Black crowded her vision as her lungs screamed. With one last burst of effort, she swung her suitcase up and back. It cracked against her assailant's head. The lock split. Clothes tumbled out all around them. Pirazzo fell to the floor, a large gash bleeding from his head and splattering red droplets on her satin knickers.

Esme clawed the cord from her neck and heaved in great gulps of air, hissing out unladylike names to the prostrate bull at her feet. He wouldn't stay down for long. Grabbing a pink-and-yellow silk scarf that clashed horribly with her navy travel suit but had managed to escape blood splatters, she wound it loosely around her neck to cover the red line burning against her throat and slipped out of the waiting room, closing the door firmly behind her. She cradled her handbag to her chest and made her way through the crowd, blending in as another hurried passenger on their way to and fro. Exiting the station's front doors, she hailed a taxi.

"Gare du Nord," she told the driver without thinking.

The auto rumbled into the traffic heading to the 10th Arrondissement, but Esme's legs didn't stop shaking until several streets later. She relaxed against the leather back seat. She had to leave Paris immediately. All the trains from Gare du Nord went north. Belgium, the Netherlands, Lille. Lille wasn't far from Calais. And Calais wasn't far from the shore of England. A short boat ride across the Channel and she could arrive in London in a matter of days.

There was no better place to lay low or get lost in than the East End.

A tremulous smile fluttered across her lips as she eased the scarf from her tender neck. Home. She would go home. To most people the thought of home would conjure images of lace curtains, a warm oven, a familiar creaking door, but to her it was the smell of grease paint, warped stage boards, and zozzled gaffers cursing up a blue streak because the curtain was stuck again. Wouldn't Mimsy be surprised? Her stomach soured. Best not to think about Mimsy until it was absolutely necessary.

The site of the former Bastille and the Crowne Plaza Republique flashed by her window. She took a shuddering breath to calm her ricocheting nerves and unclenched her purse from her chest. The silver beading caught the weakened rays of sunlight and bounced them off the taxi ceiling.

She fingered a loose thread near the bottom seam.

"Drat." Several beads had been ripped off in her struggle with Pirazzo. Squashing another unladylike word, she unclipped the purse's clasp and peered into the satin-lined interior.

"You're proving to be a handful." The Valkyrie's diamonds winked up at her in shared conspiracy. Before Jasper had awoken the previous day, she'd taken the precaution of dismantling the wings from the head circlet as the tiara was less conspicuous to pack that way.

A smile, a real one, tugged at the corners of her mouth. "How do you fancy a trip to jolly old England?"

16

Calais, France

EITHER HIS GLASS WAS SPINNING or Jasper wasn't drunk enough. Taking no chances, he signaled the bartender for another whisky and downed the golden liquid in one gulp. It no longer burned his throat, merely offering an intoxicating caress of oblivion.

He propped his tuxedo-clad elbows on the polished bar and breathed in the heavy scent of cigarette smoke permeating the dimly lit room. It was the kind of hole-in-the-wall joint where patrons secreted away for a real drink after being forced to sit through a formal dinner with in-laws or a boss. Here, ties loosened, dress hems rose, music swanned, and drinks knocked a man back. Here, everyone grasped after pleasure, wanting to lose themselves while silently hating everyone for acting as a mirror to what they despised most about themselves.

Jasper didn't hate himself. Nor did he hate anyone else in the room for seeking escape. He had passed the years and hours in the fragrant arms of pleasant women as they danced the night away, but always the wretched quiet followed when the music stopped and the alcohol dried up. And the silence summoned *her*.

She strolled out of the haze just as she had the day they met. Armistice had been declared and all the bells in Paris were ringing. People young and old flooded the streets, cheering and clapping, hugging and crying. Jasper had been on leave with a few of the lads from his unit when word came that the war was over. They'd joined the celebration sweeping along the Champs-Élysées where a brass band had set up among the waving flags.

The first chords of "Daisy Bell" were playing and suddenly there she was. Long dark hair rolled and pinned up at the nape of her neck, a red skirt and jacket, and a hat tilted to the side. She'd walked straight up to him, kissed him full on the lips, and then with a saucy wink she'd disappeared into the crowd.

His world had turned upside down.

Hours later his mates dragged him into a café for a pint and there she was again. Tucked into a corner booth laughing with four other girls. He and Esme had found a quiet booth of their own and talked until night fell.

"What if I told you I might fall in love?" he'd asked, drowning in her sky-blue eyes.

She'd taken the pint from his hand, sipped it, and smiled. *"What if I told you I'd break your heart?"*

"I'm lost either way."

An hour later they were married. A passionate kiss, a ring on her finger, a photograph, and the nearest hotel they could find, and the rest, as they say, is history. And history, as they also say, is bound to repeat itself.

"Isn't that the truth?" Reaching into his wallet, he plucked out the shiny gold band he'd slipped on her slender finger. Not twelve hours later she'd given it back, and like a sentimental fool he'd carried it around for four years. Imagining that one day he would find her and she would want it back. "Joke's on me."

He dropped the ring into an empty glass and rattled it around to catch the bartender's attention. "Another."

A frown flickered across the bartender's face, but he was too much of a professional to stop a rummy from spending more money and poured another shot as the jazz band tripped into a song Jasper had never heard but that sounded an awful lot like the hollowness groaning in his chest.

A newcomer slipped onto the barstool next to Jasper and nodded to the freshened drink in his hand. "What's your poison?"

The man took on a vaguely familiar form. Jasper blinked in concentration. Fair with a missing right arm. Mond.

"Loneliness." Jasper saluted his friend with the glass. "It started off as barely controlled rage." He pointed to the first empty glass lined up in front of him. "Then disbelief." He pointed to the second. "Then my own idiocy—a double for that. It's a game I'm playing. I drink to see how much it takes before Glenfiddich's finest starts pouring out of the hole in my heart."

"Don't swallow the ring. It'll hurt like the devil coming back up." Always a dry wit, that Mond.

Jasper drained his glass dry, catching the ring with his teeth. He spat it back into his hand. "Did I say heart? I meant pride."

Mond took the empty glass and added it to the expanding row. "Oh no. I think your heart got roped into that golden circle long ago. Otherwise you would have pawned it for something more useful."

Jasper appreciated the straightforwardness he shared with Mond. Most days. Today was not one of them. "Why are you here?"

"You sent me a telegram." Mond pulled out a yellow slip of paper from his breast pocket and waved it in Jasper's face. "Urgent you claimed." He dropped it on the counter and flattened it with his palm.

Jasper blinked at the telegram and spotted his name typed at the bottom. "Oh. So I did. And it is. Urgent." He frowned at Mond's empty hand. "Do you want a drink?"

Never one to turn down a refreshing drink, Mond signaled to the bartender. "Scotch and soda, s'il vous plait."

As the bartender gathered the requested order, Jasper didn't linger on unnecessary niceties. "I've found Esme."

Mond sighed and shook his head at the soda the bartender was about to add. "I've changed my order. Neat."

"She's eluded me for the past month. At first I thought she'd traveled to Milan to give the tiara to that woman who hired her, but none of my contacts had seen her heading south. Nor did anyone spot her in Milan."

"Neither did mine," Mond added.

"Then I asked around in Paris." Warming to the topic of a chase, Jasper's mind pulled itself from the whisky-induced haze. "She was spotted at Gare de Lyon. When I arrived and questioned the stationmaster, he claimed Esme had been there a month ago and purchased a ticket but never boarded her intended train to Milan."

Accepting his drink, Mond sipped the amber brew. Lucky old sport. He didn't have need to toss it all back in one go. "She probably knew she would be too easy to track using the train and only bought that ticket to throw you off."

"I considered it a possibility until the stationmaster checked his logbook and found a gendarme report from the day she was supposed to depart. An Italian man was found bleeding and unconscious in one of the platform's waiting rooms, and a woman's busted-open suitcase and clothing were strewn all about. It was Pirazzo, Countess Accardi's goon."

Mond frowned. "Why would Pirazzo show up in Paris if Esme was taking the tiara to Milan?"

"Obviously the countess has trust issues after Esme handed her a fake one last time."

"Esme wouldn't double-cross the old broad, not when she had a payout coming."

"Unless the countess had no intention of paying and sent Pirazzo to collect the tiara and dispose of Esme." Fingers clamping around his glass, Jasper stared into the emptiness. No amount of drink could blot out his shock and anger upon hearing the rest of the report for the first time.

"A cord shaped into a garret was found with dried blood on it. The beast tried to strangle her."

Mond let out a low whistle. "Bad luck for her mixing up with that lot."

Jasper forced his grip on the glass to relax. Shattering glass in his hand was counterproductive to his line of work and he needed all the advantages he could muster. He needed a cool head, and thoughts of Esme in danger only made his blood boil. He'd warned her to cut ties with that old gorgon. Impulsive minx that she was, Esme hadn't bothered heeding his warnings. And now look where she was. On the run from a hit man and a barmy old diva, leaving a trail of scattered breadcrumbs for Jasper to track across the English Channel.

At first he'd thought crossing paths with his estranged wife over the Valkyrie was an odd and twisted set of circumstances, but now he was convinced this was no coincidence. *"A posh aristocrat's mistress, an Italian opera singer."* Duke had a number of affairs, many of them with Italian women and many of them performers of some sort, so it seemed conceivable that Countess

Accardi was one of his conquests who believed she was owed more for her services rendered. Such as a diamond tiara.

"Two days ago I received word from an old comrade who works the loading docks in Dover," Jasper said. "A Miss E. Fox was on a ship's manifest that landed three weeks ago. She sailed to England."

"So the question is, what's her plan for the tiara now that she's on the run?"

"I don't care about her plans." A lie. He ordered another drink to prove how much he didn't care. "The only thing I need concern myself with is tracking her down and taking back the tiara so I can be done with this job once and for all. It has caused me nothing but headaches."

"It's that woman. She's what's going to give you an ulcer. Look at this." Mond jabbed at the row of empty glasses. "You're crawling into the bottom of a bottle because of her."

"As if a woman hasn't sent you on a bender."

"Not for a month straight. My heart may break for an evening, but there's always another dish around the corner willing to soothe me."

"Heart," Jasper scoffed. "I told you my heart has nothing to do with this. Wounded pride, that is my affliction."

"Wounded pride stings. It makes you curse at the moon and go out looking for a brawl with the first sorry sot to cross your path. But a woman who has her hooks in you, well, that's a whole other set of problems. Makes you lie to yourself, for one. Listen to weepy music." Mond jerked a thumb at the band, who chose that moment to back up his statement with "Three O'Clock in the Morning." "Drink the juice joint dry. And my personal favorite, chase after her in hopes you'll get her back."

Jasper reiterated his scoff. "I'm not chasing her, and I do not want her back."

Mond raised his eyebrows in mock rebuttal.

"There are rules to be followed—*my* rules. Keep the job entertaining. Don't make enemies. There's a third . . . somewhere . . ." He tapped his head in concentration. The gold wedding band stared accusingly at him. "Oh, there it is. Never allow the job to become personal."

"I'd say you've broken that rule a thousand times over in the past few weeks."

"The Valkyrie is the only thing of importance to me. Esme and I had our chance. She didn't want me, and I should have known better—that she wasn't the sort of woman to stick around." The bartender set a freshly poured whisky in front of Jasper. He didn't reach for it as his resolve sobered. "I want someone who wants *me*."

"Then go get the Valkyrie and put all this behind you."

Jasper pinched the simple wedding band between his fingers, turning it this way and that. Dim light sparked off its smooth gold surface. Flicking it in the air, he positioned the whisky glass, where the ring landed with a splash. It sank to the bottom, along with whatever might have been with Esme.

Pushing away the glass, he dropped a generous tip of coins on the counter.

"I intend to."

17

London, England

THE RED CURTAIN FELL TO raucous clapping, whistles, and breaking
bottles. A typical Tuesday night at The Scarlet Crown. Originating
as The Spotted Toad pub, the building laid claim to several ghosts
and was where Guy Fawkes and his fellow conspirators met for a
final toast before heading off to their dastardly attempt to blow
up Parliament.

Of course, no one could prove that fact, but it made for a
good story, and pubs loved nothing more than spinning a good
yarn. A few fires and rebuilds later, the pub was converted into a
theater hosting such rousing acts such as Bottleneck Molly and
her whistling set of pipes, the Bacon Brothers and their trick
poodles, and the crowd favorite, Blow the Hatch Will, who could
guzzle any brew-filled bottle chucked at him onstage.

Esme glanced at the backstage clock. Nine forty-five. The last
performance was scheduled for ten o'clock. A classical depiction
of *Salome*. Another crowd favorite as Salome somehow managed
to misplace four of the seven veils.

"Those vests for Robin Hood's merry men were quite the treat tonight, Dora," Esme said to the costume mistress as she brushed by draped in cheap satins and carrying an armload of men's boots. "You could see all the green sequins to the back row."

"For every one sequin I sew on, they lose twenty," Dora muttered as the tape measure slung around her wrinkly neck threatened to choke her. "I blame those felt-tipped arrows. They snag on everything, they do."

"Dora!" a female voice screeched from behind a painted backdrop of a temple. "Dora! Where are me veils? There's only the two here." The Scarlet Crown's very own Salome popped out, black wig askew and rouge rubbed into red circles on her cheeks.

"Here they are. Stop your caterwauling and grab them from my shoulder." Dora sighed and rolled her eyes at Esme.

Salome snatched the silky veils. "You want me goin' on tha' stage withou' a stich, don' ya?" There wasn't enough silk in the world to cover up her East End origins.

"What I want don't matter much, do it? You've lost nearly all of 'em by night's end."

They carried on back to the dressing room, their squabbling as much a part of the backstage world as scenery props and line recitation. Others may have grown up with the lullaby of a horse and cart or a nanny's humming, but not Esme, not in the world of theater. Here was where she'd learned that calling someone "Macbeth" was worse than using a four-letter word. Here was where she'd learned how to use a cane in one swipe to knock off a too-tall hat that was blocking the stage view. Here was where she'd learned dramatic Italian phrases from *La bohéme*. Here was home.

She'd thought returning home was the safest way to lay low and get her feet under her again while she considered her next move. And what to do with the Valkyrie currently hidden in the false bottom of a costume trunk in her room above the theater.

What she was really doing was hiding. Not that she would admit that out loud. A lady was nothing without her secrets, but in the quiet after the footlights dimmed she could admit the truth to herself. Of course, in the theater the footlights never dimmed for very long, so it was a sticky wicket she was never forced to contend with at length. Thank heavens for that. However did truthful souls manage the appalling burden?

Shaking off her tinges of blue, Esme left backstage and took the side aisle, heading to the front of the house where a double staircase winged its way up to the mezzanine level that had been transformed into the bar area.

"Evenin', Esme," Frankie, the bartender, called as he juggled four glasses in one hand and two bottles of gin in the other.

"Good show tonight," she said, bypassing the worn counter and rows of glittering bottles sitting behind it.

"Tell the boss ta add more comedies," he said. "These dramas whot's too mushy for me."

"You and I both know what it's like telling the boss anything that doesn't already correspond with her plans."

"Too right I do!" Frankie laughed and waved, then turned his attention to a customer.

Continuing down a hallway marked "Private," she passed a few storage rooms before coming to a door at the end. She rapped once, then entered. The room was a decent size with light-paneled walls and the furniture upholstered in pale pinks and watery greens. Potted plants dotted the corners, while framed playbills lined the walls.

In the midst of it all was Mimsy, holding court in the center of a ring of well-heeled gentlemen. Dressed in a gown of silvery blue, she stood with one gloved elbow propped on the faux marble mantelpiece, blowing out rings of cigarette smoke. She didn't acknowledge Esme.

"Harold, lamb," Mimsy crooned. "You know The Scarlet Crown is entirely booked until March. I cannot possibly squeeze in another performer. Not at the expense and pride of one of my actors already contracted."

"Holly Featherlight isn't some two-bit actress," the man, presumably Harold, said. "She has the makings of a star. Think what it will do for your publicity if The Scarlet Crown is where she's discovered."

"I simply don't see how I can make it work."

That was the game. The theater needed to fill up its calendar and there was nothing more alluring to a talent manager's drive than filled slots. And Mimsy was aces at playing hard to get. She'd pulled herself up through the theater ranks from chorus girl, to secondary, to understudy, to leading lady, and finally to being owner. It also helped that she was the previous owner's paramour when he kicked the bucket and left all his shares in the house to her. Mimsy had mourned for promptly one hour before making changes. The theater had been somewhat profitable before, but under her ownership it had become a raging success.

"Fit her in here and there," Harold continued. "Use her as an understudy. You won't have to pay her as much as your first-rate performers. All she needs is a chance to be seen."

Mimsy's kohl-rimmed eyes gleamed at the magic words. Less payment. She tapped her cigarette ash into the unlit fireplace.

"Perhaps there's something." It was the same noncommittal tone Esme had learned to mimic to perfection. "Let me think on it and we can discuss it over lunch next Thursday at the Savoy."

Another gentleman with a belly ready to burst from his waistcoat harrumphed. "But, Mrs. Fox, you've promised to lunch with me next Thursday to discuss a new backdrop artist."

Esme stifled a giggle. *Mrs.* Fox, indeed. Both title and name as fake as the black dye coating Mimsy's marcel waves.

"Oh yes. How frightful of me to forget." Mimsy fluttered her long ebony cigarette holder in innocent ignorance. "Confer with my secretary and she'll find a convenient time. She has a tighter hold on my diary."

One of the men turned to refill his glass from the crystal-cut decanters provided on a side table. His gaze caught Esme and took her in with an appreciative survey. She wore a white number trimmed in silver fringe with two ropes of black-jet beads hanging from her neck.

"Who do we have here?" The man grinned. Drink forgotten, he slid across the floor and wrapped an arm around her waist. "You didn't tell us you had a sister, Mrs. Fox."

Esme laughed lightly and slipped his hook like a fish. "Ah, sir, but when you enter the theater, you enter a world of secrets."

Mimsy's dark red mouth curled into a tight smile. She skipped forward and linked her arm to Esme's, dragging her into the center of admirers.

"This is Esme." That was all. No relation or affiliation. And heaven knew she would rather go the way of Ophelia than admit mother and daughter. "Gentlemen, this evening has been delightful, but I'm afraid it's time for a girls-only chin wag."

An actress always knew when she was losing her audience.

After toodle-ooing them out the door, Mimsy dropped the act of refinement. "Whew! What a sack of ol' windbags. A girl stoops something awful low to keep her theater doors open." She dropped onto the delicate chaise piled with velvet pillows and kicked off her gold T-strapped shoes, closing her eyes with a blissful sigh. "Be a pet and fetch me my cigarette case."

Esme took the silver case from the mantel and crossed to where Mimsy lay. She selected a fag and fit it into the end of the ebony holder, then lit it with a match. After blowing out the match, she tossed it into the crystal ashtray with half a dozen other burned sticks.

"You smoke too much."

"Steadies the nerves." Mimsy puffed, exhaling smoke through her nose and pulling it into her mouth like a coiling snake.

"Wherever did you learn to do that?"

"Ain't it something? Learned it off one of them French actresses what come through here last year. Terrible play, but the audiences love anything exotic. Called a 'French inhale.'" She cracked open an eye, her eyelashes thick with mascara. "Thank heavens your bosom never came in. Those pearls would never hang straight if they had."

Esme tossed the cigarette case onto the table next to the ashtray and dropped into one of the matching pink accent chairs.

"That's not what you said a decade ago. I strictly remember you lamenting over my lack of a bosom when I became an adolescent. Said the lads would never go for a flat-chested beanpole."

"Lucky for you the fashions have changed since then. Now your type is all the rage while I'm left to pinch myself into girdles." Classic Mimsy. Ever so deft at dealing a compliment with a backhanded slap.

Accustomed to dodging such slaps, Esme crossed her legs and settled farther into the chair. "Is the theater suffering?"

"Eh? Oh that. No. We're doing right as rain."

"Then why play the hard-to-get card?"

Mimsy puffed her cigarette, spewing smoke all about. "All them talent managers think their starlets deserve top billing. Playing hard to get drives their asking price down. The key to a successful business is exclusivity. Same way I taught you to get a man."

"Get a man." Esme twirled the end of her pearl ropes. "Have you changed your tune about settling down to slippers and pipe?"

Smoke sputtered from the older woman's nose. "I'd be better off listening to a soprano shatter glass and stab me in the eye with it than ever tie myself down to a man. Best to have flings. No mess, no commitments. Pure freedom."

There it was. The Fox ladies' mantra. Avoid commitment at all costs. Now here they were, master free, bouncing down a line of men and living the life of swells. Wasn't it brilliant? Rising, Esme moved to the side table and poured herself a gin and tonic.

"I thought you were kicking up your heels with that banker from Whitehall." She returned to her chair and sipped her drink.

"That was over a year ago, pet. Can't let them hang around too long. They start getting ideas."

Ideas such as marriage, hardly. More like ideas of leaving and finding a younger pair of arms. Best to leave first and consider it your idea all along. It was the only way to maintain control.

Esme ran her finger around the edge of the cool glass, the drink suddenly heavy in her stomach. "What if the right man came along?"

"Learned long ago there's no such thing. Only kind that exists is the man for right now. They want too much, and guess who always gets stuck footing the bill?" Mimsy made a bump gesture over her stomach. "Us. You and me, we're not cut out for all that hearth and apron strings nonsense. Look at us, we're free."

"Yes, indeed. Free as birds." Why hadn't the gin kicked in yet?

Propping her stocking-clad feet on a plump cushion, Mimsy tapped her cigarette ash into the tray behind her head. She missed and the ash floated to the floor.

"Speaking of which, how long until you take flight again?"

"Why do you ask?"

"Concern is all."

"Let us not pretend you've ever hosted a maternal bone in your body. Motherly concern is not your style." Ah, there it was trailing through her at last. Nothing like the tranquil cooling effects of a good gin.

"Don't use that dreadful word." Mimsy shivered as if the image of a doting Madonna terrified her more than panning in front of a full house. "My only concern is to keep you from moping too long. You only return home when your tail is tucked between your legs. Because of a man or an art deal gone wrong, so I want to know how long it'll take this time."

It was true that Esme didn't often step foot in The Scarlet Crown when life was jolly. She was far too busy plying her trade in jewels and art, a trade she had neither confirmed nor denied as being on the up and up to Mimsy. They had an unspoken policy of not asking, and therefore needing no explanation. Yet in coming home, there was always an admission price of sorts to pay.

Esme drained her glass dry and prepared herself for the inevitable. "Out with it."

"With what?"

"With whatever task you wish to employ me in."

A moment's hesitation and finally out it came. "Thelma is out sick—"

"No."

Mimsy sat up straight, kicking the cushion away from her feet. "She has only a few lines in the second act. You'd be onstage less than a few minutes."

"Do you not remember the last time I was forced into a performance? I tossed my cookies before uttering a single line."

"That was ages ago." Mimsy waved her hand as if it were no concern at all. "Surely you can muster the strength to push through. After all, the show must go on."

"It can go right on without me." Standing, Esme moved again to her newest best mate, the loaded side table. "Backstage, I'll lend a hand. Out front, no. Find someone else."

Mimsy pounced on the offer. "I do need a prop master. Wallace got smacked in the head with Tybalt's sword during last week's *Romeo and Juliet*. You can fill in until he returns from hospital."

"Swell." Three cubes of ice this time. *Clink, clink, clink.* Such a magical sound they made falling into the glass.

Knock. Knock.

Quick as a flash, Mimsy swung her legs off the chaise and strapped on her heels. She pinched her cheeks and casually angled herself on the cushions with one arm thrown carelessly over the back of the seat. She never let an acting opportunity pass her by.

"*Entre*," she called in her best Gladys Cooper voice.

The door opened to reveal one of the Crown's ushers, dressed in a smart uniform of scarlet and navy.

"Excuse the interruption, Mrs. Fox. There's a gentleman here to see you."

"Who?"

"He didn't give his name, only said that he's your husband."

"Husband?" Mimsy's drawn-on eyebrows pinched together. "Someone is playing a cruel joke, for I am a widowed lady."

The usher shrugged. "Sorry, ma'am, but he said he was here to see Mrs. Fox."

"*Miss* Fox," came an altogether too familiar voice from the other side of the door. "A mistake easily made."

The door swung all the way open. Jasper glided past the usher and into the room. His eyes swept the space until lighting on Esme with cool directness.

"Hello, darling wife. Did you miss me?"

18

It wasn't often that Jasper had witnessed an unsettled Esme. The woman was always on guard, ready with a rapier-like quip, batting away any inconvenience as if it were nothing more than an irksome fly. So it gave him great pleasure to watch her deep crimson lips part on a strangled noise and the glass slip from her hand, bounce off the plush rug, and slosh gin over the tips of her satin shoes.

She didn't notice. "Wh-what are you doing here?"

He strolled farther into the room. "Not delighted to see your husband? I admit I dreamed of you throwing your arms around me with a welcoming kiss, but you seem rather shocked." The kiss he could fend off, but having her close enough to bind and gag would be a welcome prospect. A taste of her own coldhearted medicine that he would gladly ladle down her throat.

"Husband?" The woman on the chaise, her mother if he had to guess, popped up from her lounging position. A long cigarette holder dangled limply from her ringed fingers. "Esme, why didn't you tell me you were married?"

Esme kept her knifelike stare pointed at Jasper as she answered. "I'm not. I mean, we were—*are*—but not for much longer. We're divorcing as soon as possible."

"Divorce or not, aren't you going to introduce me?" The mother wiggled her shoulders back in a move he wasn't accustomed to seeing off a dance floor.

"No." Esme threw her own shoulders back, but this move was made in defiance, not flirtation. She marched toward him. "He's leaving."

"Don't be testy, darling." Jasper dodged her as she came to shove him out the door and made for the mother. This would be easier than he'd thought. Taking her hand, he brushed his lips over her knuckles. "Jasper Truitt, a pleasure."

"How utterly charming. Maud Fox," the woman tittered. Her legs were not quite as long as Esme's, but she had the same black hair and striking bone structure. "Esme, how dare you go on about the right man not ten minutes ago and here he stands. Whyever have you kept him hidden?"

Thunder rolling in her eyes, Esme crossed her arms. "Because we had one too many on Armistice Day and thought the only thing grander than ending a war was a wedding. It didn't take long to realize we were better off going our separate ways."

"That was before we crossed paths in France not long ago," Jasper added, smooth as acid. Drip by drip he would get her to crack.

"And now you've come to win her back," Maud gushed.

Esme aimed her knives at her mother. "Was it not *you* ten minutes ago going on about being as free as birds?"

Maud trailed her hand down Jasper's sleeve. "That was before this tall, cool drink of fizzer waltzed through the door."

"He can waltz right back out it."

Heaving a dramatic sigh that rolled with exasperation, Maud crossed her legs, flashing a glimpse of her rhinestone garter. "Mr. Truitt, you must forgive her. She's not quite herself today."

Jasper smiled, though he felt anything but humorous. "It's quite all right, Mrs. Fox. I've become accustomed to Esme's cool shifts in mood."

"You must call me Maud. 'Mrs. Fox' sounds so ancient and attached. Neither which aptly describe me, wouldn't you agree?"

"My dear Maud, there are no words that can truly describe you."

She tittered again as if he'd given her the greatest compliment, although he had done nothing of the sort except to increase the steam shooting from Esme's ears. Maud noticed and rolled her eyes.

"How and why you plan to win this one back is beyond me. She has her own spot of troubles at the moment, and she'll do nothing more than drag you down. I've always told her commitment isn't her strong suit, and wouldn't you know it, as soon as times get tough, here she comes with her tail tucked between her legs like always."

"Mimsy!" Esme's cheeks blazed red.

"Don't deny it, pet." Flicking off a used cigarette stub, Maud tucked a new fag into the holder. "Of course, I can't say I had no influence in that. Women not graced with a social position must learn to find their own way, but the difference between us is that she hides while I brazenly display it out in the open. A true thespian of the grand stage knows how to smile through it all." Flashing this infamous smile, she angled the unlit cigarette up at him.

Taking his cue, he struck a match and lit her cigarette.

"As for my plan, Maud, I prefer to keep those cards close to my chest. But there are a few things Esme and I need to settle between ourselves. How that goes will instruct which hand I play next." After blowing out the fire licking its way toward his fingers, he dropped the spent match in the ashtray, then turned his attention to the true purpose at hand.

"Is there somewhere we might speak in private?"

Esme stormed toward the door, flung it open, and marched out without a word. He took it as indication for him to follow.

"Do come back, Jasper!" Maud called through a cloud of smoke. "We have so much to talk about."

Halfway down the hall, Esme opened an unmarked door, entered, then kicked the door shut after Jasper had followed her in. She yanked on a cord, and a lightbulb flickered on overhead.

She squared off like a gladiator in the arena. A very cramped, dim arena with hundreds of costumes crammed onto racks hanging on each side of them.

"Drop the charisma act. How did you find me?"

He squared off right back. She may have had displeasure on her side, but he was outright narked.

"My job is hunting down elusive objects. Don't think you're anything special."

"You should've taken the hint back in France that I didn't want to see you again."

He shoved aside a feather boa dangling in his face. "Don't flatter yourself, sweetheart. I'm not here for you. Now where is it?"

"As if I would tell you." A sequined sleeve fell over her shoulder. She smacked it away.

He stepped forward. She stepped back.

"I know about Pirazzo. I know you came here because you have nowhere else to run. I know that by crossing the countess and not giving her the tiara—which clearly you have no intention of doing, otherwise you wouldn't be here—she wants you removed for good." He took another step, crowding her against a petticoat wall. She wasn't fleeing until he got what he came for. "Hard to tell anyone anything when you're dead."

A series of emotions flashed across her face, like one of those nickelodeons where the silver images moved so quickly the watcher marveled at the speed. But watch he did. Disbelief, panic, fear, confusion, resolution, and finally his personal favorite, haughtiness. Her prized armor.

A warrioress ready for battle with her crimson smirk and crinoline frothing all around her.

"What a dreary future you've painted. Here's something you should know about me, *sweetheart*. I always find a way out of a predicament. This is no different."

"You have a hit man after you." Reaching out, he lifted the string of pearls away from her throat. A thin red line circled her neck. "From the looks of it, I'd say he was nearly successful."

She jerked away, repositioning the pearls to cover the faint scar. "Nothing I couldn't handle."

So sure of herself. Outwardly at least. A defensive tactic he knew intimately, one that served to distract from the soft underbelly they were both so desperate to hide.

"One day there will be something you can't handle."

"Is that concern peeking through? Here I thought you were only interested in the Valkyrie and how well its sale is going to line your pockets."

His own pockets, ha! The Valkyrie meant little to him beyond earning a respectable name and place among his blood family, but such a confession would invite a swift kick to his own soft underbelly. She'd kicked him down in France, a pain he'd managed with the copious help of whisky, and he wasn't about to set himself up for a second go-round with her. This time he knew to stay well out of kicking range.

"You're right. My only interest is the Valkyrie, and it will be much easier to find if you're alive to give it to me."

Tilting her head, she blinked those thick black eyelashes at him. "You're a clever man. I assume you can sort out my response to that."

"I will have it, Esme. If you think to run, I have people watching every door of this theater. You won't get far." Newsboys and prostitutes made the best lookouts as long as you greased their palms, and Jasper was a considerate tipper. "Why did you decide not to give the tiara to the countess?"

"She planned to kill me all along. Imminent death seemed as good a reason as any for a double cross."

"What sort of plan do you think will get you out of this double-crossing mess? Especially now that your name is mud."

"That is my own business."

"Ah, so you have no plan. I thought as much. You're more of a figure-it-out-on-the-run kind of girl."

The coquettish tilt of her head straightened with a snap. "Why don't you mind your own bloody business for once?"

"That is precisely what I am trying to do, but you keep getting in the way." He hissed through clenched teeth. "Being done with the Valkyrie cannot come soon enough for me because we can finally wash our hands of each other. The only thing I'll ever need from you is a signature on the divorce papers."

She jabbed him in the chest with her finger. "Oh no you won't because I'll sign them first. In fact, finding a solicitor is the first item on my to-do list tomorrow."

"I'll have my pen ready." Wheeling on his heel, he yanked open the door and stalked out of the closet.

"See that you do!"

He slammed the door shut behind him.

"BLACKHEATHE-492, PLEASE." JASPER ADJUSTED THE telephone's earpiece as the operator made the connection all the way to Surrey. The newfangled contraptions for communicating had yet to gain in popularity in the East End, but he'd managed to find a hotel with one only a block from The Scarlet Crown. It wasn't the nicest or cleanest of accommodations, considering its clientele were late-night theater folks and sailors on leave, but everyone minded their own business and that was good enough for him.

Laughter and clinking glasses echoed from the hotel's dining room across the hall. He pulled the privacy screen tighter around him to cut off the noise, but all it managed to do was amplify another problem. Without the scent of lemon cleaner, beer, and cigarette smoke, the orange-blossom perfume wafted freely to antagonize him. It had nearly overwhelmed his senses in that costume closet an hour before, teasing him, digging into his brain, undermining his nerve. Much like the woman who wore it.

Yanking the handkerchief from his tuxedo pocket, he blew his nose to dislodge the lingering scent. He needed a clear mind for this conversation.

The line crackled with static. A voice stumped through. "Linton Hall." Corby.

"I need to speak with the duke. It's urgent."

"I am afraid His Grace is unavailable at this time—"

"This is Jasper Truitt."

A miffed pause. "One moment please." More static.

Tired, agitated, and not looking forward to the conversation to come, Jasper wished he'd taken time for a pint first, if only to shave off the edge of at least one of his competing problems. He unbuttoned his top shirt button and tugged at his bow tie. Exhaustion clung to his bones—miles and miles of train travel and a boat ride did that to a man—but rest would not be easily gained. Not until that cursed tiara was handed over. After that, he planned to book a luxury hotel room somewhere warm, Rio or Valencia, and not leave his room for a month except to refill the ice bucket.

The line crackled. "Where is it? I'm in the middle of arranging the last details for my birthday celebration in three days and I don't have time for more of your excuses." Duke's voice barreled into his ear.

"Good evening," Jasper said dryly. "I'm quite well, thank you for inquiring, as long as you don't take into account being thwarted at every turn, outfoxed by a chicken, and sidestepping an Italian hit man."

"What is this about a chicken?" Leave it to Duke to skip over the danger and focus on the absurd. "Never mind. Where is it?"

"I don't have it."

"What do you mean you don't have it? You've had two months. More than enough time to track down a silly crown and return it to Surrey."

Jasper ground his teeth. If it was so silly, why bother at all? "There have been unexpected complications."

"Yes, your man Mond has been fobbing me off with excuses."

"Mond has not been fobbing you off." Well, he sort of was at Jasper's request. "The tiara is quite the collector's item, and you're not the only one in want of it."

"Who else?" Duke snapped. Patience was low on his list of key virtues.

"Half the treasure collectors in Europe. Greedy aristocrats." Jasper steeled himself. "My ex-wife."

"Ex-wife?" The squawk trumpeted in Jasper's ear. "You've never mentioned matrimonial entanglements before. I thought I taught you better than to allow yourself to become embroiled in affairs of the heart. A wife is only for the legitimacy of heirs. Otherwise, keep mistresses. They're more expensive but infinitely more entertaining."

"What can I say? Esme Fox caught me when my defenses were lowered." He didn't want to bring her up, but Esme had a way of forcing herself in against his better judgment. "Turns out she's a jewel thief as well and after the Valkyrie. She led me on a wild-goose chase all over Europe, then double-crossed me and snuck off with it." Orange blossoms tickled his nose. "I've tracked her to The Scarlet Crown theater in London."

"Snuck off, did she? Am I to understand that your defenses were lowered again at the time?"

Silky black hair against his pillow. Her fingers tangled with his. Her warm breath across his neck.

"I'd rather not discuss that." Jasper snorted into his handkerchief.

"My boy, let me tell you something about— What is all that honking racket? Are you ill?"

"In a manner of speaking." He tucked away his handkerchief. "Please continue."

"One thing about women. Not a one can be trusted." A pause stretched.

Jasper waited. "Is that all?"

"Learn from my experience, boy. When I was your age I met a beautiful Italian girl, an opera singer. Rossalina was the most alive, divine thing I had ever seen. All the men clamored for her, but it was me she chose. For her debut as lead soprano, I had a one-of-a-kind piece crafted from the Roxburgh jewels to symbolize her titular role in *Die Walküre*. She was glorious with it shining atop her red hair, but all good things must come to an end. When I told her I was taking a bride and needed the tiara returned, it holding family jewels and all, she went quite mad."

Rossalina Accardi. The very countess Esme was employed by, and consequently, the same one trying to bump her off. He'd had an inkling all along that she was Duke's infamous mistress from long ago, and it turned out his instincts were correct.

Putting aside that wrinkle, he focused on the other pressing issue. The tiara wasn't just some long-lost pretty trinket. It was part of Duke's legacy. And legacy was about the only thing the old man took seriously.

"So you want the Valkyrie not because of sentimental value over your deceased wife but because it has the Roxburgh jewels?"

"Of course," Duke said. "Its value is beyond monetary. I've lavished enough money on mistresses over the years. Furs, pearls, necklaces, furnished apartments. Never meant a thing, but this crown is the only one I want returned. That I *need* returned."

"Why was a second one made?"

A disgruntled intake of breath.

Jasper forced his voice to remain calm. He didn't like going into a job and being made to look the fool when he could have been forewarned.

"Duke? Why was a fake made of the Valkyrie if it was intended to be one-of-a-kind?"

"Blame my wife for that." A few inappropriate words may have been muttered but the miles muffled them. "It was Clarice's twenty-seventh birthday. I threw a large party for her here at Linton Hall, but instead of the entertainment I hired, my operatic ex-mistress showed up. Caused quite the scene for which my wife never forgave me, so she had a jeweler create a replica tiara and sold the real one to spite me.

"She had the gall to look me in the eye and say I would never see the Roxburgh jewels again, and each time she wore the Valkyrie I would know it was fake just like our marriage. I spent years passing off the replica as the real one, all the while searching for it. After Clarice died, I sold the fake. It wasn't worth much, but there were a few real stones mixed in with the glass ones, and they got me by for a time."

Jasper didn't bother controlling the sharpness in his voice. "That information might have been useful to me two months ago."

"You hardly needed the sordid details of the past to track down an item." There wasn't an ounce of regret or apology in the old man's rambling. He enjoyed holding all the strings while those tied to the ends of the strings were left to clack about to his tune. "I have used every tool, curator, and thief at my disposal, but all have come up empty-handed. Until two months ago when I got wind that the jeweler Clarice hired to create the fake died and the real tiara had slipped back into existence along with several other items of value he'd been hoarding. That was when I pulled you out of jail and sent you on the trail."

"A last-ditch effort, I seemed to be."

"Though no different from the ones before you. Failures. And you, allowing yourself to become entangled with some woman who swiped it out from under your nose."

"I hardly think you're one to judge on that account."

"Yes, well, perhaps we have more in common than originally conceded, but the point of the matter is that you were to succeed where the others failed. The Phantom, they call you. The best in the game. If you truly were the best, you wouldn't be scrambling all over the Continent and phoning me with excuses." Duke scoffed. "I've a mind to let the police throw you back in that cell."

Temper rising, Jasper scoffed right back. "If I'm back in that cell, then good luck getting your diamonds. Or better yet. Go find new ones and forget about that cursed Valkyrie."

"The Roxburgh diamonds cannot simply be replaced. Not even if I had a mind to, which I do not."

"Why, Duke. I didn't take you for the sentimental kind. Especially over a pair of cold rocks."

"Those cold rocks are the only hope of saving this family's fortune." Each word was chopped with precision. Jasper imagined the old man's jaw tight with each one spoken because his own, regrettably, did the same thing when he was on the edge of blowing a gasket.

"The war cost us everything, like all the noble families. At first I wanted them returned as a matter of family honor, but now they're crucial to keeping us afloat. It would bring in a handsome fortune on the auction block, well enough to keep the Loxhill title in comfort for some time."

Tied to Duke's strings indeed. Jasper was tired of clacking about to his tune. He'd thought if he went along, his grandfather might finally recognize his worth, but Duke recognized only accomplishment. And Jasper had not lived up to his mark. How could he have been so desperate to believe Duke might actually have welcomed him into the family proper if he'd succeeded in retrieving the Valkyrie? More fool him.

"You say 'this family' and 'us' as if your fortunes are in any way tied to mine."

"You're my blood. Retrieving the Roxburgh jewels should mean something to you."

"Why? I'm not a Roxburgh. You've made that very clear over the years."

"Here I thought might be the opportunity to prove yourself more than a common by-blow."

There it was. Truth straight to the gut. "Once a bastard, always a bastard. Something else we have in common."

"Now you listen to me, that tiara—"

"What was that?" Jasper blew into the mouthpiece. "I'm sorry. I can't hear you. There must be something wrong with the connection." He hung up.

Flinging back the privacy screen, he crossed the hall into the dining room and sidled up to the bar. He didn't know how many pints awaited him before the night was out, nor did he know how he was going to find the Valkyrie, and Esme . . . Well, he'd be an even greater fool to claim he knew anything about her. But one thing was certain.

He was not giving the Valkyrie to Duke.

19

LONDON WAS AWAKE IN ALL its shades of gray and blue with tints of light peeking over the rooftops. Sitting on the alley curb behind the theater, Esme sipped her tea and smiled. She'd missed this. Not the grime or cloudy skies but the familiarity it brought.

Somehow she could never forget the impressions of childhood, good or bad. As much as she hated the soggy newspapers clogging up the gutters and the smells of ship smokestacks and fish drifting up from the Thames, they were ingrained in her. Without this, she never would have pushed herself to be more, so she was grateful for the hardships and treasured the quiet mornings like this before the theater world came alive.

Then again, all theater mornings were quiet since no one rose before noon thanks to late-night performances.

As for herself, she'd tossed and turned all night. The scent of cedarwood cologne had kept her awake. They were alone together for barely a few minutes in the costume closet, yet Jasper had managed to infuse her with his scent until it choked out all possibility of restful dreams. Drat the man. He probably did it on purpose, if such a thing was possible. She wouldn't put anything past him when it came to getting under her skin. Especially after her repeated betrayal.

She glanced down at their wedding photograph resting innocently in her lap. A bit more creased and curled at the corners, but the fresh faces staring back at her were as happy as they always were. Her melancholy moods had a habit of dragging out the photo to torment her.

However, in this case she deserved the vexation.

She'd tried to justify her actions and outrun their consequences, but there was the truth punching against her heart. She'd wronged him and for one of the few times in her life, she regretted thinking only of herself. It was a new feeling, but one that hinted at a possible goodness lurking within her all along.

How Jasper would laugh at that diagnosis! That thought alone made the corner of her mouth tick up.

The feeling was fleeting. Reminiscent of their time together in France. His blasé coolness about the matter when he'd arrived at the theater—looking too handsome for his own good in that tuxedo jacket with his hair combed devilishly to the side—had riled her to no end. So much so that her usual quips refused to come to her rescue, forcing her into a situation she disliked more than anything. One of vulnerability.

Then again, she wasn't the only one.

Jasper's words had been aloof as he carelessly tossed them out, but she saw the pain stuttering behind them, for it was precisely the armor she donned when she was too close to breaking.

"Find one beautiful, good thing and I break it before it breaks me." She traced a delicate fingernail around Jasper's sepia face. "Typical."

"What's typical?"

Esme jumped as Mimsy came up behind her. Tea sloshed onto her knee. She quickly swiped it off and tucked the photograph back into her garter. Safe from curious eyes.

"Typical how some things never change."

"Stick around the theater and that's true enough. The more things change, the more they stay the same." Mimsy raised a gloved hand to her powdered and colored face. "Except for the amount of face paint I require. That increases daily."

Esme took in the smart cranberry day dress with cream trim, stylish cloche hat, and figure that was the envy of women half her age. The smoke and mirrors of theater life was a grand education in how to present one's best image, and Mimsy had perfected the art.

"You don't look a day past chorus girl."

"Oh, how you flatter."

"I learned from the best."

"Speaking of flattering, where is that charming husband of yours?" Mimsy's dreamy gaze drifted upward to Esme's third-story window.

Esme's heart gave an involuntary double thump. "Not there."

"Whyever not? If I had a man like that, I'd lock him in and never let him out." Mimsy dragged over an empty crate and dropped it next to Esme, then sat.

"He has a knack for wriggling loose."

"Then you're not keeping a tight enough hold on him."

"Who says I want a hold on him?" The words soured on Esme's tongue. Odd. They once tasted of conviction and relief. Something was off with the tea.

"You married him, didn't you? Not to mention that photo you hurriedly stuffed away."

Esme glared into her cup, searching for the offender who was twisting her insides into some unrecognizable state of flustered. A common state when Jasper was involved.

"The two have nothing to do with each other."

"Then whyever did you marry him?"

The woman was annoyingly persistent. Forcing Esme to confess feelings she'd done her best to bury. Run away from or bury, her most refined instincts when she got caught in a situation over her head. Marrying Jasper was the epitome of in-over-her-head, so she had run and quickly buried all the might-have-beens between them. Only now they were wriggling loose.

Esme did her best to wrangle them before things got out of her control. "I was khaki mad, like most other women when the army came sauntering through. Simply could not resist all that masculine charm neatly bundled up in a gleaming uniform."

"I understand the temptation. I've had a number of gleaming uniforms step through my theater doors. None tempted me enough to tie myself down with apron strings."

That caught Esme's attention. The woman she knew only as a free bird contemplating marriage was as absurd a concept as that of King George skipping around Piccadilly in naught but his skivvies.

"Would you have accepted if they had offered a ring?"

A girlish smile flitted across Mimsy's powdered face. "Years ago maybe, but my youthful idealism wanted a duke or a lord, and they weren't interested in marriage. At least not to me. Actresses were little more than acceptable mistresses. They already had their fine ladies to call wife while I was little more than a distraction. A jolly good distraction, but never suitable for respectability. So I waited and waited for my prince charming to come along and sweep me off to his castle and leave all this behind." She gestured to the dank gloominess around them.

"But I was never truly loved by any hand that touched me. The years passed and I realized my prince was never coming, so I set out to become ruler of my own kingdom. And now here I am, a queen with her own Scarlet Crown."

"What if the prince were to come along now?"

"He'd find out he was too late. The boredom of hearth and home isn't for me. Something I've tried instilling in you since before you could talk. Men promise the moon, kisses, and love, but all they really want is someone to wash their socks. Where's the excitement in that?"

Esme dropped her gaze to her left hand where a small gold band once briefly rested. Her thoughts filled with the man who had put it there.

"What if there was a man who lived for the same excitement as you?"

"Show me the man and I'll show you a smooth liar."

"Jasper is the one man who I believe could lasso the moon if he wished. He's rather obnoxious about his capabilities." It was devilishly attractive.

"Then why are you so eager to toss him aside?"

Attention snapping up, Esme raised incredulous eyebrows. "It's what you taught me, remember? Best to exit the stage before the trapdoor swings open under you and all that. No one wishes to be left lying broken in the sawdust."

"And has he left you broken?"

"I thought about breaking but couldn't quite get the pieces apart."

"Stubborn."

Esme gave an unladylike snort. "Pardon me, but I've heard you refer to that as self-preservation."

Mimsy primly crossed her ankles. A move she used onstage to indicate righteous authority. "It is when the man doesn't want you. The man I met last night looked to be very much in love with you."

"Your eyes are going bad because that man wanted—*wants*—to throttle me."

"More to my point. Why is he so angry?"

"Because I made him believe things were possible."

"Do *you* believe they're possible?"

The question prickled under Esme's skin, scratching against her so-called refined instincts and revealing furrows of fear. Fear that she might actually care for him. Fear that they could be something great together, but if she allowed herself to care, it gave him power. Power to hurt her, to break her heart, to leave her. She refused to live in that kind of helplessness.

"Would it be so terrible if we fell in love?" Jasper's words whispered in her ear, racing a thrill through her heart. For the first time, the mention of love didn't send her into a cold sweat.

"I want to," she said softly.

"Then believe."

"This from the woman who told me not to be led around by my heart. Who told me to always be the first to leave because commitment is a death sentence."

Mimsy flapped her hand. "I say a lot of things, but I've also seen a lot of things. I know the difference between a man in lust and a man who's had his heart bruised. And you, my girl, have ground his beneath the heel of your expensive shoes—which you must let me borrow sometime. They are quite divine." She pursed her dark red lips and looked at Esme with rare clarity. "I see yours is smarting too."

"There are too many things . . . We can't . . . I've betrayed him too many times."

"If that were true, he wouldn't have chased you down."

"He made it very clear he's not chasing *me*. There's something else . . . unfinished business between us. Once it's settled, we're going our separate ways."

"Far be it from me to offer reasonable advice on relationships, but I will tell you that life is too short for regrets."

A question burned in Esme's mind. One she'd been too afraid to ever ask. It was too personal, and she and Mimsy were never personal, but she couldn't allow the moment to pass. It might never come again.

"Do you ever regret my father?"

Mimsy's thickly caked lashes fluttered in surprise. "Your father . . . ah yes. Stan Littlespick, or Littlesbrick, something like that. A stevedore from Wapping. Great big hands, sky-blue eyes, and coal grime behind his ears."

"So not an aristocrat."

Mimsy laughed. "Furthest thing from it, but we had a few good laughs and a few months later, you came along. He was long gone by then. I still think of him from time to time, but the image has gone all fuzzy." Her mouth quirked in a dreamy way before softening as she looked to Esme. Quickly squashing that sentiment, she pulled her cigarette case and lighter from her purse and lit a fag. "You on the other hand, have managed to stick it out."

"A delight for you, I'm sure. A snot-nosed kid is what every aspiring actress craves hanging onto her costumed train."

"You were snot-nosed a great deal of the time, but we made it, you and me. We're fighters, Esme." Grinning, Mimsy tapped her ashes onto the concrete curb. "We're never down for long. And now look at us, like sisters we are."

An awareness swept over Esme that went far beyond distinctive, familiar bonds. It was an understanding of seeing someone familiar in a new light, as if a side of them that had been hidden in shade had finally been uncovered. A side she was proud to understand as a piece of herself.

"Fighters, indeed."

Never one to dwell too long on a scene, Mimsy ended the moment by standing and shoving the crate back against the theater wall.

"I have the fight of the century on my hands. Tad Barker, the baritone, is coming to ask me for a raise later today, and negotiations won't be pretty, so I need a new hat to suffer through it. You're going shopping with me before the shops are overrun with housewives. Come on."

With one last long puff, she tossed her cigarette into a puddle between the uneven cobblestones and marched back toward the door.

"Housewives," Esme said, standing and following her inside and up the stairs to their private rooms. "You mean those respectable women who wouldn't be caught dead on the same footpath let alone the same shop as actresses."

"Those old biddies cluck away, but it's my theater their husbands come to because they're bored stiff at home."

Esme breezed into her room and opened the wardrobe where a handful of new dresses hung. After escaping France with barely more than the clothes on her back, several shopping trips had been required to replace what she'd lost.

"I wonder how they feel knowing it's their husbands' money going to pay for all your new chapeaus."

"I don't care how they feel, and I adore my new hats." Mimsy studied the pink hat atop her head in the mirror with a satisfied smirk. It was a confection of bows and ribbons she'd purchased the previous week for when the health inspector came for his yearly investigation. All the ruffles managed to distract him from writing up violations, or so Mimsy claimed.

Esme chose a forest-green number with drop waist and pleated skirt and a woven picture hat that perfectly framed her face. She crossed the room to where her purse lay on the costume trunk and noticed the lock had been removed.

Her heart gave a little jump. She flipped open the lid. The old costumes inside had been shifted. Her heart gave a double jump.

"Has anyone been in here?" Kneeling, she dug through the jumbled clothes to the bottom and pressed the lever for the hidden compartment.

Empty.

Her heart dropped through the floor.

"Hmm?" Mimsy turned her chin for a better angle in the mirror. "Oh, that was me. I was looking for Cleopatra's wig and remembered putting it in one of these old costume trunks. Can't find a thing in all the mess, but then I remembered that one has a false bottom. No wig but I did find the most delightful tiara. Like a pair of wings. I've never seen it in one of our productions before, but maybe one of the costume designers stashed it there."

Horrifying spots danced in front of Esme's eyes as she ran her fingers over the bare wooden bottom in disbelief.

The Valkyrie was gone.

"Where is it?"

"What?"

Esme slammed the lid shut. "Mimsy! Where is it?"

"I took it to Stockton's yesterday. The stones on the tiara didn't look like our paste ones so I asked for his assessment."

"The tiara is mine and you took it to a pawnbroker without consulting me?"

Mimsy frowned in the mirror. "Really, darling, quit shouting. I didn't realize it was yours, though honestly you should thank me for having an estimate done. The thing wasn't worth a brass farthing."

"Stockton told you that?"

"He sent a note round yesterday afternoon saying not to bother coming back for it. Not worth my time. I might though. Could be a nice addition for one of our King Arthur shows." After tucking away a wayward strand of black hair, Mimsy spun to face her.

"What's wrong with you? You've gone all peaky."

Esme shot out the door and barreled down the stairs. Not worth a brass farthing. Stockton knew his onions, so why claim the tiara was worthless as paste?

A terrifying truth lodged in her gut. Stockton would have known immediately the Valkyrie's value. That slippery eel also would have known which buyers' noses to waggle it under for a profit.

Her stomach churned with sickness as she raced out of The Scarlet Crown, Mimsy's shouts falling behind her, and hailed a taxi.

"201 Gower's Walk, please," she said to the driver, climbing in and slamming the door. "And hurry."

An excruciating twenty minutes later, the taxi screeched to a stop near a worn brick building sagging against its neighbors. "Stockton's Pawnbroker" was painted in faded black above the door. Esme paid the driver and hopped out, then marched straight into the store.

The bell tinkled violently as she swung open the door. It was a cramped, musty space with a glass counter at the back and the walls lined with shelves stuffed to the gills with odd junk. Castoffs from the desperate in need of a quick coin.

A younger man with a pock-marked face slipped out from behind the curtain separating the front room from the back. "Need help, lady?"

"I'm looking for Mr. Stockton."

"He's busy in the back." He jerked a professional thumb over his shoulder. "Got a few of granny's pearls to pawn off?"

"Not today. An item was brought in by mistake yesterday. I want it returned."

His ratlike face lit with interest. "Is that so? Well, we don't give away our business for free."

Her fingers strained against her purse handle. Calm and cool, that was how she would remain no matter how sorely she was tempted to behave otherwise.

"I'm certain once Mr. Stockton learns of my unique situation, he will gladly rectify the oversight for me."

"I'm good at rectifying things for ladies. Just say the word and I'm at your service." He leaned a scrawny elbow on the counter and looked her up and down like prized beef.

Calm and cool were overrated. "Say another word like that and the only service you'll be rendered is a sock in the jaw."

Miffed, the boy straightened. "Look, lady. Mr. Stockton don't like to be disturbed—"

"I do not care for his whims. I demand to speak to him at once."

The curtain flapped open. A lanky man with thinning white hair and glasses thick as jam jars stepped out.

"Get in the back, boy. That's no way to speak to a lady." Curling his lip at Esme, the boy scrambled out of sight. Mr. Stockton locked his attention on her. Sharp brown eyes peered out through the glass lenses. "Apologies. After the war customer service has become appalling."

"Quite."

Adjusting his glasses, Stockton, too, had the gall to give her the once-over. His at least was less perverse than the boy's.

"Well, well. Esme Fox. It's been some time since you've graced my shop. Last time I believe you were here with a pocket watch and silver-capped cane."

Memories of her petty thievery still touched a sore spot deep inside her. She shook it off, not allowing her stare to drop from his inquisitive one. "I've been out of the country."

"Trying foreign pockets now?"

"They're a bit fuller than British ones."

"An odd coincidence you showing up today when I had the pleasure of seeing your mother only yesterday." He rubbed at a smudge on the counter with his jacket cuff. The smudge merely spread.

"Yes, she told me. For an erroneous transaction." She tapped her toe with impatience.

"Erroneous? No, my shop prides itself on honorable deals."

"We both know that's a lie. Honor has very little to do with turning a tidy profit, otherwise you wouldn't have told Maud that tiara was a fake. You should know better than anyone it's the real deal."

"What will you give me for it?" His eyes gleamed behind the jam jars.

He could gleam all day. She wasn't giving an inch. She'd worked too hard to be thwarted now. What her plans were for the Valkyrie she had yet to decide, but they certainly didn't involve being misplaced into the grubby hands of a pawnbroker.

"Nothing. It was taken without my consent; therefore, the transaction is null."

"That is not how this works, Miss Fox."

"Listen here, you slimy eel—"

The front door pushed open, tinkling the bell. Esme turned and readied to tell the newcomer to buzz off for his ill-timed entrance. Until she saw it was the last person on earth she needed to come calling at that heated moment.

She leveled an icy glare at Jasper. "Of course you pick this moment to waltz in."

"I told you. My spies are everywhere, and if you think I'm about to let you jump into a taxi and speed off without raising my curiosity, then you have not been paying attention to my determination." He strode right up to her.

She backed up, bumping against the counter as his toes nearly touched hers.

"How many times are we going to act out this scene?"

"As many times as it takes," he said.

"Stubborn."

"Reckless."

He smelled positively delicious. If they weren't under a time constraint, she might devote a moment longer to the way his lips—

"If this is a lovers' discussion," Stockton rudely interrupted, "take it outside. You'll scare away all the customers."

Esme rounded on him. This interview was getting wildly out of hand. She had to keep her head on straight. "Your usual customers are too busy sleeping off last night's pints."

Jasper's expression darkened as he glanced around the shop. "Why are you at a pawnbroker?" His mouth flattened like the edge of a sword. "Where is it?"

She nudged away from him. "Don't stand there accusing me."

"There's no one else to accuse," Jasper said.

"If you must know, none of this was my doing, but it has become a situation that I am working to correct."

"Then allow me to assist you." He pinned his stare on Stockton. "I presume you have the tiara and refuse to return it."

Stockton jutted out his wrinkled chin. "It's mine. A deal was made."

"By someone who did not have the authority or my permission," Esme corrected.

"If I needed permission for every object to cross my counter, my shop would have closed long ago."

"You old swindler!"

"As if your scruples have climbed so high out of the mud." Stockton sneered. "I remember your filthy face pressed against my window when you were no higher than my knee. Wanting all the shiny things you could never afford, so you pinched them instead. You and your mama strutting around giving yourself airs. Ha! Heifers dressed in silks."

Esme balled up her fist and reared back.

Jasper caught her intended punch in his hand.

"He's no more than a bag of bones," he said with irksome calmness. "You punch him and he'll likely crumple into dust, and then we'll be forced to comb through this filth hole in search of the item ourselves."

He dropped her hand, then leaned across the counter and grabbed the front of Stockton's smeared shirt, yanking him forward until they were nose to nose.

"You say one more word like that to the lady, and I promise a broken nose will be the least of your worries. Do we understand each other?"

Stockton's mouth flopped open like a fish's.

Jasper shook him until the old man's head wobbled back and forth. "Well?"

"Y-yes."

"Good." Jasper released his grip. "Where is the tiara? I won't ask again."

The door crashed open, sending the bell flapping wildly.

"Oh for the love of applesauce and crackers—" Esme whirled around to tell off the latest intruder, but six police officers stormed in.

A bully sergeant with a gleaming badge elbowed his way to the front of the group, a billy club swinging in his hand.

"Esme Fox, you are under arrest for the theft of the Roxburgh diamonds."

20

JASPER JUMPED TO BLOCK THE police officers, but they shoved past him and grabbed Esme, wrenching her arms behind her back. She cried out in pain.

"What is going on here?" He reached for her, but they wrestled her away. "By what authority do you take this woman into custody?"

A cocksure grin widened across the sergeant's face. His billy club swung around in lazy circles. "She's a known thief who's been running us in circles for years. A tip-off finally came through, and she'll be going away for a long time."

"I've never even heard of these Roxburgh diamonds," Esme protested. "If you're looking for a thief, arrest him!" She pointed and glared at Stockton. "He's been conning people for years."

"So long, lady light fingers," Stockton crowed from his safe place behind the counter. "And don't worry. I've taken good care of your merchandise. Its owner is delighted to have it returned."

The police hustled Esme out of the shop despite her shouts of outrage.

Jasper charged after her. Two black autos waited on the street. The sergeant opened the back door of the second auto and waved at his men to put Esme inside.

"Where are you taking her?" Jasper demanded.

"To the precinct where she'll be charged with a laundry list of items stolen." The sergeant puffed out his chest as if he'd just nabbed Jack the Ripper himself. "I might even get myself a promotion off this one. Yes, sir. The prosecution'll throw the book at her."

Esme's panicked eyes latched onto Jasper. "Jasper?"

"Esme! Don't say anything until I can get you a solicitor."

"Jasper? Jasper Truitt? Eh, you're the man I should be thanking for this roundup," the sergeant continued as he rocked on his heels. "Without the tip we might never have caught this one. Slippery, she is."

Jasper could have slugged him in his fat mouth. But the anger at being outed was nothing compared to the gut-wrenching look of betrayal morphing across Esme's face.

"*You* did this to me?"

"No!" Her strangled voice nearly broke him. "Esme, I swear I had nothing to do with this."

The officers shoved her in the auto and slammed the door shut. She collapsed against the back seat like a limp fish, the backbone ripped out of her. A ripping she blamed him for.

"Good job, Romeo." The sergeant slapped him on the back and ambled toward the first auto.

The engines revved and off they zoomed. Everything in him propelled him down the street, chasing their bumpers, but his feet pivoted back to the shop.

He needed to hit something. Hard.

Inside the shop, he leapt over the counter and shoved Stockton up against the wall.

"Who did you sell the tiara to?"

"Its owner." The old man didn't even wheeze. Probably not his first time being knocked against a wall.

"There's only one owner, and I know for a fact he doesn't have it."

"The Valkyrie's whereabouts no longer concern you, signor." The back curtain parted. Out came a pistol and a black-gloved hand, followed by a man in a black suit with oily hair.

"Pirazzo." Jasper cursed and backed away from the gun pointed at his chest. "I might have known your harpy mistress had you on the trail. Tell me. How did you escape France? Last I heard you were found unconscious by the gendarme with a goose egg on your forehead and taken into custody."

"Countess Accardi has her connections."

"Do her connections reach all the way to a swindler's shop in Whitechapel?" Jasper's glare cut to Stockton.

The old man shrugged and patted down the creases Jasper's fists had formed in his shirtfront.

"She toured London many years ago. We struck up a correspondence for collecting the unattainable. Her man here traveled all night to get here after I wired her yesterday. Of all the shops"—he cackled—"her prized possession dropped into mine."

"You son of a—"

"It is time for you to leave, signor." Pirazzo waved his gun at the door.

"This isn't over." Jasper backed toward the exit.

"*Sì.* And you have lost," Pirazzo said. "Do not let me see your face again. Or Miss Fox's. It will not end well for you."

Jasper trembled with rage as he stepped out on the street. Rage at being caught out, exposed, and falsely accused. Mostly he raged against himself. If the Valkyrie was to be his downfall, he would gladly take the consequences of his actions. Esme had her own consequences to deal with, but she didn't deserve his.

They'd done a great many underhanded things to each other. That was the game of their profession, but there was an undercurrent of honor among thieves, and she had leveled him flat with the perception of him violating that code.

No, not just a code. That was too impersonal.

The way she'd looked at him struck to the core of what existed between them . . . stabbing it apart like a white-hot knife that speared straight into his gut.

He couldn't let them end that way.

THE PRECINCT IN WESTMINSTER WAS fine enough as far as jails went, and Jasper had seen his fair share. Still, stepping inside was enough to make his blood run cold, no matter which side of the bars he stood on.

He'd taken a taxi straight from Stockton's only to learn from the Whitechapel police station that Esme had been taken to the station in Westminster. Ordinarily it could take up to an hour to cross town, but he'd paid the taxi driver double and arrived in half the time, only to be shown to the waiting room to sit for two hours while they processed her.

Processed. Like a common criminal.

A female guard in a starched uniform and a severe bun walked into the room. "Mr. Truitt. You can see the prisoner now."

She led Jasper down a cement-block corridor to a room with a single, high window and a small table with a chair on each side of it. A door with bars stood on the opposite wall. The guard unlocked the door and swung it open.

"Get in here," she barked.

Chains rattled as Esme shuffled into view. She'd been stripped of her fine dress and shoes and shoved into a gray sackcloth with oversize brown brogues fit for a granny's feet and shackles around her wrists.

"Five minutes," the guard grunted, then slammed the door shut and stood glaring at them from the corner. Clearly privacy was not to be had.

Silence ticked.

Jasper grasped at the first words that came to mind. "One thing's for certain. You make that drab uniform fashionable."

Esme's expression remained deadpan. "Hello, traitor. I'm surprised to see you here. Thought you'd be out celebrating a victory. That is what you do, isn't it, when you reel in and hand over one of your own?"

"I swear to you I had nothing to do with your arrest."

"Odd. That rotund sergeant gave the impression that you're quite chummy with them. Thieves aren't typically considered high class, but that was a low move even for you." She cocked her head to the side. Her black hair fell away to reveal that even her earrings had been confiscated.

"You and your Romeo charms. Boy, what a sap I was to fall for it."

"I have never used— Wait a tick. You found my charms worth falling for?"

"Don't play coy. That's my bit."

"Four minutes," barked the guard.

Esme's comment sparked a nagging need to know more, but Jasper pushed it aside. He was no better than an addict when it came to her. Swearing her off yet craving the next moment with her. If he couldn't uphold his own word to stay away from her, what kind of man was he?

"We'll come back to that charm point later—"

"Charm of a snake," Esme said with a huff.

"Believe me or don't, but it wasn't me who informed the police."

"Who then? Countess Accardi? She's never mentioned anything about Roxburgh diamonds."

Pieces clicked together. Pieces so glaringly obvious he felt the fool for not seeing the whole picture sooner.

"The countess has the tiara. Stockton tipped her off, but she wasn't the one who turned you in. It was Duke. He must have told the police you were trying to take the tiara from me, and they most likely confused the whole bit, thinking I gave the tip-off. Which I did not."

Integrity was not one of the old man's shining virtues, but neither was allowing credit to go to others for his own doings.

"Who is Duke?"

"The Duke of Loxhill. My grandfather."

She blinked slowly several times as if he'd announced he was flying to the moon.

"You're a lord?"

"No. I'm the illegitimate son of his illegitimate son, remember? I'll draw the family tree for you later."

"Why does your grandfather want me arrested? How does he even know about me?" Her eyes narrowed and she took a step toward him, chains rattling. "Jasper, how does this duke, your never-before-mentioned grandfather, know about me?"

Here it came. The shameful truth he was none too pleased to divulge, but a man in his predicament couldn't afford to scrimp now.

"Because he's the one who tasked me to retrieve the tiara and return it to the family. It should have been a simple job, only I was thwarted by a Valkyrie with gossamer wings who had designs on it herself." He gave her a pointed look she ignored. "Duke isn't known for his patience and has been breathing down my neck this entire time. Then last night . . ."

She crossed her arms, her face summoning the same challenging expression from their chat in the costume closet. "Last night what?"

If his confession from moments before was shameful, this was about to be downright despicably sordid. "I updated him on the turn of events and my being in London. One thing led to another, and I may have mentioned you, and a marriage, and you running out on me, and you being a competitive jewel thief."

"Oh no. You didn't." Esme clutched at her chains.

"Two minutes," the guard said.

Jasper backed up a step, putting the table between them lest Esme think to lasso her chains around his neck.

"We can have a row over all this later. I need you to listen. The countess is Duke's old mistress. He gave the tiara to her for her performance on the stage thirty years ago, but when it came time to marry a proper wife, he took the tiara back and gave it to his new duchess.

"Only, the duchess found out about his trysts and sold the tiara out of spite. Now you and I are here thirty years later caught in the middle of an old lovers' tug-of-war for diamonds."

"Your grandfather is the double-crosser? Oh, the irony." Esme turned toward the window. It was too high up to offer a view of any kind, but weak sunlight filtered in and rested atop her head.

"The countess considered it hers all this time. And now she has it just in time for her big return to the stage celebration where she plans to recreate her performance from Wagner's *Die Walküre*." She spun around. "If your grandfather is the double-crosser . . . Jasper, she's planning to kill him."

A chill crashed over him. "How do you know?"

"She told me the night I swiped the fake tiara. A violent ending worthy of a Valkyrie's kill, she claimed. If your grandsire is her intended target, what celebration is she planning all of this around?"

"Duke's birthday is the day after tomorrow. Fireworks, dancing, food. Music." Just when Jasper had decided to wash his hands clean of all this tiara business, Duke, and whatever announcement he kept threading Jasper along with—the whole tangle caught him by the ankles and yanked him back into the fray. Cutting off one's ill-reputed relative was one thing, but allowing them to swagger straight to their death was another.

"So her plan all along has been to crash his birthday party." Esme shook her head, tutting. "A real revenge stunt—showing up to her former lover's home wearing the jewels he's been searching for. Not that I feel sorry for your grandfather. You don't give a woman diamonds and then snatch them back."

"Duke has never been one to struggle over ethics."

The guard jangled the keys. "One minute."

"Then they make the perfect pair." Lines creased Esme's forehead. "But no one deserves what she's planning. You must warn Duke."

"I'll ring him straightaway. Though with a party looming he has the bad habit of leaving the telephone off the hook due to so many caterers and well-wishers calling." Which would leave Jasper no choice but to travel to Linton Hall in person. The very thought set his gut to roiling, but this wasn't the time for personal feelings to hold sway.

"When you speak to him, be sure to tell him how much I appreciate my new accommodations."

"I'll get you out. I promise."

"Time!" The guard jammed the key into the barred door and swung it open.

"Why bother?" Esme flicked him a sad smile. "This could be a fun party story when you tell everyone how your ex-wife got locked away as a jailbird. I'm sure many men wish their wives were so easily disposed of."

"Time to go," the guard growled as she reached for Esme's arm.

"No, wait!" Jasper pulled out his wallet and grabbed a tenner, then shoved it in the guard's scabby hand. "Two minutes more. Please."

The guard frowned, then pocketed the money. "Two minutes." She waited outside the cell, tapping her baton against the wall as a warning against the time ticking away.

"This isn't what I wanted for us," he rushed out. If he didn't say it now, he would never summon the guts again. "We started out with so much promise. How did we end up here?"

Esme slowly shook her head. "We started out with a dream of champagne. In the morning the bubbles were all dried up."

"You didn't stick around long enough to discover if we could have faced it together."

"Because if I had, I wouldn't have been able to leave." She crossed her arms. A defensive move as if protecting herself. "You were entirely too tempting, and giving in to a man's arms means nothing more than entanglement."

"I've watched you waltz in other men's arms. You did mine once. Why not now?"

"Because you are the one man who could trap me." Wetness glossed her eyes.

"I don't want to trap you. I wanted to love you." His own insides felt watery.

"That's what all those men told my mother. 'Come on, honey. I'll take care of you.' 'My wife means nothing. You're the one I want.'" She wiped her lower lashes. "Or my personal favorite, 'You'll never want for anything ever again.'"

"I'm not those men."

"No. You're simply the kind to have me arrested."

"We can keep doing this same old dance, Esme. Pushing each other back and forth, and this is how we will end, with you and me bent."

"I'm already bent."

"So am I." It was like fighting a brick wall. One he kept throwing himself against. Bruised, scratched, and defeated. He felt it all.

"You, my darling, float through life like a scarf on a trace of perfume. Beautiful and captivating but directionless. Only now you've floated behind the bars of a jail, but you've been in a cage your whole life. One you built yourself, terrified of what it might mean to break free and take chances. Real chances with broken hearts and unseen tomorrows. Here . . ." He reached into his jacket's inner breast pocket and pulled out a folded handkerchief. He shook the fabric over the table and out fell a ring.

Her ring.

It bounced on the dull wooden surface, spiraling lazily until falling flat on its side. He'd intended on leaving it behind in that whisky glass, but Mond had fished it out. *"Worth more pawning off than leaving for a drunk to find later,"* he'd said, handing it back to Jasper.

"I've been carrying that around for four years. I don't want it anymore."

Tucking away the handkerchief, he turned and left.

21

Nighttime at the jail was a noisy affair. Cups clanging against metal bars, drunken singing, moans of despair, guards shouting to keep quiet. It wasn't unlike a night in the East End.

Esme could endure it all except for the tiny intruders crawling about her sackcloth of a dress. As soon as she'd satisfied one itch, another popped up on her opposite shoulder. Then hip. Then elbow. Turned out to be quite the losing battle.

Perhaps it was punishment for all the wicked deeds and lies she'd supported herself on over the years. If that was the case, the enormous bite on her arm driving her to distraction must have been courtesy of Jasper.

That man.

That man . . .

She dropped her chin to her pulled-up knees on the cot and sighed. That man had become the brightest color in her world, and she'd let him get away. He had offered every part of himself, and what did she do? Closed herself off and ran just as she always did. A reaction that had kept her safe and one step ahead of the game, but Jasper wasn't one for lagging behind.

He'd been right next to her, matching her step for step, and she had reveled in their equal footing. He was the only man to keep up with her. All along she'd been waiting for him to tie her down and shove her in a box, yet being with him was exhilarating in a way she had never experienced before. Swiping Empress Josephine's emerald brooch had been an incomparable high—until the night she and Jasper rode horseback through the French countryside with the Valkyrie tiara perched atop her head. She'd thrown her arms wide and laughed with all the freedom of a victorious warrior.

Free. That was how he made her feel.

And that scared her more than anything. So she ran.

Checking that her cellmate still snored on the cot in the opposite corner, Esme reached into her brassiere, scratched a bit, and pulled out her wedding ring. If the guards had seen it, they would have confiscated it like all her other belongings, but Esme's light fingers had stowed the ring before their greedy eyes caught sight of it.

Holding it up, she inspected it as the dim corridor light shone through the gold circle like a halo. Halos never suited her. Then again, they didn't suit Jasper either. Two sides of the same coin, they were. One flipping over the other until they blurred together into the same image.

Conspirator. Thief. Charmer. Thrill-seeker.

But never liar.

Well, she stretched the truth from time to time, but Jasper did not. He was unflinchingly honest for a thief. When he had come to see her after the arrest, perhaps if she had remembered that odd characteristic, they would have parted very differently, but the thought of his betrayal had pierced her blind. She'd felt helpless, taken advantage of by the one man who had come closest to touching her heart, and all her worst fears had consumed her. She'd pulled them close, a familiar comfort to staunch the hurt pouring through her.

If there'd ever been any doubt she was cut from Mimsy's cloth, her survivalist reaction toward Jasper was the irrefutable proof.

Now, sitting in this dank cell with unseen vermin making a meal of her, all she had for comfort was this cold metal ring and what it could have been. What would happen if she stopped running? If she took Jasper for all he was and not what her fears twisted him to be?

"Would you take me back?" she whispered to the ring. "Would you forgive my foolishness? Or am I too late?"

Her cellmate snorted. "Put a cork in it, will ya? Trying to sleep." Flopping on her belly, she snored against the wall.

Esme quickly tucked the ring back into its hiding spot, just over her heart. She didn't want to follow in Mimsy's footsteps, a bright smile pasted over a lonely existence, forever seeking fulfillment yet never finding it. Late or not, she would confess her true feelings to Jasper.

He would demand groveling, the louse, but she could distract him with a kiss. A real kiss with her entire heart behind it. He deserved that after all the misery she'd put him through and the time squandered keeping them apart. If groveling and a kiss didn't do the trick, well, she had plenty of time cooped up behind these bars to think of other persuasive means.

No matter how long it took, Esme Fox always got her prize in the end.

22

LINTON HALL WAS A GRAND old estate built sometime during the seventeenth century and home to the dukes of Loxhill for just as long. It rose majestically out of the Surrey countryside, all sharp corners, towering columns, and grand stairs. An architect could better describe the feats of such a structure, but to Jasper it was like a museum. A place he politely entered from time to time, but was never allowed to touch or linger, its holdings far too valuable for the likes of him.

When his telephone calls had gone unanswered, Jasper had no choice but to race north on the soonest available train.

Upon his unexpected arrival the day before, a distracted Duke had seen fit to offer him a small guest room in the farthest corner of the house. Next to the servants' stairs. It was a step up in accommodations considering his previous overnight stays had been relegated to the tiny room over the stables.

"Did you bring something suitable to wear?" Duke eyed him in the dressing room mirror as his valet finished tying the white bow tie. He was the perfect picture of an old-world gentleman with his silver hair and towering height. "This is a party and we require appropriate dress here in the country. Despite the fashions in London or Europe."

Arms crossed, Jasper leaned against one of the three wardrobes packed into the mahogany-paneled room.

"Apologies. I didn't have time to pack my top and tails. I was rather preoccupied with getting here to warn you because you couldn't pick up a simple telephone." He waved his hand in annoyance.

"The contraption rings too much. Barkley, have a jacket and tie laid out for Mr. Truitt. Can't have him spoiling the evening looking straight off the boat."

"Yes, Your Grace." Barkley bowed stiffly and retreated from the room without straightening.

Grabbing an ivory-topped cane that was purely for aesthetics, Duke strode out of the dressing room and into the main corridor. Jasper followed. The walls were papered in red damask with gilded frames of Roxburgh generations looking down their long noses at those daring to pass beneath them.

"Have you not listened to anything I've said?" Jasper asked as they descended the sweeping staircase to the ground level of the house. Servants bustled all around carrying fresh flowers, trays of drinks, and cloaks and hats from the guests starting to arrive.

"If I tucked tail and pulled down the window shade on every spurned lover I've had trying to confront me, I would have been a shut-in at two and twenty years of age." Duke paused on the bottom step and looked back at him. "That first one came at me with a sharpened chandelier pendant. She married a year later, some railroad baron in America."

"This particular lover most likely won't be coming for you with a light fixture."

"Very well. A sheet of music for a nasty paper cut. Rossalina and I were over years ago. She may still hold a grudge, but your gasping is a lot to do about nothing."

They crossed the polished floor of the grand hall, took several more turns through a number of fancy rooms, and exited through a set of double doors that had been thrown wide open to the summer evening. The back terrace and garden glowed with thousands of lanterns while the air was perfumed with jasmine and roses. A small orchestra plucked out a gentle tune that hummed beneath the laughter and chatter of a dozen guests. In an hour the space would be packed with little room to move.

"Gasping am I?" Jasper maneuvered around a long table laden with crisp fruit, sugar-dusted pastries, intricately rolled charcuterie, cheese wedges, and enough liquor to fill a lake. An ice sculpture of a swan perched in the center of it all.

"When this little paper cut sets into infection, don't come crying to me. In fact, don't bother coming to me ever again. I've done everything I can to make something of myself, to have a name I can be proud of. At one time I had hoped it would be your name, but I don't need that approval any longer. Nor do I need you muddling up my private affairs."

"If you are referring to that woman again—"

"Esme."

"I have already apologized for the misunderstanding. How was I to know that police sergeant would assume I was you when I called to have her arrested?" Duke smoothed the table's linen cloth with the tip of his cane.

"She believes I'm the one who had her arrested."

"Another case proving my point that women leap to dramatic conclusions. I'm confident in your ability to whisper a few honeyed words into her ear and all will be forgiven and forgotten."

"Goodbye, Duke." Jasper turned on his heel.

"Wait! You can't leave."

"Difficult to accept when the tables are turned, is it?"

"I had hoped we could discuss my announcement this evening. As gentlemen. It's rather important, involving you."

"'Gentleman' is a title that has never been afforded to men like me and is too honorable for men like you. Don't start appropriating it now. Say hello to Rossalina for me."

Jasper bounded up to his room and swept the few items he had unpacked back into his suitcase. From the bed, the freshly pressed evening clothes mocked him. A fine cut from Saville Row with a white silk waistcoat and bow tie. The garb of a gentleman. He'd worn the like before, either while traveling with Duke or blending into the rich crowds he intended to swipe from, but it never fit him correctly. He was nothing more than an impostor playing the role. All this finery around him and the swells gathered downstairs—he didn't belong here and he would never be accepted because of the manner in which he'd been born. On the wrong side of the blanket.

Heading downstairs, he took the back halls to avoid the crush of people spilling in through the front doors and made his way outside to the garage. Duke's chauffeur could take him to the train station. With any luck he could make the nine o'clock train for London, and from there . . . He'd figure it out on the way.

Rounding a hedge, he collided into a woman. His suitcase popped open and spilled its contents.

"Ow!" the woman cried.

Jasper lunged to grab her as she tottered on her heels. "I'm terribly sorry. Forgive me, I wasn't paying atten— Esme?"

One slender penciled eyebrow notched upward. "First imprisonment. Now assault. My, you enjoy keeping me guessing about which horror I'm to be subjected to next."

For a moment Jasper felt as if he were the one tottering about. Of all the surprises he might have encountered, her showing up dressed in the same clothes she'd worn when she was arrested was the last one he would've placed odds on.

Releasing her, he stepped back. "What are you doing here?"

"Something I never thought to do. Help you."

Correction. *That* was the most unexpected surprise. "You came here to help me?"

"What can I say? Prison changed me." She shrugged a shoulder as if she couldn't believe the odds either.

Kneeling, he gathered up his spilled belongings and stuffed them back in the suitcase. "How did you get out? That came out wrong. Mond told me it could take him several days to file the paperwork."

"I suppose paperwork is unnecessary when the Duke of Loxhill personally requests your release." She scooped up a pair of his underpants and dangled them out to him on her forefinger.

He snatched them off and shoved them into the case. "So Duke managed one good deed."

"Yes, you had your chance to lock me away for good and you blew it."

He slammed the lid closed and stood. "I never wanted that and you know it. Locked in a closet for a few hours, perhaps, but not in that awful place. The food is terrible and the service leaves much to be desired. Especially when I was *not* the one to put you there."

"I know you didn't."

"So now you believe me?"

Her gaze dropped to her scuffed shoes. "I was too angry at the jail. Too betrayed."

His hand curled tight around the suitcase handle. "Hurts like hell, doesn't it? Betrayal."

"Only until I remembered you're not like me. You don't turn on people, and I've never had reason not to trust your word."

"Despite my being a thief?"

"You are the most honorable thief—*man*—I've ever met." At last she met his gaze. No mockery. No sly wink. Merely sincerity. "Truly, Jasper."

They stared at each other with a thousand what-ifs passing between them. Not one could he put into words, but he felt them all. With no clue about what to do with them. Until one corner of her red lips curled up, followed by the other corner. And just like that he was smiling back. The perfect response as talking had never been their best means of communication.

Music playing in the garden floated around the side of the house. A lovely piece heavy with strings.

"Is this what the high set considers party music?" Esme cocked her ear toward it. "I know that piece. It's from the first act of *Coppélia*. Mimsy played one of the villagers when the theater tried to turn it into a play. The East End doesn't really go for ballet. The show didn't last long because there wasn't enough skirt hiking." Grinning, she scampered to the side of the house, beckoning him. "Come on. I want to see the toffs in action."

Jasper tucked his suitcase in a bush. No use encouraging a drunk guest to trip over it and spill his unmentionables again.

He joined her peering through a vine-clinging trellis at the party scene behind where the people had tripled since his departure.

Esme's finger curled over the twisting plants. "Oh my. This is how you grew up?"

Gazing upon the scene, he realized what it must look like to her. The amount of wealth swirling about in diamonds and black jackets, the dozens of servers with their silver platters, the pops of champagne bottle corks. To all the world it was the epitome of grace and luxury, but Jasper knew it for the hollowness it was.

"I told you," he said. "The life of a bastard is not nearly so glamorous. I can act the part, but this isn't my world."

"We seem to do a lot of that. Acting. Though I must say we pull it off rather well."

"Acting has lost its sparkle for me."

Esme pulled a face. "Much like this music, I'd wager. Heavens, can't they cut a rug to something from this century? This is going to put everyone to sleep."

"There is nothing new or exciting about this place. It's maintained as a mausoleum to the past and that's where it intends to stay. For how much longer I don't know. I don't even know how Duke is footing this bill."

The Roxburghs' pockets had always been deep, but Duke's spending had cut them severely short. It had taken a long while for Jasper to look behind the reverence he'd once held for this style of life he'd been cut out of. A family name to belong to, a history to give him roots. He now saw the cracks, and cobwebs, and tarnishing.

"The man is entertaining with empty pockets. A common occurrence among the rich."

"Could have fooled me."

"It's why he tasked me with retrieving the Valkyrie. He needs the Roxburgh diamonds to pay off his debts."

Esme gave a low whistle that summed up the ridiculousness of the situation. "Good luck wrestling it out of the countess's clutches. Better yet, let Duke wrestle it away from her. We can sit back and enjoy the spectacle for once."

Shaking his head, Jasper turned his back on the soiree and leaned against the side of the house. The cool stone pressed through his jacket, offering relief to his overwarmed skin.

"I've no intention of watching anything. Duke can go hang for all I care. Him and that tiara."

"This from the man who chased that tiara all over Europe?"

"My priorities were misplaced. I've since seen the light."

The orchestra switched to a new tune, this one slower than the last and to which Esme offered another disappointed frown as she muttered about King Oliver and the Original Dixieland Jazz Band.

"What priorities were those?"

Priorities. What a laughable notion now. He'd acted like a child begging for handouts of acceptance or acknowledgment, a hope that he had become a man worthy beyond the confines of his low birth. All nothing more than achievements to impress someone else. He was done with that.

The shame of his eagerness to please would linger in judgment, but somehow he didn't believe it would cross Esme's mind. Altruism and compassion were not her top strengths, yet she was never one to thump another on the nose for making bad decisions. She understood what it was like to twist yourself into what was needed to get by in the world. For that reason he didn't hold back his crushing embarrassment.

"Thinking I might have a place here among the illustrious Roxburghs if I returned as the triumphal savior to the dynasty."

If he was waiting for judgment, she didn't offer it. Merely twitched her eyebrows in amusement while continuing to watch the spectacle through the trellis.

"Ah, you thought bringing back the tiara might put you in Duke's good graces and he would name you as his heir."

"Heir to a crumbling kingdom."

"You could make something magnificent of it."

She spoke of the future as if it glittered within his reach. As if it were one he dreamed of to go with the loving family and happy home he had so longed for. Dreams that were all but dust grinding beneath the heel of life. Wasn't that where they had left their relationship? Another speck thrown beneath the tread of humanity. What was she doing sweeping it all up again?

"What are you doing here, Esme?"

Sighing, she relinquished her fascination with the party and turned to him. In the rising moonlight the smudges under her eyes darkened to purple. Jail had the rather unrefined habit of robbing one of sleep, though she managed to carry it off with aplomb.

"I told you. I'm helping. Although, after hearing this new information I'm quite at a loss as to what we should do once we steal the tiara back. Neither of them deserves it."

"There's that 'we' that has been so distasteful to you in the past." He waited for a rebuttal but surprisingly got none. "I have no intention of stealing anything. I'm leaving on the nine o'clock train. You shouldn't be here either. If the countess is coming for her revenge, it's too dangerous. I'll alert the authorities—"

"Well, I am here."

"And your plan is to what?"

"Prevent a murder? Spare the cream of British society the atrocity of having their ears bled dry by a geriatric diva past her prime?" She shrugged. A nonchalant motion to the untrained eye. To his eye, however, it was one of her tells. A cover-up to the tenseness she was loath to display.

"Honestly, as soon as I was released I came straight here. I didn't even stop to pack my toothbrush. Whatever happens tonight, I don't have a plan for it. I just knew that of all the places to be, I needed to be here. With you."

The words tumbled around, settling slowly in his mind as if they weren't quite sure it was safe to sink in. "With me."

Her shoulders dropped, taking with them the coy flutter of lashes and the smirk of full lips to expose a raw vulnerability.

"You told me this isn't what you wanted for us. I had a great deal of time to think behind those bars—the real ones and the ones I built around myself. What if it isn't what I want either?"

His heart may have lurched. Traitor. Did it fail to understand they intended to boycott her?

"Then what do you want?" His pulse decided to commit treason as well and sped up.

Her lovely eyes poured into his as she took a tiny step toward him, brushing her fingers against his knuckles.

"I think I might have fallen in love— Pirazzo?"

That wasn't what he'd expected to hear. "You love Pirazzo?"

"No, look!" Those lovely eyes that had been all his seconds before had narrowed as she pointed through the vines to the oily man creeping though the crowd. He had spiffed himself up into a tuxedo that looked ready to burst at the seams like an over-stuffed Italian sausage. His head twisted this way and that.

"The countess must be here," she whispered.

An ill-boding sign. And one he couldn't ignore no matter how loudly his instincts shouted for him to leave this mess for someone else to clean up. Then there was that other persistent factor damning him to stay. Bloody code of gentleman's honor.

Shouldering that unprecedented mantle, he strode to the side gate hidden between the vines that opened to the back garden.

"Find Corby. Tell him to alert the authorities."

"I don't know who Corby is."

"The butler. Look for the man who eats starch for breakfast. Hurry!"

She marched over to him. "You tell him. Pirazzo and the countess began as my problem. I'm the one who will see this through."

"Now isn't the time to put on the sackcloth and ashes."

"As if I would wear such a hideous ensemble on purpose." She slipped around him and through the gate.

Given no choice but to follow, he hurried after her. Partygoers gave them quizzical looks as they were clearly the most under-dressed guests in attendance. Esme in her wrinkled day dress, and him in a regular tie. The scandal!

Esme stopped near the edge of the dance space where the orchestra began trilling out another dusty old tune.

"Do you see him? I can't see past all the feathered headpieces."

Jasper craned his neck, but it did little good as there was no greased-back head to spot. He grabbed a passing server who doubled as one of Duke's footmen.

"Find Corby. Tell him to alert the authorities at once to suspicious activity here on the estate."

The footman's face creased with concern. "But, Mr. Truitt, I'm not supposed to leave my post."

"Would you rather be here to witness a possible disaster?"

The food tray wobbled in the boy's gloved hand. "Wh-what disaster?"

"Find Corby. At once. And do not breathe a word of this to anyone. If you do and cause a widespread panic among His Grace's guests, I guarantee the only position you'll have references for will be washing tankards at a roadside inn."

"Y-yes sir." The footman gave a little bow and scurried off.

"So authoritative." Esme brushed her shoulder against his. "A divinely attractive quality in a man."

"Don't swoon yet because you're about to see recklessness. Look." He nudged his chin toward the platform where the orchestra was situated. Pirazzo was motioning to the conductor to bend down.

"I don't think he's a qualified musician," Esme said as Pirazzo shoved what looked to be a payoff into the conductor's hand.

"Likely he's setting up the diva's entrance." Jasper faced her and put his hands on her shoulders. "Stay here. I'm going to—"

A silver tray loaded with filled crystal glasses wedged between them. "Champagne?"

"Not now!" Jasper shouldered the overzealous waiter out of the way. Quite a feat considering the little man's head barely reached Jasper's shoulder and was completely blocked from sight by the large tray.

"You are going to what?" Esme said, ignoring the intrusion. "Confront him on your own? Not bloody likely. I'd wager you don't even have a weapon."

"Gave them up after the war. Too much of an invitation for someone to shoot back."

"Overcome your moral quandary for the evening and take mine." Bending down as if to check the seam in her stockings, she dipped her hand under her skirt and fished out a derringer.

He took it, weighing the toy in his hand. "What do you expect me to do with this? Hunt mice?"

She sniffed indignantly. "Beggars do not have the luxury of choosing. I'll shimmy up front and create a distraction. Surely dancing the Charleston will stop everyone in their tracks, including that greaseball. You sneak around behind him and whack him on the back of the head. Or shoot him, because if you don't hit him hard enough, he'll likely pull his own gun and shoot you dead."

"Your confidence in me is astounding. Unlike your ridiculous assumption that he won't shoot you dead first."

"My dancing is hardly offensive. Besides, do you have a better plan?"

"No, but the last thing I need is a dead wife who didn't have enough common sense to stay out of the way."

"Why, darling, you do care." She tweaked him on the chin. "If I get killed, it'll be your fault for not whacking him in the back of the head quick enough and you will be forced into the sackcloth for the shame of it all."

Applause erupted around them. The orchestra blared a jingling to gather the party's attention to the platform. Duke, grinning broadly and waving benevolently to the plebs before him, swept up the short flight of stairs to stand next to the conductor. Pirazzo had disappeared.

Duke held out his hands for silence. "Welcome, my lords and ladies, my friends. Welcome and thank you for my wonderful birthday celebration."

"Huzzah!" The crowd cheered. Plied with spirits they would cheer anything.

The orchestra suddenly jumped into a rousing rendition of "For He's a Jolly Good Fellow" to which the crowd joined with enthusiasm. Duke blushed and grinned through it all, soaking up the glorious celebration of himself.

"Thank you all!" he said when the song ended. "How unexpected to be serenaded so well by my dearest friends." He droned on. The audience listened with rapt attention. Another blessing of title riches. People would listen to whatever nonsense a titled person gasped about for fear of offending them and being cut from the "in" crowd.

Jasper shuffled through the sycophants, inching to where he had last spotted Pirazzo near the platform.

"Stay back there!" he hissed at Esme.

She rolled her eyes. "I have yet to listen to you and will not break my record by starting now."

"How am I supposed to concentrate while having to worry about you at the same time?"

"Easy. Don't."

"Esme, I swear—"

"Which is why I am proud to announce that Jasper Truitt—where are you, dear boy?" Duke's voice cut through their argument. He squinted out at the audience, his gaze roving over heads until landing on Jasper's. "There you are!"

The crowed peeled away, leaving Jasper and Esme standing alone in the center of the dance floor, their noses inches apart in heated debate.

"I am proud to announce my grandson, Jasper Truitt, as my heir and the next Duke of Loxhill."

23

"Darling, smile. They're all watching you." Thank the stars above, Mimsy's lessons kicked in right as the proverbial spotlight hit them in the middle of the dance floor, shoving Esme's shock and disbelief deep down and conjuring a smile of pure delight.

Jasper, the future duke and her estranged husband, wasn't quite so quick on the uptake. He continued to stare at her, his expression at war with itself, his eyebrows drawn into a sharp V still punctuating their argument while his delicious mouth flopped open rather stupidly. She resisted the urge to press her finger under his chin and close it before some undukelike noise came forth. Hardly the best way to accept his new title.

"Come up here, my boy." Beaming like a puffed-up rooster, Duke beckoned at Jasper. "Come so I may properly introduce you as the new Earl of Westcott, a title that has gone unused for far too long."

"Close your mouth, pet." Esme smiled brightly and gave him a little push. "Go on before he sends a footman to collect you."

Gathering himself, Jasper pressed his lips into a somewhat pleasant line that belied the anger beginning to snap in his eyes. Mimsy would have declared him a star pupil. The crowd parted for him as he made his way to the platform and stood next to Duke. To the crowd it was the most astonishing of spectacles. An unheard-of heir emerging from the woodwork to claim one of the land's most coveted titles. Who was this man?

They picked apart his grubby day suit while cooing at the curl over his forehead, missing the flash of annoyance in his eyes. They noted the casual way Duke slung his arm across Jasper's shoulders. They did not notice the way Jasper stiffened. They saw two strapping men with power and prestige laid at their feet. They did not see the rejected little boy who had craved acceptance and fought to make his name one of worth.

But Esme saw. She saw the man who had nothing to prove to anyone. And for that her heart swelled and her hands clapped. Not because of some title, but because of who he was without all that fuss. She should have kissed him when she'd had the chance. In the four years of their separation she had never felt more distanced than she did now with this earldom stretching between them.

Duke patted Jasper on the shoulder, presenting him like a boy who had just won his first ribbon at a pony race.

"Do you wish to say a few words, my boy?"

Jasper's gaze locked on her. "To say this was unexpected is an understatement."

"Quite so, quite so!" Duke laughed. "Come, let me introduce you." He hustled Jasper off the platform and he was lost to Esme, swallowed up in the purring and cooing of the other aristocrats more than willing to welcome one of their own into the flock.

Esme was elbowed out of the way until she found herself once more at the edge of the dance space. She nearly laughed at the irony. One minute, the center of it all with Jasper at her side, and the next, tossed out like yesterday's newspaper. If that was the case, it was up to her to make a new headline. Something she was rather good at.

"In honor of His Grace's birthday celebration we have a special guest here tonight," the conductor announced.

An icy finger zinged down Esme's spine. As if she needed the warning.

"A world-renowned sensation and star of the stage, she has performed Puccini's 'O mio babbino caro,' Mozart's 'Der Hölle Rache,' and Bellini's 'Casta Diva.' Tonight she graces us for one night only for an enchanting remembrance of her center-stage debut in Wagner's *Der Ring des Nibelungen*. Please welcome Countess Rossalina Accardi!"

Applause exploded. Countess Accardi swept onstage in a fanfare of glitter and feathers. Dressed in black-and-purple velvet with draping sleeves that dragged the ground, a purple turban wrapped around her head with three long, black feathers curling over the top, and black sequined slippers, she looked like a fortune teller escaped from the caravan. A very expensive caravan, but a sideshow nonetheless.

Reaching the center of the stage, she gazed upon her audience with adoration shining from her kohl-lined eyes. She placed a veiny hand over where a heart might have beaten had one ever had the misfortune of being there and dipped low into a curtsy. The applause continued but thinned. Ever the consummate performer sensitive to her art, the countess stood, raising her arms over her head in a plea for silence. Her sleeves rolled back and the bangles circling her wrists clacked together.

"Grazie! Grazie!" She smiled widely. Her dark red lipstick looked nearly purple in the evening light, a color bruising her mouth.

"How welcome you have made me feel tonight after such a long departure from the stage, and how wonderful it is to return on this most auspicious occasion. My dream was to go on performing forever, but alas, time decreed my voice had finished its song and it was time to step aside for newer voices to arise."

A murmur rippled through the white hairs in the crowd. Doubtful any of them considered relinquishing power and stepping aside once their time had passed.

"Do not weep for me, *i miei amici*. For while a younger ingenue may rise to take my place, it is I who owned the part first. That is something that can never be taken away." Her eyes glittered as she stared straight down at Duke, who, for his part, looked positively gobsmacked.

His arrogance countenanced no warnings or threats, preferring to believe his rank kept him untouchable. The countess flashed a gleaming row of teeth and opened her mouth. Out soared Brünnhilde's battle cry solo from *Die Walküre*.

Subtle, the woman was not.

Esme snorted. She had seen the opera once before in Copenhagen while pricing the Johannes Vermeer collection and didn't recall the lead soprano's voice cracking nor sagging skin flapping about under her chin as it did with the countess. Some gifts did not age well, but the diva sought to overcome that disagreeable obstacle by singing louder, forcing the notes out no matter their reluctance. The audience didn't appear to mind as they burst into applause when the last note shot from her mouth like a discharged cannon.

Peering between heads, Esme searched for Pirazzo or any ill indication of what was to come but saw nothing. Until a stout waiter rolled close to the stage. The same one with the champagne tray that had blocked his head. Esme squinted. How tall all the other servants were. This one's shape could only be described as . . . egg-like.

The little ball turned his head and winked at her. Lamb!

That sneaky devil. Of course he was here to throw a new wrench into the debacle. She scowled. He gave her a sharp grin and wiggled his fingers at her, melting into the crowd.

Wonderful. Three against two. The odds were not in her and Jasper's favor. Still, she had been in worse predicaments, though considering a hit man and deranged killer were involved perhaps this was the worse.

Jasper, where are you?

Sweeping her ringed hand to her heart, the countess curtsied again. She gave nothing away of her true intent. And that was when she was at her most dangerous.

"Grazie." She straightened and reached up to her turban, then one by one plucked out the feathers and blew them into the audience. People scrambled over one another to grab them, which delighted the diva all the more.

Then she began to slowly unwind her turban.

"Most of you will be unaware of the special connection I have to our host. A lifetime ago we were well acquainted. You might say our, ah, destinies were entwined for a time." She winked and the audience roared with laughter.

Evil and deranged, but brilliantly captivating.

Esme inched toward the stage. She'd given away her gun, but a shoe would do in a pinch.

"I was his queen, his inspiration, his angel of stars and wings." The countess gave one last tug on her turban and the bindings fell away to reveal the Valkyrie perched atop her henna-red hair.

The diamonds glittered like a thousand stars under the glow of candles and moonlight, like a living being breathing in its adoration from a stage once more.

On a strangled cry, Duke pushed to the front of the crowd. He seethed with horrified anger. "My Valkyrie! How dare—"

She flicked her wrist, and the orchestra kicked in, blaring the epic charging force of "The Ride of the Valkyries."

Duke shouted, but the music drowned out his rage.

Acid shot from Countess Accardi's eyes as she stared him down, daring him to speak again.

He dared.

She silenced him momentarily with another of Brünnhilde's battle cries.

"You thieving raptor!" Duke's insults rang out as the music hit a low bar.

"You lying reptile!" screeched the countess.

"That tiara belongs to my family!"

"*Mortacci tua!* You had it made for me and then you snatched it back and gave it to that *puttana*."

"Clarice was not a whore! She was my wife!"

The crowd gasped. The orchestra skipped a measure.

"It is same thing." The countess trembled with rage. "You gave to her what was mine. What *is* mine."

Duke's face reddened. "I don't know what delusions you've fed on for thirty years to think you have any claim, but the Valkyrie belongs to me. Hand it here. At once!"

Sensing the musical moment had soured, the orchestra petered out.

"No, but I will give you what you truly deserve. *Bastardo*." From one of her long sleeves, she pulled out a gun.

Women screamed. Men shoved one another out of the way. Instruments honked and chairs tipped over as the musicians scrambled off the platform.

Duke threw up his hands and backed away. "Now, Rossalina. Put that away before you hurt someone. You don't really want to kill me."

"Sì, I do. I have taken tokens from each of my lovers over the years, but nothing from you because you stole it from me. I have been searching for this token for thirty years and at last it's mine."

Esme slipped behind the stage and peered through the overturned music stands. Where was Jasper? The icy finger that had trailed down her spine wrapped around her throat. What if Pirazzo had found him first? What if he was lying face down in a pool of blood and she never got the chance to tell him what she'd come here to confess? That she loved him. Wildly and unexplainedly. If he died before she told him those three little words that she should have told him from their first meeting, she would never forgive his rudeness in leaving her.

"I gave you pearls, diamonds, villas." Duke's coloring darkened to a sickly purple.

The countess shrugged. "I wanted this. Just as I want to shoot you."

"Where did you even get a gun? A stage prop? Put it away before you hurt yourself."

Hoisting herself onto the stage, Esme ducked between the overturned chairs. A plan might have been helpful before she threw herself headlong into certain danger, but then, she was better at off the cuff.

"Forgive my paraphrasing of *L'incoronazione di Poppea* when I say, 'Go to exile in bitter grief.'" The countess leveled the gun at Duke.

Duke's gaze locked on the barrel. The purple drained from his face to an ashy color. "That farewell was for Rome."

"And like Rome, you are doomed for downfall." She pulled the trigger.

Nothing.

"*Cavolo!* I never should have trusted my father's gun from his war." She smacked the gun against her thigh. Pulled the trigger again. Nothing. She tossed it aside and rummaged through her other sleeve, extracting another gun.

Esme lunged through the last row of chairs. She knocked into the old woman and down they tumbled.

The gun skittered from the countess's hand, fell off the stage, and was neatly caught by Duke.

The countess screeched, clawing after it with her bony hands.

Esme sat on top of her. "Cease with the tantrum, you old crone."

"You stupid, stupid girl!" The countess wriggled like a caught fish. Small as she was, she had a good amount of fight in her dusty bones. "I should have killed you when I had the chance."

"Then we never would have had this thrilling reunion."

A string of Italian cursing burned Esme's ears. "You have ruined everything!"

"If you had slipped in quiet like and knifed the duke while he was sleeping, you wouldn't be in this predicament." Duke made a strangled noise at this suggestion. Esme shot him an apologetic look and continued. "But no, you had to take center stage and act out the greatest revenge scene since *Hamlet*."

"A fellow craver of limelight, how *magnifique*." Lamb, still clad in his waiter attire, popped up on the stage. "Though any good performance should have only one star, and I'm afraid that will always be me, in which case, I'll take that." He swooped down and plucked the tiara from the countess's head.

Or tried to. The countess clamped onto the wings with all her scrawny might.

"It's mine!" she hissed. "After all these decades I will not allow some snub-nosed amateur to take it from me."

"Give it to me!" Lamb pulled harder.

The countess held on for dear life, veins straining in her neck and eyes bulging. "Unhand it!"

A tug-of-war ensued, each opponent equally matched in determination. It wasn't going to end well.

Esme leaned in, reaching to swat their hands away. "Enough! It's over. Neither of you—ow!" She jerked her hand back. Teeth marks dented the back of her hand. "You bit me!"

Lamb latched his teeth next into the countess's hand. She screamed but held on. He bit again, this time clamping down on her thumb. The tiara tumbled free.

Snatching it up, Lamb pressed his prize to his heaving chest. "Winner takes all. Ladies, it has been a pleasant evening, but I must bid you all a fond adieu."

He tossed something at his feet. A puff of smoke erupted.

Esme coughed and batted away the smoke.

Lamb was gone.

"You little sneak!"

His laughter rippled across the empty dance floor as his black coattails disappeared around a bush.

"My prize!" the countess shrieked as if she'd been stabbed.

"Come back here at once!" Duke shouted. "Thief! Thief!"

Lamb did not obey the command, nor did anyone move to go after him, the audience and waitstaff too enthralled by the unusual spectacle. Typical. Most people preferred the safety of spectator rather than the unknown of participant.

Click.

Esme swiveled her head and found Pirazzo pointing a gun at her from the rear of the stage.

"A pleasure to see you again, Miss Fox," he said.

"I can't say the same." Panic thrummed but she wouldn't give him the satisfaction of having her at a loss. The countess squawked beneath her.

"Move away from Countess Accardi now or I will be forced to remove you by other means."

Bam!

A gunshot exploded behind Pirazzo. His gun tumbled from his hand.

Before he could even blink, Jasper appeared behind him. From ground level, his arms snaked out and grabbed Pirazzo by the ankles, yanking him off the stage. The sound of fists smacking and grunting echoed up. If he was any hit man worth his salt, Pirazzo would have more than one weapon on his person. Esme's little gun held only one shot and Jasper had used it.

Forgetting Lamb, the Valkyrie, and the murderess jabbing pointed fingernails into Esme's leg, Esme scrambled to her feet and lurched to the rear of the stage. The two men had regained their feet and were slinging fists.

Bruises bloomed on both their cheeks. Blood trickled from Pirazzo's lip. Jasper swung and ducked, punched and bobbed with all the sleek concentration of a panther. Pirazzo was more of a boar, his meaty hooks lacking style but connecting with punishing blows to Jasper's upper body and jaw.

Ducking low, Jasper drove his shoulder into Pirazzo's stomach, knocking him backward. Jasper jumped atop his opponent and rained down a series of pummels, cracking the Italian's nose sideways. Pirazzo threw up his arm to block the blows while his other hand squirmed down to his belt.

In a motion quick as lightning, he whipped out a silken cord and lassoed it around Jasper's neck, yanking tight. Jasper's face flushed red as he clawed at the cord. Cackling in delight, Pirazzo heaved up and shoved Jasper to his back.

Pirazzo leaned over Jasper with a pointed grin, blood dripping from his mouth and nose. The bright red splattered against Jasper's neck, an ugly color against the purpling of his skin.

"I have you now, little Phantom."

Esme looked around for a weapon of any kind. Grabbing a music stand, she jumped off the stage and brought it crashing down on Pirazzo's head. He juddered from the impact but didn't break his hold on choking Jasper. She swung the stand again, cracking it against the side of his head.

Down he went, sprawling against Jasper in an unconscious heap. Scrambling out from beneath the oily mass, Jasper tore the rope away from his neck and gasped.

"Darling! Are you all right?" Esme threw herself at his side. His purple face faded to blue, then red, then ashy. A nasty shiner ringed his eye and a cut trickled blood from his cheek, but at least he was still breathing.

He nodded, sucking in air.

Esme grabbed the cord and tied Pirazzo's hands and ankles behind his back, securing them with a knot to make any sailor proud.

"Where did you learn to do that?" Jasper rasped.

"A good thief must always know how to prevent another pickle," she said. "Besides, I saw it in an American cowboy act that toured the East End once, and I always wanted to try it. He used a hay bale with horns, so I believe I pulled off the more difficult stunt. Wherever did you learn to fight like that? I assume fisticuffs would be strictly forbidden in a gentleman's upbringing."

"Thanks goes to the army. Amateur boxing champion of the First Battalion Royal Warwickshire Regiment at your service." He tried to grin but winced as the gash on his cheek split wider.

She dabbed at the cut with her sleeve. "How splendid. Boxing and shooting. That was quite the shot you made, though I personally would have aimed for his meaty head."

He grimaced. "I did."

"Oh, well, we can't all be sharpshooters." The rush of action that had propelled her moments before left in a whoosh, leaving her trembling all over. Tears pricked her eyes.

"Don't ever frighten me like that again." Throwing her arms around him, she peppered his face with kisses.

His arm slipped around her waist. "Your doubt in my survival is touching." He pulled back a bit but didn't quite drop his arm from around her. His other hand reached up and swept back the mussed hairs clinging to her cheek. "My brave little vixen."

Another swell of tears started. How close she had come to losing him. How her heart ached as she imagined never looking into his understanding eyes again, never brushing away that stubborn curl from his forehead, never scraping with him again. The only man who could rival her in all the ways she needed.

"Jasper, I love—"

"Here they are!" Duke's voice cut through the moment with all the subtleness of Big Ben tolling on New Year's. Rounding the stage, he took in the scene with a scowl and shake of his perfectly combed silver head.

"Leo! Harry!" Two footmen scurried after him. "Take this . . . this creature to the wine cellar along with Countess Accardi and guard them until I alert the authorities. It might be some time before the badges arrive."

"Mr. Corby has already alerted the authorities, Your Grace," one of the footmen said, grabbing the deadweight Pirazzo by the legs. "Mr. Truitt issued the order some time ago."

"Back when I tried to warn you." Jasper pushed himself up. Esme stood, grasped his arm, and helped him stand. "Remember? Something about death threats."

"Yes, well, the point has been made and we are all safe now." Duke's eyes narrowed. "Except for my tiara. Some no-necked waiter spirited it away during the hullabaloo."

"Lamb," Esme said. "He snuck in and seized the opportunity."

Jasper huffed a laugh, wincing as he touched his throat where purple fingers printed against his skin.

"We never should have allowed him to slip our minds. Of course he would want retribution after we took it from him in France."

"There's that infamous 'we' again." Esme curled her arm through Jasper's, smiling up at him. "I'm starting to like the ring of it."

Jasper's expression was inscrutable. A mix of surprise, hesitancy, suspicion, and amusement. "Are you now?"

"Ahem." Duke cleared his throat. His complexion had returned to a more natural British paleness, but his eyes were bright with excitement as they locked onto Esme. "Are you going to introduce this extraordinary young woman who foiled my murder, or must I conduct my own pleasantries?"

Jasper arranged his facial features to an acceptable politeness. "Duke, may I introduce Miss Esme Fox. Esme, His Grace, the Duke of Loxhill."

"Enchanted." Duke grasped Esme's hand and swept it up to his mouth for a brief kiss on the back of her knuckles. A practiced move if ever there was one.

"Esme Fox . . . Where have I heard your name before? Oh yes! My, my, *you're* Jasper's wife." He looked her up and down appraisingly.

"Soon to be ex," Jasper corrected.

Esme's heart thudded. "I need to talk to you about that," she whispered in his ear.

"Ex?" Duke boomed incredulously. "You are off your crumpet to toss aside such a treasure. She was in league with Rossalina, but I can forgive the lack in judgment for her bravery displayed here tonight. You are a credit to the Roxburgh name, dear lady."

"Um, thank you," she said before hissing furiously at Jasper. "I need to speak with you *now*."

"That is how I saw to your release from jail," Duke continued as if noting nothing amiss. "Your name."

Esme stared stupidly. "My name?"

"You are wanted as a known thief by the name of Esme Fox, but the lady they held in their cell was Esme Truitt. A small but critical mistake in identity."

Jasper's politeness disappeared into a frown. "Here I thought you simply threw your title at them and made it all disappear."

"Certainly I did that, too, but only after I clarified the name. I like to prove them wrong and make them sweat before I drive the nail into their coffin." Duke turned to Esme. "By the way, I wish to offer an apology for all that muck up."

"You mean when you had me arrested," Esme said dryly.

"Yes, that. I can blame only my sore temper revolving around this tiara business and my previous experience with ensnaring women. Of which you are not."

"An apology, my, my. Perhaps there's hope for humility in the men of your family after all. Though I surmise it will be a short-lived victory."

Duke rocked back and forth on his heels, eyeing her as if he were a boy in a candy shop. "By golly, you will make an excellent duchess. Witty, charming, lovely, unafraid—"

"Excuse us for a moment please, Your Grace." She tugged on Jasper's arm before she lost the nerve to say what she'd come here to confess. "Jasper, *now*."

Pulling him around to the hedges, she put her life into her hands and spilled the depths of her heart before her cornered husband could escape.

"I have been running my entire life and am no longer quite certain of where to go, only that it's after you. Once I've gotten to wherever you're leading me, I'm standing there until you make me move."

At the beginning of her speech, his expression had been inscrutable, but by the end it began to fray at the edges. "Esme, please don't. We can't go through all that again. It's time to accept the loss and go about our separate lives."

"I know I've hurt you. And I'm sorry. I am so sorry, Jasper. At first I thought I was protecting myself by leaving before you could abandon me. Then I left because I thought I was protecting you, and, well . . . I've made many mistakes and I'm bound to make many more, but the greatest mistake I could make would be to let you walk away before telling you I am absolutely mad about you. Desperately, hopelessly, incandescently, maddeningly in love with you."

Reaching into her wrinkled blouse, she pulled out a simple necklace of gold. On the end dangled her wedding band. "You said you wanted something different for us, something shiny and hopeful. So do I."

He stared silently at the ring for a moment, then lifted his gaze to her eyes. Solemn, reserved, and coolly dispassionate. "You'll run."

"If I do, I'll make sure it's straight into your arms." He raised a questioning eyebrow. She sighed in exasperation. Declaring one's feelings was more exhausting than she'd thought. "This won't work if you don't trust a little. You do remember how to trust, don't you?"

"Vaguely." Frowning, he reached out and touched the ring. It swung gently back and forth on the chain. "Say it again."

Her fingers shook as she grasped him lightly by the lapels and met his unflinching gaze with an honesty that threatened to buckle her knees. "I am maddeningly in love with you."

"Not that part. The bit about you being mistaken and sorry."

She dropped her hands. "Is that the only thing you took from my speech? I admit it wasn't poetry, but it was heartfelt. If you're going to stand there and mock my arduous declaration, then I shall take the opportunity to tell you what a low-down—"

"Has this sudden declaration anything to do with an announcement about my becoming an heir?"

"If you recall, I tried to declare myself to you before Pirazzo popped up and before Duke proclaimed you his heir. A smooth move on his part so you wouldn't make a scene and refuse him outright."

"I suppose you were on the verge of admitting something to that kind of feeling," he grudgingly conceded.

"It's no dice, Esme. We're no good together. You're a liar and I'm a thief. You run and I chase after things that don't belong to me. We've hurt each other, trampled each other, made questionable decisions together, destroyed our livers by drinking to forget each other, backstabbed, stolen from—"

"Jasper." She plunked her hands on her hips. "I haven't slept in four days. I have a bruise blossoming on my backside where the countess's bony hip stabbed into me, and I hear the coppers beating at the gates. Now, tell me quick, do you love me or not?"

He snorted and stamped like a horse with a rope about his neck, raking his fingers through his hair until it stood at all sixes and sevens, and muttering under his breath.

"Great balls of fire. I'm afraid I do."

"Finally." Looping her arms around him, she gave him a kiss of promise. It wasn't sweet nor was it gentle, but then, what about their relationship was? It was full of fire and passion and an equal desire to melt the other right down where they stood. She nearly succeeded until his arms came about her, drawing her tight to his chest and scorching her insides with a possession she happily retaliated with.

At last she came up for air, drawing in cooling breaths to temper her racing blood. She traced a fingernail lazily along his charmingly chiseled jaw.

"Shall I tell you what a blackguard you are for making me fall in love with you?"

A lazy smile curled his mouth, tempting her all the more.

"Shall I tell you what you are for seducing me so thoroughly?"

"Do tell."

He put his mouth to her ear. The words whispered warmly over her sensitive skin and prickled her all over with delicious anticipation.

He pulled back, grazing his cheek over hers. "What do you think of that?"

She laughed and cupped her hands behind his head, drawing his mouth to hers as happiness bubbled like champagne fizz, frothing over her insides in golden splendor.

"You haven't seen anything yet."

24

Jasper could have seduced her all evening right there in the hedgerow, but his name being shouted repeatedly by searching footmen combined with the heavy boots of police officers stamping all about the garden barking questions at eyewitnesses was enough to put him off romance. For the time being.

"I'm here," he called, stepping out of the bushes, his fingers laced between Esme's. The satisfied glow on her face of a woman properly kissed delighted him to no end.

One of the footmen, John, spotted him and darted through the crowd. "Sir." Out of breath and red in the face, the boy looked ready to drop. "His Grace is looking for you and requires your presence in the front drive."

Weaving through the guests who were discussing wildly varying accounts of the evening's drama, Jasper led Esme through the house and out the front door. Blazing torches lined the gravel drive, throwing the manicured lawn and clipped trees into flaming orange. Six black automobiles were jumbled together with thick tire marks behind them as if the police had raced to the front door. A likely scenario as there was little excitement to be found in Blackheathe.

Duke stood in a ring of coppers with little notepads and pencils, each trying to pitch their questions to be heard over the others.

"I've given you my final answers." Duke's voice rose above the noise. "If any more questions should arise, you may direct them to my solicitor. I thank you for your prompt attention to this disruption as I expect nothing less from the fine men of Blackheathe's law enforcement. Ah, Jasper, my boy!"

Like a gaggle of honking geese, the police turned and rushed as one to surround Jasper and Esme, lobbing question after question about the attack. It seemed an age before Jasper had answered all of their inquiries and could finally step away. He thought briefly of stealing Esme away and finding the nearest dark spot to canoodle in, but she looked perfectly at ease surrounded by those men hanging on her every word, each one spoken further enchanting them. The wrinkled blouse, tousled hair, and chipped manicure could not dim her sparkle. And he never wanted anything to.

Duke came and stood next to him in the towering shadow of the house. "Tell me again why you're so quick to toss out such a woman."

Esme threw her head back and laughed as one of the coppers asked if she had formal training in taking down crooks. It wasn't the coy, stilted laugh she gave when toying about, but rather a full-throated laugh of joy that set everything right in Jasper's world.

"I've changed my mind on that account," he said, noting the way her wedding band caught the torchlight. The gold dazzled like a beacon of fire.

"Glad to hear that. The Roxburgh men need a level-headed woman in a crisis from time to time."

Jasper's pleasant thoughts of romance and wedding bands came to a screeching halt. "Why are you so eager to tie me into the Roxburgh line all of a sudden? Twenty-eight years have gone by, and you were happy to keep me as 'Truitt,' hidden away and only summoned on occasion to do your beck and call."

"Beck and call?" Duke's trimmed eyebrows flew up to his combed hairline. "What were all those trips I took you on? Buying wardrobes in Italy. Wine tastings in France. Polo matches, yacht sailing. Greek, Latin, and German tutors. What was that all for if not to prepare you to become my heir?"

"You could have done the same for my father. Why didn't you recognize him?"

"Your father was a womanizing drunkard. He never had what it took to be a Roxburgh. He would have squandered the family legacy."

"And you haven't?"

"I may have overspent my coffers," Duke admitted with a grunt. "But I knew you would be the one to fill them again. You are resourceful, charming, efficient, keenly intelligent, and possess the rare ability to see straight through the veneer to the core of a situation. All elements of a successful man yet rarely seen in aristocrats. I may have failed to give your father a better life, but I didn't wish to repeat the mistake with you."

"Or rather, you knew your options for a legitimate heir were dwindling and accepted that a bastard grandson was better than none at all." Deep down Jasper had known the ugly truth all along, but there had always been a part of him that clung to the hope of being accepted for his own merits rather than as a last resort. It was why he had perfected his Greek with those tutors. Had watched the boring rounds of polo. And why he had chased so long and hard after the Valkyrie. All for acceptance.

But he was no longer that little boy craving recognition from a family that couldn't bother to invite him to Christmas. He was a man responsible for his own way, and of that he could be proud.

"I would be lying to deny the truth in your statement. I should have recognized you from the start, and for that lapse in judgment I am sorry. This society in which we live is cruel. Everything hinges on one's birth, and for you to be born on the wrong side of the blanket . . . Well, society makes it their mission to grind you beneath their privileged heels. The weak don't survive, so I wanted to toughen you up, thicken your skin so their barbs could never penetrate once you stepped into place as my heir, which I have reserved for you all along.

"Perhaps it was not the best course of action, but I could think of no other who would train you for success. And, my boy, you have surpassed my greatest expectations." Duke settled his hand on Jasper's shoulder. A gesture he often used to signify power, but there was nothing of that in the touch now. "It's high time the Roxburghs stand proudly where we are today and not linger in the glory of generations past. You are the one to bring us forward."

It was everything Jasper had dreamed of hearing, yet his dreams had shifted. Instead of excitement rushing in his blood, a great reluctance chugged through.

"You could have had the decency to tell me before publicly announcing my inheritance."

"I knew you would balk. As any self-made man would rightly do."

"A self-made man doesn't need a title to determine his worth in the world."

"He does not, but a worthy man taking on the title could make it great again. Respectable, a beacon of strength, a power for good. You've become that man, Jasper. The man I'm proud to call my blood."

All his life Jasper had been told of his less-than worth. As if his very existence was nothing more than a dirty smudge on the underbelly of life. For most, he still was, but Duke never considered him that. He had educated him, allowed him to travel, and given him opportunities to forge his path through the world in his own way. He'd also allowed Jasper to fall, get kicked around, and even tossed in jail. All to thicken his skin for what lay ahead as Duke of Loxhill. It was a completely and utterly daft way to train one's future heir, but the old man had never been conventional. His choosing Jasper was proof of that.

The scars deep inside him twitched as the bitterness stitching them together withdrew its hooks. All this time, he, Jasper Truitt, had been chosen, but it had been his own abilities that proved him worthy.

"I never wanted the title," Jasper said slowly.

Duke rocked back unsteadily on his heels. "You refuse the dukedom?"

"I—" Jasper's answer was cut short by a screeching of Italian.

Two officers emerged from the house escorting Countess Accardi. Two more trailed with Pirazzo in handcuffs.

"You!" She turned wild eyes on Duke. Black mascara drained down her rouged cheeks. "I will see your liver boiled in oil for this!"

"You were always quick with words in your heated temper. How I shall miss that, Rossalina." Duke sighed with what sounded like regret. "Perhaps next time you'll finally pull that trigger successfully. Best out of three. What do you say?"

"You mean she's tried to shoot you before?" Jasper asked.

"Of course. The summer of 1893—no '92. We'd sailed my yacht to the Amalfi coast. She caught me speaking with one of the local girls and pulled her gun on me. Oddly enough, I believe it was the same gun she used tonight. I told her the sea air would rust it out. Perhaps that's why it didn't shoot." He sighed again over the memory. "Keep that in mind should you ever take an Italian lover."

Jasper's gaze shifted to find Esme's eyes on him. "I already have the ideal lover. I need no other."

The countess continued her hysterics worthy of Lady Macbeth, thrashing about and trying to bite at the hands clamped around her arms. She was ushered to one of the waiting autos. The police thrust her into the back seat and slammed the door shut. Pirazzo was stuffed without ceremony into the auto idling behind hers.

Esme skipped out of her ring of admirers and over to Jasper and Duke.

"At last it's curtains closed for the old diva. Perhaps she'll find a new audience behind bars." She waved and blew a kiss to Countess Accardi, who had her hateful face pressed against the window.

"Your Grace!" A footman rushed around the side of the house, polished shoes slipping on the manicured grass. "Your Grace! I have it!" In his outstretched, white-gloved hands was the Valkyrie.

Skidding to a halt and nearly bowling into his employer, the young man gasped for breath. "Me and Muloney caught him . . .

gasp . . . the thief . . . *gasp* . . . over near the garage." He panted, normal color returning to his red face. "Muloney got him by the legs. Down the thief went, and the tiara flew out of his hands. I grabbed it and Muloney tackled him, but the nasty fellow bit poor old Muloney and took off into the trees. We couldn't catch him, sir."

Duke took his prodigal prize and turned it over to inspect the *R* inscribed on the inner headpiece. At last, the original had returned home.

"A fine job the both of you did. You cannot know what this means to me. Thank you."

The relief and gratitude on Duke's face held nothing of the greed Jasper had associated with him. Withholding the tiara would have deepened the bitterness crusted into Jasper, shackling him to a poison that would eat his soul. He was done with that.

As the footman bowed and walked away, Duke grinned like a boy on his first pony.

"If you'll excuse me, I'm going to lock this in the vault before anyone else gets an idea to swipe it tonight. I half expect another lunatic to jump out of the hedge."

"Or a chicken." Esme shuddered.

"I beg your pardon?"

"Nothing." She waved him away.

After a few steps, Duke paused and turned back. "Convince your husband to take the title. I have a sense you would look ravishing in diamonds, Mrs. Truitt."

"As do I." Esme beamed and looped her arms around Jasper's neck.

"Ow! Careful, woman. I've been strangled."

"My apologies." She loosened her grip while still holding him close. As Duke disappeared into the house, Esme looked at Jasper with a frown. "What's this about the title?"

He slipped his arms around her waist and pulled her closer. It was pure heaven on earth to hold her when she wasn't attempting one of her disappearing acts.

"I don't want the title. Nor the diamonds. The only thing I want is you. Disappointed?"

"Not in the least."

"Not even about the diamonds?" he prodded.

"The only bit of jewelry that interests me is right here." Trailing a finger across his cheek and down his chest, she pulled her hand back and tapped the ring resting at the base of her throat.

He took the ring and gave a slight tug. The chain broke from around her neck. He slid the cool band of metal off the chain and onto her finger.

"Better than any tiara."

"I'll say."

He kissed her, slow and deep and full of promise. Promises he had no intention of breaking and every intention of surpassing. She smiled against his mouth, her body warm and soft, pressing into him as the scent of orange blossoms filled his senses.

He'd held her before but never like this. A wall of defense had always stood between them, breached only momentarily in fits of passion yet remaining solid in resistance. This kiss shook the walls. The bricks and stones and cracked bits of mortar tumbled at their feet ready to build a new foundation. One on which they would stand together. If she made him chase her around a turret or two for old times' sake, he would hardly mind that.

Too soon she leaned back. Her fingers dragged through the hairs on the back of his neck, sending chills over the grazed skin.

"But, Jasper, you will take the title."

"Now, Esme, we've been through this. I never wanted to be a duke. All I wanted—*want*—is a family who is proud to call me one of its own."

"I'm proud to call you mine." Her finger traced over his ear. "And Duke has been strutting around all evening eager to present you to these snobs, to tell them you are undeniably his chosen heir. The man is going to pop a button if he swells with anymore pride. Quite different from the tune you thought he was whistling all along."

Jasper grunted. "Yes, it turns out I was wrong about his motivations."

"Oh my! Two Roxburgh men admitting their faults in one evening. Can the world withstand such earth-shattering confessions?"

"Joke all you like, but I don't belong here. I don't belong anywhere. Not thieving and not as a duke."

"The devil with belonging. We'll create our own world and rules, and you will make something wonderful of it. After all, you've proven yourself quite the champion of lost causes." She smiled and tickled the back of his neck with her nails. "You are what this stuffy old place needs, and I will be supporting you every step of the way."

Leaning his forehead against hers, he tried to hide the smile insistent upon curling his lips. Lips that were most eager to return to hers.

"You mean you'll be running the show."

She gave a dainty shrug that in every way said yes.

"Are you trying to convince me just so you can wear the Valkyrie?"

Not bothering to hide her own wide smile, she brushed her lips across his.

"Why, darling, a girl would be out of her mind to chuck away diamonds."

EPILOGUE

Two years later
Linton Hall, Surrey

"DARLING, HURRY. WE'RE LATE AS it is." Jasper's irritated voice entered the dressing room two seconds before he did.

"I'm nearly finished," Esme replied, swiping on her lipstick in front of the vanity. She capped the tube and stood to present her back to him. "I need a fastening."

"You need a watch," he grumbled as he crossed the room and set to work on the dozen buttons floating up the back of her cream frock spangled with gold sequins.

"A watch would clash with this outfit. Besides, my being fashionably late is one of the things you adore about me."

"I love you for all those sentimental reasons men aren't supposed to admit to. The way you reach for my hand when you're excited. How your mouth curls at the corner when you say my name. When you swirl strawberries in your champagne." He looked up and caught her watching him in the mirror. The dimple flashed in his right cheek. "Notice that tardiness is not on that list."

"Fine, but they can hardly start the evening without us. We are the hosts."

"Your mother has other ideas about that."

Esme waved a hand, her freshly lacquered nails shining bright red in the lamplight. "Mimsy always thinks she's in charge, and this is her show tonight, but what good is opening Linton Hall as an art space if the Earl and Countess of Westcott are forced to arrive on time?"

"Politeness to our guests?" He tugged on a particularly stubborn button.

"Tosh. We'll be ten minutes late at most. Besides, it gives the crowd more opportunity to gawk about the place."

A week after Countess Accardi's arrest was splashed across the newspapers, Esme and Jasper had renewed their vows in a proper church with a proper vicar. Duke had beamed and Mimsy had pretended to shed a tear. A real one would have devastated her makeup. The newly minted earl and countess enjoyed a proper honeymoon sailing on Duke's yacht from the Azores islands to Egypt, Cyprus, and through the Aegean Sea. Esme never did find her sea legs, but she'd learned to keep peppermint candies on hand when her stomach tilted sideways. Which had been often.

Returning to England with golden tans and even more golden memories of their sea-scented nights together, they accepted the keys to Duke's London townhome on Belgrave Square and Linton Hall. Duke then declared himself a citizen of the world and sailed off for the Amalfi Coast on the yacht that had barely finished unloading Jasper and Esme's trunks. So far, no rumors had surfaced of him taking an Italian mistress.

The newlyweds settled in Belgrave Square, where drinks and dancing were never far from their doorstep. During one particularly rousing evening at the American Bar in the Savoy, a group of bright-eyed artists had wandered in complaining of their modern art not being acceptable to the stuffy crowds in museums. Esme had lit up like a Guy Fawkes firecracker and within one year turned Linton Hall into an art gallery that welcomed artists of all shapes and forms to display their talents.

The ground-floor rooms held rotating exhibits that ranged from art, photography, and sculpture to dance and singing. Second-floor rooms were rented for private classes and studios, while the third floor had been blocked off for the family's use when they came to view an exhibit. The transformation was an enormous success, and soon the Roxburgh coffers were overflowing with enough money to fix the leaking roof, replace rotting floorboards, and rewire the entire house with electricity.

Jasper finished the last button on her dress and kissed Esme's bare shoulder.

"You look beautiful tonight." He kissed her other shoulder. "Perhaps I'm overthinking our tardiness. A few more minutes won't kill them." His arm wrapped possessively around her middle, drawing her back against his chest as his mouth explored the curve of her neck.

She sighed and angled her head to give him better access, thought seriously for a moment about continuing the delay, then reluctantly pushed away.

"Mimsy will be up here before long to drag us down by our ears. Remember the last time?"

Jasper rubbed his ear and muttered something about knocking before entering.

"I'll make it up to you later." She winked and pulled on gloves that perfectly matched the deep red of her lips. "Promise. Are you ready, my lord?"

"After you, my lady." Jasper ushered her through the door and out to the landing. Taking his offered arm, they descended the three flights of stairs to the ground level of the house.

Most of the guests had taken their seats in the ballroom, but a few stragglers remained to observe the paintings in the converted dining hall and the sculptures in what had been the sitting room. Once, this place had been stuck in the past with dusty old lords and ladies shuffling about with their aristocratic noses shoved so far in the air they couldn't be bothered to look down and see the need around them.

Esme squeezed her husband's arm. They had done this together. No longer a relic of something Jasper could never be a part of, Linton Hall had been made new into something he could be proud to add his name to. The Roxburghs were lucky to have him.

As was she.

"What's that look for?" he inquired.

"Just thinking how proud I am to be standing here with you."

"Here I thought it was pure smugness. Not every woman can pull off a tiara with such stately elegance."

She touched a hand to the Valkyrie perched victoriously atop her smooth bob. With all the money coming in from Linton Hall plus selling off two of the three yachts and his prize-winning racehorse, Duke saw no reason to barter off the family diamonds and happily gave it to Esme. *Diamonds and women are more beautiful when paired together,* the old smooth talker had explained. Smooth-talking or not, Esme didn't need to be convinced to wear the extraordinary tiara at every available opportunity. She had saved it from complete ruination after all.

Leaning close, her husband whispered in her ear, "How about later you model it for me? I heard an angel makes an appearance in the play tonight. We could borrow the wings and—"

"There you two are!" Mimsy's accusing tone rang through the great hall. "Lord and lady you may be, but I have a schedule to keep. The show must go on."

When they had informed Mimsy of their plan to turn Linton Hall into an art museum and performance space, she had immediately declared it an extension of The Scarlet Crown. It had taken a great deal to convince her that the house was open to all artists and not for the monopolizing of one. She had conceded somewhat with grace by leasing the ballroom every quarter to stage one of her new shows. To see if it was up to snuff for the refined tastes of the East End, she'd declared.

"Apologies," Esme said, kissing the air on either side of Mimsy's cheeks. "My buttons needed done up."

Mimsy eyed Jasper with suspicion but didn't pounce. Instead she cast stormy eyes about the hall. "Where is Ollie?"

Oliver Winston Truitt Roxburgh, Viscount Ardley, future Duke of Loxhill, and their son. One year old with a mop of golden-brown hair and large blue eyes, he was the apple of his family's eye.

"With Duke and Mond in the garden," Jasper said. "I left them making leaf boats to race in the fountain."

"He does it on purpose, you know," Mimsy fumed. The clipped peacock feather attached to her sequined head bandeau quivered. "That man whisks my Ollie off to who knows where always on my opening nights."

"He's still too young to sit through an entire play." Esme deployed her most soothing voice while resisting the urge to correct her mother that "my Ollie" was in fact *her* Ollie. Well, Jasper's as well as he had a part to play in the matter. "Come to think of it, Duke shares the same problem. It's best they both get the wiggles out beforehand."

"Stop complaining, Maud. We're here." Duke strolled in through the front door, hoisting little Ollie on his shoulder. Ollie wriggled all about, slapping his great-grandfather on the head and giggling as his luscious little curls danced about his chubby face.

"The boy is a natural sailor," Mond said as he twirled a fat oak leaf with his one hand. "My bet is on him for the Cowes Week regatta."

"Come, precious. Mimsy is here." Mimsy snatched Ollie off Duke's shoulders and cradled him against her chest. The little boy barely had time to peek around her to wave at his mum and dad before his grandmother swept him down the hallway to the ballroom.

"You'll just come watch the show with your Mimsy. Afterward we'll have cake and biscuits and jam. Then I'll show you how to take a stage bow. You'll be darling at it, my love. All you have to do . . ." Her instructions faded down the hall followed by Ollie's agreeable laughter.

Duke shrugged and rolled his eyes before following them. It was a dance they had been squaring off to for some time with no end in sight. Not if Mimsy had anything to say about it.

"Think about it," Mond said. "You could make an entirely new art addition to the south wing with all the silver cups your boy would win."

"That will be for Ollie to decide when he's older," Esme said. Unlike his parents, their boy would have ample opportunities to choose his own life. *Legal* opportunities.

"Speaking of opportunities," Mond said. "I was in Claridge's just the other day when the hotel bartender let slip that a Frenchman had checked in the previous afternoon. A rather eccentric, egg-shaped Frenchman who'd ordered enough champagne to drown the Eiffel Tower for a party he's hosting on Saturday night."

"A party, you say?" Jasper grinned at Esme. "Darling, when was the last time we attended a champagne shindig?"

"Simply ages," Esme said.

"Shall we make it a date?"

She twirled the ruby bracelet around her wrist. "Indeed. I have a few baubles I'd like to flaunt in front of the little devil. Perhaps he'll be up for a friendly game or two for old time's sake."

Mond laughed, waving his hand as if to fend them off as he walked ahead. "Just leave me out of it this time."

The opening strains of an orchestra floated down the hall from the ballroom.

"Is that . . . ?" Jasper cocked his ear. "'Daisy Bell'?"

Esme shrugged innocently as she hummed along to the tune. "Perhaps."

He raised an inquisitive brow. "What do you know about this new play?"

"Not much. Only something about two former lovers. An enormous diamond. And a jewel heist of some kind."

"That sounds rather coincidental."

They strolled down the hall and stopped outside the ballroom doors. She smoothed his tuxedo lapels. Dapper as always.

"Don't get too excited. A benevolent and wildly attractive theater owner saves the day and is presented the diamond for her efforts. The lovers are happy to sustain themselves on, well, their love alone. The end."

"I suppose everyone deserves their version of a happy ending."

"I'm certainly glad to have mine."

The corner of his mouth curved up as he slipped an arm around her waist and lightly took her hand in his, slowly swaying them to the music. Just as they had done so long ago in the middle of Paris. People and celebrations all around, but all they saw was each other.

"Is it everything you expected?"

Esme laughed and pressed her cheek to his.

"Now, darling, you know me better than that. Where's the fun in expectation?"

ACKNOWLEDGMENTS

To put it bluntly, the Jack and Ivy novels were a doozy to write. And survive. Coming off of all that heartache and whirlwind action and a global lockdown, I needed something fluffy. Characters easy to love, a breezy plot, and full of spirited glamour. Jack and Ivy were many things, but easy breezy was not one of them. That's when Esme and Jasper waltzed into my life, and boy am I grateful! Their banter and flirty lashes were exactly what I needed, like a piece of dark chocolate filled with marshmallow crème. So now that we're all properly hungry for something sweet, I've some people to thank.

Rachel McMillan, you swept in right when I needed you. Not only are you a gracious spirit, endless champion, and eternal romantic, but you're a darn good friend too. This story would have languished if you hadn't offered to step in and find it a home. You are one in a million and I'm so grateful to have you in my life. That and it makes my day when you send me pictures of bunnies.

To The Powerhouse, you ladies keep me going when I'm having a bad day/week/month and want to throw in the towel. We've laughed and cried and ranted together, and I hope that never stops. To my wonderful publishing house and all the fabulous people I get to work with: Laura, Kerri, Margaret, Amanda, Savannah, and too many more to name. This book would not exist without your support and guidance.

To my long-suffering yet somehow understanding family. When we sat eating pizza and I couldn't come up with a ridiculous game for an eccentric millionaire to play on his unsuspecting guests, you came through for me with some off-the-wall ideas. Including a chicken of doom. Thank you for making this wild ride even wilder. XOXO.

DISCUSSION QUESTIONS

1. Esme and Jasper had very different upbringings yet share much in common. In what ways have their paths been similar and how have they varied?

2. Brashness plays an important role in Esme's decision-making. How would you have handled the choices she made in following her cheeky nature?

3. The Valkyrie Tiara is an extraordinary bit of jewelry. Would you have been tempted to keep it for yourself?

4. The world was still recovering from the Great War and the Jazz Age was on the brink of swinging into high gear. Do you believe this time in history influenced any of Esme's and Jasper's decisions and the choices they made?

5. Esme is often faced with choosing between her head and her heart. How does her upbringing influence this?

6. Jasper and Esme seem to work better together as thieves than apart. Why do you think that is?

7. Do you think Jasper should have given up the title and inheritance that Duke finally granted him? Why or why not?

8. Given the unorthodox nature of their marriage as well as their individual reputations, do you truly see Jasper and Esme settling down to hearth and home?

LOOKING FOR MORE GREAT READS? LOOK NO FURTHER!

THOMAS NELSON
Since 1798

Visit us online to learn more:
tnzfiction.com

Or scan the below code and sign up to receive email updates
on new releases, giveaways, book deals, and more:

@tnzfiction

ABOUT THE AUTHOR

Photo by Bryan Ciesielski

Bestselling author J'nell Ciesielski has a passion for heart-stopping adventure and sweeping love stories while weaving fresh takes into romances of times gone by. When not creating dashing heroes and daring heroines, she can be found dreaming of Scotland, indulging in chocolate of any kind, or watching old black-and-white movies. She is a member of the Tall Poppy Writers and lives in Virginia with her husband, daughter, and lazy beagle.

jnellciesielski.com
Instagram: @jnellciesielski
Facebook: @jnellciesielski
Pinterest: @jnellciesielski